D1177287

Standing Stones
Book 1:
The McDonnell Clan

Beth Camp

For Allen,

Rachel, Nick, and Leda

Always.

Cover designed by Angie Zambrano

ALSO BY BETH CAMP

A Mermaid Quilt & Other Tales

CONTENTS

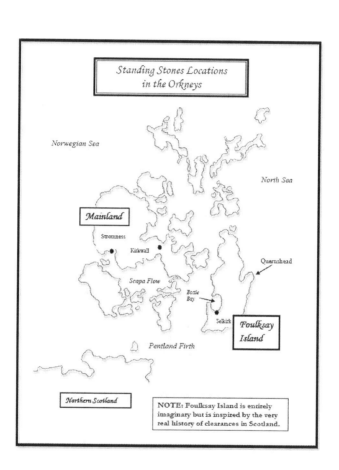

Standing Stones Locations
in the Orkneys

Norwegian Sea

North Sea

Mainland

Stromness

Kirkwall

Queenshead

Scapa Flow

Bottle
Bay

Selkirk

Foulksay
Island

Pentland Firth

Northern Scotland

NOTE: Foulksay Island is entirely
imaginary but is inspired by the very
real history of clearances in Scotland.

BOOK 1: FOULKSAY ISLAND

Spring - Summer 1841

> Some hae meat and canna eat,
> And some would eat that want it;
> But we hae meat, and we can eat,
> Sae let the Lord be thankit.
>   ---Attributed to Robert Burns

CHAPTER 1: FOULKSAY ISLAND

A few cold and slimy cod lay in the wheelbarrow. Moira gutted one, washed it in salted water, spread it on the drying rack, and turned back for another. Her back hurt. She had worked steadily all morning, ever since she helped her brothers pull the *Star* up on the beach.

A steady north wind kicked white caps into the cove and blew along the beach. Sea gulls screamed and fought over fish guts spilled on the rocks close to the water.

Along the rocky beach, women called to each other as they cleaned and racked the morning's catch on low work tables cobbled together from stone and driftwood. A few laid the cod directly on the sand in neat rows or put them into creels to sell later.

Moira rinsed her hands in the bucket of salty water, the cuts on her fingers stinging, as Dougal came up to her, his brown face as familiar to her as the sea.

"The ferry's here." Moira wiped her wet hands on her skirt. "Help me check the knots." Together they bent over burlap-wrapped bundles of dried fish waiting for transport to the Mainland. Dougal pulled on the twine; the knots held firm. "Let's get them down to the boat," said Dougal. He put one of the bundles of dried cod into the empty wheelbarrow and picked up another, laid it on his back, and turned down to the beach, leaving Moira to drag the wheelbarrow to the shore. *I wish he would carry two bundles once in a while,* Moira thought. *His back is big enough.*

Moira wrestled the wheelbarrow down to the shore, her skirts gritty, her boots and the wheel of the barrow sinking into the sand. She'd been hauling fish as long as she could remember, bringing wet fish ashore to dry in the wind, taking dried fish back to their boat, and watching her brothers take the boat out to the ferry or over to the market on the Mainland.

"Look," said Mac pointing to the ferry holding steady at the edge of the cove. "We don't usually get visitors."

Moira struggled to pull the wheelbarrow to the side of the *Star*.

"Aye, and I wonder who's coming ashore." Dougal tossed his bundle of dried fish up into the boat where it landed with a thump.

Moira pinched a blister on her finger and leaned against their boat to rest.

"Colin, over here," called Mac. "Help get these bundles into the *Star*. Then take the wheelbarrow up to get the last of them."

Always bossy, Moira thought. *It's because he's the oldest.*

Colin ran back up the beach, the wheelbarrow bouncing behind him.

"Look at that energy," said Dougal. "It's past time we should be taking him out with us."

Jamie looked up from the net he was untangling. "Mac, can I go?"

Mac and Dougal looked at each other. Mac shrugged. "Only one of you this time. Jamie, you stay here with Moira. Colin's older. Maybe next time."

Jamie worked the net, his head down.

"Come, Jamie. Let's see who's coming to land."

Moira stood on the beach with Jamie, a little apart from the last-minute bustle on the beach, her hand pressed to her lower back. "Looks like a woman and two men."

"Yep," said Jamie, his eyes on the bobbing boat. "'Tis the new laird and his lady, I bet you."

"And how do you know that?"

"I heard it from Gibson. He brought the buggy down."

Mac and Dougal stood mid-calf in the surf, waiting for the longboat. They locked their arms together, making a seat to carry the strangers ashore so their feet wouldn't get wet. They carried the older man ashore first, and then the remaining two.

Moira edged closer. The woman looked to be about her age. Moira watched as the woman smoothed the skirt of her gray traveling suit and pushed aside her heavy veil to whisper something to the man at her side. They laughed. The travelers from the ferry looked everywhere -- at the beach and the island, and at the fishermen and their women, but they spoke to no one.

The woman held a handkerchief to her nose as the strangers made their way up the beach to dry ground, where a horse and buggy waited. One of the men, the shorter one who held the woman's arm, walked with a slight limp; his feet sank into the sand.

Moira wondered if the strangers would stay. For the first time, she looked down at her apron, smeared with fish. She probably did smell.

"'Tis Lord Gordon, the new laird, his lady, and his factor," Dougal said, coming up to her. "They seem proper enough folk."

"Told you," chimed in Jamie.

"Proper enough," said Mac. "But they didn't part with a penny, did they? Most likely we'll be taking them back out to the ferry at week's end, soon as they settle with Hargraves." He clumped wet sand from his boots. "Moira, Jamie, what are you standing about for? Give us a hand then, while we take this out to the ferry."

Their boat loaded, Colin and Dougal hopped aboard as Mac, Moira, and Jamie pushed it off the sandy beach. Mac clambered up the side of the boat with the ease of long experience, and the *Star* was afloat. Dougal pulled up the smaller sail, which quickly caught the wind, and the *Star* slid over the breakers, to the waiting ferry.

Moira picked up the grass-lined creel she'd filled with fresh-caught cod and strapped it on her back, the lines cutting into her chest and belly. "Are you ready?"

Jamie nodded and grabbed a pail with a few more cod in it, covered over with seaweed. Together they walked up the slight incline of the beach to town. Moira wondered how far they'd have to walk past Selkirk to trade for butter and milk and how many fish she'd have to hang by their cottage door to dry in the wind when the day was done.

Today she just wanted to get cleaned up. She couldn't stop thinking of the young woman in a gray traveling suit, wearing a veiled hat and holding a pink handkerchief.

CHAPTER 2: BOTTLE BAY

Late the next morning, Mac scanned the sky. Sea gulls and cormorants squawked overhead, the ocean gray as far as he could see, with not a flash of light. Long waves rolled up and broke on the beach and then returned as the tide came in. A few barefoot boys raced along the beach, pelting each other with clumps of wet sand.

Everywhere the beach was littered with small boats, some a little larger than the *Star*, simple two-masted open boats, their bows sharpened to a point, double the size of a rowboat. Older boats, no longer seaworthy, had been upended atop walls of stone, packed with grass, and made into storage sheds. The men gathered beside the sheds. Some checked the fine mesh nets used for cod; others untangled the long lines needed to catch flounder.

"I want to be first this year," said Mac, as he began to untwist the 1,200 foot line tangled at his feet.

"Why worry about being first out at the grounds?" Dougal settled on the sand

"If this season goes well, I want to trade up for a skaffie," said Mac. He shook out another section and ran his hands down the thin line, his fingers checking for knots. He coiled the smooth line neatly into a large woven fish-basket as he worked.

"Each in its own season. Herring is months away." Dougal pulled a section of line free from the tangle at his feet. "You don't like Da's boat anymore?"

"I never have. It swamps too easily, as you well know. You almost slithered off last time out, and now I have to worry about Colin. We do have to take him out. It's past time."

"We don't have the money for a new boat," said Dougal.

"We didn't have money for your violin, did we? But we got it." Mac untangled the line without stopping. "I was talking to Sean over at the Pig's Head. He's willing to work with us. He'd let us trade the *Star* up for a skaffie if he comes in for a share."

Dougal tugged another section of line straight, careful to avoid the hooks, flicking the old bait onto the sand. "It's only five years since Da died. We're doing all right."

"That's what you say." Mac stopped working and looked out again across Bottle Bay, at the clouds hugging the horizon. "You weren't there when the storm came up out of nowhere. You didn't see Da washed off the deck like he was some kind of flying fish."

"Don't be getting mad all over again. It happened."

"Everything changed with that storm and Da gone." Mac's fingers stilled. He'd had no complaints when his father had needed him on the boat. Fishing seemed a good life then, at least better than grubbing on land.

"I miss Da too."

"She's too small to stand the winter storms," grumbled Mac. He stood and slapped the bow of the *Star*. "She runs low in the water."

"She'll do."

"She still runs too low in the water."

"You remember why Da named her the *Star*?"

"I remember."

"Well," said Dougal. "She's good enough for us, then."

"It's still something to have a bigger boat." Mac settled down on the sandy beach and picked up another bit of line, untwisting the tangle. "And I wouldn't mind being first to get to the grounds tomorrow."

"We'll be ready." Dougal cleared another lump of tangled line.

An afternoon wind straight from the north pushed the sand along the beach, stinging Mac's and Dougal's faces as they sat in the lee of their boat. Their hands moved constantly, knotting hooks on their two lines now untangled, over 1,000 hooks on each line. The cold air smelled of the sea.

Mac watched the waves roll up on the shore. "Another storm's coming in." He wondered if they would have enough money for a larger boat at the end of the herring run. He didn't really want to go shares with Sean. "Let's hope she blows over before we go out."

"Aye. And where's Colin this afternoon?"

"Over at the Mercantile," said Mac. "Unpacking boxes. He's a good worker."

"I know. He takes after me," said Dougal. He poked Mac's shoulder lightly.

"He should come with us tomorrow. He needs to learn the marks."

"He'll learn. And Jamie?"

"We'll take him one day. He's young yet. After all, Colin's almost a man. What were we doing at sixteen?"

"Jamie still wants to go with us, you know."

"I know. In spite of his books." Mac rested his hands on his knees for a moment, several hooks gleaming on his left palm. "I heard some folk got evicted the other day."

"Here, on Foulksay?"

"No. Down by Sutherland. Gibson told me they're bringing in sheep. The people had no food and no work. And no way to pay the rents."

"We have enough," said Dougal.

"If it happened there, it can happen here."

Moira and Jamie started down the hill toward the boat, both nearly bent over from carrying two tin pails filled with dead fish. They settled on the sand near Mac and Dougal and began twisting fish heads onto the hooks.

Mac jabbed Dougal's ribs and pointed toward the beach. "Look there. 'Tis the new laird. That must be his factor, for it's not Hargraves, 'n not any one we know."

Their hands still for a moment, Mac and Dougal watched the two men walk along the beach, one limping. The factor pointed at the headlands and the cart path that led up the hill, and then, as if they were alone, they walked slowly back to Selkirk.

"I wonder what they were doing."

"Nothing that brings us good," said Mac. He threaded another hook on his line.

CHAPTER 3: WESTNESS

Lord Gordon stared at the marble bust of Wellington, a gift from his father. His collection of leather-bound books on India had been properly arranged in the floor-to-ceiling bookshelves that filled three walls. As he glanced around his office at Westness, he sensed Perkins at his back. Hanging oil lamps flickered occasionally as the wind blustered around the east side of the house. Hargraves sat in front of him.

"Hargraves, my uncle thought well of you," began Lord Gordon. "His trust has been answered by many years of service, especially this last year following his death." Gordon looked at the man perched uncomfortably on the cushioned chair in front of his desk, the estate account books balanced on his lap. "Nevertheless, the revenues are not at all what I anticipated."

"Sir, times have been hard." Hargraves shifted again, deep brown circles under his eyes. The account books slid on his lap; little slips of paper stuck out between its pages. "The people are good workers, sir. They will not disappoint you."

"That may be," said Lord Gordon. "But I want Perkins to take over the accounting. You will be paid through quarter day. Whitsunday, I believe." He turned back to the stack of letters Perkins had opened for him.

"Sir, am I not wanted, then?"

"Perkins will call you if you are needed. Give the accounts to him on your way out." Gordon did not look up.

Hargraves handed the books to Perkins. "I served your uncle over thirty years, sir."

"And they were good years, I am sure. I will send for you if you are needed. Perkins, see him out."

Hargraves turned and followed Perkins out of the office, his back straight.

Gordon looked around his office again. A life-sized painting of Lord George Alexander Gordon in battle dress, the fourth earl of Selkirk, hung over the fireplace. Alice had placed a row of blue and white Chinese urns on the mantle atop the marble-faced fireplace, where a peat fire burned behind brass andirons. Perhaps not as nice as his brother's office in London, but it would do. At least it was entirely his.

"Your review with Hargraves is complete?" asked Gordon as Perkins came back into the office. He wondered again if Perkin's very large nose made him so obsequious.

"Yes, sir."

"And your findings?"

"The holdings are extensive, sir, as we had discussed. But, as you said, sir, the returns are low."

"Is there any flaw in Hargraves' accounting?"

"No, sir. But overall, the income's not the same as Lord Alexander's estate in the south."

Gordon's mouth twisted as he thought of his brother. "To the task, Perkins. What do they farm?"

Oats and bere, sir. Potatoes."

"Bere?" Gordon raised his eyebrows. "What's bere?"

"A kind of barley. They make a grainy flour out of it for bannocks or biscuits. You can use it to make malt for beer or whiskey, though I don't think that's done here." Perkins rocked on his feet and stared at the oak beams above him as he recited what he knew. "They feed it to their cattle, sir. They use the straw for thatching. It grows fast with little work, even in the thinnest soils, though harvests are generally poor."

"Much room for improvement, then. You've brought the map? Good. Here, look with me." Gordon spread out the map of his island on the desk.

The map showed Foulksay Island at the very northern tip of Scotland, in that unexpected clump of islands called the Orkneys, so named by the Norse for seal islands.

Lord Gordon studied the map, imagining how the hills rose to a crest at the center of the island, how grasses grew in the upper valleys, and how crofters farmed narrow fields separated with small dikes of tilled soil and stone. "Are you having problems finding workers, Perkins?"

"I've got a small crew now, but the fishermen will leave in May when they chase the herring."

"Does that bring me an income?" Gordon replied, smoothing the creases on the map.

"It comes back to you in rents, sir."

"How long will they be gone?"

"Some four to six weeks, sir, at the most, if they just go for the first season. Most come back before Lammas in August, and the rest in September. If the herring run well, a fisherman makes eight times what a crofter will make raising cattle and sowing fields."

"The market's good for herring in England and in Russia. We could raise their rents."

"Yes, sir. But sometimes they come back with close to nothing." Perkins pointed to the map. "Here, sir, I've marked where the fishermen live, a smattering around Selkirk, close on the beach. Some here up along the coast. A few hold their own land. Others rent just enough land to get by. There's some ten or so families that don't pay rent."

"Why not?"

"Perhaps your uncle's charity, sir. In the storms of '39, twenty-seven men and ten boats were lost. "

"What about these?" asked Gordon, pointing to the map.

"The crofters are pretty much scattered haphazardly, all inland. Most pay rents, but not here and here." Perkins tapped the map.

"More who don't pay rent?" Gordon rubbed his leg.

"Perhaps at one time, they did. When the harvests are poor, the men go south to work on the canal or the railroads, or in the new textile mills. Or they'll take to the sea on a whaler. A few sign on with Hudson's Bay. If the men don't return, the families grow what they can, barter for the rest, and hope their men send money home."

Perkins pointed to a line of hills that cut through the middle of Foulksay. "The crofters let their cattle loose in the high grasslands here during the summer." Perkins moved his finger down the map. "They cut their peat here in the bogs near Barr Auch. Below, in these run-rigs, the crofters plant their oats, potatoes, and bere in the early spring, just about now, sir."

At Gordon's nod, Perkins continued. "Most years the planting is done before the herring begin to run. The harvests could be better, but without proper fencing, when they drive the cattle back in the fall, the cattle trample the crops, leaving barely enough for subsistence. The spring is the hardest time, between Beltane and Lammas. They call it the hungry time."

"Why ever don't they fence the land? Silly not to." Gordon remembered the country estate in the south he'd loved as a boy. Neat fences there. All that belonged to Alexander now.

"Not enough trees on the island. And it's not been done in the past, sir. Some have built stone and dirt walls, really a kind of dike, to enclose the cattle here and there, but there's no incentive for them to do so."

Gordon's finger traced the outline of the island. "They'll have to pay the rent. That will make incentives."

"Yes, sir. We have ample grasslands for sheep, should you choose to go with the Cheviots. The land could be cleared and leased to herders from the south as Lord Alexander did."

"My brother wrote me of this. It's a better income than rents." His finger stopped at Selkirk. "Maybe. But we need a pier. The cove is deep enough. I want the ferry to stop here at least once a week. We could set a fee for using the pier."

"They won't pay, sir."

"Then we'll charge them for using the beach."

"Yes, sir. But these people don't have ready money. You saw when you landed. The whole family cleans and dries the fish close to the beach. A few families use a smokehouse; most use the wind. Then, the fishermen take the dried fish out to the ferry, every few weeks or so from spring to early fall."

"That's not very efficient. And in the winter?"

"The island's pretty much cut off then, from what I hear," Perkins replied.

"Storms?"

"Unpredictable, sir," replied Perkins. "They come in suddenly, winter storms. Those from the North Sea are fierce, but the worst storms come in from the southwest, off the Atlantic. I've heard them talk of howling winds that near bend you in half when you walk outside. Even the cold air freezes white. Few fishermen venture out in winter, lest need drives them."

For a long moment, Gordon closed his eyes. "It's a long way from India."

"Yes, sir," Perkins said.

"The boats are old-fashioned. They need to be retrofitted." Lord Gordon pointed again to the map. "Tell me about Selkirk. What have we there?"

"This line of cottages close to the beach is protected by the Bottle Bay," Perkins replied, pointing to the map. "Mostly fishermen here, sir. In the town, about fifty stone houses, close up together, and about 200 people. You have rents coming from about half of the households in Selkirk proper, with the rest being independent landholders. St. Ninian's is staffed by Pastor McPherson. He lives in the manse behind the church and directs the school." Perkins rocked forward on his toes. "The Grammar School's open a full day from late September to early May, which means most can read and calculate. Once the children are twelve, they can attend half-days, but few do so. They work with their families or are apprenticed out."

"I saw the church. It's still Presbyterian, I trust?"

"Aye. McPherson serves at your pleasure."

Gordon grunted. "What about commerce in the town?"

"Not much, sir. There's no market. William Scott has owned the Mercantile for the last twelve years. Your uncle brought him in from Wick. Scott sells fishing supplies, house wares, and staples through the year. He's the center for any trade or barter."

"They barter? You said that before. Barter for what?"

"The crofters are as self-sufficient as they can be, but they'll barter fresh produce or grains for cloth, salt, medicines. Things they can't grow for themselves." Perkins shrugged. "Scott delivers the mail and helps Hargraves collect rents and taxes. They both earn a bit from that. Then there's Gibson and his brother Henry; they run a smithy. They also have one of the larger land holdings on the island. The MacLean widow bakes; she's open five days a week, and a few women weave. A one room tavern, the Pig's Head, is right close to the cove."

"I'll tour Selkirk this afternoon."

"Sir, the weather looks nasty."

"No matter. I've been out in the wet before. Have Lady Alice come in."

"Yes, sir. I'll have the horses readied." Perkins tucked the estate books under his arm and closed the door as he left.

Lord Gordon thumbed through his letters, picking out one from Gray. He read Gray's report and quickly calculated he would need nearly 1,000 pounds to cover his part in outfitting three ships to India. But if the returns were anything close to what Gray had suggested, he could pay Alexander off completely.

Gordon studied the report again. *Alexander will want to know we've arrived safely, and he'll want an accounting. He doesn't understand it's another world here.* Gordon leaned down to rub a cramp out of his left leg.

He thought of the weeks spent sitting in the gardens at Laurel House near St. James Park when he first returned from India, still shaken by fevers at night, echoes of long ago summer days around him. How he, Alexander, and Peter had once hunted imaginary elephants in those quiet gardens. But a second son had few prospects. At fifteen, he enlisted in the East India Company and left London for a decade.

On a home visit, in a swirl of parties, he and Alexander had fallen in love with Judith, but Alexander was first born, the heir. Gordon frowned. Finally retired from the Company. Dratted leg. Laurel House again. Several stilted conversations with Alexander over his future had led to one loan and then another. Gordon glanced around his library without seeing it. Their uncle's death had been a blessing. Alexander had given him the island.

Gordon had traveled north immediately, to see the Edinburgh lawyers and to find a wife. He wanted sons. He wanted to make Westness equal to Laurel House. His eyes focused on the statue of Wellington. *No more India. No more intrigue. No more loans from Alexander.* He rubbed his leg and returned to his letters.

CHAPTER 4: A CROFTER'S COTTAGE

Catriona heard her father, as he poked the fire up in the main room of their cottage. *I should be up as well.* She eased from the pallet she shared with her younger sister, slipped a thick skirt over her pantaloons and tucked her hair back into a semblance of order, covering it with her kerchief.

"Morning, Da," she said, coming from behind the screen that hid her bed.

"Ah, good you're up, Cat. Dish the porridge, will you. I'll rouse the boys." Jacob Brodie, a tall thin man with wiry muscles, called to his sons in the loft built up close to the roof. "Up, boyos. Breakfast is near ready. We've a lot of work ahead."

"Yes, sir." Suddenly the main room was full of noise as three boys spilled down from the loft into the main room, pulling their coats on over their shirts. They stood close to the central fire, eating their porridge, with little jabs to each other, angling to stand closer to the fire.

"Elspeth," called Catriona. "Come to breakfast. I need you to help with the eggs this morning. Mother's abed still." The little girl wiggled from behind the screen, pulling her skirt and smoothing her hair.

"Boys, boys," said Jacob. "Save some of that porridge for your sisters."

Matthew, the oldest at seventeen, looked at his father. "I'm to go to Westness, Da, to work on the new wall."

"Aye, son." Jacob nodded at his other two sons. "We'll take the rest of the potatoes down to Scott's this morning. Luke, let the cows out after milking. Mark, come with me to load the barrows."

Catriona pulled Matthew aside. "Say hello to Dougal if you see him, will you, Mattie?" She could see little flecks of sleep sand still in Matthew's eyes, and she wished she could go with him into town.

"No daydreaming now, Catriona," Jacob said. "I dinna want you running off when your ma needs you."

"Yes, Da," Catriona replied. Matthew held her hand for a moment and then was gone. Catriona shook her head. The smoke from the peat fire burned in her eyes as the cold air from outside blew into the cottage.

"See to your mother and the baby."

Catriona filled a cup with hot tea. "Elspeth, clean up here. We'll help Da and the boys in a few minutes." She entered the small closet-sized room Da had added on last summer. "Ma, are you awake?"

Freya moved restively. "I should be up. 'Tis late."

"Have some tea, Mother. No need to be up. I'm here." Catriona handed the cup to her mother and bent over the straw mattress on the floor to take the baby. "He's very cold, mum." The baby lay unmoving in her arms.

"He didn't wake in the night. He didn't wake this morning."

Catriona held the baby close. "He's not going to wake now, Mother."

Outside the cottage, the sky had lightened, but a cold mist settled over the land. Matthew, his cap low over his eyes, walked along the ditch to the path that led to Selkirk, six miles away.

Jacob pulled his jacket close as he glanced over his holding. The farthest fields had been left to a mix of bere and grass. The nearest rows would be replanted in potatoes in the spring. Close to the cottage, Catriona and the girls had pulled turnips and onions from the kitchen garden, now layered with straw. Jacob nodded. The once neat stacks of peat were depleted and would need replacing.

A trio of black and white barn swallows dipped behind the cottage, as Mark hurried out, pulling his cap on. "Da, will we take them all?"

"Aye, whether rain or no, son."

They entered the shed, their hands in their pockets to hold off the cold, their breath showing in little white puffs. They had dug the potatoes from the field and piled them here, ready for Scott's Mercantile. Jacob inspected some of the tubers, holding them up in the dim light. A few seemed soft and rotten. He threw them to the side. His heart fell as one after the other turned soft in his hands. He worked with Mark to load the barrow as the cold morning mist turned to rain.

CHAPTER 5: WESTNESS

Gordon rifled through his papers as shifting afternoon light filled his office at Westness. He picked up his pen, dabbled the point in the inkwell, and set it down again. *Alexander will not be pleased.* He began the letter to his brother.

Dear Alexander, Thank you for your many kindnesses during our visit.

Gordon snorted to himself. *We were lucky to have been given a suite of rooms at Laurel House.* Judith had been more than formal. He hadn't been able to speak to her alone, yet he found himself watching for her. Even Alice had noticed, new bride that she was.

We arrived safely after a grueling trip by coach to Edinburgh and a visit to Alice's family there. We took a ferry across the Pentland Firth in rough seas to find Westness and Foulksay Island desolate and perpetually cold.

I might as well tell him the conditions as close to the truth as possible, though I doubt he'll believe me. Gordon looked at his study once again as if the very walls would change before his eyes.

The people live in hovels; the land itself remains unimproved. Uncle Henry was not well for several years before his demise, leaving Westness House in need of much repair. In short, the estate has changed little from what we remember so long ago.

Perhaps that will alert him to how it is to live here. We will not winter here. That I can promise. Gordon rubbed his leg again and continued.

Despite my initial reservations, your man Perkins has been invaluable, especially in assessing potential income. I've read your instructions on planting wheat, hay, potatoes and turnips with interest. I fear I have an unreliable workforce, mostly fishermen and crofters with little training and primitive tools. I estimate it will take more than one season to produce a good revenue.

That should suggest I'm not a grubbing farmer. But that is the rub. If I can make this land self-sufficient, we can live permanently in Edinburgh and pay off Alexander. I want nothing of his money. He glanced again at the Gray's letter inviting investment in the India trade. *One thousand pounds. Alexander didn't need to know everything.*

I'm considering investing in Cheviot sheep, much as you, the Sutherlands, and others have done so successfully. The funds you advanced are sufficient and have been deposited in Edinburgh, truly the city of lawyers. I shall write you a full report of our expenditures on the estate.

Gordon rubbed his hands, his knuckles swollen slightly from the damp. *If it weren't for the monsoons, I would wish I were back in India and out of this blasted cold.* He continued writing:

The winds here blow unceasingly. We will most likely winter in Edinburgh, though I miss the warmth of India. My health improves somewhat but would do better in a Mediterranean climate. Please give my regards to mother. I shall look forward to your packet of London papers and remain your devoted brother, Gordon.

He laid the pen aside and looked up to find Alice sitting quietly before him. "There you are. I didn't hear you enter."

"You were busy."

"I've been writing to Alexander."

Alice brightened. "Please thank him for his hospitality. It was good to meet your family at last. I enjoyed parts of London very much."

"Yes, the stay at Laurel House was pleasant." He stared at her. "I pray mother's health continues well. But, to matters here, I want you to complete an inventory of Westness. Put all in order. You may give Perkins a list of any repairs."

"I will do so, Gordon. Could I could ask a favor?"

"Yes, yes, go ahead."

"I would like to invite my sister, Diana, for a visit. It's a little more isolated here than I anticipated."

Gordon shook his head. "I have much to do on the estate. I want peace and quiet for my work. You'll be seeing Diana soon enough. We'll go to in Edinburgh for the winter. Otherwise, madam, we keep the schedule I set in London. You are settling in well, I presume?"

"Yes. The front rooms are quite sufficient; my books have arrived safely. Your rooms are satisfactory?"

"The house remains as I remember from many years ago."

"The staff seem competent. I would like to add a few more servants to help with the cleaning."

Gordon looked at Alice as if his glance could penetrate her clothing. "Do what is needed. And your health, madam?"

"I am a little tired but well, thank you."

"No change? That is, are you with child?"

Alice flinched, but she looked steadily at Gordon. "No change, my lord."

"Yes, well, have Perkins hire additional staff. Let him know where repairs are needed as soon as possible." A flush crept up Lord Gordon's cheeks. "Additionally, I want you to meet with Pastor McPherson and inspect the grammar school. Report any needed improvements to me. Note that he serves at our pleasure. Should he not prove satisfactory, he can be replaced. I want you to keep an eye out for the character of the people."

"Very well. If I may ask, when do we leave for Edinburgh?"

"Possibly October, but no later than mid-November. We'll return here in the spring, March or so. I'm not ready to winter at Westness. Yet."

"Will we be close to the University?"

"I've been rereading Drummond's study. New Town is quite modern. I've leased a house on

Hanover Street near St. Andrew's. I'm sure you will find it pleasant."

"That's the other side of the city from my family. If we're going to be here until October, I really would like to send for Diana."

"Perhaps. Just not now." Gordon picked up another letter, this one from Hyderabad. "Ah, news from India."

For a moment, the office was quiet. Gordon heard Alice's skirt rustling as she rose and left, shutting the door behind her.

Alice spoke to Mrs. MacNaught about dinner and directed Perkins to hire two day workers. Alone in her rooms, she drew the heavy hangings open. Cold air seeped through the glass. She stood close to the peat fire in the fireplace and stared at the closet that connected her rooms to Gordon's bedroom.

Her rooms had high ceilings and wooden panels; they were bright and airy despite the dark furniture that looked as if it had been imported from the mainland many decades before. The Persian carpets they had brought from London bloomed underneath her feet as she paced back and forth. She pressed her stomach. *I wish I could send for Diana.*

In the beginning, Lord Gordon had seemed romantic. Alice, the second daughter of Dr. William Butler Wheaton, professor at the Edinburgh School of Medicine, had attended a lecture at the Great Hall. There, Lord Gordon, short of stature and with a slight limp, enthralled the audience with his tales of battle in the remote mountains of Afghanistan,

27

his visits to the Deccan courts in southeastern India as an attaché, and his descriptions of the *musselmen*, their harems, and the threat of pirates along the coast of West Africa.

His reserved and courteous manner struck her, and she welcomed him when he called later that week. He talked with her father about exotic plants and herbal medicines and took tea with the family. Everyone liked him. The following day, Gordon brought a ginger plant from India, calling it *Inji*, from its Tamil name, and demonstrated how to make a kind of pickle from its roots, to counter the effects of the heat, he said.

Over the next several weeks, Gordon visited frequently. One evening after dinner, he strolled with Alice out into her mother's expansive garden. "I am a simple man," he said, drawing her into a gazebo.

Alice could hear her younger sisters, Sarah and Rebecca, talking as they picked flowers nearby.

"I've returned to Scotland, God willing, to make my home. I am searching for a wife, one who is well educated, and of a calm and virtuous temperament." He took her hand. "You appear to be such a lady."

"I had not thought to marry, Lord Gordon." Alice replied. "My sisters and I, we've had a somewhat different upbringing. I fear some would call us bluestockings. Our parents have encouraged us in our studies and in our charitable works."

"I applaud your independent mind. Forgive my bluntness, for I have returned to England only recently from many years in India. I have holdings in Scotland." He looked at her with the compelling gaze of one who has commanded many. "I estimate we could manage quite well together."

"Perhaps," Alice replied.

Gordon pursued her with military exactness over the next month, escorting her to lectures and amusing her with anecdotes of his twenty-year stay in India. He professed interest in her small library. She was finally won over by his gift, a small leather-bound copy of the *Enquiry Concerning the Principles of Morals*, by the Edinburgh philosopher, David Hume. They were married by her father in the garden she so loved.

How she missed her home in Edinburgh, her mother's garden and glass house filled with ferns and orchids, her sisters' good humor, their daily noisy routine, even their weekly charity work at Magdalene House. She missed Papa's office, the mornings set aside for patients, and the afternoons, his desk muddled with papers and his work interrupted by constant visitors from the university.

But she was far from Edinburgh. In the last year, Gordon had stopped smiling. She didn't understand why. She knew his leg pained him in damp weather, but he never complained. He withdrew immediately after dinner to his study, professing paperwork. She suspected he smoked his hookah there. He did visit her very late at night, but his embrace seemed forced, as if he performed a duty.

Alice watched from her window as Perkins gave a small boy a slip of paper and sent him off on an errand. The boy scampered over a patch of ground protected from the harsh winds by rock walls.

Funny to miss a garden. She stared out the window. *Certainly it would be possible to grow roses here.* Even in this isolated island, one could make a glass house, though the very elements seemed to be at war. Alice returned to her desk, the quiet in her room broken by an occasional rattling of the wind at the windows. She began a letter to Diana.

CHAPTER 6: STROMNESS

"Nothing like an excursion to shake you from your doldrums." Gordon looked out at the busy port from the fourth floor window of the Stromness Inn. "I shall return in time for dinner. There's a garden behind the hotel. Try some walking today. It will do you good."

Alice turned over on the bed. She tried not to cry as he left the room, the floorboards creaking at his every step. Every noise he made hurt her head. Why couldn't she have stayed home? She cringed when she thought of the journey. It had taken a full day of sailing to come from Foulksay Island to the port town of Stromness. They would stay a week and then return. She was still not ready to travel, yet Gordon had insisted. *Diana would have known what to do.*

Gordon had left the window partly open. Outside, people shouted. Something about the carter not bringing beef. She fell asleep again.

When Alice awoke, clouds darkened the sky, and the wind blew fitfully. Someone had closed the windows. She finally got up, washed her face in the porcelain bowl provided, and dressed. She was still so tired. She thought of that long night, the miscarriage, Gordon's disappointment, and her own. *Perhaps I shouldn't have married. I only wanted what others seem to have so easily, a home of my own, a child.* Alice lay back on the bed and stared at the ceiling. *If I'm being honest, I'm fortunate. I have my books. But not a child.*

"Still malingering, are you? Don't know how you slept through that rain. But it's finally lifting." Lord Gordon stumped into their rooms. "Good view of the harbor we have from here."

Alice shut her eyes. She didn't want to be awake yet. She didn't want to be here. She didn't want to talk to him.

"Come here. Have a look. A ship from London's taken shelter." Gordon rapped his cane on the floor.

Alice peeked out the window. A three-masted barque had docked at the pier, its outlines barely visible in the dusk.

"It's the *Rajah*. I know her captain. I met him in India before I returned home. A good man. He'll join us for dinner." Gordon consulted his watch and then looked at Alice. "You'll come to dinner, won't you?"

Alice shook her head tentatively. The headache was gone. "Yes, I'll come down. I do feel better."

"Good. You'll be back to yourself before you know it."

"Will you send Sheila up?"

"If I can find her. Worthless girl. I saw her all the way over to the docks when I was there. Business went well, though." Gordon patted her arm. "It's good to see you coming back to yourself."

Alice rested her head against his shoulder for a moment and then turned away. She didn't want to talk about anything. Outside the rain began again, dripping on the casement.

The private dining room was well lit by candlesticks and sconces on the wood paneled wall. A long table and a sideboard took up nearly all the space. Captain David Ferguson had brought two guests, Dr. James Donovan, a young ship's surgeon hired from an Edinburgh medical school, and Miss Kezia Hayter, a slim, almost child-like woman with large dark eyes. Gordon had invited his man of business as well. The six guests sat congenially around the table, while the owner of the Stromness Inn brought another steaming platter in. "Lobster, sirs, fresh caught. And there's oysters baked in a pie, with beef rump and country mushrooms to follow."

A hum of appreciation rose.

"What a pretty name," said Alice to Kezia.

"Thank you. I hear you're not well."

" Lord Gordon brought me over from Foulksay Island for a change of scene." Alice didn't want to talk about herself. She felt suddenly as if sitting at the table were more than she could do. She put her fork down. "Tell me about you. What are you doing on the *Rajah*? I hear it's a prison ship, and you're going to New South Wales?"

"Yes, I am," said Kezia. "Actually we're bound for Van Diemen's Land. We have 180 women on board from Millbank Prison. They're a pretty sad lot after that storm."

The clink of wine glasses and silverware continued.

"Conditions must have been very bad for the ship to shelter here in Stromness."

"The storm was ferocious. Captain Ferguson locked us in our cabins, and the women below, I was told, could not even have a light for fear of fire. Praise God we put in here to avoid the worst of it." Kezia shuddered. "Even in my cabin, I felt at the mercy of the sea. I couldn't stay in my bed, and my trunk flew open, scattering everything. I wasn't sick, but many were."

"I feel guilty for our easy trip over from Foulksay. You must be very brave to venture out in the open sea."

"I don't feel very brave. This is my first trip. Captain Ferguson has offered me every courtesy. He has been most kind, a paragon to make the way smooth for my mission."

Alice glanced at Captain Ferguson, seated at her left in full dress, gold epaulets shining at his shoulders, deep in conversation with Lord Gordon.

"He is very nearly heroic," Kezia said in a lowered voice, almost to herself. She leaned closer to Alice. "Elizabeth Fry recruited me for this voyage. I'm to report back to her on the conditions of women prisoners in Van Diemen's Land."

"Elizabeth Fry?" queried Alice.

"You've not heard of her? She's rather well known for her advocacy of women in prisons. She looks unassuming, but when she speaks, her words fill you with compassion. You cannot imagine the changes she has brought. She first took Bibles to prisons in London. Then she took groups of ladies through the prisons. Once we saw the conditions, we were compelled to work, just as she did. She has changed my life." Kezia's eyes gleamed. "Perhaps we should wait to talk until after dinner."

Alice nodded and turned to her companion on her left as a flustered servant offered her a platter of oysters. "Mr. Gray, I understand Lord Gordon met with you today."

"Yes, m'lady." Gray served himself another helping of steaming oysters. "Lord Gordon visited me on business for Sutherland."

"Ah, you're the agent for Lord Sutherland."

Mr. Gray nodded as he dexterously stabbed a large oyster and popped it whole in his mouth.

Alice cringed. The man looked rather small for such an appetite. "Do you live here in Stromness?"

"Oh, no, m'lady. I came over from Inverness to meet with Lord Gordon. My family's near London." Mr. Gray ticked on his fingers. "Two brothers, one at the Registry and the other in the military, currently in India. Three sisters, all happily married." He blushed. "I'm an uncle five times over." He patted his mouth and politely burped behind his napkin as laughter arose from the other end of the table.

"Congratulations, I trust." Alice felt faint. "Have you been to India?"

"Oh, no m'lady. I wish I could go. My brother's in India." He blushed again. "Sorry, m'lady. I told you that already." He put his oyster fork down and leaned over his plate, his sleeve catching on the edge of his plate. "I'm sure Lord Gordon's told you about our venture. We're outfitting several ships for trade to India. It should be an exciting voyage in spite of the nasty weather, eh?"

"Lord Gordon has long had interests in India," replied Alice. She surveyed the table. The dinner was going well. She felt her spirits lift. Gordon gestured enthusiastically as he talked to the ship's surgeon and Captain Ferguson, quizzing them on their last voyage to India. *Good enough*, thought Alice.

Gordon rose from the table. "We hate to leave you lovely ladies," he said. "But 'tis time for port and a bit of a smoke." He nodded courteously to Alice and Miss Hayter. With a courtly bow, Captain Ferguson rose as well. William Gray bumped against his chair and hurriedly joined the other men as they ambled from the room to smoke in the bar.

Alice felt her headache returning. She wished she could return to her rooms alone. She pushed the plate away from her.

"Let's not bother with this," said Kezia. "Can we go somewhere the air is fresher?"

"I was just wishing we were home so I could show you my garden. Shall we go up to my sitting room?"

The two women sat on a small verandah overlooking the gardens at the back of the Stromness Inn. Night had fallen, and the rain had stopped. A few stars seemed to float clear and sharp above the clearing clouds.

"Lord Gordon was saying your health is not well?" Kezia began.

"I'm improving. It's difficult to talk about, but, yes, we had a disappointment very recently. I'm feeling sad just now," Alice said, pulling her shawl around her shoulders. "You were telling me about Mrs. Fry?"

"I met her through my cousin at a lecture last year. She recruited me to work at Millbank Prison as a matron. She feels that these women should be separated from male prisoners and male guards. I spent ten months there."

Kezia leaned over to Alice. "You would not believe how grateful the women were. They had been used to so much worse. Only a few were so depraved that they missed Newgate and Pentonville. But at Millbank, they had their own rooms. We set up projects so they could earn money by working. They could attend school. We held services. And we provided better food. It was edifying to see them blossom under these better conditions. Mrs. Fry believes in reform, not punishment."

"I have a hard time seeing you as a prison matron," said Alice.

Kezia laughed. "So did my father. He nearly didn't allow me to leave home, but Mrs. Fry was very persuasive. Mrs. Fry asked me to meet with Lady Franklin in Van Diemen's Land and to work with her to improve the lot of women prisoners. I hope I shall be successful."

"I hope so too." Alice replied. "Your courage is inspirational."

"Once we're aboard again and truly on our way, I'll believe it's really happening. Oh, I meant to tell you of our project. We're to make a quilt." Kezia's face brightened in the lantern light. "Just patchwork at first. Some of the women need to learn how to sew."

"You're making a quilt while on board? Is this possible?" Alice couldn't imagine sewing on a constantly moving ship.

"Oh, yes. Mrs. Fry's ladies' society gave each woman a Bible, toiletries and a sewing kit. It was quite a bit of work to put the kits together, but we did it. Each kit has 100 needles, scissors, pins, several kinds of thread, and two pounds of cotton and chintz scraps. Mrs. Fry felt the women would find the journey less arduous if they were busy with a project. If we could encourage them to be industrious, perhaps their life in Van Diemen's Land would be different."

"You've just come through this terrible storm, and yet you still feel this way?"

"I sincerely do. Beginnings are always the hardest. Ah, you should meet the women. They are the ones with courage. Perhaps not all of them will survive this journey. I worry most about those who are with child. But somehow, with the help of Providence, we will reach Van Diemen's Land. And these women will begin anew."

For the first time, Alice did not cringe when the talk turned to women with babies. "When I was home with my sisters in Edinburgh, we worked at the Magdalene House. But we never imagined such a journey as yours. Here I have been thinking of myself and my hopes for a child, but that's not important, not really. Perhaps I was meant to come to Stromness – to meet you. You make me think there's quite a bit more I could do on Foulksay. I'd like to write to you."

"Please do. Captain Ferguson will be at Hobart Town, but I don't know for how long. I'm not sure exactly where I will be staying. Send letters in care of Lady Jane Franklin in Van Diemen's Land. She's the Lieutenant Governor's wife. I think I shall be staying at Government House, at least at first." Kezia patted Alice's hand. "And I shall hope for good news from you."

The two women sat quietly, each thinking of the future.

Downstairs, close to the fireplace, Lord Gordon and Captain Ferguson lingered over their port, long after the other two men had excused themselves. The tap room of the Stromness Inn was empty.

"Very different from India, eh?" queried Captain Ferguson.

"Too damn cold here. My bones will never recover. But this voyage of yours interests me. Why would the government pay to transport these women to Van Diemen's Land?"

"Have you been to Newgate? " asked Captain Ferguson.

"No, but my brother Alexander served on a Commission for the General Prisons Board last year. They studied Newgate. He reported pure chaos. Corruption everywhere. Gaming, prostitution, drunkenness, and filthy, lewd behavior." Gordon brushed his hands. "Men and women prisoners mixed together. Not even fear of

Johnny-the-headsman could stop them from creating hell on earth."

"That's why the government is willing to pay. The prisons throughout the country are crowded beyond belief. It's cheaper to transport them to Australia, than to build separate prisons for men and women and then to staff the women's prison with female matrons."

"Like Miss Hayter?"

"Yes, like Miss Hayter, though I think she's an exception." Ferguson smiled and then frowned. "Some of the matrons I've met are little better than the prisoners they keep. The costs are high. Over 500,000 pounds for Millbank Prison. It's a brilliant design. Built in the shape of an octagon. Guards stationed in the center. Separate wings for men and women. Absolute silence enforced at night. Most of the prisoners at Millbank are held over for transportation, like the women I'm taking to Van Diemen's Land. But they don't know what they'll be getting into. Nothing like Millbank or Pentonville there."

"Will they have work once you land?" asked Gordon.

"Oh, they'll work all right." Ferguson tamped his cigar. "They'll be assigned to landowners, if they're lucky. If any are recalcitrant, they'll be sent to Port Arthur to work in gangs or one of the factories. But women are still in very short number. Once their time is served, most will marry. Better than prison or living on the streets of London."

The two men were silent for a moment.

"I'm thinking of clearing my land for sheep. I'll see more returns from sheep than from subsistence farmers. But the people have to go somewhere." Lord Gordon cleared his throat. "I've heard of a few landowners who've arranged transport to the Americas or New South Wales for their people. How does this work?"

"It depends." Captain Ferguson frowned. "Transport costs have to be paid up front for each person. But, before leaving, the immigrants can sign indenture papers for five to seven years. For example, if you paid the transport costs, you could be reimbursed by the ship owner at dock or later, when the indenture papers are bought up by local landowners. This way, your costs are reimbursed. And, after serving their indenture, the immigrants can work for anyone in one of the towns or claim land in one of the newer settlements. So they benefit as well."

Lord Gordon leaned back in his chair. "Could I arrange such transport, if needed, for say several hundred people?"

"Lord Sutherland's agent has the details. Benefit from Gray's experience."

"I shall think on it. God send you a good voyage."

"Thank you. I'm proud to be taking these women to Van Diemen's Land. Their chance for a better life is great, and Miss Hayter is an exceptional woman."

"Yes, she is. And a pretty one, in her own way. Those eyes."

"Yes, perhaps. The prisoners respect her already. We should have no trouble on the *Rajah*. I predict a good journey south, despite this storm. We'll be in Hobart Town in under three months."

"So quickly? I thought the voyage took longer."

"Not since we time our voyage to benefit from the southern trade winds. The hard part is getting out of London, going against the tide in the Channel. That's what drove us north."

"And here to Stromness. You've given me much to consider, Captain Ferguson."

The two men shook hands.

Later, Lord Gordon thought of his crofters as he watched Captain Ferguson walk out into the night with Miss Hayter on his arm.

CHAPTER 7: BELTANE

Moira woke earlier than usual. She took a handkerchief from her basket by the spinning wheel before letting herself quietly out of the stone cottage. She didn't want anyone with her this cold and foggy morning.

Moira walked north to the headlands near the great standing stones, and, as Granny Connor had taught her, she swept the handkerchief in circles north, south, east and west, and began to gather the dew.

She walked to the center of the circle made by the old stones and washed her face with her damp handkerchief. She raised her head and spoke to the sky: "If you're there, old gods, bless me with love this year." She felt a little silly. "And we could do with a little more to eat."

The heavy morning fog muted the sounds of the ocean below. She picked a few sprigs of blossoming purple heather and turned away from the headlands to home.

"Up early you are this morning, Moira," said Mac as he built up the peat fire on the open hearth and set a pot of water on the fire.

"It's cold out. I've brought some moor flowers for Beltane."

"Better cold dew than tears," said Mac.

Moira shrugged and scraped the last of the oats from the meal chest, setting some aside in a small bag for Beltane. She poured the oats into the boiling water to make a porridge and stirred.

"We've the cattle to take up later," Mac stood close to the open hearth. "'Tis glad I am this day has come."

"Mac, I want to go harvesting this year after the herring run. Susan and Jane said they'd take me with them down to the Jameson farm on the mainland, near Dunbeath. I'd earn some money."

"You're old enough." Mac squatted and pushed another bit of peat onto the fire. "Both Susan and Jane are going?"

"I talked to them yesterday. We're to sleep in tents in the fields and travel to farms all along the coast." Moira stood away from the smoke rising from the peat fire.

"I know, I know. I've been harvesting before." Mac was silent. "So you're not stepping out with the MacTavish?"

"Don't talk to me about Peter MacTavish. All he wants is a mother for his children. He's old."

"Is that so bad?"

Moira couldn't tell what he was thinking. She looked around their cottage. All she could see was work to do. The smell of smoking fish hung in the air. She felt as if she couldn't breathe. "I want to go off island. It's more than a day trip over to Kirkwall or Stromness. I'd be gone from when the herring run to near Lammas, that is, if you give me permission to go."

"And how would I be stopping you?" Mac shrugged. "We'll manage on our own. But remember you're a McDonnell. No going off with the young men, no matter how handsome they are."

Moira laughed. "None could be more handsome than my brothers." She put her hand on Mac's arm. "Thank you."

"You'll be home by Lammas?"

"I give you my word."

They grinned at each other. Moira saw new lines in Mac's face. She thought he was a man to break hearts, strong and fair, even sitting on his stumpy half-stool this early morn. She spooned up the porridge and passed the salt.

"Up, boys. Break the fast," Moira called. "'Tis Beltane today."

"Beltane," shouted Colin. He came down the ladder so rapidly he nearly fell. Jamie followed, half-asleep.

Moira heard Dougal moving in the loft, pulling rough blankets over the straw pallets. "A few more minutes," called Dougal. He clambered down for the last of the porridge.

"You're near as tall as me, Colin, but your bones are sticking out," said Mac. "Eat up. We've work to do."

Moira watched her brothers at their breakfast and wondered what their mother would have thought of them had she lived. The brothers stood around the small fire in the center of the room to eat their oatmeal, warm from the fire.

"Might as well get started," Mac began. "Colin and Jamie, see to the cattle. God willing, 'tis a grand day for us all. Is all else ready?"

"Aye. In the basket by the door." Moira had woven sprigs of rosemary and heather into small crown-like garlands. Dougal and Colin had carved animals from bits of driftwood.

Everyone gathered around the hearth and watched as Moira spread the peat out and extinguished its fire with sea-water. The smoke lingered in the large open room as the cottage quickly cooled. "Earth to fire, water to fire, all to rest," Moira murmured.

Mac and Dougal were first out of the house. The morning was raw, with clouds scudding in from the north. They walked the span of their four narrow fields behind the cottage, keeping their hands in their pockets against the cold morning air. They had enough of a holding to grow oats and bere, just around Beltane, marking the turn to spring.

"Let's hope weeds don't overtake us this year," said Dougal.

Mac scanned the horizon. "Rain, I think, and a strong wind. Not a good day for fishing or planting."

"'Tis time to cut peat, this coming week."

"Gibson will tell us when."

"I'll ask him about bringing his mule to plough," said Dougal, crumbling a bit of earth in his hands. "It would be good to have the planting done before the herring run, if the weather holds."

The two men fell silent, looking back down the sloping fields to their cottage, built nearly into the ground, often called a black house for its smoke-stained double walls six feet deep, made of stone and packed with earth and rubble. Its heather-thatched roof was anchored here and there with flat sandstones.

"Ready?" Mac called into the cottage.

The McDonnells drove their last two cows along the winding path towards Barr Auch, the highest point on Foulksay Island. As they walked up the gradually increasing slope of grassland, they watched crofters come from every part of the island, bringing their cattle to the fires of Beltane.

Not everyone came. Some said Beltane was silly superstition, an ancient Celtic spring festival. Those who came were silent, each thinking of the hard work to come, worried if there would be enough to eat in the hungry months before the grains flowered and ripened.

At the top of the hill, smoke poured from two large peat fires tended by Henry Gibson and his brother, Thomas. Granny Connor stood in a place of honor, chanting in Gaelic those prayers that would bless the people and their cattle, keeping them safe and prosperous in the coming season.

Moira followed the shaggy red cattle through the smoke between the two fires; the smoke stung her eyes. She scattered the very last of the oats from their meal chest into the Beltane fire. It was enough to hope for a good year. Her younger brothers were growing up so fast. The herring would soon run. Who knew how the harvest would be this year? And who knew what the sea would bring or take away?

"Blessings on the coming year," she whispered to herself. "May it be a good year."

On the other side of the bonfires, Moira looked over at Dougal who stood close to a dark-haired girl. *There's Catriona.* She smiled. *Dougal's got a girl.* She tapped their two cows with a switch to keep them moving forward, their shaggy reddish flanks steaming in the cold morning air.

Moira and Jamie herded their cows down from Barr Auch to the open grasslands above their holding. Dougal caught up, looking pleased with himself, but he didn't say a word.

Here, under the shadow of Barr Auch, their cows would graze freely on the common grasslands over the summer months. Already, cattle from several families mingled and spread out in the green spring grass. Jamie raced about with excitement. Moira swept cobwebs from the inside walls and ceiling of the *sheiling,* while Dougal and Mac piled flat stones and newly cut grass on the roof. That afternoon, they returned to their cottage.

Then down from Barr Auch came the young men, Colin among them, bearing brands of fire from the twin fires of Beltane. They ran sun-wise around the stone cottage and the McDonnell fields. They came into the cottage to relight the hearth-fire. Moira handed out gifts from her basket; Dougal played sprightly tunes on his fiddle, and it was warm again.

In the morning, Mac, Dougal, and Colin took their barrows, creels, and spades, long-handled tuskers, to the upland bogs to cut peat. They spent the next six days with the other men from Selkirk parish, to dig oblong sausages of peat and lay them flat on the moor to dry.

"We'll come back after quarter day. But these, we can take now," said Gibson, pointing with his head to one section of peat, stacked end to end, the long sides exposed to the cold, damp wind. He divided the peat among those who had worked. "Mac, take some over to Granny Connor," he said. "Tell her to let these dry a bit more."

"Aye," replied Mac. "She'll know." He piled his wheelbarrow high with the wet peat and headed back down the path, the barrow bumping on the rough ground. Colin ran alongside, steadying the load, both with full creels tied on their backs.

Dougal stayed behind, stacking the wet peat for their cottage into barrow-sized loads. Once the peat fully dried, they would return here for the rest. Each man would cart his share home, layering the peat again into a neat beehive behind their cottages.

The men worked steadily as they cut, hauled, stacked, and then carted and carried some of the peat logs away. Mac and Dougal took turns wheeling their barrow down to their cottage and back.

Gibson blew on his hands to warm them. He took Mac aside. "They say the rents are increasing."

"We'll find out Whitsunday. If not, he has to tell us at Lammas."

"We don't know this new one, him and his wife. Looks as if they're staying. They say he's a hard one."

"We'll be finding out. He can't draw the blood out of our bodies," Mac said.

"I hear they need workers at the house."

Mac nodded. "I'll tell Dougal and Colin. Me, I'd rather be out on the water." He smiled and pulled his cap closer to his head. "And chasing the devil while I'm at it."

Gibson laughed and slapped Mac on the back. "See you at the Pig's Head? It's a cold moon tonight."

"Aye," Mac replied. "A cold moon."

CHAPTER 8: THE HERRING RUN

"They're running," Dougal called. "Come on, Moira."

Moira turned to Colin and Jamie. "You're in charge now, of all that's here and the cattle above. I'll be back close to Lammas." She hugged the two boys and gathered her things, already packed in a small bundle by the door. "Remember to take Granny Connor milk. Be good, boys. We're depending on you."

"Don't worry," said Colin. "The old house will be standing when you get back."

"We'll miss you," said Jamie.

"Remember who our friends are," Moira called. She hurried down the hill, trying to keep up with Dougal. Her bundle thumped against her skirts as she ran. Her boots slipped on the cobbled streets, as she dodged people rushing to the boats, for the herring were running at last.

Moira settled herself near the center of the *Star*, her bundle tucked under the seat next to several large creels, as Mac and Dougal pushed off. They moved fast to unfurl the sails and raise them to the top of the mast.

"Watch the sail," Mac called. "Moira, you've got your money set aside?"

"Yes." Moira felt her waist. The coins were pinned safe beneath her belt in a cloth bag.

Dougal dropped a line over as soon as they cleared the island. Moira knew any fish they caught would become their dinner. The line sank down, weighted with fish heads, and trailed out behind the boat, fast moving as the wind pushed them south.

The *Star* made its way down Stronsay Firth, past the Mainland. The waters darkened and the spray-filled wind blew in Moira's face. They skirted the coast along the edge of the North Sea.

"We'll pull in at Copinsay for our first stop. Maybe South Ronaldsay by tomorrow night," called Dougal.

Moira nodded, too excited to say another word. As their vessel cut through the water, she looked ahead at the sparkling wind-tossed waves and at what seemed like hundreds of other small boats like theirs, all following the herring schools headed south. There was no worrying now about if they'd have enough to eat, or where she'd sleep, or how many fish they would catch. The season had begun.

Mac and Dougal took the boat out at dusk from Copinsay, but they returned after a few hours "We're too far behind. I can see the birds following them further out," said Dougal. "Maybe tomorrow."

They sailed on to South Ronaldsay the next morning and spent the afternoon setting up at Needle Point. At dusk, Moira hiked her skirts up and helped to push the boat into the water. Mac and Dougal stood ready at the sails, their drift nets neatly folded at their feet. Moira settled her skirts, cold and wet, and sighed as the *Star* sailed out on the graying sea until it disappeared in the gloom.

Around her, some twenty women from the boats built small driftwood fires. Moira could smell fish soup cooking, made from haddock caught earlier, and realized she was hungry. The beach was quiet now the boats and the men were gone. Jane waved to her from their campsite. Susan sat bundled in a blanket, close to the fire.

"It will be busy tomorrow. I can feel it," said Jane.

"You and your feelings." Susan pushed another piece of driftwood onto the fire. "And how big a catch do you see?"

"A good one. That's what we need. I've had enough of being hungry."

"Me too," said Moira, even as she filled her tin cup with fish soup and began to drink the hot salty broth.

The next morning, Moira stayed close to Jane and Susan. They waited with the other women on the shore, but it was no longer quiet. Carters and curers came over from St. Margaret's Hope, the men carrying large empty wooden barrels and bags of salt down as close as possible to the water's edge. The women from the islands stood in tense circles around the curers. Their voices rose until a price was set for the herring.

"Here's where we get to work. Moira. You'll be a gutter with Susan. I'll pack. We can trade off later. But expect to work fast." Jane stamped her feet to keep warm. "Here, bind your fingers up. You don't want to cut yourself." Jane handed Moira cotton strips torn from her underskirt and showed her how to twist the rags around her fingers.

"My fingers feel like fat worms. This won't work," Moira said.

"You'll see. You'll be fine."

"They're coming in. There's the *Star*," cried Jane.

The rest of the morning passed in a blur. The men from Orkney had fished all night. They pulled their boats onto the rocky beach, racing to unload their fish and get back out. Mac and Dougal threw their herring in a great pile near the three women, and then they were gone.

Susan and Moira cleaned the fish as quickly as they could move. With one slash of their knives, they flicked fish entrails onto the rocks by their feet and tossed the cleaned fish into a large bucket filled with sea water. Jane sloshed the fish in the murky water to wash it, then packed the fish in layers of salt. Her hands moved so fast, they looked like they were swimming. As soon as one barrel was filled, the carters wheeled it away and brought another.

Mac and Dougal went out twice more that first morning, following clouds of sea birds that hovered over the herring. Each time they returned, they dumped the herring near Moira and Susan. Moira's back ached from bending over, yet she kept gutting the fish.

"They say a good packer can pack 10,000 herring in a day," said Jane. "I've already done ten times that, eh? How many barrels? Three? Five?"

"Four," said Susan. "You've done four barrels."

"Feels like thousands," said Moira. "How many times more will they go out?"

"They're done for today. I bet we move down the coast tomorrow."

"Aye," said Susan. "Watch the knife, there."

The herring bellies shone white in the sun and then red as the women sliced each fish open and pulled out its entrails. Moira's hands burned from the salty water, one finger partly swollen where her knife had nicked it.

Mac and Dougal untangled their nets and checked them for tears to get ready for the next run. Then they rolled into their blankets and stretched out to sleep on the *Star*, oblivious to the roar of work on the beach.

As the sky darkened, the men awoke and ate their soup. The women hiked their skirts up to push the boats out again, for it was still cold, and the men couldn't risk wet trousers out on the boats with no way to dry them. The herring rose again to the surface of the sea at night to feed. Dougal said he could see them just under the surface of the water, hundreds and hundreds of herring they'd nicknamed the silver darlings for the money they'd bring.

Now all the work Mac and Dougal had done on the nets paid off as they swung the nets out over the black water, the *Star* moving up and down on the swells. They waited until the tugging weight nearly tipped the *Star* and the nets were full before they pulled them in, dumped the fish out onto the bed of the boat, and returned to shore.

And so it went for the next six weeks. At each landing, the men fished, the women made camp and washed their bits of rags, laying them out to dry on small bushes. They rested on the rocks when they could. When the boats came in, the women worked in groups of three to gut, clean and pack the fish, still cold from the sea, until the carters had taken all away, the gulls clamoring around them like angry, hungry children.

Each night, the women built small fires from scavenged driftwood and cooked fish with bartered potatoes into a soup until Moira could hardly drink the broth. When they wanted to sleep, they rolled themselves in blankets along the shore. Some landings had temporary huts to sleep in when it rained. Sometimes they slept on the boats anchored in the cove, if the men came in again at night. At night the women told stories and drank bitter beer. A few women slipped off with the men to walk along the beach. Under the moon, tucked between Jane and Susan, Moira slept deeply, tired to the bone.

At every landing the carters and curers came, sometimes bringing whiskey to sell. One night, as they sat on the *Star*, Mac brought out a bottle. "We all need a bit of the devil to keep us warm," he said, spilling out some whisky in the sea before pouring a bit in Moira's tin cup.

"I've never seen you do that," said Moira.

"You've never been fishing, girl." Mac filled his own cup to the top. "Just as well to keep the old gods sleeping."

Moira was quiet. Her hands were cracked from the brine, and her clothes smelled of fish, but she didn't care. She wrapped her fingers in bits of cloth like the other women did, and tied her sharp fish knife to her waist.

The next morning, a cry went out, "They're moving south. To the boats! To the boats!" The women ran to the boats, their blankets and bags flapping behind them.

The small boats followed the herring past Mull Head, along the Point of Ayre, to Burray, then past South Ronaldsay to Old Head, across the open sea at Pentland Firth to safe landing at Duncansby Head, then along the coast to Wick. Some went further south to the bigger ports of Peterhead and Aberdeen.

Moira never tired of looking at the islands and the sea, even when it rained and the wind blew her face raw. As the boats skirted the mainland proper, she pulled the blanket around her for warmth, and the wind blew rain into the boat. She tied a handkerchief tightly around her head and tried to stay out of Dougal and Mac's way, admiring again their skill in maneuvering the two sails to catch the wind that kept them apace with the herring fleet.

Each afternoon, the boats landed, and the women went ashore. Throughout the day and at dusk, the men went out and came back in with the bottoms of their boats filled with herring. It was a good run.

Then the six-week season ended, as abruptly as it began. The herring turned east and south to the open North Sea, and the smaller boats held close to Scotland's shore.

"God willing, they'll be back next year," said Mac, shading his eyes as he looked around the port.

They stood on the *Star,* tied up at Wick's dock, surrounded by the unrelenting noise of a seaport in high season, the docks crowded with hundreds of small boats like theirs mixed in with several large flat steamers from Holland and Germany. Set with square-shaped sails and dragging nets for trawling, the steamers unloaded their catch by the thousands.

Mac scanned the port and spat, "That is, if we're lucky, and those Dutch bastards don't take every last little fish that ever was."

Mac and Dougal turned to Moira, for the moment of parting had come.

"We'll settle up now with the curers," said Mac, "and then we'll take you back up to Dunsbeath for the harvesting, you and Susan and Jane. We'll meet you at Kirkwall the week before Lammas, for that's when you promised to come home."

Moira nodded. She couldn't speak now, knowing they were going home without her. She hugged each of her brothers. "At Lammas then."

CHAPTER 9: DEIDRE

Deidre stood in the entry to Scott's Mercantile, her two travelling bags heavy in her hands, the familiar smell of burning peat from the central stove mixing with the scent of wet cloth, tobacco and fish.

Her father, deep in conversation with a fisherman, lifted up coiled line and a handful of fish hooks. The store was unchanged, its shelves stocked with tea, meal, barley, salt, eggs, dried peas, and dried fruits. Behind the counter, nets hung near another row of shelves lined with fishing tackle, and on the top shelves, a few bottles of beer and whisky. At the very back of the store, animal hides, seal, otter, and goat, lay stacked on the floor next to bundles of dried fish and burlap bags of bird feathers. Deidre could reach out and touch knitted stockings, caps of several sizes, and several lengths of rough woven cloth.

I shouldn't have come back. But Da had written her, and she had returned. *Perhaps only for a visit.* Foulksay Island seemed smaller to Deidre. She took another step inside the store. William glanced up, saw her, and dropped the fish hooks on the wide wooden counter.

"Deidre. Ah, here's my girl. Home at last." He gathered her into a great hug. "Are you well?"

Deidre couldn't speak for a moment. She felt as if she could stay in her father's arms forever. "Yes, father, I'm fine. I'm not sure about the position you wrote me about, but if they want me," she glanced upstairs, "I'll stay."

"Yes, of course you'll stay. Who's to tell you not to stay? Mac, come and say hello to my favorite daughter, home from teaching in Inverness." William couldn't let go of Deidre's arm.

"'Tis a pleasure to welcome you home, miss." Mac took her hand formally and shook it. "I remember you from school days. You haven't changed."

"Thank you," Deidre replied. She could barely take her eyes away from her father.

"Too long it's been, that's what," said William. "What a day for celebration."

"Da, I'll be upstairs. Are Penelope and Charlotte at home? And Mother?"

"Yes, yes. I'll finish up here. Go up. They're all expecting you. We didn't know exactly when you would arrive. We hoped it would be soon."

The two men watched Deidre go to the back of the store. "Ah, she really is my favorite daughter," William said. "I can't believe she's home."

"She was a pretty girl when she was younger, and she still is," Mac said. "'Tis glad I am she's home, William."

William nodded and began recoiling the wire. "She's been gone too long. Six years it's been. You say you want four lengths? And the hooks?" He smiled as the running steps echoed overhead and they heard squeals as his family reunited.

"Aye. And she's come home to stay?"

"Yes. That's my hope. Mayhap she'll teach in the Grammar School." William looked at Mac. "It's been breaking my heart she's so far away. We've got a chance to bring her home."

"I'm wondering is she married now?"

"No. And don't be getting any ideas."

"Me? Would I have ideas? I'm just a poor fisherman."

"Right. And chasing every skirt on the island, you are."

"I'm an old man now. I don't chase every skirt. There's no harm in asking." Mac paused as he took up his parcel. "Put this on account. I'll settle up at Lammas."

"Things be changing," said William. "I was up to Westness. He wanted to go over all my books. He says I can't carry accounts next year like I have this. Not for anyone who doesn't pay."

"We always pay."

"Aye, but not everyone pays. Some barter."

"I've known you to take an egg or two on account. I'd not like to see that change."

"'Tis not the only change. He wants the fishermen to rebuild their boats. Close over the tops, like. Says you'll catch more fish. I'm to order in the lumber from Inverness."

"I heard," Mac said. "I don't know. We're doing all right as we are."

"You know about the pier?"

"Aye, and the fees that go along with it. Will you be collecting that as well?"

William nodded. " I'll have to hire someone to help me, either here or on the pier. I can't send the girls down to collect the fees."

Mac grimaced. "He can find ways to kill a dog without choking him with butter."

Upstairs, Deidre was delighted to see her sisters. "You've grown so much. You're truly young ladies, both of you. Ah, I've missed you both." She twirled Penelope and Charlotte into her arms for another long hug. "Hello, Mother."

"You look well, Daughter," said Anne. "Your father arranged an interview with Lady Alice. You're to go up as soon as you're able. He tells me if you get the position, you'll be staying here with us."

Deidre glanced up. Her mother's face in repose was a study in lines: two dissected each side of her mouth, and a third line connected dark eyebrows. "How have you been, Mother."

"Well enough." Anne fluttered her hands. "Girls, that will be enough. Go down to your father. Find something to keep you busy in the store, for I wish to speak with your sister."

"Yes, Mother," Charlotte replied. She and Penelope raced down the stairs, calling for their father as they went.

"I remember when they were smaller," said Deidre. "Our house always seemed noisy."

"The house is still too noisy. They forget themselves at the least provocation." Anne smoothed her skirt and beckoned to Deidre. "Come sit for a moment."

Deidre looked around the upstairs kitchen. Not a single napkin or a bowl was out of place. She followed her mother into the tiny front parlor where they sat on facing chairs.

"Your father has prospered. It's he who wanted you home."

Deidre raised her head. She should have known her mother would not forgive her.

"If you teach at the Grammar School, you'll have a room here, but I expect you to be a good model for your sisters. No immoderate laughing. No walking out at night."

"Mother, you've read my letters. I taught girls just like Penelope and Charlotte at Mrs. Neill's Academy for the last five years. I am a good teacher."

"I'm not talking about your teaching. It's grateful I am you have a profession after all that happened. I'm talking about you and your sisters and our standing with the new laird."

"I'm not sure they'll offer me the job." Deidre stared at her mother. "I'm not sure I'll be staying."

"Oh, your father, he talked to Lord Gordon. There's a need for another teacher at the Grammar School. You'll be staying. There are too many children at that school, and I think too many women like you."

Deidre felt her face flush. "What do you mean, mother."

"You know what I mean. There's no need to discuss it." Anne stared at her daughter. "You may want to live elsewhere, but your father won't hear of it. You can pay room and board as long as you're with us, but I want you keeping proper hours. I want you to be circumspect with the girls. They don't need you, the prodigal daughter, wrecking their chances."

"Yes, mother." Deidre wondered what chances her sisters had on Foulksay Island.

Anne stood. " I expect you will want to freshen up before your interview. Best to go over to Westness sooner rather than later. I've put you in Charlotte's room, that's your old room. She'll share with Penelope for now, and then we'll see." She rose. "Supper is at six then."

"Yes, I should like to freshen up." Deidre wondered again if she was making the right decision.

Her mother nodded and left the parlor. Their talk was over.

Deidre sat on the iron bed in her old room, the door to the rest of the upstairs apartment closed. Like old friends, she recognized the carved cabinet beside the bed and the colorful rag rug on the polished wooden floor. A small mirror had been hung on the whitewashed walls. Someone had placed a small bookcase for her books next to the window, white lace curtains obscuring the view. *Father*, she thought. *He hadn't forgotten.*

How she had loved that window at the front of the store. She used to spend hours looking out over the street and down the cove to the sea. It still hurt to think of the baby she had lost and the man who had made promises so long ago and then left her.

She watched the afternoon wind push clouds across the sky. *If I get the job, I will stay for my sisters and my father.*

It didn't take her long to finish unpacking, to wash her face and to comb her hair, tucking her long black hair into a serviceable bun. Deidre tied on a sturdy gray woolen hat bedecked with a bit of white lace and two small cloth roses. She took her woolen cloak and looked again around her room. The bookcase now held her precious cache of books. She pinned her spectacles to her waist and put on her gloves. She was ready.

"There you are. You look entirely grown up, my dear," said William, holding out his arms for another hug. "Already off to Westness? No worries, child. The interview is a formality. Once they meet you, they'll love you just as I do."

Deidre thought about her father and mother as she walked up the hill to Westness, the wind billowing in her skirts. Her father still saw everything with a golden glow. He seemed shorter, though, and she could see gray in his hair and more lines on his face. Her mother was ageless, standing straight and proper as any lady she had seen who came visiting Mrs. Neill's Academy.

How she missed Mrs. Neill, but once the letter came from her father, Mrs. Neill had said, "There's nothing really here for you, my dear. Too many know of your stay at Magdalene House, before you came here. Best you return to your island and your family."

Deidre stared at the outside of Westness, so large, its windows from four stories facing the sea. A few old men pushed wheelbarrows of stone to the back of the house, their narrow black coats buttoned against the wind. Somewhere inside that house, she would meet Lady Alice.

The large wooden door opened suddenly. "There you are," called Mrs. MacNaught. "Come up. Come up. We've been waiting for you. Welcome home."

Tears pricked Deidre's eyes at the warmth of Mrs. MacNaught's greeting. "I don't believe it quite yet," she replied. "But it's good to be back. It seems not much has changed."

"Don't you believe it. Everything has changed, and there's more change coming." She surveyed Deidre from head to foot. "What a charming hat. Now, give me your cloak. I'll take care of that. Come along with me." Mrs. MacNaught's skirts rustled as they went up the stairs.

"I'm taking you straight up. It's that busy we are with opening up the whole house. Did you remember Sheila Trimmer and Catriona Brodie?" she asked, nodding at two young women scrubbing the wooden floors with flannel cloths. "Extra day help from inland."

Deidre shook her head. She felt overwhelmed by the number of people she'd seen, faces she could almost recognize, names of people she once knew, and some she did not know at all.

"Never mind, dear. You'll like Lady Alice. She's very kind. Not that I should say anything, but she is. And your mother? How is she? No, don't tell me. I already know, but you'll be all right." Mrs. MacNaught patted Deidre's hand. "And here we are," she said, showing Deidre into Lady Alice's upstairs parlour.

"Good morning. Welcome to Westness," said Alice, rising from her desk. "You must be Miss Scott. Come sit while we talk."

Deidre murmured a greeting and tried not to stare. Lady Alice looked almost like a schoolteacher herself in her simple gray morning gown. Her dark hair had also been pulled into a bun, with a few tendrils escaping by either ear.

"I understand you once lived on Foulksay?"

"Yes, mum. I grew up here. For the last five years, I taught at Mrs. Neill's Academy for Girls in Inverness."

"And you have a letter of reference? May I see it?"

Deidre handed over the letter Mrs. Neill had so carefully prepared. She waited and tried not to fidget. The room was very quiet.

Lady Alice folded the letter. "Mrs. Neill says you have special strengths in teaching reading."

"Thank you, mum."

"Pastor McPherson has more than sixty children in the Grammar School. When Lord Gordon and I learned from your father of your teaching background, we thought it a perfect fit. I know you've come all this way, but perhaps only to see your family? Are you interested in staying on Foulksay?"

"Yes, mum. I think so."

"Why would you leave a comfortable position in Inverness with certainly more of an income to return here?"

"Mrs. Neill has been most kind, mum, but the school is a charity school. Those who can find other positions make way for the younger ones, those coming in. As you say, my family is here."

"I see. Tell me more about Mrs. Neill's Academy."

"Do you know Inverness? The Academy's out Culduthel Road, atop the hill overlooking the city. The building's not as grand as Westness House, mum, but bigger in a rambling kind of way, big enough for our hundred students. About half of the girls are day students. The rest live at the school. Classes meet in the central building with two wings extending around a walled garden. We teachers had our own rooms and served as monitors in the dormitories on each wing."

"And the curriculum?"

"All had instruction in reading and writing, with some arithmetic. At first I helped with these classes; later, I taught them. When the girls become twelve or thirteen, they're apprenticed or placed in service as soon as Mrs. Neill can find positions."

" It doesn't sound like many were from wealthy families."

"Actually, very few came from wealthy families. Two doctors, Dr. Cummings and Dr. MacLeod, started a school for boys. They funded Mrs. Neill's Academy to help girls who were thrown out by the mills or sent to the workhouse." Deidre wasn't sure if she should continue. For all she knew, Lord Gordon owned mills.

"I know of the conditions in the mills. My sisters and I helped a similar school in Edinburgh, though that included young women as well as girls." said Alice.

" We did have some older girls, but the children would break your heart, mum," Deidre replied. "Some started at the mills when they were six and seven. They took their shilling and made their X on a paper that committed them to work until they were 21. They stood at their stations from five in the morning until eight at night, all day, a little tin of oat cakes next to them. At night, they were locked up so they wouldn't run away. Most of the children were very sick when they first came to the school."

"I haven't seen anything like that here on Foulksay," said Alice.

"On the island? We have no factories. But the children work as soon as they can toddle, mum."

"Mrs. MacNaught speaks well of you," said Alice. "And, of course, your father does as well. Is there any reason I should not hire you?"

Deidre knew the moment had come, but she didn't want to tell Lady Alice of her first year in Inverness or of her baby that had died, stillborn. The old gossip would fly over the island soon enough.

"I can't think of anything, mum. Mrs. Neill was very kind to me. This job at the Grammar School seemed a good opportunity to come home." Deidre watched as Alice rose and walked to the window, her back to Deidre, the letter of recommendation folded in her hand. She hoped Alice would give her a chance.

"That was was a difficult time in Inverness, so far from your family."

"Yes, mum."

Alice faced the young woman seated before her, her eyes downcast, her hands clasped in her lap. "Do you know Pastor McPherson?"

"Yes, mum. He came the year before I left the island. Both my father and mother think highly of him."

"You will do well. The school is my special interest, especially the children. I would very much like you to teach at the Grammar School." Alice put the letter down on a side table. "Please visit with Pastor McPherson about the facilities and the curriculum. I will arrange with Perkins for your salary to be paid quarterly, if that is satisfactory."

"Thank you, Lady Alice."

"Call me Alice, please. I think we shall be friends."

CHAPTER 10: END OF THE HARVEST

The oat fields were nearly bare at the small farm outside Dunbeath. The workers lined up for their pay before they left to search for the next harvest. Moira fingered her scythe and the tin cup tied at her waist. "Let them go along," she said to Susan. "It's time to go home."

"Not a bad summer, right?" Susan replied, her dark hair pulled back tight behind her ears, her face brown from the sun.

"We made some money. Tell you true, I loved every moment. But I miss the boys."

"Miss the boys? They were here last night."

"Not those boys. My boys at home." Moira laughed as she thought of the young men from the field who had come to their tent last night. They'd brought a fiddle and sang songs until late. The music made her think of home and Dougal with his fiddle. The night air had hinted at cold.

"Jane's going south, down past Golspie or Cromarty, maybe to Inverness. She says you can find work in the mills there."

"Will you go?" asked Moira.

"Me work in a factory? Not likely. I hear they keep the women locked up at night, and the noise from the machines yammers so you can't hear. 'Tis ready I am to go home."

They joined the line for their day's pay, putting their coins away and tucking their purses into their bodices. Moira looked at the setting sun across the open fields and felt the slight edge in the evening air. She pulled her shawl tightly around her and linked arms with Susan. They walked back to their tent at the corner of the field to sleep.

Early the next morning, the women gathered to eat porridge provided by the farmer. Moira bound an oat cake in her waist. She was ready. "If we leave now, we can maybe find a ride to Dunbeath today."

"Give me Da this, and tell him that I'm all right," said Jane. She handed a small purse to Moira. "I'll send more money when I can. I'll find work in Inverness if I have to go that far or else somewhere along the way."

"I will," said Moira, taking the purse. "You're sure this is what you want to do? You can come back with us."

Jane settled her shawl around her shoulders and tied it tightly around her waist. "'Twas bad last year. Too many of us at home. Not enough to eat. 'Tis the right thing, though tell me Mum I'll miss her and all of them. Say a prayer for me, girls." She turned quickly away and walked along the road south, her head bent.

"We could go with her," said Susan. "We could stay with Jane, you know, and find work. We could send money back. I hate to see her go by herself."

"I promised Mac I would come home. That's where I'm going."

Susan took a last look at Jane, nearly out of sight. "Let's for Dunbeath then. I heard Market Day is the day after today."

Moira nodded. "It would be good to bring a little something home, something for my boys, something to remember the summer by."

The next week passed quickly as Moira and Susan made their way north to Land's End where they arranged their passage home to Kirkwall.

On the appointed day, Moira sat in the center seat next to Susan, her feet propped against a wooden crate of chickens. The small open boat pitched up and down large waves as they crossed the Pentland Firth to Kirkwall. She knew why Mac and Dougal went out on the sea nearly every day, regardless of the weather. *I love the sea. I could fly in this wind.* The Firth looked wider than she remembered, and the mainland behind her small on the horizon.

"Not to worry, lass. You'll be in Kirkwall before you know it," Old Jack shouted in her ear, as he scrambled past her, ducking under the boom.

Moira nodded. She wanted to scream in the wind. Her heart seemed bigger than her chest. They were close enough now to see the Orkneys ahead of them, flat floating islands on the edge of the Northern Sea. Another hour or so to sail around the edge of Scapa Flow, depending on the wind, and they'd be in Kirkwall. They'd catch a ride to Foulksay or send word over to Mac to come and get them. They'd be home in another day at the latest.

Two days back on Foulksay, and Moira felt as if she'd never been away, the familiar routine wrapped around her as if the island were her only home and the sea her only horizon. She untied her creel and stood admiring the beach. The tide was well out. Cockles scattered on the surface of the sand amid patches of seaweed, their shells gleaming pink and white in the early morning light.

"Look at them, just laying on the top there, waiting for us." Lenore set her creel down and hiked up her skirt.

"It's never enough," said Moira. "We'll still have to dig." She untied her rake, a narrow wooden rake with thumb-sized digits. "Jamie, use your rake."

The two women walked barefoot out on the tidal flats as Jamie ran ahead.

All along the cove, women, children of every age, and old men retired from the sea walked barefoot out on the tidal flats. The women hunched over and began to rake gently, digging just below the surface to feel the shell. With a twist, they pulled the cockles onto on the surface of the sand and threw them into their creels, working steadily until their creels were full.

"Watch the tide coming in," said Lenore. "We don't want to be cut off out here."

"You heard that Scott's won't take barter anymore?"

"Aye." Lenore slung another cockle into her creel. "Sean tried to talk to Scott, but he won't carry us on account."

"We'll still eat." Moira prodded a cockle with her rake. "Have you cooked these?"

"Aye. They're a little tough to chew, but they make a good soup."

Their creels full, the two women walked back up the shore, letting their skirts down as they came to dry sand.

"Let's work here, by the shed." Moira put her creel in the shade to keep the cockles alive as long as possible. "Jamie," she called. "Bring Sean's line over here." She sank down on the ground, pulled out Mac's fishing line already set with hooks, and began to bait the line.

Moira picked up one of the heart-shaped cockles and inserted her knife into its narrowest part, twisting sharply to open the shell. She threaded a hook through the meat of the cockle, tossing the shell behind her and dropping the baited line neatly into a creel for Mac to use in the morning. When she lifted her head to stretch, she could see a fast tide coming in. Jamie was bent over, his rake busy, his back to the sea.

"Enough, Jamie. Come help us."

"I don't like the color of the sky or the sea," said Lenore, pointing with her knife.

"Neither do they," said Moira. A few women had come down to the shore and stood watching the sea. The sky had lightened, but a strange brown color held to the horizon, and the sea was a sickly green. The women stood, wrapped in their shawls as the wind picked up from the east, and the sky darkened.

"They're late," said Moira. She brushed the sand from her hands. She walked down to the water's edge and stood with the women until the first boats could be seen. The women began to talk loudly;

each returned to her lines and her baiting. Moira remained at the waterline, ready to help pull their boat to shore.

Mac and Dougal grinned and shouted at Colin as he let the sails down by himself.

It must have been a good catch, she thought. Mayhap it would be good enough.

CHAPTER 11: MOIRA

The peat fire on the hearth had died to embers. Moira savored the last warmth as she turned the knitting in her lap and started another row. This made the third cap she could take down to Scott's. She listened to Colin and Jamie rustling above in the loft. *Home again with my brothers. At least the night is mine, and tonight the moon is full. Let them yell at me about the dangers of the summer night. Oh, sure, in this wild country, someone could kidnap me or carry me off to India.*

Moira peeked out the open door at the rolling grasslands and the path that led to the cliffs overlooking the sea. *Not a soul in sight.* Their stone cottage held the only bit of light as far as she could see. She heard a slight movement from the loft above.

"Jamie, Colin," she called up. "Are you done with your talking?"

"Colin's asleep," Jamie whispered back.

"And you'll be sleeping in the morning when it's time to go."

Moira wrapped her shawl tight and slipped out the front door to walk down along the moonlit path. She picked her way first through the moors, the heather undulating in the wind like the sea, then along the rim trail above rocky cliffs that led to the cove below and the beach. Moira felt close to the sea in a way she felt her brothers would never understand, even though Mac and Dougal had spent their lives fishing.

77

Moira watched the waves in their insistent rhythm. The rare clear night, the stars wheeling above, the smell and sound of the sea, all brought a sense of peace. Then, just as the stars were at their brightest, Moira turned toward home, hearing again the words Miss Deidre had read from Lord Byron's book of poems at the Grammar School: "So we'll go no more a-roving so late into the night . . ."

Later, she lay in bed, eyes closed, yet remembering the stars. She was just slipping off to sleep when Mac and Dougal came in, their voices filling the cottage until the walls seemed too small to hold them.

The next morning, Moira awoke to a quiet cottage, for her brothers had left well before dawn. Already her memories of the summer were fading, as if she had never followed the harvest and brought money home. She hoped the harvest on Foulksay would be a good one. They could trade fish for potatoes through the winter, if all went well. That and eggs, a little milk from their two cows, and more fish meant they wouldn't go hungry. She added an onion, stirred the fish soup, and set it on the edge of the hearth.

Moira looked out the window again, checking the weather. Clouds had gathered, but the *Star* wasn't due back for another hour or more. Moira began to pack her straw basket with eggs, layering them with grass to protect them.

"Halloo," cried a voice. "Are you home, Moira?"

Moira looked up to see Peter MacTavish walking into their yard. He carried a burlap bag over his shoulder. She had forgotten how tall he was.

"Brought you some potatoes," he said, handing her the bag.

"Thank you." Moira felt self-conscious. "I was just going down to Lenore's."

"I'll walk you down then."

Moira felt a rush of exasperation. "I'd rather go down by meself."

"All right." He leaned back on the cottage wall, watching her, his eyebrows pulled in a perpetual scowl.

Moira put the potatoes in a box, checked her soup, and closed the cottage door. "Here's your bag back. We all thank you."

"I want more than thanks, you know. I'd like us to marry. I'm willing to wait until Lammas. But I need a wife."

"Take the bag, then." Moira looked straight at his bristled face.

"I'd rather have an answer."

"All I'm offering is the bag. If you want your potatoes back, I'll get them."

Peter MacTavish towered over her. "I'm willing to wait. There's no so many who are asking. I have my own holding. You know my girls."

"I'm not ready. For all that, I may never be ready. Tell Ellie and the rest I think of them."

"Don't be so quick to say no. Think it over." Peter slung the burlap bag on his back and slowly walked down the path to Selkirk.

Moira watched him go. How could he just ask her, as if she were another cow for his farm he was thinking of buying? And to live with him, day past day and night past night. It didn't bear thinking of. She felt as if a dark shadow had passed over her.

Moira clambered over the rocks that led down to the beach and walked in front of the row of two-room stone houses at the north end of town. Several old men sat in a group around a shed, their beards damp with morning fog, their gnarled fingers mending nets. At the very end of the row of houses, closest to the water, Moira saw Lenore hanging laundry on a line strung next to her house; the diapers caught in the wind like tethered white sails.

"Moira. I wondered if you'd come today. Thanks for the eggs."

"They're from my summer chickens. And you're pregnant again."

Lenore laughed, and the two friends hugged.

"Come sit for a minute." Lenore settled on the porch, taking Mary on her lap. "Sean works so hard, but with the new baby coming, he's worried." She shrugged. "When the fish are running, we have a grand life." Lenore wiped Mary's face with her hand. "And when are you going to marry, my dear?"

"Probably not at all. Definitely not the MacTavish," Moira replied. "He came up the hill this morning."

"He didn't. Did he tell you he's the new constable?"

"No, he didn't. Since when do we need a constable?"

"I don't know. But he's older than Mac, at least. And all those children." Lenore looked at Moira speculatively. "You're thinking about it, aren't you?"

"No. I'm not thinking about it." Moira shivered again at the thought of sleeping with Peter MacTavish, no matter how many bags of potatoes he brought, no matter how sweet his girls were. "I don't know if I do want to marry." Perhaps she should have gone south with Jane. But then she wouldn't have come home. This island, her brothers, this is what she had dreamed of all summer. Now she was home, and all she could think of was getting away.

"I heard they're hiring up at Westness."

"I heard," Moira replied. "Dougal's girl, Catriona, works up there sometimes."

"Working at Westness would be better than marrying the MacTavish." Lenore lifted Mary up into the air. "Such a pretty one, you are. Maybe we'll have a brother to take care of you."

"They're coming in." Moira jumped up and ran down to the beach. She hiked her skirts up and waded out to wait for their boat.

"How did it go?" she called.

"Good enough," Mac said, throwing her the tie line from the front of the boat.

CHAPTER 12:

THE MCDONNELL COTTAGE

Mac shoved a bit of stone with his foot. "He's going to raise the rents. I know it."

"All the more reason for me to work. We need the money." Moira sat on a stubby stool and leaned against the outside wall of their cottage, a fishing line coiled in her lap. Dougal pulled another stool out and settled beside her. Together they straightened the knotted lines.

"It's not that simple. You'd be working at Westness, for him," said Mac, pacing in front of the cottage, the door open to the warm summer night. "You'd be serving him food and taking his leavings, but he's not for us. Not in the way the old laird was. This one wants us to put decks on our boats, but we have to pay for the lumber and all. There's to be fees for using the new pier. I don't see the end of it. 'Twill be worse if he raises the rents."

"All the more reason for me to go to Westness," said Moira.

"You may as well keep your breath to cool your porridge. There's no point to worrying," said Dougal.

"Somebody has to worry. Since Da died, it's me."

"We all worry, Mac." Dougal watched his brother pace. "There's no good of worrying. What will happen, will happen."

"I want to go." Moira spoke up. "Lenore told me they were looking for help. The pay is good, and it's steady. I'd be paid every quarter day."

"I know, I know. But where's all this taking us? Da wouldn't have liked you going into service. It's too many changes. Perkins wants us to ship our fish out fresh, not dried. How are we going to do all that if you're up at Westness?"

"Colin can do more. Jamie's older too. It doesn't have to be me."

Mac kicked the stone again. "Jamie's no got fish blood running in his veins. Always his nose in a book. And Colin's near a man. He'll be out with us before long. And you, you'll meet someone and go off and get married. Then what will we do?"

"Don't be saying that. I just want to work up at Westness. I don't want to marry anyone. If anyone should be marrying, it should be one of you."

"You don't know what you're asking, Moira. Ever since you came back from the harvesting, you're different. I shouldn't have let you go."

"'Tis glad I am that I went. Everything's the same here. Even the wind doesn't change. Nothing changes."

"We don't see it," said Dougal, his hands still for a moment. "But change happens all around us. It's like the music. I play the same tunes, and they're like old friends. But sometimes the music becomes something I never expected. Everyone still wants the old songs, but I can't always play them."

Moira looked out over the yard, past the stone wall to the headlands and the sea beyond. She could almost hear Dougal's fiddle in the wind. "I like your playing, Dougal."

"It doesn't put food on the table," he said softly.

"Eh, we can always eat fish," said Mac. "I'm trying to think what's coming. If we ship our fish fresh, we still have to pay for the barrels. Scott will make money on that," Mac pulled out another stubby stool and grabbed one of the lines. His big hands untwisted the line in jerks and then stopped. "Aye, he's got the ferry coming more often now, every week for sure, from here to Stromness. We can earn a bit from that, but only 'till November, if the weather holds."

"Moira has a point," Dougal interjected. "We can pay at Lammas, but what about the next quarter day? If you're right about him raising the rents, where will the money come from?"

"That's just it. We don't know." Mac's hands moved again. "And forget about getting a bigger boat. We just can't. And I don't know anyone who's ready to rebuild his boat. Are you, Dougal?"

"Will it help us catch more fish?"

"They say yes, but I don't know."

Dougal looked up. His hands stilled on the fishing line. "We'll see come Lammas. He has to announce it then if he's going to raise the rents."

"So I can go up to Westness?" Moira looked at her brothers. She flicked a fish head off the line and onto the ground.

"It's not up to me," said Dougal.

"I don't like you working up at Westness," said Mac. "I'm not so sure it's a good idea."

That was as close to a yes she would get. Moira looked down at the fishing line snarled in her lap. Her fingers automatically untwisted the line. Tomorrow morning, she would go to Westness.

Moira felt half asleep the next morning, wrapping oat cakes into a bundle. Even the stars were sleeping as Mac, Dougal and Colin left the cottage. The sky was so dark, all Moira wanted to do was to go back to bed, but today she would go to Westness.

Moira cut up potatoes for the day's soup. While the pot simmered on the hearth, she pulled the tub out, washed the clothes, and hung them outside, next to a line of drying fish.

As the shirts flickered in the wind, she realized she should have gone to Westness yesterday eve. Mac hadn't exactly given permission, but he hadn't said no outright. She scrubbed her hands again and tucked her hair back into a respectable knot. She checked her reflection in a piece of mirror Dougal had hung by the window. "Jamie," she called up to the loft. "You're to look after the cattle up by Barr Auch this morning."

"Dinna worry. I'm up already."

Moira left two oat cakes out on the side table for him and latched the door behind her. She hiked past the village on the upward path to Westness, the sun warming her back, the smell of sweet heather around her. She stopped to look at the fine large house at the top of the hill.

The four-story mansion, embellished with towers and turrets, had been called Westness for as long as she could remember. A few men from the village carted stones from the front of the house around to the back.

Moira walked up the expansive drive, hoping to see someone she knew. She raised the knocker at the large oak front door and let it fall. Nothing happened.

"Go around the back, miss," said the man who opened the door.

Moira nodded. She should have known better. She slipped around the side of the house. She could hear the workmen talking in low voices, their hammers chipping the rock into a well-shaped wall. She tapped on the back door.

"Ah, Moira. You've come about the job?" Mrs. MacNaught, heavy-set, with dark hair and darker eyebrows, nodded. "We've got one open in the kitchen, and maybe," she paused, tilting her head and listening to the clatter in the kitchen, "maybe one more. Come in, come in."

Moira stood just inside the door by a great scrolled sideboard, somewhat battered, covered with china and lace. It was her first time inside the great house. She peered down the carpeted connecting halls. Thin cables hung from the wooden walls at eye level, with high ceilings above her.

"Lord Gordon's having gas lights installed," Mrs. MacNaught explained. "You can sit in here," she said, showing Moira into a small office. "I heard you went harvesting down by Dunbeath this summer and brought some chickens home with you. That was wise, now, wasn't it?"

"Yes, mum."

"You'll have to meet with the factor, that's Mr. Perkins. If he says yes, you'll meet with Lady Alice. And if she says yes, then you'll start." Mrs. MacNaught winced at another burst of noise from the kitchen. "Wait here. I have to see to this." Her skirts whirled as she returned to the kitchen.

Moira rubbed the tiny nicks and scars on her hands and waited.

After what seemed a long time, Mr. Perkins came into the little office. He had the largest nose she'd ever seen and wore a pair of eyeglasses perched on the end rather like a medal.

"I am Mr. Perkins," he announced. "And you are?"

"Moira McDonnell, sir. I heard there was a job in the kitchen."

"Hmmn," he surveyed Moira. "Hands. Show me your hands."

Mutely, Moira proffered her hands.

"A hard worker, I see," he commented. "Can you read?"

"Yes, sir. And I can cook and garden."

Perkins sniffed. "How much schooling have you had?"

"I finished the grammar school here on the island," Moira replied.

"Did Mrs. MacNaught explain the duties to you?"

"A little, sir."

"The job is simple enough. You do what you're told. You can lift, can't you? You'll be making fires, carrying up meal trays, bringing in water and peat, that sort of thing. You'll sleep in the kitchen. Each day starts early and you'll work until 9 or 10 pm. Usually."

Mr. Perkins paused to examine her clothing. "You'll have to wear a clean black dress."

Moira flushed. She leaned forward so that her skirts covered her boots.

"You will be provided a white apron and a cap. You will have Sundays off, unless you are needed." He peered at her over his glasses. "You do have references?"

Moira nodded.

"And they are?"

"Pastor McPherson and Granny Connor can speak for me."

Perkins was silent.

Moira tried not to fidget. She wanted to know how much money she could earn. "About the money, sir, how much would it be?"

"Two pounds, 6 shillings per year, paid on quarter day. Room and board included. But if you are not interested." He turned to leave the room.

Moira calculated quickly. "Mr. Perkins, please sir, I'd like the job."

"Very well, McDonnell. You'll do. I'll find out if Lady Alice can see you now."

Once again, Moira waited. She would be bringing money home. Another clatter came from the kitchen, and Moira heard raised voices. *I've dealt with worse. After all, I have brothers.*

CHAPTER 13: THE PIG'S HEAD

"I didn't think you'd really go and do it." Mac paced around the hearth. "Who's going to look after things here at the house? And didn't I say we need you when we bring our fish in?"

"But you didn't say no, Mac. I'll still be coming home on Sundays. I was gone over the summer. You all survived. Colin took on more. And Jamie's a help as well."

Mac swung his head around, as if he was trying to see the cottage without Moira. He sat on the stool by the hearth and then stood again. "Jamie's not old enough to do much."

"Mac, think of Jamie. He'll need more school in a couple of years. So I finished the grammar school here. I can read and write, and so can you, but Jamie's different. He's reading whenever he can get a book. We need to set some money aside. And there's Colin. How do you know he wants to go fishing with you and Dougal?"

"Never mind about Colin or Jamie. This is about you going to work for them up on the hill. Ah, I let you go off for the summer, and you come home all full of yourself. You'll be too busy to take care of those fancy chickens you brought home."

"Mac, we'll manage. It's not like I'm getting married and moving away." Moira said.

"Don't be spinning fancies. You'll live here with all of us if and when you marry." Mac grimaced. "I don't like you working up there. What if something goes wrong? What will you do then? And you all alone there. I don't like it. And what's this about you getting married?"

"Don't be sidetracking me, Mac. It's near three pounds every quarter day. We need the money. I thought you'd be pleased."

Mac slumped back in one of the chairs. "I know, lass. I know. I never thought you'd hire out, Moira." He looked around the cottage again. "Jamie wants more schooling, you say."

"Mac, he's only ten. He doesn't know what he wants. But he's reading. Sure you see him reading, don't you? Someone has to think ahead."

"I'm thinking ahead. More than you know." Mac pulled his jacket on and paused at the door. "I still don't have to like it."

In the early evening, Mac walked down the hill to Selkirk, following the dirt path as it widened. *Whatever was she thinking?* He shook his head. *And nothing I can do about it.* He grimaced again and turned into the Pig's Head, welcoming the comfortable dark smell of beer.

The Pig's Head had been close to the shore as long as he could remember, a room set aside as a tiny pub in Mrs. MacLean's corner stone house. A rough drawing of a pig's head hung overhead on a shingle outside, with a lantern lit in the evening to show the way. Inside a counter had been built along one wall, with three tables near a stone fireplace where a peat fire burned only in winter. Here, beer or rum could be had in small dram-sized glasses for a half-penny or trade.

On rare occasions, Willie, a small, spare man with bushy eyebrows and fish-gnarled hands, brought out the whisky that burned all the way down. The taste lingered sweet, not like sailor's grog, watered rum. When the old laird died, the men had come to the Pig's Head to make solemn pronouncements.

"There you be, Mac," said Willie as he poured a glass of ale, his three fingers holding the glass steady. "Just as you like it. Fresh from the keg and warm as mermaid's milk."

"Ah," said Mac as he took the first sip. "Almost as good as what I make. Anything new from up the hill?"

"Who knows? They're fixing everything, like the old laird lived in a cave. All new furniture coming up from London on a steamer. Workers building a wall for a fancy English garden. And they're hiring more staff."

"That I know. Moira took a job there this morning."

"She didn't."

"She's old enough I can't say no. But that doesn't stop me from getting gray hairs." Mac turned and nodded a greeting.

"Willie, I'll have me one." Sean looked around. "Where's Dougal?"

"He said he went for a walk. But he's courting."

"He'll stop back later?"

"Maybe."

"You got news?" Willie asked.

"Just more about the pier," Sean said. "It's to run straight out from Front Street. I heard Mr. Perkins and him talking when they came along the beach." Sean frowned and hunched his lean body over his beer. "I guess it's a good thing. I don't know how we'll bring the boats in and unload them. But I guess that's what he wants, more men fishing and more fish."

"And more money for him," Mac said.

"That's the way of things," said Willie. "Not much any of us can do." He turned away to roll another keg into the bar.

"And mayhap less money for us," Sean said, his voice lowered. "I heard them saying there's a fee we'll have to pay."

"That bloody Perkins taking the food off our tables," said Mac.

"Hush, man. We don't know that yet. They're going to take down a few fishermen's shacks. Not as far up as my place, though," said Sean. "They'll clear out some of the drying racks as well."

"They talk to anyone?"

"Not a soul. They come down to the beach, and they talk to each other as if we're invisible."

"We are invisible, Sean. We're nothing to them. Just the way it is." Mac took a deep sip of his ale and thought about all the years he'd been fishing with his father and his father fishing with his father before him. Now Moira was up at Westness, and mayhap Jamie someday would go to the mainland, leaving just him, Dougal, and Colin to take the *Star* out. "There's change coming," he said, shaking his head. "The old laird dies. There's a new laird, and it just gets worse and worse. We might as well be drinking kelpie beer."

Sean laughed, a short barking sound, his blue eyes keen. "Kelpie beer. Why not just eat seaweed and piss in the ocean?"

"Yeah," Mac grimaced. "We got a right proper taste for it."

Willie moved back down the bar. "You want another?"

"Nah," said Sean.

"Perkins stopped in earlier." Willie ran his rough fingers along the bar. "The pier should be done before Martinmas and to pass the word. Lord Gordon wants his taxes paid."

Mac stood. "There's no money for taxes, and there's no money for something we don't need."

"If they require us to use a pier," said Sean, "we have to pay them."

Mac poked Sean's shoulder. "There's some who'd rather pull their boats on the other side of the island rather than pay a bloody tax."

"Shush now," said Willie. "I can't be hearing what some might do. Perkins will call in the new constable and lord knows what else." He nodded to the two men and moved down the bar, his back held straight for an old man.

"What a mess we got." Mac said. "Never doubt this will get worse."

"Shall I spread the word?"

"Be careful who you talk to." Mac lowered his voice. "Might you pull in on the east side?"

"I might. Some of the time. And you?" said Sean.

"Maybe. Depends on how much they take. We're all right for now, but the new laird, he wants to lick the butter off my bread." Mac drained the last of his beer. "See you around."

"Tomorrow at dawn then, you and Dougal?"

"Aye." Mac felt as if he were in deep water and sinking to the very bottom of the sea. He looked at his hands in the dim light of the tavern. "Ah, give the beggar a bed, he'll repay you with a louse," he muttered.

BOOK 2: WESTNESS

SUMMER - FALL 1841

CHAPTER 14: STANDING STONES

The sky filled with high, fast-moving clouds as Alice picked her way up the hill to walk along the headlands. Her rucksack with drawing materials almost forgotten, she followed a narrow path east, the cool wind a welcome change. Her head down, she barely saw the heather mixed with moor grasses on the rolling hills.

She rounded a turn to find a massive stone circle on a flat hollow before her that faced the sea. Alice walked around the outside of the stone circle, measuring it with her steps. How many stories had been told of these stones – that giants heaved them here in some heroic battle when the earth was young or that druids used them in magical rites now long forgotten. The grass was smooth in the inner circle.

She leaned her ear against one of the stones, the one closest to the sea, as if she could hear why it had been made. The stone, its front scoured by wind, arched above her some ten feet. *What a marker this would have made for early seafarers,* she thought.

Alice sat with her back against the cold stone and gathered her long skirts around her legs. She quickly sketched in lines to mark the horizon and the expanse of grassy headlands around her. She then blocked in the seven standing stones, measuring the relationship of each with her thumb and the head of her drawing pencil.

When her back began to ache and her legs were cold from the damp, she walked to the center of the circle of stones. Here a small flat stone remained, dried flowers scattered on the grass before it. Alice looked to the sea and then methodically in each direction, back to the island, searching its hills and valleys for other markers or stones. She had read in the *Archaeologia Scotia* report her father had sent that these stones could be linked to other ancient sites. Turning, she spotted a slight boy in bare feet, his trousers not quite reaching his ankles.

"Hello," she called.

The boy stood at the far edge of the stone circle.

"Come here," she called again.

"You're from Westness?" he shouted back.

"Yes, I am. Come here."

The boy approached, his thin face uncertain. "I saw you drawing."

"What is your name?"

"Jamie McDonnell."

"I know your sister, Moira."

"Aye. She works over to Westness." Jamie touched his cap. "You're Lady Alice."

"Yes, I am. What are you doing out here?"

The boy pulled open a creel slung over his shoulder. He lifted a layer of grass to show a pile of small dark gray eggs. "Gathered them. Over there." He nodded toward the cliffs.

"You climb on the cliffs?"

"A little."

"Just like that, with no shoes?" Alice asked.

Jamie grinned, the gap between his two front teeth showing. "Aye."

"Do you want to see?" Alice held up her sketch book.

Jamie nodded. They sat on the ground and bent over the sketch book while Alice turned the pages.

The boy studied the drawings intently. He looked again at the standing stones and back to the drawing. "I like your pictures."

"My father taught me to draw back home in Edinburgh. He's interested in old things. Do you draw?"

"We did some in school when I was younger. I liked it well enough."

"Show me." Surprising herself, Alice handed the sketch pad and pencil to Jamie. He held the pencil in his grimy hand as if he'd never seen one before. "Go ahead. Draw one of the stones."

Jamie bent over the sketchbook and drew, his concentration so intense it was as if he were alone. The standing stone emerged on paper, the lines rough and true. Alice was content to sit beside him and watch. She wondered if she would ever have a son like this. She sighed. The boy had so much talent, yet he was hanging over a cliff to gather eggs. If what Pastor McPherson had told her was true, he would be on a fishing boat far too soon. "I've been reading about old stones like this. Are there others like this on Foulksay?"

"I know a few places. One's further up the coast." Jamie waved to the north. "One's on the other side of the island. Both are a good walk from here, though."

"Did I see you at Westness recently?"

"Yes, mum. I was looking for a job."

Alice noted his thin clothing. "Could you help me measure and draw some of these stones? And maybe take me to the other old places? I will pay you."

"Aye. I'd like that."

Alice wanted to reach out to him, to smooth his hair, to give him a warmer coat. "Tomorrow then, in the morning." She looked at the sky. "We'll hope for good weather."

"Can it be in the afternoon, mum, like today? I help my brothers in the morning."

"In the afternoon? Certainly. Come to Westness as soon as you can."

"I'll be there, mum."

Alice watched Jamie run down the path back to Selkirk, his creel tucked under his arm. So this was Moira's brother. He would spend the rest of the day down at the beach to bait hooks, she guessed. The boy was so thin she wondered if they truly had enough to eat. God willing, they could always eat fish.

By the time Alice returned to Westness, it was nearly supper and quite dark. The two maids were just lighting the lamps throughout the house. Alice pulled off her jacket as she walked up the central winding stairs to her rooms to change.

"Lord Gordon wanted to see you earlier," said Mrs. MacNaught as she helped Alice take off her wet skirt and boots.

Alice pursed her lips. "Did he want to see me before supper?"

"He said you were to come to his office the moment you came in." Mrs. MacNaught shook the wet skirt out and spread it over a chair near the fire to dry. She avoided looking at Alice.

"Very well," replied Alice. "That will do for now. I'll go straight down as soon as I've changed."

Alice tapped on the door to Gordon's office and waited for a few moments. She heard nothing. She tapped again.

"Yes, yes, come in."

Alice found Gordon with papers spread over his desk. He looked up as she entered. "And where have you been all day?"

"Out walking. I took my sketch book up to the standing stones above the cove."

Gordon stared at her, silent.

"Papa wrote me about them, asking for drawings. He thinks they may be similar to the standing stones at Stenness."

Gordon pushed a set of papers aside and sighed. "I wanted to ask you, have you seen Pastor McPherson?"

"Not yet."

"Not yet?" Gordon stood. His letters and papers scattered to the floor. "But I asked you weeks ago to work with him."

Alice was silent.

Gordon's face flushed red. "What are you, some kind of foolish girl who must be kept in her room before she does what she is told?"

"Perhaps it is better not to shout," said Alice.

"Don't tell me not to shout." Gordon slapped a book and it fell to the floor. "This is my office and my house, and you are my wife. You are to meet your responsibilities."

Alice felt a surge of anger. "This is foolishness. All this uproar. Just because I wasn't here this afternoon when you called for me. Why are you so angry?"

He grabbed her wrist, holding it tightly. "Tell me now. Are you pregnant?"

"Pregnant?" Alice shook her head. "No, I'm not."

He pulled her toward him until their faces were inches apart. Alice saw spittle shaking on his lips. "I want sons."

"Gordon, let go of my wrist." *I am his wife,* thought Alice. *He cannot do this.*

He held her for a moment longer and pushed her from him. He sat heavily on one of the side chairs. "Leave me."

Alice rubbed her wrist. Her anger evaporated. *Something was wrong.* "I don't understand, Gordon. You know we both want children. It must be something else."

Gordon turned his face away. "I can't talk about it. Just leave me."

Alice closed the office door and stood by it a moment. There were no servants in the hall, but they knew. They always knew.

Gordon looked at the papers strewn on the floor. Alice was not to blame. William Gray's letter lay crumpled on the desk. On the way back from Bangladore, one of their three ships had foundered and sunk along the Barbary Coast. The captain of the second ship had thrown much of its precious cargo overboard to survive the storm, and the third ship hadn't yet arrived in London. Gray reported that the exchange was talking of another market crash, as bad as the one in '25.

It was a disaster. He would have to travel south to ask Alexander for another loan. He could see his brother's face now, narrow and supercilious. Of course, Alexander would tell his wife about his poor brother, banished to this god awful cold and dark island with an intractable and infertile wife, yet unable to make a living even with Alexander's largesse.

Gordon felt the blood rushing in his temples. He rubbed his arm again. The pain lessened slowly. Raising the rents would not be enough. He would have to begin evictions.

CHAPTER 15: SCOTT'S MERCANTILE

Deidre buttoned a lace collar over her black dress and stepped into the kitchen. "Good morning, Mother. Are the girls awake?"

"Not quite yet. I heard Penelope stirring." Anne leaned over the stove, one of the few iron stoves on the island, her back to her daughter. "Fetch me some more peat, and we'll call them to breakfast."

"Yes, Mother." Deidre ran down the stairs and started to fill a large tin pail with peat from the bin in the storage room at the back of the store. It was cooler downstairs, but her heart felt light.

"Good morning, daughter. You're up early this morning."

"Not so early, father. I'm to see Pastor McPherson this morning." She put the scuttle down as she surveyed the store. "I should be back by noon."

"Your mother talked to me about the Pastor just last night. He's a fine man. Single, you know."

"Father, I'm going to work at the school with him, not marry him." She shuddered. "Not the Pastor."

"I know. I know. But he's an educated man. You could do worse. Here, give me that. It's too heavy for you."

"No, I'll take it up, Da. I just wanted to say good morning."

"And a good morning it is. We're busy already."

The store was a little dark in the gray morning light. Mac stood with several other men around the pot-bellied stove in the middle of the store. He was taller, and his dark hair seemed to catch the light.

"Breakfast is ready if you can come up, Father."

"All right." William patted her arm. "Boys, I'm going upstairs for a moment. Be back in a few."

Mac turned at his voice and saw Deidre. He walked to the back of the store. "And a good morning to you, Mistress Scott."

"Good morning. You're not out fishing this day?"

"Not when I could be talking to you," He grinned, and Deidre flushed. "Let me carry that up for you," he said.

"No, I've got it. I'm fine."

"I insist." He leaned close to Deidre to pick up the pail. "You smell nice this fine morning."

"Please. Let me be."

"Ah, ladies don't carry such heavy things, Deidre, and you are definitely a lady."

Deidre's heart hammered. She wondered how much he remembered about her. She gave up and followed Mac up the stairs.

"There you are, Mac," said William. "Mother, you know Mac."

Anne nodded a greeting, her eyes on the bubbling porridge.

"Good morning, Mrs. Scott. Where do you want this?" Mac held the heavy pail up as if it were weightless.

"By the stove. No need for us to keep you from your work."

"'Tis hard at work I am already, Mrs. Scott." He gave Deidre a wink. "Lifting and carrying for Scott Mercantile when I could be fishing."

"Ah, Mac, you're fishing already, fishing for compliments," said William. "Go on with you now. Mayhap you can walk Deidre over to the school since you're so busy."

"Father," interrupted Anne. "She's to see Pastor McPherson this morning."

"Toosh. Let the boy walk her up to the manse. Take your cloak, Deidre. You'll be working soon enough."

Deidre pulled her cloak on, eager to leave the warm kitchen before her mother said something irredeemable. Penelope and Charlotte whispered and stared at Mac waiting by the door, the pail of peat forgotten by his feet.

Then Deidre was outside with Mac, glad of the morning wind that smelled of the sea.

"'Tis good to see you back home." Mac looked at Deidre as they walked along the boardwalk in front of Scott's Mercantile. "Watch out for the mud here."

"I know about the mud, thank you," Deidre replied. "I didn't realize how much I missed the island."

"We think nothing changes, and then everything changes. You were off teaching. That must mean you still enjoy your books."

"You remember?" Deidre was a little surprised.

"Of course I remember. You were the prettiest girl at the Grammar School. I think I lost my heart to you."

"Those days are long gone, Mac."

"Remember how we used to hide from Mr. Carruthers to read *Ivanhoe*?"

"I remember. Do you still read?"

"Not so much. Did you bring any books with you?"

"A few."

"Jamie's a reader. He's in school, though he's close to his last year." Mac was silent for a moment, staring at the street before him.

"What will he do when he's done with school?"

"I don't know. He's young yet." Mac shook his head. "Are you coming to Lammas tomorrow eve then?"

"I wasn't planning on it. Not yet. It's too many people and too soon."

"Ah, it's never too soon to have a bit of a dance. Mayhap you'll dance with a hulking old fish like me?"

Deidre laughed, feeling as if the years she had stayed in Inverness fell away, and her only worries were over who she might dance with at the Assembly House. "Dougal still fiddles, does he?"

"So you remember Dougal, and not me."

"Who could forget his fiddle-playing? No one can listen without being moved to cry or dance. That I remember. And your sister, she was so wild." Deidre bit her lip.

Mac laughed. "Moira's working up at Westness now, but I don't like it. Me Da died while you were gone. It's just the five of us now."

Deidre took Mac's hand. "I heard. I'm sorry about your Da."

"He was a good man. Better that he went when he did than to see what the new laird is doing."

"I'm hired at the school because of him, Mac."

"Aye, but I'm thinking we'll have higher rents ahead and maybe worse."

"You don't know that, do you?"

"I've heard some things. We'll find out come Lammas." Mac grimaced. "Nothing will help if he takes the bread out of our mouths."

"My father thinks well of him."

"Mayhap I'm worrying for nothing. 'Tis glad I am that you're home. Come tomorrow eve to Lammas, then, will you?"

"Aye," said Deidre. For once, she didn't think of what might have been.

CHAPTER 16: LAMMAS

Dougal flourished his bow at the crowd. He nodded at two other musicians, and they began another reel. A few couples and several youngsters danced near the stage. Men gathered in clumps near barrels of dark home-made harvest ale at the far end of the Assembly Hall.

Moira looked over the gathering of bobbing heads from her vantage point by the musicians, her foot tapping. The hall was nearly full. Crofters had come in from all over the island, and the men were back from the second herring run. She saw a few strangers scattered among those she knew so well.

Along the other side of the hall, Lord Gordon and Lady Alice watched the dancers. Heads of households had visited Lord Gordon all day, paying the rents and taxes that were due and presenting the freshly baked harvest oat cakes that now lay sliced and ready to eat on the sideboards.

The bodhrán's steady beat compelled everyone to dance until sweat rolled down their faces. Chairs had been pushed to the side of the Assembly Hall, and the birds flew out of the rafters at the noise.

Mac brushed the top of Moira's head. "You look like our mother, with your dark hair and your blue eyes." His voice boomed in her ear over the noise of the music. "Not dancing? I see some good men here tonight."

"Aye. Too bad they're too shy to dance," Moira replied.

"Watch out the MacTavish doesn't find you." He turned, spotting Deidre. "I'm off for a bit of dancing meself."

Moira watched Dougal's fingers fly over the fiddle. She felt proud of him, and her feet tapped the rhythm of the drum. The dancing grew frantic as more people pushed into the hall. Moira closed her eyes and gave herself over to the dance, the music keening in her head and heart. A strong arm held her at her waist and twirled her around.

Moira's eyes flew open. "And who might you be?"

"I'm Dylan, from across the water, ready to dance your feet off and steal your heart." He grinned and bowed.

Dylan was much shorter than her brothers, wiry, and dark when they were fair, his hair curly with sweat. His eyes, nearly black, sparkled. He smiled again, and Moira felt her breath catch. "Dance with me?"

She gave him her hand, and they danced one set after another, until they were both breathless.

"Any others like you at home?" he asked.

"No, not a one. Just me," Moira shouted over the music, turning away and then back as he twirled her to the music.

"Ah, 'tis fortunate I am, for then I'll only have me heart broken once."

Moira laughed. His hand caught and held hers, and his dark eyes dared her to let go.

"Wait until you meet my brothers."

"And how many brothers do you have, all tiny men, as small as trolls, no doubt?"

"Four brothers," she replied on the next round. "Mac, Dougal, Colin and Jamie. All of them are giants compared to you." She glanced over at Dougal and waved. "There's Dougal."

"He looks ferocious," said Dylan. "Does he have an evil temper?"

"None of my brothers would harm a soul."

"Then why is he glaring at me like that?"

"Maybe he worries about your intentions."

"Ah, my intentions are only good where you are concerned." Dylan swung her away and back in another spin. "Care to step outside for a bit of a walk?"

Moira nodded. She wasn't sure she should go with him, but then they were outside, away from the music, the cooler night air on her face a welcome respite. "You're new to the island?"

"Aye. I'll be here a time. Mr. Scott put me in a room over at Mrs. MacLean's house, close by where they plan to build the pier."

"How come you to Foulksay?" Moira asked as they turned around the small square in front of the Assembly House, the stars white dots of light above them.

"'Tis a long story, one to break your heart," Dylan replied. "You've heard of the troubles in Ireland?"

"No."

"I remember good years. We had a small holding near Ennis, and then we lost it. We lived by hiring out and by poaching." He sighed. "'Twas either that or no food. Came a time we couldn't pay the rent. Everywhere, people was living in the lanes and starving. So we went to Ulster, looking for work, and we found it at Peterport. We scrabbled enough together to pay passage over to Glasgow for my two brothers and me. The plan was for us to work and send money back .The rest, my father, my mother, and three sisters stayed in Peterport, picking up day jobs as they could."

He couldn't speak for a moment, and then he laughed, a harsh sound in the cool night. "I'll save the rest for another time. You wouldn't believe how many starving Irishmen they can fit on one of those ferries."

Moira could feel the muscles on his arm tighten. The moon hung low on the horizon. "It's so beautiful tonight, you nearly forget the hard times," she said. "What happened in Glasgow?"

"You sure you want to hear this?" Dylan shook his head. "I was taken up at a shipyard, and Michael and Sammy got in at the railroad. We found a place to stay, crammed in at the top of a tenement seven stories high. There we slept, the three of us, sharing half a room and sending money home. Except it wasn't enough. First we got word that my youngest sister died. Then my mother and my father went. After that we didn't hear anything. 'Twas the cholera. God forgot us all."

"No, never say that." Moira wondered if words were ever enough. "My mother and father both died. There's only my brothers and me."

"Then you know."

She nodded.

"There's more," said Dylan. He cleared his throat and held her hands tightly. "In the spring, the cholera came to Glasgow. It spread through the tenements like a plague, and it took my younger brother, Sammy. All that's left now is Michael and me."

They walked in silence for a bit, holding hands. "I have two younger brothers," Moira said. "I don't know how I'd feel if anything happened to them."

"You don't die," Dylan said. "That's the hard part. They've all been black days until I saw you dancing this night."

"Your brother, Michael. Is he here tonight?"

"Ah, no. If he were, we'd be fighting over you." Dylan grinned. "He's digging track down by Inverness."

"So, how came you to Foulksay?"

"Hired I was, by the lord's factor from the boatyard over in Inverness. I'm here to help the fishermen rebuild their boats."

"You'll be working with my two older brothers, then."

Dylan threw back his head and laughed. "Lucky I am. I'll charm those trolls until they think I'm one of them, and they'll bring me home to you." He picked Moira up and twirled her around. "Let's go back to dancing, for if we stay here, I'll kiss you before I should."

Moira leaned her face close to Dylan. "Then kiss me now, for I'd like to know how an Irishman kisses."

Dylan stood completely still.

Moira couldn't take her eyes away from his. He pulled her into his arms and kissed her gently, his lips warm on hers. The tip of his tongue teased her lips, and his kiss lasted until she could no longer breathe, yet she wanted him to never stop.

The kiss ended. She wasn't sure if she should stay or run away. She smiled and so did he.

"Beautiful." Dylan stroked her hair and drew her close. "Moira, Moira. Your name reminds me of the Queen of Heaven, and that you are, queen of my heaven."

They watched the stars shine above the sea.

"You know that I'm serious about you?" he asked after a long while.

"Yes." Moira felt tears in her eyes.

"Hist, love, tears? None of that. 'Tis not a bad thing. As you see, I'm only an Irishman, and Protestant to boot, not enough to stand between us."

"It's not that." Moira wanted nothing more than to stay here next to him for the sheer joy of being close to him, smelling the salt on his body, holding his hand. A tumult of emotions ran through her. Her brothers would be waiting. After Sunday, she'd be starting at Westness or back down on the beach, cleaning fish. "We better go back."

"Not 'till this is resolved." He looked at their hands, joined together. "I want to see you again. I hear sometimes people meet out by the standing stones. Will you meet me there tomorrow eve when the moon rises?"

"Aye." Moira knew in that moment that nothing else mattered, not her brothers, not Westness.

CHAPTER 17: AFTER LAMMAS

The next morning, Moira dished up porridge for her brothers and wondered if she would meet Dylan that night at the Standing Stones.

Jamie and Colin pushed each other over who would get the last of the Lammas bread.

Mac's eyes narrowed. "I saw you with that scrap of a man, that stranger. I asked around. Is that what's bringing a silly smile to your face? You've not done anything foolish, have you, lass?"

"What would I be doing? Yes, I finally met a man. Little enough you would know, with you off fishing all day and gone all night." Moira leveled her wooden spoon at Mac. "And when are you going to find a wife so I'm not the only one here cleaning and cooking and washing and all, and now working up at Westness."

"Don't try to change what we're talking about. That man's an outsider, Moira. He's out to break your heart, and then he'll slip away like an unknotted rope." Mac's head barely cleared the beams of the ceiling. "As to the rest, you should know that I'm serious about Deidre."

"Serious? What ever does that mean? You could be serious about a person for a hundred years and never take a wife," Moira shot back.

Jamie and Colin giggled behind their hands.

"Shut your laughing," Mac growled. "I hear the Irish are coming over by the thousands down south. They're filling up the cities, and they're taking our work. Ah, what's the point. I know what kind of man he is. He's most likely gone off the island by now, with never a thought for you."

"He's not leaving. Mac, give him a chance. He's had a hard time."

"Told you a pretty story, did he? What's he doing here?"

"He's to help the fishermen rebuild their boats." Moira saw the anger rise in Mac's face. "Wait. I know that's something you don't want, but, Mac, I don't care he's a stranger or even an Irishman. I wouldn't care if he were a papist. I want a chance to know him."

"You'll know him all right if he gets his way. What did he do to you so fast?"

"Nothing. We just danced and talked."

"Out, boys," Mac said. "Stay close for we're leaving for church shortly. That's right. Off you go. Moira, stay a moment. Dougal, stay as well."

"Why do I have to go out? I'm old enough," Colin grumbled. "I could have met someone dancing."

Mac glared at Colin. "And does your head hurt? Don't think I didn't see you drinking buckets of ale last night. Out."

The stone cottage was quiet. Moira couldn't help a sense of dread. She remembered Dylan as clearly as if he stood before her, the warmth of his lips on hers. *Now I'll have to fight to see him again, but I will.* She busied herself with cleaning up, scraping the porridge pot clean, keeping her back to her brothers.

Mac and Dougal exchanged glances. "Moira, come sit. We need to talk," Mac said.

Moira pulled a stool from under the side table and sat. She glared at Mac.

"Ah, sister, dinna work yourself up. This is serious business. Did this man force himself on you?"

"His name is Dylan. We danced and talked. That's all." Moira crossed her arms.

"Is he a papist?" Mac began pacing.

"No. He's Protestant, same as you and me. Maybe not our kirk, but we didn't talk about that."

"I'll bet," said Mac.

"Moira, he's not one of us." Dougal hunkered down next to Moira. "Surely you don't want that?"

"He makes me laugh. He's kind and gentle. He lost his sisters and his family back in Ireland; otherwise, he wouldn't be here."

"I saw the two of you dancing," said Dougal. "You looked happy last night. But we don't know anything about this man."

"I want to see him again."

"First, we talk to him," said Mac.

Dougal nodded.

"I will see him again," Moira replied. "If you harm the slightest hair on his head, you won't be my brothers, not in the same way ever again. That I promise you."

"But he works for Lord Gordon," Mac interrupted. "All they want is to squeeze more and more money out of us. You might as well know Lord Gordon increased our rent. That's what he told us last night while you were all making music and dancing. And there's nothing we can do about it." Mac threw his hands out in frustration. "So we need that money you'll get at Westness, but I still don't like you working up there. And now there's this Irish man on top of it. We'll talk to him before you meet again, that's certain."

"His name is Dylan. Mac, you won't hurt him, will you?"

"We'll talk to him gently," said Dougal.

Mac nodded. "But you're not to see him again until we do. Agreed?"

"All right."

Mac stood abruptly. "Enough of this. I've got a meeting after church, Sabbath or no." Mac crammed his cap on his head and slammed out of the cottage.

"He'll cool down," said Dougal. "He's just angry about the rents and all."

"I know." Moira pulled her shawl close. "But, Dylan's different."

"We'll see." Dougal put his arm around his sister. "Come on. You'll be safe enough in church. For sure you won't be seeing him there."

Moira bristled. "You don't know that."

The McDonnells didn't talk as they walked down the hill to St. Ninian's. Inside, Moira and her brothers took up nearly the entire back row. Moira sat on the narrow wooden bench next to Jamie and Colin. She sneaked a glance at Mac and tipped forward a little to see if Dylan had come and where he might sit. Peter MacTavish scowled at her. Moira looked at her hands.

But she couldn't find either Dylan or Lord Gordon. In the very front of the church, closest to the altar, Lady Alice sat alone in the family pew, wearing a small hat with a veil that concealed her face.

Around her, the congregation rustled. Jamie fidgeted. Moira nudged him to keep him still. Maybe Dylan had come, and she couldn't see him. Maybe he would speak to her after services. She flushed. She wished her mother were alive. The wind picked up outside. Moira felt a cold draft on her feet.

Pastor McPherson came in from the sacristy, one finger holding his place in his Bible. He nodded to Lady Alice. "Today, my children, we mark the end of summer. For it is written in *Ecclesiastics*, there is a time for sowing and a time for reaping. Now we reap the bounty of our labor."

Pastor McPherson paused. "We know the future is uncertain. We do not know if we can carry the burdens that come to us. But if we have faith in God and in ourselves, we will prevail. Let us give thanks to God for our blessings. When the collection box is passed this morning, consider our neighbors. Who is in want? Who goes hungry this day? Let us pray."

Moira peeked at the bowed heads around her and at her brothers to see if they were truly praying. Only Mac's head remained upright, his eyes open as he stared at Lady Alice.

CHAPTER 18: MOIRA AT WESTNESS

Moira wrapped her plaid tightly around her shoulders and quickened her steps as she set off on the walk to Westness just after sunrise. She could barely see the path before her as the sky lightened. Cormorants cried out over a passing school of fish. The birds dove into the sea and wheeled back again, hunting breakfast. She felt like running. Today, she wouldn't be cleaning fish.

That first morning at Westness, all was chaos. Sarah Britton, sweaty, her apron stained with fresh jelly, shouted and bullied everyone who came near. Moira didn't know where anything was or what she was supposed to do.

When she thought she couldn't stand another moment, Moira thought of the higher rents due next quarter day and Jamie's love of books. She imagined Mrs. Britton out on their boat, screeching at her brothers. That made it all possible.

"You, girl, help Maggie take the trays up," Mrs. Britton said, gesturing to Moira. "Now, don't look directly at himself, and for God's sake, don't spill anything."

"Yes, mum," said Moira, as she lifted the heavy breakfast tray and followed Maggie up the dark, winding back stairs. She nearly tripped at the door to the dining room and kept her eyes on the floor as she followed Maggie over to the side table and laid out the serving dishes, eggs covered with cream sauce, kippers, black olives, and fried potatoes with tomatoes and bacon. The smells made her dizzy. So much food. Even white bread.

Moira sneaked a peek at the laird. She was to call him Lord Gordon if he spoke to her. He sat at the very end of the table, alone with his papers. Benson served tea and then breakfast. Moira and Maggie stood at attention by the great sideboard, bringing dishes over as directed. Finally, they carried the trays, cluttered with used dishes and half-eaten food, back downstairs to the kitchen.

"We'll come back up when they ring the bell. No guests today," said Maggie, with a nudge. "That means we'll have more for us later."

"What do you mean?" asked Moira.

"Didn't they tell you?" Maggie stopped on the stairs. "Now that the new laird's here, there's people coming and going all the time. We get whatever's left over. Sometimes it's not so much, but aren't you hungry?"

Moira nodded. "What about Lady Gordon? She wasn't at breakfast."

"You mean Lady Alice? She don't eat downstairs any more. She'll have something in her room. Tea and a bit of toast is all she'll eat. Most likely she'll want her tray in her room right about the time we need to bring the rest of the dishes down from the morning room." Maggie pushed a piece of white bread into her mouth and kept walking down the staircase. "You don't want to be around them when they start arguing. And watch out for Perkins. Don't let him get you alone."

Somehow, Moira got through the first day. She brought in endless loads of peat for the two large fireplaces in the kitchen, scrubbed pots, and washed dishes. She chopped vegetables and skinned meats as Mrs. Britton instructed. In the afternoon, Moira kneaded dough made up with white flour into rounds of fresh bread and brought provisions up from the cellar. She helped carry up trays for afternoon tea and dinner. She had never seen so much food, and, as Maggie had said, the staff ate some of what was left over, with scraps going to the pigs behind the stables.

At supper, Moira carried up heavy trays with platters of meat and potatoes, a soup of leeks, and a raisin pie with cream to pour over it. At the end of the day, she scrubbed the stone kitchen floor and cleared away the last pots. She was tired but happy. Mrs. Britton had stopped shouting at her. Perkins had done no more than stare at her.

Moira lay down to sleep beside the fireplace on a pallet made of blankets, warm and surrounded by the smell of the kitchen. She could hear Maggie's even breathing nearby. She looked up at the heavy beams over her head. *Had Jamie fed her chickens and remembered to check the cheese? Had they taken her finished caps down to Scott's Mercantile? Was Mac still angry about Dylan?*

Around her, all was quiet, but Moira lay awake, her back a little sore. She rubbed one finger that had gotten burned on a pot. *Dylan.* She could hardly see his face. Thick black hair she remembered, that and his warm hands. Perhaps she would see him on Saturday. Maybe Mac and Dougal had already talked to him, and he would be waiting at the house. She snorted. *Not bloody likely.* But she would go home Saturday afternoon. Maybe she could take a bundle of food as well. She fell asleep as the moonlight coming through the windows slowly faded to night.

The kitchen was still dark when Maggie gave her a push. "Wake up. We got to get the fires started afore Cook comes in, or she'll have a fit. You do this one, and I'll do the morning room." Moira quickly pulled her shawl over her dress and stacked the peat in the fireplace. Another day had begun.

On Thursday afternoon, Moira leaned against the casement outside the back door. She'd been up since dawn. The dishes and pots were clean for the moment, but she could hear Mrs. Britton clattering at the stove, starting a soup for dinner. Her hands were grimy from rebuilding the fire. She wished she had more than a moment alone. The kitchen garden stretched before her, tidy rows of onions and parsley, garlic and basil. She had filled her basket with potatoes and greens.

"Hello, Moira."

Moira jerked around.

Dylan stood before her.

"I wasn't sure you came to Westness." He was as handsome as she'd remembered.

A glint of humor edged his smile, and Dylan pulled her in his arms right there in the garden by the back door of the kitchen.

His lips were warm. Moira lost herself in his kiss and then remembered. She could lose her job. "Hist. Stop. Someone will see you, and I'll be in trouble."

"How could such a pretty one be in trouble?"

"Ah, I'm working now. And I'm supposed to be inside in a few minutes more. Did my brothers talk to you?"

"Aye, they talked. I listened. And the fairest lass of all Foulksay is mine to court."

"Did they say that?"

"Not in so many words. But they didn't say I couldn't."

"I thought of you." For a moment she leaned into Dylan's arms.

"Come out tonight?"

"Impossible."

"Such a pretty bird. I'll wait for you as long as it takes. When can you walk out with me?"

"I don't know. I'll be home Saturday afternoon. Maybe then. I've got to go in."

"Stay until they call you."

Moira was still in his arms. She could feel his heart beating. She leaned her head against his shoulder. She wanted to breathe in his scent.

"Where's the girl," Mrs. Britton shouted. "Where are my greens?"

"I've got to go."

Moira waited at the door to watch Dylan walk down through the garden, out the gate and past the barn. She could hear Mrs. Britton calling her.

"'Tis a pretty bird you are," whispered Perkins behind her, nearly at her ear. "I could have you fired for this. Already shirking and this your first week."

Moira almost dropped her basket of greens. "Just a friend happened by."

"I know him. He's the boatwright. Tight with Lord Gordon for now. He looked to be more than a friend." Perkins pinched his nose just below his glasses. "You're hired to work and not be a slut, so get back to the kitchen. Now."

"Yes, sir. Thank you, sir."

"Oh, don't be thanking me. I'll think of a way for you to thank me." Perkins turned back into his office and closed the door.

Moira's hands shook as she tightened her grip on her basket and turned back to the kitchen.

On Saturday, Moira's first week at Westness was over. She had the rest of the day and Sunday at home, then she'd be back to Westness until the next Saturday. Moira felt fortunate to have found a job, despite what Mac said. They needed the money. That added income was assured as long as she could stay away from Mr. Perkins and please Mrs. Britton.

Her best strategy was to be invisible, she thought. That should be easy with her new uniform. Mrs.

MacNaught had told her the cost would be deducted from her wages, but Moira didn't care. The dress was cut from heavy black cloth, made simply with a high neck and long sleeves. She was given a clean white apron and collar to wear each day. She pinned a tiny lace cap to the top of her head, whenever she went upstairs.

In the afternoon, she went to Mr. Perkin's office and stood in line for their weekly accounting with everyone else, even Mrs. Britton.

"Don't take that in with you." Maggie pointed to the small bundle of food Moira carried. "You can get it on your way out. Don't worry. He just doesn't have to see everything."

"Why is he taking so long?"

"He just wants to account for the week. He may make a suggestion or two. Just get through it." Maggie's cheeks were flushed.

Moira waited her turn without further talking. Maybe she wouldn't be working at Westness after today. Each person went into Perkins' office alone and closed the door. After a few minutes, he or she came out. No one smiled.

Finally, Moira entered the office where she had met Perkins that first day. He was seated behind his desk, his account book open. His pen hovered over the ledger as he looked up. He sniffed.

"Ah, yes, the new kitchen girl."

Moira nodded.

Perkins looked at her a long moment and then wrote in his ledger. "Deduction for the uniform. Deduction for new shoes. A fine for shirking work."

"But I've worked full days, every day."

"And that day in the garden?" His glasses slipped down further on his nose. "You're three schillings down. You'll have your full pay next week, won't you? That is, if you do your job without mooning over some man. Go along, then."

Moira didn't move. "I didn't do anything wrong."

"Ah, a troublemaker. McDonnell, isn't it?"

"Aye. I have four brothers, sir."

"Would they come up to Westness? That would be amusing. All of the them?" He grabbed her hand and ground the bones of her fingers together. "Don't threaten me. Now get out of here."

No one would meet her eyes as she came out of Perkins' office. Moira picked up her bundle of food and left Westness.

Moira walked along the headlands, at first just grateful to be alone. She rubbed her hand. *I hate Perkins, but I can avoid him. I don't like cook's rages, but they're spats over nothing.* She nearly tripped on the path, thinking about all the food she'd carried upstairs for so few people. *I'd rather be following the harvest and sleeping out under the stars.*

There ahead of her, at the place where the path branched down to Selkirk, Mac waited. "Did it go well?"

"Well enough. But 'tis glad I am to be coming home."

Mac took the bundle from her and together they walked home. At supper, her brothers argued over whether they should eat charity food from the new laird, but their hunger won out. The bits of meat and bread were a welcome addition to oatcakes and fish soup. Her brothers said nothing about Dylan, and neither did she.

Later, Mac and Dougal left the cottage for a meeting. Moira knew they were stopping at the Pig's Head. She didn't begrudge them. It was enough to sit by the hearth with Colin and Jamie before they went up to bed. It was enough to not be waiting for the bell to ring or Mrs. Britton to yell at her once more. She was too tired to worry about Dylan and when or if she might see him. He seemed like something from a dream she had long ago.

Moira stepped outside of their stone cottage for a moment. She stared at the moon. The whole world seemed to tilt and move toward the stars. She could hear the noise of the waves far below.

Even as the wind picked up, Moira walked along the heather-lined cliff path that led to the sea. She felt tears on her cheeks. She didn't know why she was crying. The wind pulled at her dress, making it sail out behind her, and the moon shone through the clouds.

Sunday came too soon for Moira. They honored the Sabbath, even with work left undone, though Mac said this afternoon he and Dougal would take the boys walking to the far side of the island, something about meeting the other fishermen. Her fish stew already warmed on a banked fire for the meal after services. Moira hoped the rain would hold off.

Moira settled onto the bench next to Jamie and Colin, as the congregation waited for Pastor McPherson. Lady Alice again sat in the front pew, alone. Moira looked behind her once to see if Dylan had come, but Mac scowled at her. The old church was somewhat warmer. A new door and tighter sidings on the windows meant less of a draft, but Moira's feet were still cold from the wet along the path. Her feet were forgotten as Pastor McPherson came in. *He doesn't look well*, thought Moira.

"Good morning, my children." Pastor McPherson paused, and the congregation settled to quiet. "Soon we come to the end of the harvest. With one breath, we worry about winter storms, and with another, we prepare to celebrate the birth of our Lord and His gift of redemption. We are challenged by trials on sea and land, yet keep this in your heart: We are protected by the love of Christ who will never abandon us. Let us pray."

Moira flexed her fingers and thought of clearing away the breakfast table at Westness. *Mac doesn't need to know everything.*

After church, Dylan followed the McDonnells out into the sunlight. "Have a word with me?" he called. Mac kept on walking, not turning back. Dougal stopped with Moira.

"Good Sabbath, Mr. McDonnell, Miss McDonnell."

Moira smiled a welcome and looked at her brother.

"Good Sabbath." Dougal looked uncomfortable.

"I know about the meeting," said Dylan in a low voice, "and I think it's . . . "

"Don't talk here," Dougal interrupted. "Come to the house. You need to see Mac."

Moira looked from one man to the other, their faces tense. She turned and began the walk home, just ahead of Dougal and Dylan.

When they reached the cottage, Mac was waiting for them. "Moira, go inside. This is men's business."

Moira flushed. She flounced into the cottage and slammed the door shut.

"Who can blame her?" Dougal motioned to Dylan to sit down on one of the round stools at the side of the cottage. "She thought you were coming to see her."

"And I would, if you but give me permission."

"That's not going to happen." Mac leaned back on the cottage wall, his eyes narrowed to cracks. "Tell me how you know about the meeting."

Dylan paced in front of the two brothers. "None of the fishermen will talk to me. They tell me to come to you. Then I hear there's to be a meeting tomorrow. I can't say who told me. I know it. And I know this. You're asking for trouble."

"We know how to deal with trouble."

"That may be. But Lord Gordon is serious about these improvements. He's ready to fine those who don't rework their boats." Dylan stopped and looked around the small yard in front of the cottage and the stone walls between the yard and the sea. "You risk losing all this if you don't do what he wants. And you risk more if you lead the fishermen against him."

Mac looked at Dylan and grunted. "So, you're only here for a while, then."

"That doesn't change my feelings about Moira. She's not part of this, not for me. If she'll have me, I'll stay. It's as simple as that. But if there's trouble, I'll go, and I'll take her with me."

"That won't happen. Not unless I'm dead." Mac stood, the black rage swimming up in him. "She's me only sister."

"Then maybe you'll be dead," Dylan said, not backing down. "I want to marry her."

"A hell of a time to be saying it," said Dougal.

"Aye, but that doesn't change it."

"All right, all right. This isn't about Moira anyway. It's about Lord Gordon and his damned demands. You being here makes it worse. You speak for him. But this is about us." Mac thumped his chest. "We have to decide what we should do. Yes, we're meeting tomorrow. You're right. Down on the beach, after the fishing's done. You can talk to them direct, and then we'll see."

"Tell her I would have come to see her if it hadn't been for this."

"I'll tell her," said Dougal.

CHAPTER 19: FISHERMEN MEET

The boats had landed, and the women had long finished their work of gutting and salting the day's catch. The men stayed behind. Dylan walked down along the beach, gathering the fishermen as if he pulled a net around them.

"You know why I'm here." Dylan looked at each man. "Lord Gordon wants you – all of you – to top off your open boats and add a deck. From stem to stern. This will strengthen your hulls and give you good storage for your fish. You can improve your boats and your catch."

The men stood close around Dylan. "Aye, we heard of this. We knew it was coming."

"Scott Mercantile has the wood," Dylan continued, "and I will help you with the rebuilding of decks, until you see how 'tis done."

"I told you he wouldn't stay long," whispered Mac to Dougal, as they watched Dylan.

Dougal nodded.

"An' who will be paying for the wood up at the Mercantile?" asked Sean.

"Lord Gordon's having it brought in. He'll cover the shipping. You'll pay cost. I'm told the increased yields should cover your expenses in a season," replied Dylan.

"If it's a good season," someone muttered.

A few of the men laughed.

"But if I change me boat, how will she handle in a storm?" called Robert from the back of the group.

"Aye," the men around him agreed.

"From what I've seen," said Dylan, "when you cap over the deck, the boat is less prone to tip."

"Aye, but how do we know what you've seen?" asked Sean.

Mac stepped forward. "And where will we be in the middle of a storm with no place to drop down to?"

The men around Mac laughed uneasily.

Mac leaned close to Dylan. "This is not personal." He raised his voice. "Who wants to take a chance on being blown off their boat in a storm, like me Da?"

Dylan glared at Mac. "This is personal. And you know why." He turned to the rest of the men. "If you want help in carrying out the retrofitting, that's what I'm here for. Lord Gordon is paying me to help you now. You know where I'm staying. Come to me when you're ready to work."

Dylan walked back up the beach to Selkirk, alone.

"We could do it," said Dougal. "We could be first to try."

Mac shrugged him off. "He doesn't own us." He turned to the small crowd of men. "Who's for retrofitting our boats when the bastard has raised our rents? And who knows when he'll raise them again?"

The men milled around Mac.

"We'll no change," cried Sean.

"None of us will. He can't make us," said Robert. "What can he do to us, anyway? Raise the rents again?"

The men shifted on their feet as the sky darkened.

"Aye, that's the burr that pricks me," said Mac. "You know he can. But where will it end? Do we want to change our boats or no? Go home and think on this. Come prepared tomorrow to make a decision. An' then we'll see."

Mac walked up from the beach, stopping with Sean and Dougal underneath the sign at the Pig's Head.

"We should have talked more to him," said Dougal.

"We talked enough," said Mac.

"Aye," Sean added. "I'll bet Lord Gordon hasn't been out in a storm. He doesn't know."

Dougal shrugged. "I mean we should have talked to Dylan. We promised Moira."

"What's this about Moira?" Sean's face narrowed.

"Ah, Dougal, sometimes you don't talk enough, and then you talk too much." Mac turned away. He wanted to be outside this night, under the stars with Deidre. "You might as well know, Sean. Moira's met Lord Gordon's man, this Dylan MacInerney. He's from Ireland. He's probably close to being a papist for all I know."

"But we told Moira we'd talk to him." Dougal, a head shorter than Mac, stood light on his feet, ready for a fight.

"And so we have this day."

"Moira will want more than what we've done. You know it, Mac."

Sean circled around the two brothers in front of the Pig's Head. "So she's not going with the MacTavish?"

"Pah! Don't be silly, Sean. She never went with MacTavish or any of the rest of them I brought home. Ah, you're right, Dougal. What's meant to happen will happen. I'll go see him. You can even come. But I'm no going this night."

Dougal nodded. "All right. That's good enough for me. When?"

"Tomorrow." Mac stared at his brother and at Sean. "I don't like them coming around, telling us what to do. We know how to fish."

"Will we change our boat?" asked Dougal.

"Maybe. Don't be asking me now."

"Shall we go in then?" Sean asked.

"Not tonight." Mac shrugged. "It all comes back to the rents. We dinna have the coin, Sean. Not even for a ha'penny dram."

"Well then. You don't want to stand around here all night." Sean lifted his hand in a mock salute.

"Tomorrow, we settle this, for I want an end to this wrangling. I'd rather be out walking with Deidre."

"Go along then, you old cod. Give her my regards."

The two men looked at each other, and Mac grinned. "I'll give her my regards. You going home, Dougal?"

"Aye. 'Tis too late for anything else."

"Talk to Moira. Maybe she'll come to her senses."

"I doubt that. She's a McDonnell too. Some would call us stubborn."

Mac turned away and shook off thoughts of Moira and Dylan and the meeting tomorrow. He'd probably have to apologize to Dylan and refit their boat as well. There was no hope for a skaffie this year. Mac could almost hear his father saying, 'What cannot be helped must be put up with.'

Mac walked up Front Street toward Scott's Mercantile, the street ahead of him empty in the early summer evening. Inside the closely-built stone houses, lamps were lit, and families gathered for supper. Maybe one day, he and Deidre would live in one of these stone houses. He couldn't imagine them living in his cottage. He'd have to add something on, maybe another room. But it was that serious he knew. What was he to do? He couldn't live with Deidre's parents and her sisters over the store. However large it was, it wasn't large enough for a fisherman they didn't want their daughter to marry.

Mac lifted his hand to knock on the door, but Deidre opened it before he could.

"Let's go out," she said.

"Everyone's home, then?"

"Yes. Let's just walk," she replied, already bundled up in a shawl, for the sun had dropped behind the horizon, turning the clouds red, and the evening air was chill. They walked along Front Street, down to the beach where the boats had been pulled up. Not even the wind blew away the smell of drying fish.

"All's well with you?" she asked.

"Well enough."

"Everyone's excited tonight," she explained. "Da was called up to Westness to see Mr. Perkins. They want the store to carry more provisions. Mac, we're to have a weekly ferry once the pier's in."

"A weekly ferry?" Mac said, trying to take it in. "Every week for sure?"

"Yes. Father said he's going to order from Wick and Inverness. Even newspapers. He'll have newspapers from Edinburgh."

"Mayhap we'll be able to take our fish to the mainland easier, some dried and some fresh."

They both were quiet for a time.

"Mac, I'm sorry about the rent increase. Mr. Perkins said it was for the good. That Lord Gordon felt this was the only way to get the fishermen to change their boats."

"The bully. How's someone who's not fishing at all supposed to pay higher rents? He didn't just increase the rents on us fishermen, you know. It's on everyone."

"Will you rebuild the *Star*?"

"I don't know." Mac kicked at a stone. "If we cover her deck over like they want, she might not handle the same way. You know these waters. Sometimes storms come up without a warning."

"But you're a good sailor, Mac."

"Maybe. But out there, if a storm comes roaring in, there's no good sailor or bad sailor. The waves pick up.

The wind starts blasting. There's only you and the storm. And a boat you'd better know exactly how to sail."

Deidre tucked her hand under Mac's arm. "Mr. Perkins said Lord Gordon was angry the fishermen hadn't rebuilt their boats. Especially after he brought a man over from the shipyard in Inverness."

"I met him. This Dylan MacInerney. He's dancing attendance on Moira, and I don't like it. Enough. Enough of this stranger. Enough of Mr. Perkins and Lord Gordon. I don't care he's angry. I'm angry too whenever I think on it."

They walked in silence for a while, down along the beach and toward the point.

Deidre checked her watch, pinned at her waist. "It's time to get back. I'm meeting with Pastor McPherson tomorrow."

"Again? What does he want sniffing around?"

"Mac, he's the Pastor. I work with him. That's all. You might notice that I'm walking out with you."

"I noticed." Mac took a swallow. "You know, you and me, Deidre, we should talk about getting married."

"Now might not be the right time." She looked at him, her eyes large in the twilight.

"Deidre, it never seems the right time." He traced her cheek with his finger. "I know your parents don't like me, but I will always take care of you."

"Mac, there's things you don't know, and things I'm not ready to tell you."

"I don't care about any of that."

"But I do. It's too soon for us."

Mac waited. He watched Deidre's face fade in the twilight.

"Maybe someday," said Deidre. "Maybe if Jamie goes off to school, and Dougal gets married and moves into his own house, and Moira's settled some way, and Colin, well, I don't know." Her voice dwindled off.

"It sounds like never, Deidre," Mac replied. "I'll always have my family near me."

"You could move into town. Da said the business will expand. He could use you in the store, better than Colin."

"I'm a fisherman, Deidre. I'm not giving up the sea." He found it hard to speak. "If I have to choose, I'm going to choose the sea."

"Then let's not talk of it just now. I'd never ask you to give up the sea, and I don't want to stop seeing you, no matter what my mother says."

"But I'm still a fisherman, Deidre."

"I know."

Mac passed by Mrs. MacLean's house on his way home. There on the porch sat Dylan, the end of his pipe flaring red in the night.

Mac stopped. "You want to talk?"

Dylan came down from the porch. "Aye. We can talk."

The two men walked down Front Street and sat on two large stones near the water. Finally Dylan said, "Did the men decide?"

"That's tomorrow."

"They'll do what you say."

"Aye. I know. It's a cold night to know that."

"Lord Gordon . . ."

"Don't talk to me of Lord Gordon." Mac had a bad taste in his mouth. He looked up at the stars and the fast moving clouds over his head. "Tomorrow morning, we'll go out in the boats as we've always done. We do well enough. Why does he want us to change?"

"It doesn't matter why anymore. He's thinking of reprisals if the men don't rework the boats by Martinmas. 'Tis worse than higher rents."

Mac grunted.

"If only one of you could try it. Show the other fishermen."

"It's giving in. He should just leave us alone."

"You could be the first."

"So Dougal says."

Dylan was silent. The boats along the beach shone silver in the night, with a dog or two sleeping on the sand near the fishermen's huts. Here and there an oil lantern gleamed in a window. All was quiet.

"Ah, you're right. I'm thinking someone should be the first." Mac sighed. "It might as well be the *Star*. But I'm not saying I'll do it. I'm waiting 'till tomorrow."

CHAPTER 20: WESTNESS

"You can't all come in here." Hargraves surveyed the small crowd of fishermen who'd followed Mac up the hill to Westness. The men stood in the yard by the back door. Late afternoon winds had picked up, pushing dark clouds from the southwest.

The fishermen shuffled a bit, looked at each other and then to Mac.

"You go in and speak for us," said Gibson. "We'll wait here."

"Tell him we can't just spend money like lords," said Sean. "We've got families to feed."

"You tell him, Mac."

Hargraves blocked the doorway, his large body nearly filling the door. "Mac, you sure you want to do this?"

"Someone has to speak for us," said Mac.

"Come in, then."

Mac followed Hargraves up the winding stairs at Westness. His mouth turned down at the fine woodwork and rich carpet. Mac wished he could stop sweating.

Hargraves stopped at the library door.

"Sir, Mr. McDonnell to see you."

Mac stepped forward into the large room, glancing at the rows of leather-bound books from floor to ceiling on each wall. The warmth from the fireplace made his coat steam. He hesitated at the edge of the Turkish medallion carpet with his mud-crusted shoes. Lord Gordon seemed smaller than he remembered, sitting in comfort, with a map of Foulksay Island spread out on the desk.

Lord Gordon closed the map. "Yes?"

"'Tis about the boats, sir. We canna' afford to rebuild our boats just now."

"McDonnell, is it? I've sent Perkins down with the plans and arranged to have the wood shipped here at my cost. I've brought over a good man for the retrofitting."

"Yes, sir. But with the fees on the new pier, and the next quarter day just ahead and the higher rents, we don't have enough money for the wood, sir."

Lord Gordon rose and faced the windows. "The fishermen can use terms at Scott's Mercantile to pay off the cost of the lumber over time. That should close the matter."

"But how our boats are now, this is how we fish. As far back as we remember."

"How many boats are lost each year?" Lord Gordon turned back to Mac, the wind rattling the windows behind him, his face nearly hidden in the back light.

"Depends on the storms, sir. Some years we lose one or two. In bad years, we lose more. We always lose men to the sea, sir."

"If I told you that when men simply add a deck, as I have asked you to do, and as I have generously provided resources, that fewer lives are lost and more fish caught, would that speak to your fishermen?"

"They dinna want to do it, sir." Mac shifted his feet. He wished he were outside, anywhere but in this warm room. "It's hard enough to go out in the sea. They worry it'll change how she handles in the open sea and if a storm comes up."

Lord Gordon shook his head. "That's no reason."

Mac was silent.

"So you came today, thinking I would simply let the fishermen do what they wish."

"I was hopeful, sir, you would understand. We have families to feed, and 'tis soon winter."

"And if I didn't, as you say, understand, what then?"

"We'll try to rebuild the boats then. Some of us."

"I want all of the boats retrofitted, as ordered." Lord Gordon's pale face gleamed in the firelight. "By no later than Martinmas. That gives you until November. Those who do not convert the boats by then will be fined."

Mac felt sweat gather on his back. This man was not listening to him. "But we fish every day. If we stop to build, our families will go without. If we could postpone the building 'till the weather turns and we canna' go out?"

"And when winter comes, will I hear another story?" Lord Gordon looked out over the garden where the imported trees he'd had planted bent in the steady sea wind. "Tell them Martinmas. No later."

A tap sounded at the library door. "Yes?" said Lord Gordon.

Lady Alice came hesitantly into the library. "You wished to see me?" she asked.

Mac stared. Lady Alice had the pale complexion of a woman who'd never worked outside. Her eyes were shadowed. She was wearing a sort of rose-colored dress, and her dark hair was twisted up in a knot.

Lady Alice floated past Mac; a faint smell of verbena lingered in the air.

"Out, McDonnell. We're finished. You know what I want. See Perkins in the future."

Mac took a last look at Lord Gordon and Lady Alice as he left, a sour taste in his mouth. So many rooms for the two of them. What did they know of how the people lived or died. Or how much it took to pay the rents.

Mac's stomach cramped as walked down the stairs and back out into the twilight, the cold wind nipping the warmth from his clothes and chilling his face.

The fishermen huddled together in the back yard behind Westness.

"He dinna' listen, boys. We have 'till Martinmas."

"All of the boats?" asked Sean.

"All of them." Mac pointed down the hill to Selkirk. "It's just as Dylan said. The lumber's in at Scott's. He says we have to arrange credit. If we don't, there'll be fines."

"It won't change anything. If we do or if we don't," said Robert. He turned away from the group and headed home, a little bent over to protect his face from the wind.

"I'm thinking I'll try it first," The men clustered around Mac. "We'll see how she goes, and then you can decide what you want to do."

The men nodded and made their way back down the winding road along the headlands. Mac, Dougal and Sean walked together as the sky darkened.

"'Tis a thankless job you did today," said Sean.

Mac shrugged. "I talked to Dylan last night. He'll help us, and we can show the rest, after we take the *Star* out."

"Mayhap it's not so difficult," said Dougal. "If a few of us can make the change, the others will come along. He can't penalize us if we're making progress."

"The man's about making money," said Mac. "He'll find a way."

CHAPTER 21: GORDON AND ALICE

Gordon stood by the window and stared at the workers in the garden. *Damn McDonnell for stirring them up.* "Don't hover, Alice. Sit down."

Alice sat on one of the chairs in front of his desk and waited.

His cheeks reddened. "We won't be going to Edinburgh for the winter."

"Oh, I was starting to close the house this afternoon. Of course, if that is what you wish." Alice pressed her lips together. She noted the lines on Gordon's face.

"Alice, I leave Sunday for London. I should return within two months, less if I can. If needed, Perkins and Hargraves will handle quarter day in November, and you'll be here. I'm sorry, Alice. But it's necessary."

"London?"

"To see Alexander. We need more capital. Alice, I should apologize. Certain investments haven't come through. I've raised the rents here, but even for that, I must wait another few weeks." Gordon shuffled some papers on his desk. "Bringing the estate profitable will take more than I anticipated."

"Can I help? I have some money of my own."

"Ah, Alice. We're not talking about a few pounds here and there. I need several thousand."

"I could ask Father for a loan."

"I've already asked. He said no."

"Then we won't be going to Edinburgh before Christmas?"

"No. I suppose the move to Edinburgh would have helped you. I'm sorry."

"There's nothing to be sorry about." Alice hesitated. "If anything, I'm sorry I failed you."

"We both wanted the child. But that's behind us now." Gordon rearranged the papers on his desk. "I don't want you worrying more than necessary. I'm still waiting for news about some investments. In the meantime, we'll manage."

For some reason Alice found herself thinking of the dinner with Kezia Hayter and Captain Ferguson of the *Rajah*. They must have reached Van Diemen's Land by now. And those women, the prisoners on the boat. What were their lives like now? She felt as if Westness were a boat moving into a future she could not see.

Gordon came around the desk and held her hand. "Alice, be patient. We will come through this. Just be circumspect with household expenditures as much as you can." He tucked a curl behind her ear. "I know I haven't spent much time with you lately. The paperwork's been fearsome, as has the news. But that must change now. For me, it's enough that I know you are doing better."

"The weather can't be that much worse here than Edinburgh. I've only one project that requires any spending. I'd like to send one of the young boys over to school on the mainland."

"The one that's been following you all over the island?"

"Yes." Alice smiled. "Jamie McDonnell. He's a bright boy. He deserves a chance at an education, more than the Grammar School."

"McDonnell? I know that name. No, we'll not be helping the McDonnells. God willing, one day we'll have a lad of our own." Gordon sat at his desk and picked up a letter.

"I could cover the cost from my allowance."

"I would rather you not." Gordon frowned at the letter.

"I see. Is there anything at all I can do?"

Gordon's hands stilled. He turned to her, rolling his chair back slightly. "Do you imagine you could help?" He mused for a moment. "Perhaps. You understand if I tell you some things, you must keep them to yourself. No chattering to anyone else, not even Perkins?"

"Yes, Gordon. Of course." Alice blinked. She couldn't imagine chattering to Perkins.

"Well, then." Gordon set his papers aside. "You know my plans in general. I want this estate productive. To make a home for us and our children, not here on the island and not necessarily in Edinburgh. I want us to be in London, where our children will have a future."

Alice nodded. "Yes. I know that."

Gordon paced the length of the library and stood in front of her. "But the estate hasn't generated income for many years. Alexander told me it would be a challenge, and it is. The people are set in their ways. Even small changes, they resist. Alice, I want to transform this land. I want to bring sheep here and build up trade."

"But how can you have sheep and farming?"

"We will dispense with the farming."

"What about the people?"

"They'll have to go."

"But winter's coming."

"Yes, I know. The sheep must be established no later than the end of January." He looked at Alice. "Before the spring lambs. It has to be."

"Where will the people go?"

"I don't care. Anywhere but here. They're renters, after all. If they can't pay the rents, they'll be evicted."

"Pastor McPherson tells me they've lived here all their lives. Surely we have a responsibility."

"My responsibility is to us, to our family. I can't support people who don't work. I'd like to transport them all off the island, but it's a terrible expense. Maybe Glasgow. They've new factories there. They could find work there."

Gordon began pacing again. "There may be a way that doesn't involve us making a great outlay. I'm looking into a plan that will take some of our people to the Americas, perhaps Newfoundland or Virginia. I'd have to arrange for the ships to pick them up, but when they sign papers of indenture, I'm reimbursed. You remember Captain Ferguson? He and Sutherland gave me the idea. It could mean a better life for all of them."

Alice thought of the people she knew on the island. "This will be a tremendous change."

"Alice, when the crops fail, they starve, and so do we. If I can make the land more productive, with sheep, with hunting, our income will grow. Those who are willing to work will benefit. If the fishermen rebuild their boats, they'll be fine. But the rest have to go. I will not tolerate any delay." Gordon stopped in front of Alice. "Now I've confided in you, Alice. I expect you to respect my confidences."

"I will." Alice sighed. "I'm not sure how I can help."

"I would like you to work with Pastor McPherson. He's our man, though sometimes his sermons don't sound like it."

"Pastor McPherson?"

"Yes. He knows the crofters best. He'll know which families can stay and which families can best adapt to a new land. Talk to him. I'll need a list on my return. Alice, don't look at me that way." He took her hand. "You make me feel I'm not alone."

"You're never alone, Gordon. You have me."

"This means a lot to me, Alice. Send Perkins in, will you?"

The wind fluttered in the curtains and rustled a few papers on Lord Gordon's desk. Behind him, a white mist rose from the sea, low to the headlands.

Alice rose. "I'll see to the packing for your trip. I shall miss you."

For a moment, the study was still. Alice could hear house wrens start up under the eaves as the wind shifted.

CHAPTER 22: THE STORM

Late Saturday afternoon, Moira came home from Westness to an empty cottage. She opened a window to air the cottage out, washed up dishes, put clothing into the cupboard, and swept out the floor that looked as if it hadn't been swept all week. Moira checked on her chickens. All flourished, pecking on the scraps she brought from Westness as if she had never been away. She laughed aloud. She was meeting Dylan tonight, this night, whether her brothers said yes or no.

Jamie came in with a half creel of oatmeal from Scott's Mercantile, but Mac, Dougal and Colin didn't return. The afternoon fog moved in along the coast and then darkened to dusk. Moira couldn't sit still with her knitting. She kept getting up to look out the window. *Where were they?*

After dark, Mac, Colin, and Dougal entered with a rush, filling up the cottage with noise.

"Moira, you won't believe what happened," Colin burst out.

"They said the fish were running out past Quernshead," added Mac.

Moira's heart stopped. "Ah, no. That's the one place you said you wouldn't go."

"We got caught in one of those whirlpools out there, just like they say, only worse," said Dougal.

"Don't be looking at us like that," said Mac. "Aren't we all here and fine and all?"

"So, like I was saying," said Dougal, "We got caught out there in a terrible fog. And then the whirlpool got us."

"You should have been there. Mac went over," said Colin. "And that was before we got the biggest fish you've ever seen."

"One of you! Just one of you speak," Moira commanded. "I can't tell what happened from this mish mash."

"Right you are," said Mac. "We hadn't planned to take the boat all the way to Quernshead, but we followed the birds, and there we were."

"Go on. Get to what happened. And don't tell me that you fell in the sea."

"The closer we got to Quernshead, the better the fishing got, with the gulls crying out and squawking all around us," said Mac. "Then a big fog came rolling in. You couldn't see where the sky ended and the water began. When it lifted a little, there we were, right in the nastiest part of Quernshead. There our little boat was with its fancy new deck, twirling around in a great whirlpool, her lines fanning out behind her like a veil. We could see great fishes in the deep there, Moira, like you've never seen in your life."

"That's no way to tell what happened," said Dougal. "You're scaring her right to her bones."

Mac pulled a chair out to the center of the room. "Sit."

Moira fluttered her hands. "Tell me the rest. Don't leave a word out."

"I thought we were all lost, the boat and all." Mac looked around the room, at Moira, and at Dougal, Jamie and Colin. "There we were, in the middle of a beast of a whirlpool. I thought we'd never see land again." He paused again. "This next is passing strange. But believe me, it happened, just as I'm telling you now."

"Go on," said Dougal.

Moira grabbed Jamie's hand and held her breath.

"Right in the deepest part of the hole in the water that was pulling us down, was a man. An' he looked to be smiling at us." Mac waved his arm. "Don't interrupt me now. 'Twas a selkie. That man-fish we hear about now and then. He had a good hold of one of our lines. He could see us, and we could see him. And he looked at each one of us, studying our faces. The winds were howling; the boat was turning like the devil himself had it in his hand. The deck was that slanted, you couldn't get purchase. We were shouting and crying, and the boat was twirling around. I slipped and fell into the sea. The selkie went after me. He wrapped his arms around me and brought me back to the boat. Then, he pointed at our towline, and we threw it to him, for we were lost men, and we knew it. He swam with that towline wrapped around his body, down into the center of the whirlpool and then up through the waves, and by God, he pulled us out of that sinkhole."

Mac sat down, his forehead dotted with sweat. "It was too close, Moira. We'll not be fishing off Quernshead again, rents be damned. And I'm that close to tearing off the new deck."

The room was silent.

"I don't believe a word of it," said Moira. "Except you went to Quernshead when you said you wouldn't go. You should save such stories for the Pig's Head and all your friends, and not give me such a fright."

For the first time Moira noticed that their clothes were wet. "Off with your wet things, now. Go get cleaned up. You can have supper. But don't be talking to me."

"But there was a whirlpool," said Mac. "No one would believe us if we told what happened. Not even the Queen of Heaven could make sense of this."

"I don't want to hear another word. You promised you wouldn't go to Quernshead after the last time." Moira's hands shook as she hung their wet jackets up in the byre. She hurried back to find Colin already wrapped up in a blanket.

"I'll never get the cold out." Colin leaned closer to the fire.

"But you're all right?" she asked.

"You should have been there." His blanket dropped to the floor. "The fish were the biggest I've ever seen. And 'tis true. Mac fell in."

Moira laid the bowls out on the sideboard next to the food chest.

Jamie sidled close to her to whisper. "I don't want to go out with them."

She wanted to tell him not to worry, that if all went well, he would be going to school on the mainland someday, but 'twas Mac's place and Mac's decision. "Ah, Jamie. I thought you were working for Lady Alice."

"She don't need me now the weather's turned."

"Can you find something over at Selkirk?"

"I don't know."

"I can ask up at Westness."

Jamie nodded.

"Where's me dinner," Dougal cried, as they came in from outside, their hands and faces wet from washing. "I'm colder than a selkie sleeping at the bottom of the sea."

"Don't be talking to me about selkies. Not another word." Moira waved her spoon at her brothers. She served up the fish stew and oat cakes, while they clattered on about the new deck and the fish they caught. Finally Colin and Jamie went to bed.

Moira wondered if Dylan would be waiting at the standing stones this night. What would he do if she didn't go? But Mac and Dougal stayed home, as if their own beds would finally warm their bones. Moira tossed and turned on her pallet by the hearth, long after everyone had settled in for the night.

When she slept, Dylan came to her in dreams, smiling, laughing, as he held her close, and then he vanished behind the standing stones. Moira awoke with a jerk, tears on her face.

The fog had lifted, and the moon's cold white light fell on her bed. All was quiet.

I never should have promised to meet him.

CHAPTER 23: MAC CLEANS THE STAR

Moira touched the great scrapes along the side of the *Star*. She pulled her shawl close for the morning fog had not yet lifted. "I can't believe you went up by Quernshead."

"Dinna worry, lass. It's not so bad," Mac said. "We'll be going back out tomorrow."

The *Star* was big enough for three men, 32 feet long, wooden with its beam solid. Prow and stern were built trimmed to a point, like a drift boat. It carried two large lug sails, both adapted with booms for easy maneuverability in the unpredictable seas. The wood on the new deck was unseasoned, and the caulking shone black in the sun.

They'd already unloaded nearly all of yesterday's catch. Just a few of the great fish were left in the hold, great green sea cod from the very depths. Dougal filled a sack to take up the hill. Around him, women loaded cod onto hand barrows to cart the fish to the racks of wood stretched about the curved beach.

Moira well knew the work that came next, fish dumped onto a table, filleted, then laid out on wooden racks to dry. If the family couldn't pay the penny fee to use the tables, they laid the cod right on the gravelly sand to dry. She smoothed her hands free of salt.

"These will bring a good price, won't they, Mac?" Moira asked.

"Already sold they are. And everyone's talking about the new decks as well," he replied, tapping the side of the boat to find weak spots. He ran his fingers along the new deck as if he needed to learn its shape.

"Do you think the new deck will work?"

"You saw the fish we caught. We never caught such big ones before."

"And weren't that fancy new boat over at Quernshead? I'm off," said Moira. "They'll be wondering what happened to me up at Westness if I don't get there soon." She didn't want to leave her brothers, not after seeing the scrapes on the boat and realizing how close they'd been to not coming home at all.

"Go along then."

"I'll be asking about work for Jamie up at Westness."

Mac stared at her. "Did he say something last night?"

Moira nodded.

"Ye might as well ask for him," said Mac. "I canna see him fishing with us."

"I want to go up to Westness," said Colin, leaning over from the top of the boat.

Mac tousled Colin's head as he ducked away. "You're needed for fixing lines, boy." He turned to Moira. "They'll yell at you if you're any later."

Colin banged on the other side of the *Star*.

"Let them yell all they want. They like my work." Moira lowered her voice. "I've seen Dylan a few times up at Westness."

Mac straightened up, his large hand resting on the deck. "Have you now. I hoped you wouldn't see him again."

"I was to meet him, Mac, last night. But I didn't go."

"He's working for Lord Gordon. You can't want to see him."

Moira looked at her brother. "But I do, Mac."

"It's not a good time."

"And when would it be a good time?"

Mac turned back to the boat. "We'll be stopping at Pig's Head tonight."

"With Colin?"

"It's not going to hurt him. I'll go over to Deidre's after."

"You're courting her, aren't you?" Moira was fascinated by the thin stain of red that crept up Mac's cheeks.

"Go off with you. I'll talk again to your Mr. MacInerney."

"And this time you'll be talking about me," Moira said as she waved goodbye.

Mac shrugged.

Several fishermen came up to look at the *Star*, banged up as she was, the only boat that came home with a good catch.

"Those are some fish you found out there by Quernshead," said Bruce, a wizened crab of a fisherman whose only occupation now was lining boxes with seaweed to send lobsters to the mainland and south.

"Aye," replied Mac. "But we'll not be going that way again. We almost foundered in a whirlpool. No fish is worth that. Not even these big ones." The men around him nodded in agreement, noting the great scrapes that ran the length of the boat.

"Was it the new deck that gave you trouble?" asked Sean. "I was that worried when the fog rolled in."

"I don't think it was the deck. We could fill the hold easily, and we kept all the fish we caught."

"One of us had to try it," said Robert. "Glad it wasn't me in the fog."

"'Tis the time of year for fogs," said Mac.

"We had a devil of a time getting our boats in yesterday." Sean tapped the new deck. "I heard your fish sold already. Makes it almost worth it for the rest of us to rebuild, don't you think?"

"I don't know. True, we got a good catch, but I fell in, and we almost lost the boat. I can't say it was the new deck, but it changes things." Mac shrugged. "We'll go out tomorrow."

"We'll all be dancing around on fancy new decks soon enough," said Sean.

The men returned to their boats pulled up on the rocky beach. No one needed a reminder about the higher rents due quarter day.

Dougal rested his sack of sea cod on the walk outside the back porch at Westness, glad of the chance to put it down. He stood tall, easing his back muscles, not minding the light drizzle.

"Come up on the porch, man. Don't be standing there in the rain," said Hargraves.

"Thanks," said Dougal. "I've got some fish here. Be you interested?"

"Not for me to say," Hargraves said. "I'll call Mrs. MacNaught for you."

"You working here still? I'd heard otherwise."

"They kept me on. Give me odd jobs now and then, but it's not the same." Hargraves crouched down on his haunches and opened the sack to peer inside. "These are big ones. Where'd you catch them?"

"Out Quernshead. Wasn't an easy trip."

"That's what they said." Hargraves touched the giant cod, still cold from the sea. "They'll want these." He looked behind him. "'Tis not so good here at Westness now. Next time you're over to the mainland, you might go on to Stromness. Visit the Hudson's Bay Company. They're always looking for Orkney men."

"I hear you sign on for five years. That's a long time to be away from home."

"Think, man. It's a chance to go off island, at six or seven pound a year."

"That's higher than it used to be. You get something for telling me?"

Hargraves grinned. "Aye. I get a little something." He glanced back at the closed kitchen door. "They don't know everything. But it's good pay for a young man like you who's not afraid of working. You've heard the stories. Simon came back and bought his own holding. He don't have to pay rent anymore." Hargraves lowered his voice. "I hear Mac's making trouble. He'll pull you down."

"Things will blow over. They always do."

"Not this time. I heard that he, well, these fish look fine."

Perkins stood behind him. "Another McDonnell hanging around." He touched the sack of fish with the tip of his polished boot. "As if we need fish here. We've already got all we need."

Hargraves kept his head down. "I was calling Mrs. MacNaught."

"Well, call her then, and be about your business." Perkins sniffed and walked past Dougal to the stable, tapping his riding crop against his leg.

The two men stood for a moment, watching him.

"You've always been fair with us," said Dougal. "Do you have to stay here?"

"There's nothing else for me. I'll stay as long as I can. Keep in mind what I said about the Hudson's Bay over at Stromness."

"Aye. And I'll talk to Mac." Dougal hefted the bag of fish up. "You think they'll want these?"

Hargraves nodded.

CHAPTER 24: GRANNY CONNOR

The afternoon wind pushed Moira's skirts against her legs as she walked north from Selkirk along the headlands and climbed the hill to Granny Connor's house. The village with its stone houses and the harbor, with its row of fishing boats lined up on the beach, looked tiny against the wide horizon of the sea. She followed the path along the ridge line and turned into a hollow. Immediately the wind dropped.

"Come in, come in. I was hoping for a visitor today."

"I didn't see you down at church," Moira said. She put the basket of eggs she'd brought on the settee.

Moira wondered why she felt so at home here. Maybe it was the familiar smell of the peat fire, mixed with drying fish. Two small windows, their glass nearly darkened with soot, let light in. A faded patchwork quilt covered Granny's small box bed, the door left open. Her chair, its sides built up to protect her from drafts, had been pulled close to the fire where an old sheltie dog lay. On the other side of the stone fireplace, she could hear Granny's goats rustling in the byre.

Granny winced as she leaned on her cane and then eased in her chair by the fire. "Come sit, child."

Moira dragged a low stool close to Granny. "I think I've found the man I want to marry."

"Not the MacTavish?"

"No, no," Moira said. "It's Dylan MacInerney. I met him at Lammas."

Granny Connor waited.

"He's not one of us," Moira added. "He's from Ireland."

"Ah, the sea, what it brings." Granny Connor nodded. "Is he a good man?"

"Yes."

"And when you're with him, you feel as if the entire world has fallen away?"

Moira laughed. "I knew you'd understand."

"'Tis a hard thing to fall in love with a stranger. Is he a papist?"

"No."

"And your brothers? What do they think?"

"They don't want me to see him. It's all mixed up with Lord Gordon. They hired Dylan to help us add decks to our boats. Mac didn't want to work with him. But we were the first. Yesterday the *Star* had trouble out at Quernshead."

"So I heard."

"They got caught in a great whirlpool, Granny. Mac fell into the sea. They all could have drowned. Mac said a selkie pulled them into the whirlpool and 'twas a selkie that saved them." Moira moved restlessly on her stool. "But I think it was the new deck. They caught these great fish, as if they were the selkie's own. They'll go back to Quernshead. I know it."

"Ah, child." Granny Connor took Moira's hand and held it in hers. "'Tis close to Samhain. Who knows what they might have seen."

"My brothers are going out again tomorrow, Granny. Will they be safe?"

"I don't know, child." Granny sighed. "The sea is never safe. You cannot trust the sea. Even your Dylan makes his living from the sea."

"But he builds boats, Granny; he doesn't go out in the ocean."

"You canna trust the ocean, and you canna trust men you do not know. When his job here is done, will he leave the island?"

"I don't know."

Granny looked at Moira's open face and saw darkness coming. "Would you leave your home, your brothers and all, to be with him?"

"Leave home and not return?"

"And didn't you think you would someday get married and go off to your own life?" Granny hugged Moira. "Child, it's all a part of growing up, letting go and changing. Even at the very end of life." She sighed. "If there's no work for him here, you'll be going away. Or you'll lose him."

Moira stared at the fire. Little flames curled around two slabs of dried peat. She couldn't imagine leaving the island and all that she knew.

"Give me another hug, dearie. Come see me again when you can."

Moira hugged her fiercely. "I'll be back."

Granny didn't say anything. She smiled, but her eyes filmed over as if she were looking into the future.

CHAPTER 25: MOIRA AND DYLAN

When the crescent moon had risen overhead, and all were sleeping, Moira slipped out of the stone cottage and walked along the winding path that followed the headlands to the point where the standing stones shimmered in the moonlight. She sat in the shadow of one of the stones.

Another week had passed at Westness, and she hadn't seen Dylan. Maybe Granny Connor was right. Maybe he had already gone off the island.

Moira counted the standing stones, seven of them in a lopsided circle. The monolithic stones had been a place to meet as long as she could remember. Dougal said that in the old days, smugglers and wreckers met here to divvy the spoils. She shivered.

The night wind blew the grasses against the stones and hinted at cold weather ahead. Moira looked at the sea below with its constant waves and knew that nothing mattered, that she could leave it all, her brothers and the island itself, if Dylan loved her.

The first stars came out. Soon the night sky filled with their twinkling bright lights, the Milky Way a cloudy ribbon woven above. Moira wondered how long she should wait. Then Dylan was beside her, his long hair loose around his shoulders. All her worries fled.

"You weren't here last week, love," Dylan said.

"Yes, I know. Did you wait long?"

"Ah, dear heart, I waited all night."

Moira thrilled to hear his words and thrilled again at his touch as he held her hands. Nothing had changed. "You heard about my brothers? They nearly drowned. I couldn't leave them."

"I heard. All's well then?"

Moira nodded.

"Not to worry, for I would wait a hundred nights to see you again."

"I thought you had gone."

"I wouldn't leave without coming to see you first." He tucked Moira close. "I've been all over the island, trying to work with those trolls. Your brothers are the most stubborn of all."

"It's the trouble they had at Quernshead. Dougal said it might have been the new deck."

"Lord Gordon is ready to fine them all or send them to the bottom of the sea, he's that mad."

"He can't make the other fishermen change their boats like we did, can he?"

"He can. There's something driving him. I don't know how far he'll go. I just wish Mac and Dougal would help me more with the fishermen is all."

"Mac said he would talk to you about us. Did he?"

"Some. All that doesn't matter." Dylan spread his coat on the grass. "Come here, love. I see you're shivering."

Moira snuggled in his arms, content to be close to him, warmer now that he was near. His arms circled her. She could sense the standing stones around them, with all else – the stars, the moon, and even the sea – far, far away. She felt as if she were falling off her world and into his.

Dylan groaned. He pulled her closer as if he could forget the week's frustrations in her arms.

"Dylan, I want to be with you." Moira nestled close to his neck and breathed in the salt from his skin as if it would fill her heart. She felt as if this were the moment she'd been waiting for all her life.

"Are you sure? There's no going back."

For answer, Moira unbuttoned his shirt and brushed her hand across the hairs on his chest. He gave in, rolling on top of her and kissing her breathless. Her heart began pounding. *Here and now*, she thought, *we become one.* She expected the pain when he entered her, but she didn't expect the sheer joy that thrummed through her body.

Dylan went still. "Ah, sweet. I didn't know." He kissed her neck.

"I knew. Hush."

Later, when Dylan fell asleep, Moira watched his eyelashes flicker on his cheeks. She wanted to memorize every detail in the light of the waning moon.

"You look at me as if you expect me to vanish," said Dylan, his voice raspy with sleep.

"Who can see the future?" Moira felt close to tears.

He held her close. "Come away with me." He tipped her face up. "We can go to Inverness or Glasgow, or wherever you wish."

"Stay with me, Dylan," Moira replied. "No one cares you're not an islander. You could fish with my brothers. They would come to love you as I do. Please."

"I'm working for Lord Gordon. That doesn't make me any friends." He looked to the sea as if he were smelling the salt air for the last time. "Ireland's my home. I hoped to return, but no matter. If you wish it, we will stay here."

Moira wanted to say she would go with him, for she couldn't bear his sadness.

"And if we can't stay here?" she asked.

"Then we'll leave." Dylan cradled her again in his arms. "Perhaps you already carry my son. And that would be a good thing, for I've seen too many deaths in my family."

"I'd like us to marry. With the proper words, and my family and friends standing up for us."

"Then it's decided." He kissed Moira.

Moira could taste the sea in her tears, for this was the first step to leaving her brothers and leaving the island, all that she had known, just as Granny had said.

Around them, the sky lightened, The sun lit the tops of the standing stones. Moira knew her brothers would soon be up. "Come home with me now. 'Tis time my brothers knew you."

CHAPTER 26: THE MCDONNELL COTTAGE

Mac and Dougal sat close to the hearth. Their low talk stopped the moment Moira and Dylan entered the McDonnell cottage.

"'Tis past dawn, Moira. Why did you bring him here?" said Mac, rising. Dougal stood behind him, glowering. She'd never seen them so angry.

Moira held Dylan's hand tightly. "We're to marry."

"Like hell." Mac thrust his face close to Dylan. "I'm the oldest. I'm the one who marries first. And I don't know this man."

"You can get to know him," Moira stepped in front of Dylan. "I'd be pushing up heather if I wait for you to marry first. I love him."

"And where would you sleep?" Mac gestured at the dark confines of the cottage. "There's no room here."

"What are you saying?" asked Moira. "You know we'll do what everyone else does. We'll build a little room off the side. Or we'll live up at Westness."

"He's not one of us. That's enough reason to say no," said Mac. "He never came proper to ask permission. Ye'll be damned one way or another."

"Listen to me, the two of you. He is already my husband. And that makes him brother to you. Either we stay, or we go."

"Ah, Moira, did you have to do this? Did you have to go and do this?" Mac said.

Moira gritted her teeth. The cottage felt smaller than ever she'd known with everyone standing and glaring at each other.

Dougal broke the silence. "'Tis done. We better see if Pastor McPherson will marry them."

"Aye." Mac stepped closer to Dylan, so close Moira feared they would fight. Neither stepped back.

"Can you fish, then?" asked Mac. His lips stretched into a thin smile. "I'll bet you can. You're a quiet one, though. Will you fish with us? On our little boat, the one with the new deck. The one that nearly pulled us into a whirlpool."

"I work for Lord Gordon," Dylan replied. "For now. I dinna know so much about fishing as I know about building boats and farming. But I know boats. I can help the other fishermen, if they let me."

"We do well enough as things are," said Mac. "We don't need your help."

"Lord Gordon is set on this," said Dylan. "I've seen what happened in Glasgow and in Inverness. When the smaller fishing boats, like yours, are rebuilt, more fish are caught." He shrugged. "It's a better living. More money for the rents, even here."

"'Tis enough you have our sister and not our boat too," said Dougal.

Dylan nodded once. "One day you may be glad it's me that's leading the rebuilding."

Moira looked at the three men, bristling at each other. "Not now," she said. "Not everything needs to be decided now. Dylan is here to stay. People know him already. They saw us dancing at Lammas. 'Tis no surprise that we'll marry."

"True enough," said Dougal. "Mac, let it go. He's to be your sister's husband." He shifted his attention to Dylan. "And that means to honor and to love until death do you part, right?"

"I will so honor her," he promised.

Mac reached out to Moira. "Moira, you're sure you feel this way about this man? There's no going back."

"You already know how I feel about Dylan. I didn't think you'd be so upset."

"You didn't think. What if McPherson won't marry you? Think of that." Mac threw up his hands. "No more nattering. You've taken a lover. That's all. The whole island will be talking about it. There's a chance you'll be called before the congregation for fornication. This is what you wanted. Now you live with it." Mac turned away. "We'll all live with it."

"Mac, I'm sorry."

Mac waved his hand at the cottage. "This is our home. You've brought him here. He's now part of us. Go on. Get yourselves ready for church. We're all going this morn, and we'll face them down." He stared at Dylan. "All of us."

The McDonnells filed into the church with Dylan and sat along an entire row. As they settled in their places, heads bobbed forward and back; people nudged each other and whispered, even when Pastor McPherson entered.

Pastor McPherson stood in front of the altar and simply waited. Slowly the buzz of conversation died down. He looked at his congregation, face by face, and then began, his lilting voice holding their attention.

"This morning, my children, we see a stranger among us. 'Tis not so far to St. Andrew's Day that we can't tell the story of a certain bishop." Pastor McPherson looked at his hands folded before him. The congregation settled to quiet.

"This bishop was a high and mighty man, dazzled by possibilities and nearly snared by the devil himself. He was surrounded by a crowd who approved his every word. A beautiful woman sat by his right hand, tempting him with thoughts he should not have had. At the very

162

moment he could not look away from her, a stranger came to the gate with a loud knocking."

A few heads turned to look at Dylan.

Pastor McPherson raised his voice. "The stranger is outside the gates now. The woman whispers in the bishop's ear, and he says the stranger can only enter that grand gathering if he answers three questions. 'Tis the devil in the very form of that beautiful woman who asks the first question."

"'What is the most wonderful thing God has made in a small form?'"

Pastor McPherson paused to study his congregation. "The pilgrim said it is the human face, for it reveals such wonderful diversity and uniqueness, each one different and a gift from God. Look to your neighbor. Look to those you know. Do you not see the signs of God's gift in your neighbors' faces?"

The people looked around at each other as if they were all strangers. Moira saw Lady Alice in the front pew, leaning to a nearby parishoner.

"Can you see the wonder of God's creation?" Pastor McPherson's words rang out in the church. "We hear. We speak. We smell and taste. We remember, and we reason. Each of us a little differently. The pilgrim's answer was applauded in that ancient company. And yet the gate was barred to him."

"The woman, preening at the side of the bishop, asked: 'At what point is earth higher than heaven?' Those standing near the bishop gasped. Who could answer such a question?" asked Pastor McPherson. "We all know that God's heaven is higher than earth. Yet the pilgrim pointed to that place where Christ's body, made of our flesh, and thus of the earth, is higher than heaven. We know this was no ordinary pilgrim. So too did the bishop and his company. This was St. Andrew at the gate."

"Yet a third question was asked: 'How far is it from earth to heaven?' How far is it, my dear ones," Pastor McPherson asked, "From what we know every day to what remains a mystery? This question we each must ponder in faith, for our souls to live in God's grace hereafter."

"But St. Andrew replied in a loud voice, 'I cannot answer that question. Go back to the one who sent you and ask him.' With that, the woman shivered and vanished. The bishop, with tears in his eyes, cried out to allow the pilgrim to enter. The pilgrim's answers had saved his soul. But St. Andrew could not be found."

"So, my children, how do we know what is true and what is false? Do we fear the stranger at the gate with different ways? Do we truly know those who are close to us, those we see every day? Do we trust those on high to lead us safely into a perilous future? Where is Saint Andrew with his clear, loud voice to warn us of danger?"

"We do not know if the stranger at the gate will bring good or evil. We do know we cannot step away from suffering. We face hard decisions that will bring tears to our eyes, but we know in our hearts what is right and what is fair. Winter comes. Listen to your heart, meditate on God's word, and trust in God's mercy. For that comes to us from no stranger." Pastor McPherson bowed his head. The congregation was silent.

Moira felt tears fill her eyes. Dylan sat next to her. It was enough.

After services, the McDonnell family gathered in the front room of the manse. Mac spoke first. "Thank you for meeting with us, Pastor McPherson."

"Sit, sit. I imagined we would be talking together when I saw Mr. MacInerney with you this morning."

"I'm not going to hide the issue, Pastor. It's Moira, our sister, and this man, Dylan MacInerney. They wish to marry." Mac's lip twisted. "This man works for Lord Gordon, but Moira tells me he is a good man."

"These two young people want to marry?" Pastor McPherson beckoned to Moira and Dylan to stand closer.

"Aye. As soon as the banns can be read," said Mac.

"Are you saying they must marry?" Pastor McPherson glared at Dylan.

"That's what I'm saying." Mac prodded Dylan to speak, but Pastor McPherson turned to Moira.

"So, Moira, can you speak for yourself in this? Did this man force you?"

Moira shook her head.

"Did he seduce you?"

Again, Moira shook her head.

"Are you with child?"

"I do not know, sir."

Pastor McPherson turned to Dylan. "Did you lay with this woman?"

"Aye, Pastor. I have."

"And is it your intention to marry this woman and to support any children?"

"If the banns be read, yes, we will marry. As to children, if they come, I will do my best."

"By hell," said Mac. "You'll do more than your best."

"None of that now." Pastor McPherson turned back to Dylan. "But you'll marry her?"

Dylan nodded. "I have so promised."

"The way ahead does not bode well. Not for either of you."

Moira clung to Dylan's hand. She felt as if time had stopped. What would they do if he said no?

"You understand, the two of you, that you have committed an offense against the sacrament of marriage. If I bring this to the elders, you may face punishment. As you have both made a commitment to marry, that can be set aside. It's the coming before the congregation I'd like to avoid," he mused.

Moira and Dylan held hands as they waited for his next words.

"Ah, I'll not stand in your way as you came to me and to the church first." Pastor McPherson slumped into his chair. "I'll post the banns this afternoon. Go, children, and think on this further. These days are hard enough. Before you leave, Mac, a word."

Moira led Dylan outside the manse. "I'm sorry, Dylan. I didn't think it would be this difficult."

Dougal was right behind her. "You better not change your mind."

"I'm not changing my mind. I will do whatever your sister wants, if she will be my wife." Dylan clipped Dougal on the shoulder.

Dougal glowered at Dylan. "I'm not so sure of you."

"I know. You'll see."

"Aye. I'll see. But as Moira loves you, then you're my brother. I will stand by you as you love Moira and if you stand by me."

"I will stand by her and all of you. I love her more than anything I know."

Dougal shook Dylan's hand formally. "Then, you're part of our family, you are."

Mac came out of the manse, shoving his cap on his head. "Go ahead home without me. Dougal, come with me. There's trouble."

CHAPTER 27: THE MARRYING

In the next weeks, Moira caught barely a glimpse of Dylan at Westness. When he wasn't working at Scott's Mercantile, ordering materials for the retrofitting of boats, he went out fishing with her brothers. Dougal stayed beside him, their voices together a kind of music, but Mac remained glum and withdrawn.

Dylan paid the marriage contract to the church, and the elders accepted their apology. Their names had been entered in the parish session book, and the banns read. Tomorrow afternoon, they would be married. This was her last night alone. Moira turned on her pallet. Outside, the light of the new moon outlined the heather.

Yesterday everyone had come to their cottage. First the men moved their two cows and goats from the byre into a temporary enclosure and penned up the chickens. The women cleaned the outer room, while the men set up two wooden plank tables on barrels. Then the women baked oatcakes and bannocks throughout the day. Colin carried a great pot in, borrowed from Granny Connor, and the women made a fish stew. Mac brewed ale, the small casks now banked by the hearth for warmth. Colin and Jamie scrounged for rock limpets at low tide and brought up a creel of white fish caught near the shore. Dougal slaughtered three of her precious chickens.

At night, the plank table was covered with a white cloth. The cottage filled to near capacity as the women squeezed inside. Moira sat on a low stool to the left of a half-barrel full to the brim with freshwater.

Mac knelt down. "I do this in place of our father," he said, carefully removing her shoes.

"And I do this in place of your mother," Granny Connor said, as she removed Moira's stockings. Granny Connor took Moira's feet in her hands, patted them, and made a circle over the water, murmuring a blessing. As she put Moira's feet into the tub, the women gathered close to help with the washing. The younger women pressed in first with much laughter, for they were hunting the ring Granny had dropped into the tub.

"I've got it!" Maggie cried, her cheeks flushing. She held up the small ring for all to see. "'Tis a good sign."

"And who would you be planning to marry?" asked Catriona.

"I'll be finding out, won't I," replied Maggie.

Granny Connor emptied the tub outside and leaned it against the wall by the door. "Make sure to close up the dogs and keep this in the sunlight all day tomorrow."

The party broke up slowly. "We'll see you in the morning, early," the young women assured Moira. Granny Connor and Lenore, balancing her baby on her hip, left last.

Moira turned again in her pallet by the hearth. The cottage was too quiet. The moon had risen to its highest point, its yellow light on the moors a part of her home. After tomorrow, she would be back at Westness. This, save one, was her last night at home. Moira listened to Colin and Jamie sleeping. She wanted more noise, more laughter. She didn't want to think of Mac's lined face, the meetings, the shouting, and underneath all, the worry.

Morning came, bright and sunny, a fickle reminder of fall before winter rains and the cold returned. Moira fastened a few sprigs of purple heather and a white ribbon in her hair as she looked out at the yard. It was near unrecognizable. Mac and Colin had dug a pit to roast meat on the far side of their yard. They had cleared space in the center for dancing and they had set up another long table close to the house, timbers on top of barrels. Anything that could be used as a chair had been pulled around the edges of the open space, even a few burlap bags of bere and oats.

Granny Connor was first to arrive. "May you be blessed this day, child." She tapped the white ribbon wound in Moira's hair. "Remember to give me this before you marry, lass."

Dougal was next. "Never fear. He'll be waiting for you. We made sure of that." He laughed. "He's clean to the bone and ready for the net. Sean will make sure he gets to the manse."

Then her girlfriends came, Maggie, Catriona, and Lenore. They gathered around her with a clatter of talk, making sure Moira was decked out properly in all her finery, patting and admiring the white muslin dress Dylan had brought over from Kirkwall.

Dougal picked up his fiddle and brushed the strings. "Are you ready, sister?"

Dougal led the procession with a lilting march, his fiddle music calling them together. Moira walked behind him, flanked by Mac. Their friends followed all the way down the hill, along the beach to Selkirk. Sean would lead a similar procession from Mrs. MacLean's house, with Dylan at the head. They would meet at the manse, where Pastor McPherson waited.

Moira didn't know what the future would bring, but after this day, she and Dylan would be man and wife. She looked at Colin and Jamie, improvising steps to the fiddle music filling the air. Her heart felt full as she watched them step, counter step, and hop to Dougal's music.

Mac took her hand as they walked. "Most likely, you'll be gone in a year or two, off and away, far from here. Never forget us."

Moira clung to Mac's hand. "But we're staying here on Foulksay."

"I wish you well with all me heart," Mac said. "If he's no good to you, just you come home. We'll be here."

"Mac, don't say it." She pushed his arm. "It should be your day. You should be marrying Deidre. I don't worry about Dougal. I worry about you."

"Maybe I'll ask her one of these days."

"She loves you, Mac," said Moira. "Talk to her. Don't you worry about me. I'm already happy." She looked at the people walking along the beach toward the manse. "And I can't believe it's happening." She smoothed her new dress, took a deep breath, and hugged Mac fiercely. "Never forget I love you, Mac."

Nearly everyone she knew had crowded inside the manse. Even Constable MacTavish with his long, lugubrious face and his four children slid in next to Mac's crowd from the Pig's Head. Granny Connor waited by the door for a last kiss as Moira took the white ribbon off her hair and passed it to Granny, who slipped it into her side pocket.

Moira nodded to Lady Alice seated next to Mrs. MacNaught, and then, there was Lenore with her baby and Sean. All passed in a blur, for Dylan waited for her, standing by Pastor McPherson. Moira could hardly breathe. Her heart beat rapidly. This was the moment she would marry the man she loved. Dylan took her hand, and the wedding service began.

Pastor McPherson turned to Dylan. "Do you, Dylan McInerny, take this woman, Moira McDonnell as your wife, to have and to hold from this day forward, for better or for worse, for richer, for poorer, in sickness and in health, to love and to cherish, till death do you part?"

Dylan's voice rolled out. "I do."

Moira shivered when Pastor McPherson continued.

170

"Moira McDonnell, do you take this man, Dylan McInerny, as your husband, to have and to hold from this day forward, for better or for worse, for richer, for poorer, in sickness and in health, to love and to cherish, till death do you part?"

"Yes," Moira said. "I do."

Then the Pastor's words rang out, "If anyone knows of a reason this marriage should not take place, let him speak now or forever hold his peace." His words hung in the air for a moment.

No one spoke. Not Mac, nor Dougal, or Colin, or Jamie, and not anyone else gathered in the assembly room at the manse.

"You may kiss the bride," Pastor McPherson said, and so Dylan did, holding Moira close before everyone rushed close to congratulate the newly-wed couple. Colin and Jamie struggled to be the first to hug Moira and then Dylan.

The procession formed again, this time with Moira and Dylan at its head. Dougal followed just behind them, his fiddle rang out with bright songs in the afternoon sun. The line of family and friends followed the new couple all the way back through Selkirk, down along the beach and up the hill.

As they entered the yard to the McDonnell cottage, Granny Connor broke an oat cake over Moira's head, and the young unmarried girls scrambled to pick up a piece. "We'll hold it for later, to dream on," said Maggie.

The guests carried fish cakes to put on the side table, already crowded with food. More casks of ale warmed near the hearth. Gibson brought bottles of whisky and rum. Even Peter MacTavish, with a shy smile, had brought a freshly slaughtered pig earlier to roast on a spit all day. The women added more bannocks and oatcakes to the side table. Deidre came with her father; they carried large bowls filled with scones and cheese, the bowls to be left behind as a wedding gift.

Mac and Dougal stood over the ale pot, stirring to avoid the boil and arguing. "Add more whisky," said Mac. "I'll have him senseless tonight."

"Along with you and everyone else," Dougal laughed. "Put in just a bit more sugar. It's a long night ahead. And thank Gibson for the whisky."

"Speaking of me, are you?" Gibson came over to the fire. "Are you sure you're making that right? Maybe I need to taste it. You know, to make sure."

Mac laughed. "Take this job over, old man. You've got the mouth." Gibson called his cronies over, and the old men carried stools to sit close to the fire. They tasted the brew and declared it good enough, but not quite as good as what they remembered when they were young.

Finally the wedding meal was served, for once as much as anyone could want to eat and drink. After they had finished, Mac stood up. "I thank ye all for coming. 'Tis too bad it's only tonight, but we'll make the best of it. Tonight we celebrate this marriage between me sister, Moira, and the man she loves, Dylan." He waved at Moira and Dylan. The two young people stood up to cheers and then sat together on one of the bags of bere.

"It's time to toast the bride and groom." Dougal brought out the cog, a ceremonial wooden cup, a little barrel with three handles, already filled with the groom's brew, a mix of hot ale and whisky. He properly handed it to Mac as head of household. Mac drank deep. "Tonight I am the father of you both. May you," he nodded to Moira and Dylan, "live long and be well."

"And so for all of us," added Dougal, drinking next. He passed the cog to Granny Connor on his left. As the cog made its way around the party, each made a toast and drank deep, some coughing as the strong, hot brew filled their mouths.

"I'm minded of a story." Thomas Gibson stood and surveyed the party. "And I think it's a good story to tell at a wedding. Thank you," he said as Mac handed him a small glass.

The children gathered close, and the guests leaned forward. "You see," continued Gibson. "It's about a girl who lived by the sea, much like Moira. One day, she was walking, and she met a handsome lad, and he was much like Dylan here. He was from far away, but he wasn't a working man. No, he lay on the beach, as handsome as you please. An' she fell in love with him, in the way that lassies do."

"But this wasn't just any lad on his day off from the docks or the boats, you see. 'Twas a selkie, such as visit the islands from time to time. And he wanted to take her off island, far out to his home under the sea." Gibson waved his hands. "Down where the kelp grows five feet wide, big enough to hide those giant sea horses behind. An' she was willing, but her mother had tied a golden thread around her waist, and it kept her land bound. The laddie didn't know about the thread. He just couldn't take her out beyond where the mussels latch onto the rocks. It was like she was tied to the land."

"Where her mother found the thread, I don't know, for this girl came from a good fishing family, like Moira. An' so he stayed, and though his heart longed for his home so far away now and again, the days and then months passed, and they were good. He came home every morning with a creel full of fish, and he made a good life right here. One might say they lived happily ever after. And so may it be for Moira and Dylan, many good years ahead."

With that, Gibson turned around and emptied his glass, his cheeks red from whisky or the applause that followed. Then the fiddles came out. Dougal turned his fiddle in his hands as if he'd never seen it before, examining it from one end to the other. The other musicians began tuning their instruments. A few taps of the small drum, the *bodhrán*, could be heard.

The dancing began, first a sedate Strathspey of four couples, then a wild reel. The couples swirled around with even more intricate steps, until with a roar, six young men led by Mac took the floor, outdoing each other with elaborate leaps, all in time to the music which spun them faster and faster around the space that had been cleared for dancing. A few slipped off home, the elders nodded by the peat fire, Granny Connor among them, and the rest danced as if the night would never end.

Finally, Mac brought out the bride's cog, the wooden vessel full of hot ale and whisky with cinnamon and sugar. "May the years ahead be sweet," he said as he handed the cog to Moira, for as the bride, she drank first and she drank deep. Once again the cog was passed to the left, each drinking a toast to the bride and groom. Dougal put his violin down and was the last to drink from the bride's cog.

For this night Moira and Dylan would sleep in the box bed in the kitchen, and in the morning they would leave for their new life at Westness as man and wife.

A melee ensued as the friends of the bride and groom undressed the bridal pair. Those standing for the groom attempted to steal Moira's stockings, but Moira hopped into the box bed, safe.

Finally, the door to the box bed was closed. All was dark and quiet. Moira turned to Dylan, who folded her in his arms. She wished the morning, now so close, would never come. "We're truly married. It seems a miracle."

"And a miracle it is. I will love you always." Dylan smelled of smoke and whisky.

Moira touched the smooth skin over his heart. "Hush, love. 'Twas not so hard to fall in love with you. I'd do it all over again."

He stroked her cheek. "If the time comes that I cannot stay on Foulksay, will you come with me?"

"Yes, husband."

"And e'en if all your brothers say no?" he asked.

"Yes," she replied.

BOOK 3: THE CLEARANCES

WINTER 1841

CHAPTER 28: ALICE

Alice wondered if Gordon had decided to stay at Laurel House now that winter had come. Of course, he could be on his way home now. She sighed. Outside a blustery west wind rattled the windows.

If he were coming home to Westness, he'd have to contend with the roads, muddy and nearly impassable. Crossing the Pentland Firth was always difficult. Perhaps he would come up from Aberdeen or Leith on the new steamer. Still, she worried. And when he came home, would he ask her right away if she were pregnant? She pressed the small of her back. She wasn't.

She would have to write him about Martinmas. She was sure that Perkins would have his own version. Her mouth tightened.

She had gone to Assembly Hall to observe the paying of the rents on quarter day. These were her people as well now. As each fisherman or crofter came in, bits of money in their dirt-worn hands, some were angry, but most were afraid, for they hadn't enough. Perkins had written notes in his book, his officious little head bobbing. He made sure everyone knew that Lord Gordon would not be pleased.

Alice put the letter from Gordon aside and reread Diana's. Mother was ill again. Outside, the steady west wind pushed again against the windows. The first snow masked the tops of the rolling hills behind Westness. Alice checked the watch pinned at her waist and rang the bell for Mrs. MacNaught.

"I'll have soup up here later." Alice instructed. "No need for fussing about when it's just me."

"Pastor McPherson's here, mum. Do you wish to see him?"

"Yes, I'll come right down." Alice quickly surveyed her rooms. Where had she put her purse? She slipped several sovereigns into her pocket and hurried down the winding stairs.

Pastor McPherson stood as she entered the parlor.

"I didn't expect to see you until Sunday," said Alice.

"I've come to ask for help, Lady Alice. You heard the harvest was small?" At Alice's nod, he continued. "With this wind, no one's been able to fish, not out past the bay, and there's little enough to find along the rocks. The people are going hungry."

"But they have cows and chickens. They've dried fish."

"No house has enough this winter. There have been a few deaths already."

"Can they buy on account from Scott's?"

"He will not give more credit, Lady Alice. It's a long way to spring yet."

"Why can't he give credit? Hasn't he done so in the past?"

"Not this year. Lord Gordon has instructed otherwise."

"I see. I'm not sure what I can do. Lord Gordon's not returned yet. Could you stay for supper, then?"

"I'd rather not." Pastor McPherson wouldn't look at Alice. "I thought you might help."

"You know I will somehow. Here, use these as best you can." Alice thrust the sovereigns at him. "Do you have the list you promised? For Lord Gordon?"

"No, not yet." He hesitated. "Will you come with me to see for yourself? Tomorrow? In the morning?"

"Yes." Alice reached out to Pastor McPherson's arm. "Will you finish the list if I come? I must have it before Lord Gordon returns."

Pastor McPherson shrugged. "I'll try."

"Thank you. Come up to Westness at ten. Let's hope for dry weather."

Pastor McPherson ducked his head, still not meeting her eyes, and left, his black coat billowing behind him.

What a shame. How could Gordon believe the people would not be affected by his decisions? Alice wondered what had really brought the Pastor to Westness. "Mrs. MacNaught," she called. "I'll take supper in here."

The next morning began clear, though dark clouds lay on the horizon and snow still coated the higher hills. Alice could hardly keep her horse still. Little cold puffs blew from the mare's nostrils and hung on the air. Alice wanted to let the brown mare fly but checked her as Mrs. MacNaught came out.

"Are you sure you have to go, Lady Alice? Surely not out in this? You'll come back all wet and cold."

"We'll be back well before dark, won't we?"

Pastor McPherson nodded.

"Should you take Hargraves with you, just in case?" Mrs. MacNaught handed up an extra cloak.

"In case of what?" Alice bundled the cloak behind her saddle. "Stop worrying."

The two horses stamped their feet. Pastor McPherson's long legs hung over the sides of the spotted pony he'd borrowed. He carried a burlap bag in front of him. "Best be going."

The two rode down the hill and made their way through Selkirk. A few poked their heads out of their stone houses to see who passed by. They raised their caps to Pastor McPherson and stared at Lady Alice. Pastor McPherson turned inland and followed the winding path up to the grasslands, now barren. Barr Auch gleamed white in the foggy morning light.

Alice coughed from smoke as they entered the first cottage. A crofter leaned over a bare wooden table, his five children gathered close around a small peat fire in the middle of the room. A woman lay in a makeshift bed along the far wall, her teen-aged daughter beside her.

"Pastor." The man said. He nodded to Alice. He didn't stand up.

"We've come to see how your missus is, MacFarland." Pastor McPherson placed a small bag of oats on the table.

"Fine. She's fine. She'll be up and around in a little."

"And you have enough to eat here?"

"Sufficient."

Alice glanced at the children close to the fire. Their faces were thin. No pot warmed on the hearth. The air seemed stagnant, and the smell of so many bodies in such a small space made her dizzy.

"Good. We'll be going then."

Pastor McPherson and Alice stepped back out in the cold air. They walked to where they'd tethered the horses, past a ramshackle shed where chickens once scratched and nested. Alice could breathe again. She didn't want to talk. She didn't want to think about what she had seen, the children so thin.

They visited eight more houses along the small valley, until the bags of oats Pastor McPherson had brought were gone. In each house, the men sat with idle hands, stunned by the expanse of winter that faced them. They looked at the small bag the Pastor had brought as if it were a chimera soon to disappear.

A cold rain began. Alice pulled the extra cloak over her head. "How will they survive the winter?" Alice finally asked. Water beaded along the top of her cloak. She flicked it off.

Pastor McPherson stopped his pony and turned to face her. "Did you see the potatoes?" At the last cottage they'd visited, they'd looked into the shed to see a mound of small black potatoes crusted with mold, inedible, yet held over for seed. McPherson had picked one up, and it crumbled in his hand.

He spat. "Winter won't kill that rot. They should have burned them all. They'll let their cows wander on the grasses for feed, and they'll make a porridge out of the seed they should have planted. The cows will be too skinny for any good market price, if they last the winter. Few will be able to pay their rents at Candlemas, and the older folks will die."

Alice looked around the foggy moor with its rolling grasslands, the stone cottage behind them closed up against the cold. She could still see the people huddled inside. *No work and no food.*

"I still need the list of crofters." Her mare shifted its weight from one foot to another. Alice lifted the reins, and the horse stilled. "Names and ages. How many in each family and some notes about their skills and their health."

"I'll bring it tomorrow."

"Thank you." Alice flicked the reins and turned her horse toward Westness. She would be ready when Gordon returned.

CHAPTER 29: THE SHEEP

The sun sparkled on the waters of Bottle Bay in the cold January morning. Deidre, bundled up in a thick woolen shawl atop her cloak, leaned against her father as they watched men unload sheep onto the new pier. The sheep tossed their heads, frisky after their long confinement.

"Sheep, Da. Where will they go?"

"Somewhere inland. Lord Gordon thinks to try a new breed. Look, they've brought in their own herders."

A small band of men marched past the sheep and stopped outside the Pig's Head on Front Street. Hats pulled low, they joked and jostled each other.

"Who are those men, Da? They don't look like sheepherders." Deidre stood even closer to her father, as if she could make herself invisible.

"Ferry-loupers. Over and back, if we're lucky. Perkins said they're hired some guards to work with Constable MacTavish. They're here to protect us." He spat.

"Protect us from what?"

"I don't know. They serve Lord Gordon."

"And where will they all stay?" Deidre asked. "Not up at Westness, will they?"

"Some. A few here in Selkirk. Your mother didn't tell you? We'll have three of them at our house. Don't look at me like that. We'll be paid for room and board."

"Da, it's not about the money. They'll stay at our house? Why? Why are they even here?"

"Perkins said it's a precaution." William rubbed his hands in the cold and gazed at the small boats ferrying the off-islanders to land. "And while we're just the two of us, your mother asked me to say a word about Mac. She wants you to stop seeing him."

"Father, how could you ask?"

"I hear he's making trouble."

"You know Mac, Da. He's not a troublemaker. It's been a hard winter. It doesn't look any better with this." Deidre pointed to another group of men now disembarking, an occasional gun glinted in the sun.

"Don't forget I work for Lord Gordon and so do you." William paused, his hand heavy on her shoulder. "You're not stupid, lass."

"But we've never had guards and soldiers on the island before, not like this."

"Lord Gordon has plans. Since he's returned, 'tis all changing, and we're in the middle. For now, that means we'll have those guards in the store and in our home. I'd like you to keep an eye out for your sisters. And help your mother. If you must see Mac, you'll see him. That's all, and that's enough for me." He turned away to walk back up the hill to the store.

For the first time, Deidre saw gray in his hair. She turned to follow him, the sun warm on her shoulders. Behind her, drovers pushed the sheep onto land, and clusters of guards walked up the muddy streets of Selkirk to form ranks in front of Pig's Head.

"Don't make a fuss, now," said Anne, as she plumped the pillows on the makeshift bed in Charlotte and Penelope's room. "We'll have two guards upstairs and one down in the storeroom. That's only three. I expect I'll need more help. You'll be away from the house most of the time anyway. Not that I need you, but I would like you to watch out for your sisters."

"Yes, so father said." Deidre folded another blanket. "How long will they stay?"

"Don't be asking me," replied Anne. "Your father is the one who has the ear of his lordship. There, that will keep you well enough. Now come help me with supper. The girls will be home soon enough."

They looked at each other as they heard men come up the stairs. "That will be your father," Anne said. "Stay here for the moment." She closed the door to the bedroom. Deidre sat on her new bed and listened to the rumble of voices as they moved past her door on down the hall to the front bedroom.

Anne stuck her head back in the bedroom. "You might as well come out. They're wanting something to eat right away."

"This is Miss Scott, one of my daughters. She teaches over at the school," said William.

Three men gathered around the kitchen table and nodded at Deidre. One winked at her.

"Now, none of that," said the tallest. "Mr. Laughton will call you out."

"More bread, please," said the youngest, ducking his head.

Deidre sliced the bread, handed it over, and watched the leftover chicken from last night disappear. She ladled out another bowl of bean soup.

Deidre and Mac walked down the hill to Selkirk, its narrow lanes and stone houses ahead of them, darkening in the early evening light.

"What do you mean you have strangers sleeping at your house?" Mac asked.

"That's what I'm trying to tell you," said Deidre. "They came in this morning with the sheep."

"I heard, but there's only talk. Why are they here?"

"Mac, I don't know. Perkins made the arrangements. I don't think Father's too happy about it."

Mac stopped walking. "I'm worried about you."

"That should be the least of your worries. Who's going to look at an old maid like me?"

"Ah, now that's a different question." He drew her close. "I'd like to spend the rest of me life looking at the likes of you."

"Mac, Father said you're getting a reputation. Mr. Perkins told him you were trouble. He doesn't want me to see you any more."

"And how do you feel?"

Deidre looked at Mac. In the last few months, she had seen him almost every day. No matter what happened, he always made some time for her. They would walk through Selkirk, down to the sea and then back to the store, as dependable as the sun rising or setting. She sighed. "I think you know how I feel about you. Aren't we out walking?"

"Ah, but sometimes a man needs to hear." He waited.

The sun had just dipped down over the ocean, and the wind increased a bit. Deidre shivered. "I've got to get back. Especially tonight. My sisters will be curious about our boarders."

"And you, will you be curious?"

"Mac, I love you, but my family needs me."

"Those are the words I was waiting to hear." Mac twirled her up in the air. "Ah, lass, you near made me stop breathing."

"Put me down, Mac. This is serious. I don't like those guards, or whatever they are, and I don't like them in my house."

"I am being serious. It doesn't bode well for any of us. Do you be careful, please."

For a moment, Deidre lay her head against Mac's chest. "I will."

CHAPTER 30: GRANNY CONNOR

Mac moved as quietly as he could in the gloom of early morning. He set the newly coiled lines for cod in his creel by the cottage door. He couldn't shake the feeling that something was wrong. The new deck worked well enough, he supposed, but the fish seemed to have vanished. No doubt a troll at the bottom of the sea was sneaking them off the line. Maybe he should try Quernshead if the fog lifted. They had to eat.

The sound of running footsteps outside startled him. He leaned against the door to listen. He eased it open to find Sean with arm lifted, ready to pound the door.

Sean stood in the rain, his face wet, his chest heaving. "Mac, they've tossed Granny Connor out of her cottage."

"No. Don't say it. Come in, come out of the wet." Mac roared up to the loft. "Dougal, get down here. We've got trouble."

Dougal skidded down the ladder so fast he almost fell. Colin and Jamie tumbled behind him.

"She's an old woman," said Mac. "Why would they evict her? There's no enough land there for his fancy sheep."

"It wasn't about the sheep. Perkins wanted her house for those guards to stay in."

"God's bones, I knew it." Mac pounded his thigh. "Ever since Lord Gordon came back, it's nothing but trouble."

"Where is she?" asked Dougal. "Is she all right?"

"Granny's at my place for now. Perkins came so early this morning, it was still dark. They carried her out, scattered her possessions in the yard. They beat her when she tried to go back inside. No one heard her screams until she managed to come into town. Lenore's taking care of her now," Sean took a deep breath. "She's pretty shaken."

Mac shook his head. He couldn't imagine Granny Connor screaming. "How many men?"

"I don't know. Someone saw a group of them, maybe four or five up at Westness yester night, but there could be more."

"There's three of them quartered at Scott's Mercantile. Was Perkins about?" asked Mac.

"Granny said he was in the thick of it, riding his horse through it all." Sean sat on a three-legged stool and then jumped up again. "She said they just took over her cottage, laughing and strewing her things all over the yard and tramping up her garden. When we went back up to see what happened, Perkins said we'd better keep her away. He said she couldn't have her house back. It's the same cottage she's lived in since I can remember. Even Jack Connor's Da and Grandda lived there, and before that."

"Dougal, come with me to Sean's," Mac said. "If we can, we'll bring her up here, out of town. She can sleep in Moira's old place."

"I want to go with you," said Colin.

Mac shook his head. "Not 'till we know what's happening. Go over to Westness and find Dylan or Moira. Hargraves will help you. Wait until you're alone, and then tell them what's happened. Then come back here as quick as you can."

Colin tugged on his coat and left, slamming the door behind him.

"What about me?" Jamie buttoned his trousers. "Can I come with you?"

"No, Jamie." Mac ruffled Jamie's hair. "Keep an eye out. If Perkins comes here, just get on the moor. We'll find you. We'll be back as soon as we can."

Granny Connor stepped into the McDonnell cottage, still leaning on Mac's arm. Tears filled her eyes as she saw the fire banked on the hearth. "He called me a witch. He said I could burn in me house, if I chose to. Me own house." Her hands moved restlessly over the rough gray blanket someone had thrown over her shoulders. "What would Jack say? Where are my things?"

"Never mind that, Granny. Come sit. We'll take care of you now." Mac eased the old woman into a chair set close to the fire.

"They came all of a sudden. So many of them. Jack wouldn't have let them hit me."

Mac didn't know what to say. He stared at the purple mottling her cheek and wanted to bash something. "Granny, you'll stay with us for a time, and all will be well. You'll see."

Granny tried to get up from her chair. "I must get my things. My things are still in the yard all scattered."

"We'll take care of it. You'll stay with us, Granny, like I said. Give us a chance to find out what happened."

The door opened sharply, and Dougal and Colin came quickly to the fire. Dougal leaned close to Mac. "We've news. Willie said there's some thirty or so of those guards all over town."

"What's that?" cried Granny. "They're coming here?"

"No, no, Granny. Not now. Nothing to worry about," said Mac. "Try to rest." He tucked the blanket around her. "You're safe here, Granny." He lowered his voice. "Dougal, Colin, outside." He looked at Granny's hands still clasped in his own, and a rage built in his heart. For a moment he couldn't see. "Jamie, stay with Granny."

Outside, Mac leaned against the stones of the cottage and took a deep breath. "He's no evicted any fisherfolk as yet, so we may have ground to stand, but stand we must 'ere we're next. If we can see him. If we can get past Perkins. I don't care. I want to throttle him."

"You and everyone else," said Dougal. "Willie's got a house full. I didn't want to say inside, but Willie told me this is the third eviction this week. He hasn't heard anything about the families up by Barr Auch or out in the valley. Otherwise, it's quiet, like everyone is waiting, but they're angry about Granny."

"I saw the guards at Westness," said Colin. "They all had clubs and guns. Hargraves said they plan to go inland. I talked to Dylan but not Moira. He said he'd get word to Moira, and she'd come as soon as she could."

"Well done, Colin."

"How is she?" asked Colin.

"How would she be?" said Mac. "Colin, can you stay with Jamie just now and help with Granny?"

"Aye."

"We'll meet tonight, after Moira and Dylan are here," Mac said. "Sean will come, I think. And others. Best to have as many as we can."

"Meet at Willie's then?"

"Nah," said Mac. "Here."

"Should we ask McPherson?" asked Dougal.

"I don't know," said Mac. "He's likely already up at Westness, having tea with that sodding bastard. Did you hear anything about Catriona and her family?"

Dougal shook his head.

"Then we'll find out as we go," said Mac, his anger rising again.

Dylan watched the men talk in small clusters as the meeting broke up. It reminded him of Ireland, not enough food and too much violence. The men walked down the hill in groups of two and three, Mac and Dougal with them.

For a moment Dylan saw his sister's face. He paced along the stone wall in front of the cottage, not looking at the sea. Maybe the boatworks would take him back. If not in Inverness, maybe Glasgow. He could stay with his brother. Or try the railroad yards.

Moira came out of the cottage, shutting the door behind her. "I got Granny settled. I think she's going to be all right."

"'Tis a dark day," said Dylan.

"Looks like more to come," said Moira.

"'Tis lucky we are with no little ones just now."

Moira was silent.

"I may have to go to the mainland for work."

Moira blinked and pulled her shawl tight.

Dylan felt like swearing. He didn't want her to cry. "I don't want to leave you. You know that. But I cannot see a way out of this if I stay." He stood with his back to the sea. "I dinna like to say this. Your brothers work hard, but Mac's trouble."

"They always come to Mac when things go wrong."

"It's different now at Westness since Lord Gordon came back from London. You see it. If the fishermen stop working with me, I don't have a job. I've got to find a better place for us."

"I can't come with you?"

"I don't see how. I won't have enough to keep you."

"I know how to work."

"I know, dear heart." Dylan remembered the choking stench of the room he shared with his brothers, high in the tenements of Glasgow. He shook his head.

Moira sat down heavily on the stone wall near the house. "You don't have to go now, do you?"

"I'll hold out as long as I can." Dylan smoothed Moira's hair, wanting to touch her.

"Things could change."

"With evictions in the winter? I don't think so."

"You'll go then without me?"

"Aye," said Dylan. "But I don't like it."

Dylan sat next to her on the stone wall. He remembered saying goodbye to his mother and father, and then his sisters and his brother. He leaned on the stone wall and held Moira's hand. "Maybe not until the herring run."

Moira made no answer.

CHAPTER 31: WESTNESS

Gordon scattered the list Pastor McPherson had so carefully prepared. "You think this is adequate?" Gordon snorted. "I expected more from you, Pastor."

McPherson straightened in his chair. "I've served here seven years, sir. I know I remain or go at your discretion. All I'm asking for is an increase in my allowance over the next few months. The people are hungry."

"You want me to mollycoddle these wastrels, these do-nothings? Let them feel the sword of Damocles. If they work, they eat. I will not give false charity. You, sir, have a responsibility to support my directives." Gordon peered at Pastor McPherson. "Do you understand me?"

"Christ himself would understand you. But He fed the multitude with a basket of fish and a few loaves."

"Will it make them more amenable to emigration? Then I grant your request this once and no more. Don't mock me. For it is also written that every man shall bear his own burden. Understood?"

Pastor McPherson nodded. "Thank you." His hands lay still on his lap. After a moment, he rose and left the room.

Lord Gordon returned to his papers. "I must persevere. I have no choice," he muttered.

Alice tapped on the door of Lord Gordon's office.

"I didn't expect to see you, not after this morning."

"I wanted to talk with you about the evictions."

"Oh, that." Gordon's mouth pinched into a straight line. "Haven't we had enough excitement over you going to Edinburgh?"

Alice flushed. "I appreciate your allowing me to visit my family. But I've been down to the parish house again.

It's inadequate for the numbers of people coming into Selkirk. People are sleeping in the streets. Children are going hungry."

"Come, come, my dear. Don't upset yourself. I've just made arrangements with Pastor McPherson to provide additional resources. He's helping with emigration. Those who remain will have better lives. In time, they'll adapt." He stood closer. "I don't like you going to Edinburgh."

"You already said that this morning. I haven't seen my family for nearly a year." Alice stepped to the window. Outside, an old man sprinkled straw on the muddy garden, his hat pulled low against the constant rain. "How can you look at this weather and not think about those who have been evicted?"

"What do you mean?" Gordon raised his voice. "By God, are you defying me? You may wish to remember that I make the decisions on this island, not you."

"But I see them starving," Alice replied. "Everyone's frightened of us."

"That's more silliness. They'll manage until the ships come. I want my sheep settled on my land well before spring," said Lord Gordon. "And no crofters about to steal them."

"If my opinions don't matter, perhaps the opinions of your peers will count. Have you seen these articles?"

Gordon scanned the newspaper she thrust at him. "The *Gazette*. What do you expect from a liberal rag like that?"

"Lord Overton is setting up a fund to help the crofters. Some of the money will be used to resettle them to the Americas or New South Wales. They're asking for subscribers."

"I don't see the difference between his plan and mine."

"But the people don't have to be indentured."

"Bah! He's a bleeding Chartist. That's no solution. If you give money to the poor, they'll just breed, and we'll have more of them. Where'd you get those papers anyway?"

"If you must know, my father sent them. And I don't agree at all with Malthus and his theories of the poor. We're the ones clearing the land. We can't just leave the people to starve."

"Alice, we've talked about this before. Why do you think I went to London? The ships are on their way. Those who have skills will find a better life."

"But we can't just throw them out of their homes."

"You don't understand. These people are like children." Gordon set his teacup down with a rattle. "Don't fret yourself, my dear. They're simple, but sturdy. They starve every winter. They don't feel pain in the same way we do."

"I don't believe you. Surely we should be doing more."

"There's no 'we' on this matter. You've had your say, but these are my decisions." Gordon stood. "I'm changing this island in ways my uncle never thought of. It's not easy, but it's necessary for our survival and theirs. Now, leave me."

Alice stood. "May you never know hunger." She closed the office door behind her. *Thank God for Edinburgh. God willing*, she thought, *I will not return.*

Lord Gordon looked down at the garden from his office. The workmen had gone. *Alice is a proud woman,* he thought. *A good mother she will be to my sons, if she would only become pregnant. What a fuss over the evictions. These people hadn't paid their rent; it wasn't as if I owe them anything. Our income will be assured with sheep. If the crofters wouldn't change, then they damn well couldn't squat on the land. Better they go elsewhere. It was just like India. If you weren't firm, they would take away what was rightfully yours.*

"There you are, Perkins. Have you distributed the broadsheets?"

"Yes, sir."

"And?"

"Well, sir," said Perkins, "Most of them you'd want to go, they don't have money to pay the fees." He adjusted his glasses. "As you said, sir, we can arrange their passage if they sign letters of indenture here. Once they've landed, they'll be purchased as bondsmen. Their passage can be repaid through an agent."

"Perkins, I want them to sign up as families. Send the women and children as well. Not just the men. Keep me informed of your progress. Include those fishermen who haven't retrofitted their boats." Lord Gordon settled in his chair, wincing as the all too familiar pain snaked up his arm. "I'll give you a commission for each person who signs up, perhaps enough to purchase the land you've wanted."

"Thank you, sir. I'm pleased to serve you," said Perkins.

"Are the patrols still needed?"

"Yes, sir. The crofters keep going back to their houses."

"Have them pull the houses down, if necessary. I don't want them having a reason to return."

"Yes, sir. Scattered stones, like you said, sir. We should be through afore summer's done."

"End of summer. That's too slow." Gordon leaned over his desk to consult a newspaper. "The ships to take them to America will be here by the beginning of May. I want the people out of their houses and gone. Continue with the eviction notices. More sheep will arrive within a fortnight." Lord Gordon turned away from Perkins. "That will be all."

"Yes, sir."

Lord Gordon massaged his left arm. Nothing but aches and pains. He looked around the study with distaste. *At least it's more comfortable than when Uncle George lived here alone, but the house overall is simply too big and too cold. Too many improvements are needed. I'll be damned if I ever go to that tiny church.* He rubbed his arm again. *Let Alice represent us when we return next summer. If we return. And let her stew in Edinburgh for awhile. It will do her good.*

He opened the *Gazette*. So the Emigration Society Commission was concerned about the plight of the poor in Glasgow. He snorted. More likely they were concerned about the numbers of the poor. Lord Gordon tossed the newspaper on his desk.

CHAPTER 32: QUERNSHEAD

Mac and Dougal hiked along the headlands above Selkirk. A blustery wind swirled around them and flattened the heather. Mac and Dougal kept their heads down before the wind.

"It's too cold. I'm thinking the herring will be late this year," said Dougal.

"If they come at all," said Mac.

A long straggling line of crofters came toward them, with bundles or small packs on their backs. Mothers carried little ones on their hips and led others by the hand. Some limped, and some leaned on each other.

"Halloo, William. Is that you?" Mac called to an older man at the head of the group. "What's happening?"

"Mac. Dougal. I never thought to see this day. We've been beaten out of our homes." William stepped out of the line. "They tossed us out in our yards, helter skelter, all a mess. They set afire what we couldn't carry."

"It's happening then, all along the valley?"

"Aye. We can't go back. They boarded up what's left of our houses and posted guards at the doors. They said we have to go to the headlands, near to Quernshead." William pointed north with his gnarled finger. "I don't know where we'll sleep or what we'll eat."

Mac saw families he'd known all his life. A few stopped walking, dazed, their clothing sodden in the rain. Most kept moving. The children were silent.

Dougal grabbed William's arm. "Have you seen the Brodie family?"

"They're on the east side of the island, right? I saw smoke along the horizon. They could be behind us."

"Didn't any of you fight?" cried Mac.

"Fight? At dawn with babies crying and men kicking the door in?" William's voice quavered.

A light rain began, and the stragglers pulled closer together. Some wrapped blankets around the elders. A toddler fell on the ground, and her mother picked her up and smoothed her hair.

"There's nothing out at Quernshead."

"Aye," replied William. "We dinna know what else to do. Only that they'd come and beat us if we stayed. A few went into town, but we're going where they said." He motioned the group to keep moving. "Can you come with us? Help us make shelter?"

Mac made a quick decision. "Aye, we'll help. Dougal, go to McPherson. Find out what you can and try to get some help up to Quernshead."

"All right," said Dougal. "Can you keep an eye out for Jacob Brodie?" At Mac's nod, Dougal turned away from the straggling line of crofters and ran down the path to Selkirk.

"William, I have room for three or four at my place," said Mac. "Whoever's most hurt. You can drop them off on the way."

"Thanks, but we'll stay together." William looked at his hands. "We're to make our way fishing until the ships for America come, Perkins said. I know farming. But I don't know fishing."

Mac looked over the column. "You've got how many here, about sixty?" At William's nod, he continued. "I'll go ahead with a few of your men to get started. Come to where the creek runs near Quernshead. We'll manage."

The morning sky darkened, and the rain continued. Mac hurried ahead with three young men, trying to think what could be done. "We'll build *sheilings*," he said as they walked. "It's summer shelter, but better than nothing."

All through the afternoon, they dug stones from the ground to make small walls and packed them with heather, grasses, and mud. The women sorted the people into two groups, those who could join the work and those who needed patching up. Dougal brought several more up from Selkirk to help. As each little shelter was finished, those who were the oldest or the most hurt moved in. Some held babies as they sat on the ground in the cold.

"Have you no food?" asked Mac.

"We've a little, what we were able to take away with us," said William. His words were carried away by the wind.

"I'll see what I can gather up for you. We're meeting tomorrow night at my place. Can you come?"

"I don't know," William replied. "Aye, I'll try."

They looked around the clearing they'd made on the headlands. People hunkered down in their temporary shelters. The makeshift roofs of blankets rippled in the wind. The constant waves below filled their mouths with the taste of salt.

"We'll start tomorrow, just after dusk."   Mac surveyed the clearing once more, a bitter taste in his mouth. "Dougal, come on. We're for home."

CHAPTER 33: CATRIONA

Mac and Dougal walked along the headlands away from Quernshead.

"I don't understand why he did this," said Dougal. "How are those folks going to make a home? There's nothing there. And if they're to fish, there's no easy way down to the beach."

"He can't just toss people out," said Mac. "Surely the bastard's got enough."

"Did you see how many were hurt?" asked Dougal.

"I saw." Mac was silent, walking fast. His breath came out in puffs of white. "Look ahead," he said. "Is that your Catriona?"

Catriona stood outside of the McDonnell cottage, waving her arms.

Dougal broke into a run. "Thank God you're here. I was worried about you. Is everyone all right?"

"No, we're not all right. They're inside." Catriona tried to speak and couldn't.

"Hush, hush. Talk can wait." Dougal took her in his arms and patted her, as if she were a child. "I've been looking everywhere for you."

"We were just up at Quernshead," said Mac.

"Yes, Quernshead. Some were to go there," said Catriona. "But Mother's not well. Da didn't want her sleeping outside. We didn't know where else to go."

"Dinna worry, my Cat," Dougal's hands hovered over her bruised face and tucked back a straggling hair. "You don't have to talk, unless you want to."

"No, I want to. I have to tell you. We have no food, Dougal," she said. "She never got over losing the baby.

Me mother can barely walk for grief. And Da, they beat him down. Right in front of us all."

Dougal pulled her close to his side. "Ah, Cat."

"They tore our house apart as if no one lived there. And then they made us walk with the others, past all those houses with fires in the front yards burning everything up. They said we had to go live at Quernshead. We couldn't go back to our homes. What's left they boarded up, with guards left standing in the front of each one." She tugged on Dougal's arm, her face a mask of worry. "We came over to the headlands. No place to sleep. Me ma won't speak."

"You did right to come here." Dougal looked at Mac over Catriona's head as he held her close. "Don't be worrying. We'll get everyone settled. Shush. You're here now."

"We've got to get more food and blankets over to Quernshead," said Mac.

"Aye, Mac. We'll work on that later," said Dougal, not letting go of Catriona "Let's see to the Brodies first."

Colin had built up the fire. A fish soup simmered on the banked peat and smoke hovered near the ceiling timbers. Everyone stood or sat as near to the fire as they could get. The fire blinked red at times and cast an eerie light. Catriona went to her mother, who rested on a pallet next to Granny Connor.

"Welcome, welcome," said Mac. "Don't you be worrying. My brother and me would not be happy to see you elsewhere. We'll manage just fine."

At this, Jacob's face eased. "I thank you," he said. "Catriona said you'd see us in, but I dinna know." He sank onto the stone floor and eased his arm onto his lap as he leaned back against the stones. "Some of us need a bit of binding."

Granny bent over Jacob's arm. "There's no bone sticking out. You'll heal." Granny talked Dougal and Catriona through the gritty process, directing them to pull the arm straight to reset the bone. They wound a white cloth around two sticks to hold Jacob's arm steady.

"That should do it," said Dougal. "You'll be fishing with the best of them before you know it."

Jacob leaned against the wall as if he couldn't move any further, and he touched the white cloth on his arm, smudging it. "That's something I know nothing about."

Dougal bent over Jacob. "Dinna worry about that now. You'll no have to go fishing tomorrow."

"Aye," added Mac. "You're to stay with us. I've sent your two oldest boys with Colin down to see what help we can get for those out at Quernshead."

"They're good steady boys," said Jacob. "Catriona, see to your mother."

"Yes, Da." Catriona turned away and helped Granny Connor back to her pallet. "Thank you, Granny."

"Tish, child. I've seen worse," said Granny. "What have those murdering bastards done to your mother, with her looking so pale?"

Catriona whispered in her ear.

"Well, they're still murdering bastards to treat you all so," hissed Granny. "I remember the day I lost me own home." The two women settled on the pallets next to Freya, who had fallen asleep.

Mac hunkered down by Jacob. Dougal sat down on his other side, leaning back against the cottage wall. "Do you want to stay inside?" asked Mac.

"Ah, I think it's better than moving just now," Jacob replied. "I wanted you to know what happened."

"Catriona told us some," said Mac.

Jacob lowered his voice. "That Mr. Perkins evicted us. Said we had to go to Quernshead, but there's no houses out there, nor land to grow anything. So how can we be owing them rent?"

"It's rent for the land, such as it is," said Dougal. "That's the only thing I can think of."

"How many men did Perkins bring with him?" asked Mac.

"Too many to count," said Jacob. "No, 'twas about twenty. They went from place to place. They tore up the yard and ran off me last cow right through the fields that was just starting. Everything is trampled."

"We can hope it's not all gone," said Dougal. "And the house?"

"They made a fire in front of the house and burned whatever we couldn't grab away from them. Then they wouldn't let us go back inside. They just shoved us away. They used axes and whatever they could to break it down. That house has stood there for as long as ever I can remember. And my wife. She was in bed yet. You heard we lost a child? If we hadn't got my wife out, she would have burned." Jacob rubbed his eyes.

Dougal and Mac looked at each other.

"Things will sort out," said Dougal.

"Stay here and rest," said Mac, rising from the floor.

"Aye," said Dougal. Dougal stood as well, surveying the room. Granny Connor had made pallets close to the hearth for Catriona and Freya. The two youngest boys, Luke and John, would sleep up in the loft with Colin and Jamie. And he would be sleeping downstairs this night with the older boys. "Mayhap we'll need to stand watch tonight."

Jacob grinned, despite his pain. "And that would be outside, yes?"

"Good idea. We'll take turns," said Mac. "Will you be all right here at the cottage alone for a bit?" he asked

Jacob. "I can't imagine anyone would come here, but if they do, just get out. We'll be back as soon as we can."

"We'll be all right now. I thank you for taking us in." Jacob's voice broke.

"None of that," said Dougal. "I think you know we're family here."

Dougal stepped outside. Near evening had come. From outside, the windows glowed softly in the fading light. *How many cottages were filled as their cottage was this night,* mused Dougal. He followed Mac down the path to Selkirk.

CHAPTER 34: ST. NINIAN'S

On the side of St. Ninian's opposite the cemetery, the crofters had assembled a long shelter with poles. They tacked blankets to the church wall and made partitions with rugs and plaids. A few older people napped against the church wall, bundled in blankets or cloaks. Some lay groaning. Two women built a fire of peat taken from the large beehive-shaped stack kept at the back of the church.

"Catherine," cried Agnes McGill, nudging her kettle onto the fire with her toe. "Come over. I didn't see you when we came in." Agnes pushed a child a little away from the fire. "Watch yourself, now." Several children gathered close, holding their hands out to the flames. "Don't shove," she said. "Maggie, bring me that large pot and get these children away from the fire." Agnes turned to Catherine. "How's your grandsir?"

"He's sleeping now, worn out. He can hardly walk." Catherine looked around the small yard, two small children pulling on her skirts. "Did your man go to Quernshead?"

"Can't catch me. Can't catch me," cried Timmy. He ran behind Agnes.

"That's it. All of you, away from the fire. Go make yourself useful." Agnes gave Timmy a shake. "Maggie, where are you?"

"I'm coming, Mother." Maggie carried a baby on one hip as she dragged a large pot over.

"Good, girl. Now, please take these kids elsewhere. Bundle them up and tell them stories or something."

"Are you making a soup, Mother?" A smile broke out on her face as Agnes nodded. Maggie called the children together. "Let's make a tent just for us," she said, "and I'll tell you of the smuggling Dons of Westray and the treasures they found."

"Where were we?" asked Agnes. "I can't think with all this racket." She stooped to pick up an onion and began cutting it up for the pot.

"The headlands. I was asking about the headlands." Catherine stripped an onion of its outer skin and threw the parings into the soup. "What is it like out there?"

"Jack said there's only a pinch of land for each family, not enough for any farming. I don't know how we're going to make a living there. They said we have to fish somehow. How can we fish? We have no boat. We never fished. The house is gone, part burned and part boarded up. Jack, he went over to the Pig's Head."

"I heard some of the families were taken in. Granny Connor's over at the McDonnell's."

"Wish he had a bigger place. We'd be there instead of here." said Agnes. "I guess I could do laundry, you know. Maybe those pigs who tossed us out need their shirts washed. I could send some of the younger ones to pick up the clothing. Maybe Pastor McPherson will let us use the tubs from the church, or we could walk to the river. They've got to let us do something."

"Aye. Just don't go over alone or too late, if you know what I mean. I hear they pay for other things too, if you're hungry enough."

"We're not that hungry."

"Some are. I hate to think what will happen if they're found out."

The two women were silent.

"Not my daughter," said Agnes. "She's too young."

"Aye, but she's a pretty one and sweet," said Catherine.

"Too pretty for her own good these days," said Agnes. "I'll keep her close."

The back door of the manse opened. Pastor McPherson stepped out to survey the group of crofters camped in his back yard.

"You canna stay here," Pastor McPherson called out. "Lord Gordon has given you new lands. You're to settle at Quernshead until the ships come."

Agnes and Catherine watched a few men gather by the Pastor. They strained to hear what was being said.

"Pastor, we no can live there. It's not but rock and grass and the cold wind. There's no place to sleep."

Three more men walked over to join the circle that tightened around the Pastor.

"There's no food out there," called Willie, "and the wind blows cold. We just thought we'd stay here for a bit."

Pastor McPherson began shaking his head.

"Aye," chimed in Thomas. "We're not going to be any trouble. We'll just take a bit of shelter, until things settle and we get our lands back. 'Tis the church, a place of refuge as the Bible says."

"Don't blaspheme," cried Pastor McPherson. His sonorous voice echoed in the small yard.

"Have ye no seen what they've done? It's not right, turning us out of our homes like that," called Thomas.

"And for what? For sheep?" Ronald shouldered his way forward. "We're Christians, not animals."

"God rot you, Pastor," cried Bruce. "Look at your people. You should be fighting for us. Not whimpering behind Lord Gordon and hiding in the church. Look around yoursel'. We need shelter. We need food. We've got hurt people here. We need help to bind our wounds. We should be planting, not roaming everywhere looking for work that's na there."

The crowd shifted. Ronald pushed closer. "Some of us are going over to the mainland, to look for work, but we have to leave our women and children behind. Who's to care for them?"

"We're not the sinners," cried Thomas. "'Tis Lord Gordon who's sinning against us. All we want is our place back. Where we've all lived for as long as we can remember. Can ye help us, or have you abandoned your flock?"

The men fell silent, daring the Pastor to ignore them. Some of their women drifted over to stand behind their men. They waited, their faces thin with exhaustion, their cloaks and skirts flapping in the cold spring wind.

"You must know I've spoken to Lord Gordon already." Pastor McPherson waved his hand at the parish house behind him. "I've never seen so many go hungry. But Lord Gordon is bringing progress to us. God's will is working through him. You don't own the land that your homes were on, none of you. Maybe in the past, the old lord overlooked it when times were hard. But 'tis your duty to pay the rents or to face evictions."

"But he raised the rents to where no one can pay. How is that progress?" asked Thomas.

"It's his legal right. Ye canna' stay here. You have to move out on the headlands with the others," replied the Pastor.

"Have you even been out to Quernshead? Have you seen the bits of land where he wants us to live? There's nothin' there." Thomas leaned on the man next to him. "You can't grow anything that close to the sea, not even grass."

"What about the beatings? Me granda can't walk. What about me children? They're going without food." cried Catherine. "This can't be God's will."

Pastor McPherson looked at the churchyard filled with makeshift tents and bedraggled people. "I'll do what I can," he said. "I'll meet with Lord Gordon again. Mayhap he'll help. I'll try. I have food for you today, but you can't stay here. You have to move."

He didn't have to say another word. The people turned away and began to take down their tents.

STANDING STONES

CHAPTER 35: CROFTERS PROTEST

Occasional sparks from two peat fires lit the faces of the men and women crowded into the yard in front of the McDonnell cottage.

Jamie lay on the roof of dried peat and heather with Luke and John, peering down at the crofters and fishermen who had come from all over the island, now sitting in groups, squeezed into every possible space.

"Thank you all for coming." Mac stood up behind the fire and looked at the faces turned toward him. "We couldn't meet in town, for the guards are everywhere, even at Scott's Mercantile."

"Aye, he knows which side his bread is buttered on," called out Sean. "He's put up three of them in his place."

"Anyone in town is suspect," said Mac. "For the day has eyes, and the night has ears. But you know why we're here tonight. We're here to protest the evictions and the wanton destruction of our homes."

A shout went up from the crowd.

"We've got to go directly to Lord Gordon. He's the magistrate. He's responsible for keeping the order. If he doesn't listen, then we'll go to the Mainland."

Mac looked around at men and women he'd known all his life. "It's your families who've been tossed out of their homes. Anyone could be next. You've all heard of the people out at Quernshead. Some of you saw the tents behind the church before they were taken down. No one can live like that. I don't care what Pastor McPherson says. You just can't put people out like that."

"There's no potatoes for seed this spring," said Robert, a steady mumble of voices adding to his. "They crumble to dust in your hand. We don't have food, and we can't pay his bloody rents."

"The cows are too thin to sell, but not too thin to eat," said Bruce. His beard gleamed white in the firelight. He spat in the fire. "Perkins and his guards evicted us and ran our cows off. No warning."

"Lord Gordon wants those who were evicted to fish for their food. How can they fish without boats?" said Dougal. "Even when we rebuild the boats the way he wants them, we can still only put so many men on them."

"Aye," murmured the crowd.

Mac thought of the men who would drown in the coming weeks as they tried to fish in waters they didn't know. He looked again around the crowd gathered by the twin fires in front of the cottage. "We've got to start somewhere. We canna leave our neighbors to go without food."

"They'll be needing lines and baskets and shovels," said Dougal. "They can go for crab and clams along the coast. That's something."

Moira stood by her brothers. "Whatever you can spare, bring to Quernshead, or here. We'll take it out to them. If you have meal, that would be a help."

"We'll bring what we can," said Kate, a tall older woman with gray streaks in her hair. "I remember yet those who brought food when we needed it."

"Aye, and we'll tend those who are hurt," said Agnes, standing up beside her.

"Good," said Mac. "In the morning I'm going up to Westness. And I'm asking you now if you will come with me."

"I'll come," said Dylan. A group of men stood up and raised their hands. Bruce raised his hand as well, and the men with him shouted approval.

"I'll bring as many as I can from Quernshead," said Robert.

"I'll come," said Moira.

A chorus of hisses broke out. "'Tis no place for women," said a man from the back.

"We're going hungry too, us and the children," cried Agnes. "We should be there."

"'Tis time for us all to go before Lord Gordon," said Mac. "Men and women. Even children. But I'd be lying if I said we face no risk." He gave a bitter laugh. "He's got to see that we won't just go along. We can't live on nothing. We've got to see to our families."

The crowd was silent. Mac could see those he'd known all his life now filled with anger and some with despair.

"Now is the time to speak up. There may be something we haven't thought about, something that will satisfy Lord Gordon and give us our lands back. Give us work, and we'll pay his blasted rents." Mac raised his hands to the crowd. "Meet me tomorrow morning by the path to Westness."

"Aye," the crowd shouted, and they gathered around Mac, their faces hidden and then revealed by the flickering fire.

Dougal leaned close to Dylan. "I dinna think we'll see any changes," he said in a low voice. "But we've got to try."

Early the next morning, Dougal and Colin hiked down the path and out along the rocky beach to the far side of the cove where they had set traps for crab. The sun broke through the fog, just warming their backs, and the smell of the sea was sharp in their nostrils. Colin pulled five woven traps in, as Dougal opened each one and grabbed the crabs by their two back legs, transferring them to his creel. A few crabs skittered in the bottom of each trap. Not all of them were large enough to eat.

"'Tis a small catch today," said Dougal. He tossed a yellow starfish back into the sea.

"Aye. Too many people setting traps now."

"We've got enough to make a stew of this," said Dougal.

"I'm sick of eating the dregs of the sea." Colin bent over the crab traps and baited each one with a fish head. "I want to go over to the mainland when the herring runs. I want to work the harvests or go south, somewhere. Can you talk to Mac for me?"

"You should talk to Mac yourself," said Dougal.

"I heard Dylan is going to Inverness or maybe Glasgow," said Colin. "There's no work here. Too many men standing about with a ready hand."

"You're right. There's no enough work." Dougal stood. "For sure today will show us if we can stay here, in this place, our home, or go."

"I hate it here. I hate the guards and the way they look at us, as if we were nothing. I hate not having enough to eat."

Dougal looked at his brother and tried to remember how he felt when he was sixteen. "Ah, Colin, you're like Mac. You know we're going up to Westness today. Maybe something will come of it. If not, we'll need to talk. You, me, Dylan and Mac."

At that, Colin smiled. "Thanks, Dougal." They tossed the traps back into the cove and carried their creels up the hill.

At the McDonnell cottage, gray clouds hung close to the ground. Mac brought peat inside for the fire. "'Tis a raw morning," he said to Moira.

"Granny's not so well last night," said Moira in a low voice. She poured the last of the broth into a cup.

"You'll stay with her then?"

"How can I not?" Moira turned back to the pallet on the floor where Granny lay.

Mac nodded to Dougal and Dylan. "Colin," he called. "Stay here this time." They left, with Dylan closing the door behind him.

Colin hissed to Moira, "How can he just do that, pretend I'm still a kid?"

"Hush, Colin. He does what he thinks is best for everyone. Look around you. Do you think these people knew they'd wind up sleeping on our floor?"

"It doesn't matter. I'm going up to Westness." Colin slammed out of the cottage.

Moira settled on the floor where Granny lay, the cottage quiet around her. "Take this, Granny. Mayhap it will ease you."

Granny opened her eyes. "Best you drink it for the little one, dearie," she said raspily. "I won't be needing such where I'm going."

"How did you know?" Moira asked.

Granny's hands lay still on the rough blanket. A faint smile edged her thin lips as she opened her eyes again. "How could I not know? I only regret I won't be here when she's born. Ah, Moira, I see dark days ahead for all the McDonnells. Dark days." Her breath rattled in her throat as she struggled to breathe.

"Try to take a sip, Granny," said Moira. "Dinna worry about all that. Just rest."

"You should tell him now. Tell Dylan. About the baby."

"I can't."

"Ah, then, you always were stubborn, the most stubborn of them all." Granny closed her eyes again, as if they were too heavy to hold open. "Stubborn."

"Rest, now, Granny."

"I'll be resting soon enough. Stay with me a bit more."

Moira set the cup aside and took Granny's hands in her own. "I'm here," she said.

A light rain fell as the crowd of men and women gathered in the yard at the back of Westness, which loomed grand as ever. Mac jumped atop on a small stone fence near the house, and the men pressed close to hear him.

"He'll see me this day, or we'll set up our tents in his very yard," Mac shouted.

A roar went up from the crowd.

"We don't have to live like animals in the dirt. He's going to listen this time."

The men pushed closer.

"Hey now, you can't come here like this. Be peaceable, man," called Hargraves from the door. Dorsey stood behind him holding a club.

Mac glared at Hargraves. "We want to see Lord Gordon."

"He's not seeing the likes of you," sneered Dorsey.

Hargraves put his arm out to hold Dorsey back. "Mac, Perkins went to get the guards. You should leave. You know what will happen."

"We're past the time to be quiet," cried Mac. "He has to know what he's done to us."

"Give it up, Mac," said Hargraves. "Let your men go back to the headlands afore there's real troubles."

"We're the ones who've lost our homes," yelled one of the men behind Mac. "Our children are going hungry." The men began to mutter and move toward the house.

"He's thrown us out of our homes." Gibson slipped a little in the muddy yard. "We want work. We want our homes back."

"Tell him we want to see him," shouted Mac, leaping down onto the ground.

The men crowded around him, their shoulders bumping. "Now," they growled. "We want our homes back."

Perkins, mounted on horseback, trotted into the yard. A crowd of guards ran behind him and blocked the way out.

"Disperse. All of you," bellowed Perkins.

The crowd turned to face the guards. They were boxed in, the great mansion towering behind them. Their faces mirrored dismay. The women, who had been at the back of the crowd, scattered to the sides of the yard, pulling their children with them.

"Not until we've seen Lord Gordon," cried Mac. "'Tis time he listened to us."

"You'll not be seeing him this day." Perkins signaled the guards to move forward. They paced toward the house in a line against the crofters, their muskets and clubs held ready.

Mac knew they wouldn't stop.

"No," cried Agnes, reaching for Timmy.

A guard pushed her down. The line of guards rammed against the crofters and fishermen. Men and women shoved and grunted, fighting back and stumbling in the mud. A few children pelted guards with stones, sometimes missing, sometimes hitting their own.

Mac struggled to get to Dougal. They stood back to back as the yelling guards rushed the men. Mac pushed a heavy-browed guard to the ground and grabbed his musket to use as a club.

Another guard hit Dougal over the head. Dougal fell to the ground and curled in a ball as guards kicked and hit him over and over again.

Mac roared and slammed his club right and left as the fight surged across the yard. Every direction Mac turned, more guards came at him. He couldn't feel his knuckles. A tremendous blow hit his arms and back.

Perkins held his horse steady at the side of the yard, shouting commands. The crofters and the fishermen, covered with blood and mud, fought back against the guards with their hands.

A few children fell underfoot, Timmy among them.

Mac fought his way to the side, shook himself loose, and leaped at Perkins on the edge of the yard. He yanked Perkins down from his horse.

"We only wanted to talk, you bastard. We only wanted a chance to work." Mac pummeled Perkins again and again until the guards pulled him off.

The fight was over. Everywhere Mac looked, crofters and fishermen lay clubbed and beaten. Dylan and Colin had pulled Dougal to the side. Some of the women were crying. Agnes sat bowed over in the mud, keening. Timmy's body lay on her lap.

"See what you've gained here," said Perkins. He leaned against his guards, his chest heaving, his thin face bloody. His large nose quivered. "Ye haven't accomplished anything. Now 't'will get worse. Hold him."

Perkins kicked Mac in the stomach. "You wanted to see Lord Gordon? He'll see you now."

CHAPTER 36: THE MCDONNELL COTTAGE

"What did you expect?" asked Dougal, his face an angry mass of bruises, one cut over his eyebrow. "We got beat up. We got fined. In my opinion, we got off light, maybe because there were so many of us. Maybe because of Timmy." Dougal paced in front of the McDonnell cottage and then sat next to Dylan and Moira.

Mac ran his fingers along his ribs, wincing when he breathed in too deep. "I regret Timmy's death more than you know. " He was silent a moment, wishing he could forget the dark moments when they laid coins on Timmy's eyes. But 'tis worse than a fine. The crofters have nothing. I can't see what next to do."

"We'll go fishing," said Dougal. "We'll do the best we can. It's what we've always done. What canna be helped must be put up with."

"What you've always done doesn't work anymore," said Dylan.

Mac looked at him with surprise. Dylan looked back with a steady gaze, not backing down from what he'd said.

"There's guards here now," said Dylan. "Those fancy sheep are running in the grasslands where people once farmed. Lord Gordon's going to turn the screws tighter and tighter. And he doesn't want to wait for the fishermen to come around. Not after yester eve. I'm done. I'm going to the Mainland to find work."

"We guessed you'd be leaving," said Mac. "Do ye know when?"

"I'll be going over to Kirkwall after church."

Moira rested her head on Dylan's shoulder. *Granny,* she thought, *you were right. I should have told him, but I can't now. What canna be helped must be put up with.* She closed her eyes and saw again the two graves they'd stood beside that morning. One for Timmy and one for Granny.

A small silent group had gathered at the church, with Pastor McPherson saying words none of them wanted to hear. The people had stood in the cold spring rain and then drifted away, not speaking to each other after the short service.

"Dylan's right. It's going to get worse for all of us," said Dougal. "We may all have to leave."

They sat in front of the cottage, not looking at each other.

"Maybe we're feeling this way because Granny died," said Moira. She didn't feel she could say any more, but she could still see Granny's face, her eyes closed in her final sleep.

Mac shook his head. "It was Granny's time. Best she didn't see any of this. And it's best to be happy while you're living, for you're a long time dead. So, are ye staying, Moira?"

"We've talked about it." Moira glanced at Dylan. "I'm up at Westness for now." Only Granny knew she would rather go with Dylan. Her mouth twisted. One less to feed. Not that Granny ever ate so much. And one more mouth coming.

"I don't like you working there," said Dougal. "Not now."

Moira felt Dylan tense beside her.

"It's needed," she said. "I'll do it as long as I can."

Dylan leaned closer to Moira. His hand rested on her skirt. "I'll be sending for her when I find work."

CHAPTER 37: MOIRA

Moira walked around the rough circle of standing stones. The clouds hung close to the ground. The heather, just beginning to bud, was wet with mist, and the sea birds quiet. *Ah, Dylan, where are you now?*

She leaned against one of the standing stones and felt the cold damp rock. She imagined going on the boat she'd taken last summer, across the Firth and down the coast, all the way to Inverness and then to Dylan. Moira picked at the loose threads on her blouse and worried them between her fingers. She touched her belly absentmindedly and turned home.

She entered the dark cottage as quietly as she could, but Mac was already awake and standing by the fire.

"You're up early," he tried to whisper, but those sleeping on the floor on the far side of the hearth, shifted and then turned over, pulling their blankets over their heads. "Breakfast ready?"

"Such as it is." Moira put a small amount of porridge into a bowl of porridge for him. "We've only a small bit of oats left. Can you get more today?"

"I'll try. I'll stop off at the Mercantile on the way home." Mac realized he'd have to ask for credit, and most likely, Mr. Scott would say no. At least he'd have a chance to see Deidre. "Mayhap some of them can help a bit," he said, nodding at the sleepers. "Ask before you go. And you might as well ask up at Westness too," he said gruffly, pulling on his coat.

Moira nodded. After Mac left, she brought a small basin of water to Freya and helped her wash. The others began to stir. She dished up a bowl of porridge for Freya, the smell curling up into her face and making her nauseous. *I can't be sick*, she thought. "Here, Freya, take this."

Moira ran outside and threw up just outside the door. When she finished, she felt as if she could never eat again. She wiped her mouth on her skirt and laughed wryly. *What a waste with so little in the house.*

Freya looked at her questioningly.

"'Tis nothing. I'll be going up to Westness," said Moira. "If anyone comes to the house, do what Catriona says. Don't argue with them."

"Aye, and thank you." Freya's face was still too pale. "I'll be getting up today with the rest of them," she whispered. "Do you have to go?"

"I'll be back before the sun falls into the sea." She patted Freya and folded a shawl around her thin body.

Moira felt another wave of nausea as she opened the the back door at Westness. Shouting echoed down the hallway from upstairs.

"Quick, get in here." Mrs. MacNaught pushed Moira into a large closet at the foot of the stairs. "Just fold the linens. Don't let Perkins see you this morning."

"It's never like this, not even on Cook's worst days," said Moira. "What's happening?"

A bit of morning light from a tiny window close to the ceiling showed new lines on Mrs. MacNaught's face. "Some fool stole eight of his Lordship's sheep last night. The guards have been in and out all morning." She wrung her hands. "And now, they've drug in Bruce Miller for questioning."

"But why should I hide? I don't know anything," said Moira. "They'll need me in the kitchen."

"You're a McDonnell. That's enough this morning, trust me," said Mrs. MacNaught. "Stay in here until I tell you otherwise." She slipped from the closet, closing the door behind her.

Moira stood in the dim light for a moment and then refolded the linens, listening for any sound on the stairs. She wished she were anywhere but at Westness.

Hargraves stood at the door to Lord Gordon's study, his face solemn. "Constable MacTavish has a person of interest in the matter of the sheep, sir."

"Send them right up."

Hargraves turned and left the study.

Two guards dragged Bruce Miller into the study, Constable MacTavish following. A third stood at the doorway. Miller looked small next to the guards, his head down and his light brown hair showing a bald spot.

"We found the sheep, sir. We caught him with them." MacTavish stood at attention, as if he were a soldier.

"By damn, you didn't take my sheep, did you?" said Lord Gordon, his limp more pronounced as he walked close to the man the guards held so tightly.

"No, sir. No, sir," said Miller, keeping his eyes down. "A man sold them to me, sir, down by Selkirk. Said they just came over on the ferry, he did."

"A likely story. And where did you get the money to buy sheep when you can't pay my rents?"

"My sons came home from the cannery over on the mainland. We were coming to pay the rent. We had the money. We thought we'd buy the sheep and pay the rents as well."

"A likely story. Did he have any money on him?" Lord Gordon asked, turning to MacTavish.

"Not a pence."

"But I did," cried Bruce. "They took it." He began to struggle in the arms of the guards.

Lord Gordon turned to MacTavish. "And his sons?"

"He was alone, sir."

"The sheep were recovered. All of them?"

"All eight, sir."

Lord Gordon leaned close to Bruce Miller. "Did anyone help you in this scheme?"

Bruce stood silent.

"Ah, you wouldn't tell me anyway."

"But there's nae to eat."

"That doesn't give you the right to take my sheep. You stole my sheep." Lord Gordon turned away. "I don't need to hear more. As Magistrate, I could sentence you to death for stealing. I won't have poaching on my estate."

The room went quiet. Lord Gordon wrinkled his nose at the smell of sweat. He pulled out his large leather book of accounts and wrote an entry, the pen scratching on the thick paper.

"MacTavish, take him down to the square and have him flogged. Tie him up in the stocks for the day, then send him over to the jail at Inverness. They'll probably transport him. A minimum of seven years on my recommendation. Let that be a lesson to the rest of them," he said, shutting his book of accounts with a snap.

"But, your lordship, my children," cried Bruce. "What about my wife?"

"You should have thought of that before," Lord Gordon replied. "I'm being generous in giving you a chance at a new life. You'll avoid the gallows and gain free passage to Van Diemen's Land."

"They'll starve without me. They're starving now."

"No more of your insolence. Take him away." Lord Gordon waved his hand to MacTavish who signaled to his men.

The guards dragged Miller out of the study. The small man went quietly at first and then struggled. "Mercy, sir. For God's sake, 'twas for my children." A scuffle ensued on the stairs and then groans.

"You can come out now, Moira. I think the worst is over." Mrs. MacNaught looked both ways in the hallway. "Best to stay in the kitchen as much as you can today. And for heaven's sake, don't go anywhere near Perkins or Lord Gordon."

"What happened? Was someone caught stealing?" asked Moira as she stepped into the hallway.

"Aye. He sentenced Bruce Miller to a flogging. And then transported." MacNaught glanced again both ways down the hallway. "The poor little ones. I fear 'tis only the beginning. How is it your way?"

"Our house is full just now. Mac and Dougal are helping those out at Quernshead. Do you think there's some food to spare? I hate to ask, but it's needed, as much as I can carry."

"I'll do what I can. Just stay low today. Come to me before you go."

"Thank you. I'll see if cook can stand me today." Moira grinned. "She'll yell at me for being late." For a moment they looked at each other, then Moira hurried down the hallway to the kitchen at the back of the house.

At the end of the day, Moira folded the extra food Mrs. MacNaught had given her into a bundle as she readied herself for the walk home.

"What's that, girl?" asked Perkins as he came into the hallway. "Taking things with you?" His nose quivered as he came close, his face still yellow with bruises. "I know you. You're Mac McDonnell's sister." He turned back down the hall. "Mrs. MacNaught. Come here at once."

"Give me your bundle," he said, holding out his hand.

"It's a bit of leftover food from the kitchen, sir." Moira felt a flush start up from her neck. "I wouldn't take it if it hadn't been given me."

"We'll see," said Perkins.

Mrs. MacNaught came rushing down the hall, her skirts flying.

"What's the meaning of this?" he asked, laying out the small bundle on the hallway table, revealing bits of bread and meat.

"Just some leftovers, sir." Mrs. MacNaught picked at her apron.

"I'd rather see this fed to our pigs than given to the McDonnells. Take it away," he commanded. "And you." He turned to Moira. "You're fired. Don't be coming back here again."

"Surely, sir, you can't hold her accountable for her brother," said Mrs. MacNaught. "She's a good worker."

"Mrs. MacNaught, are you questioning me? Is this something I should be bringing to his lordship?"

Suddenly, Moira was angry. "I'm going. And glad I am me brother pounded you. Don't worry, Mrs. MacNaught. The McDonnells will be fine." She gave the back door a slam and that felt good.

Already the sky had darkened to night. Moira picked her way through the yard and came around the front of Westness, candles gleaming through the large glass windows. Despite her anger, tears came.

BOOK 4: THE LEAVING

SPRING 1842

CHAPTER 38: A COLD SPRING

Mrs. MacNaught opened the back door at Westness. Agnes and Maggie waited on the bottom steps, a cluster of children close about their skirts, their bare feet mired in mud.

"Good morrow, Agnes, Maggie. "'Tis sorry I was to learn of Timmy. How can I help you?" asked Mrs. MacNaught, glancing behind for Mr. Perkins.

Agnes straightened her shoulders, her thin face unsmiling.

Maggie stepped forward, a girl child hanging from each hand. "Do you have any work for us? Or if you have no work, have ye any food?"

"Where are your men? I thought they were out fishing this last week."

"Not last week," Agnes replied. "They went to the Mainland chasing jobs at the ironworks and anywhere else they could think of. They haven't come back. We dinna have anything to eat out at Quernshead, nothing at all. We come up here on the chance you might have something."

Mrs. MacNaught looked at the little girls standing so close to Maggie, a young girl herself.

"Let me see what I can find in the kitchen." Mrs. MacNaught closed the door and hurried down the hall to the kitchen. "Sarah, do we have anything I can give away without making much of a fuss? I have a few hungry ones at the back door. Any bread at all?"

"Mayhap this." Mrs. Britton pointed at the leftover bread covered on the table. "And there's some patties that no one ate from yester e'en."

"Is Perkins in the house? He's always sniffing away at what we do down here."

The cook tightened her apron around her belly. "It's enough we're feeding ourselves, without those others coming around. Why do they come here to take the food out of our mouths anyway?"

"This isn't much," said Mrs. MacNaught, wrapping the bread and patties into a cloth bundle. "I wish Lady Alice were here. The children are so skinny they don't look like children anymore."

She hurried back up the hall to the back door. "I'm sorry I don't have more."

"Thank you anyway," Maggie quickly took the bundle. "Everything helps just now. We'll just go back to town and ask around there again."

The women walked away from the house, the cold spring wind blowing their skirts. Before they reached the stables, they stopped. Maggie pulled the bread from the bag, dividing it among the children first. They ate standing there, bent over and huddled together.

"What a sad sight." Mrs. MacNaught closed the door, unable to watch any more. She straightened her apron and turned to find Mr. Perkins staring at her, his hands tucked in the waistcoat of his black suit.

"Mrs. MacNaught?"

"Just some women from Quernshead," she said. "No work, they said." She looked him right in the eye. "And nothing to eat either."

"Let them emigrate, then. You should tell them so. What was that you gave them?"

"Just a little food from the kitchen, sir."

"No more of that, Mrs. MacNaught."

"If we have some left over, we can share it, so Lady Alice said."

"Lady Alice isn't here now, though, is she?"

"Yes, sir. I mean, no, sir."

"Not one crumb more. Do you understand, Mrs. MacNaught?"

"Yes, sir."

"I don't want to see beggars littering up the yard again." He opened the door. "You there," he shouted. "Be off with you. Don't come back."

The women turned away from Westness as rain began to fall and the wind picked up.

Mrs. MacNaught sighed. Wind mixed with rain tapped at the windows as she walked down the hall back to the kitchen.

Moira hurried along the path to Selkirk, her shawl wrapped against the light rain. She glanced at the greening heather and the gray waves below the headlands. She could barely see Shapinsay in the lowering clouds.

She stumbled a bit. A woman and daughter lay on the path as if sleeping, their mouths stained with grass, their arms like bones, gaunt, their clothing riffling in the wind.

Moira looked about the twisting path. No one to help. She wrapped her hands in her skirt to grip their legs and pulled the bodies of the woman and her child from the path. She closed their eyes and covered their faces with her shawl. Their bare feet lay exposed.

Moira couldn't feel the tears on her face as she ran to Selkirk. She pushed into St. Ninian's, not quite sure how she came there. "Pastor McPherson," she cried. "I found them laying on the ground. They're dead."

"What happened? Who's dead?"

"I don't know. A woman and a child, just laying along the path down from our place."

"Hush. I'll send someone to take care of them."

Moira looked around the vestibule as if she didn't recognize it.

"Have you eaten this morning?"

"Some," Moira said. "I was going to Deidre and then down to the beach to wait for Mac and Dougal."

Pastor McPherson left the room, returning quickly, a cup of tea in his hand. "They should have come to me. Even if Lord Gordon has said they can't stay here, I still have food for those in need."

"Mayhap that's what they were trying to do," said Moira. The hot black tea stung her throat. She wiped her eyes. "There's so many going without."

Pastor McPherson bowed his head. "'Tis sorry I am you're not working up at Westness. At least you'd have food to eat."

"That food is no food for me. Tis tainted with sorrow," said Moira.

Pastor McPherson glanced at her slight stomach protruding from her dress. "You sound just like your brother. You cannot question the ways of God, child."

Moira wanted to say it wasn't about God, that the island had changed in the year since Lord Gordon came. That she was a married woman with responsibilities and a child of her own coming.

"I'm not a child, but I thank you for the tea." She shrugged. "I canna' go back to Westness. Perkins fired me. For taking food that was given to me."

"I wondered what happened."

Moira was silent.

"I understand the Brodie family's staying up at your place. If any are hungry, send them to the kitchen in the back. We'll have something here."

"Thank you, Pastor. I'll stop back later for my shawl." Moira stood in the small vestibule and knew the day was closer that she would leave the island.

The sun hurt Moira's eyes as she walked along the cobbled road past the two storied gray stone houses into the center of town. She skirted around strangers who jostled each other as they went in and out of the bright blue door at Mrs. MacLean's bakery. Two soldiers sat on the ground and tore the loaves into chunks as Moira went around to the back, the smell of the fresh bread hurting her stomach.

"Good morrow, Mrs. MacLean," Moira called. "I've come to see about any work you might have."

A small dark woman with sweat on her forehead and flour on her dress opened the screen door to her stone kitchen.

"I hear you've got people staying at your place now." Mrs. MacLean wrapped up two loaves of oatmeal bread that had been baked into rounds and handed them to Moira. "Take these." She nodded her head at the guards outside. "I'm baking every day now."

"Thank you, Mrs. MacLean. I'll bring you some fish from Mac and Dougal later this afternoon."

"And grateful I'll be for it, e'en so. You said you're looking for work? And with a little one coming? Mayhap I could use some help on Saturday early. Will you come back?"

"I'll be back." Moira tied the bread in her apron; her fingers scraped the rough oats crusted on the top. Moira walked slowly down the street, past the new pier that jutted out into Bottle Bay. A few men unloaded another herd of sheep down by the dock, their staffs kept the sheep bleating and milling forward on the narrow wooden pier. Finally she stood in front of Scott's Mercantile.

"Good morning, Moira," called Mr. Scott. "You'll find Deidre in the back, in the garden."

"Thank you, Mr. Scott. I'm hoping for a letter."

"A letter? The packet just came in. Give me a moment." Mr. Scott finished dickering over the price of a new knife, and turned inside.

Moira followed him into the store, her eyes blinking in the dark. Every space was taken with stacks of cartons and bales of goods.

"Mac was here earlier, you know. I've had to limit your credit."

"We knew it was coming."

"I don't like to do it." Mr. Scott fussed with a package and spilled letters out on the counter. He went through each one slowly, reading the names written on the front. He peered at Moira over his spectacles. "Best you go see Deidre. There's nothing here."

Moira nodded. She felt her face flame as she left the store and walked the few steps down to the street. She really hadn't expected a letter.

"There you are," said Deidre, standing and brushing the dirt from her hands and skirt. "Come sit with me, and we'll pull weeds." The garden filled the back yard, with young carrots and cabbage starts, but no potatoes.

"You aren't teaching this morning?" Moira asked as she settled next to Deidre and began weeding.

"Only Tuesdays and Thursdays now. Not so many come to school these days." Deidre looked upstairs. She could see her mother through the kitchen window, staring down at her. "You've heard from Dylan?"

"Nothing." Moira thought of the two bodies she'd found that morning. "Dougal's talking about the Hudson's Bay Company."

"But Mac and Dougal, they're still fishing, aren't they?"

"Aye, but the catch is not enough to feed us. We've got a crowd staying with us. All of Catriona's family and some from up at Quernshead."

"Mac didn't tell me."

"Mac doesn't want you to worry. When did you see him last?"

"He stopped by last night. Mother was furious." She looked up again at the window. "Come on, let's get to the cabbages. Were you at Westness when Lady Alice left?"

The two women moved further down into the garden where the weeds pushed up around the cabbages. Moira shook her head.

"I heard she went back to Edinburgh to her family."

The two women worked silently for a while, the sun warming their backs and their hands as they pulled weeds.

"I'm thinking of leaving," said Moira. "Maybe to Inverness."

"Can you do that now?"

"I'm thinking I have to. There's no' enough to go around. Maybe I can find Dylan. He said his brother was working on the railroad there."

"Have you talked to Mac yet?"

"No," Moira replied. She shifted a little on the ground to get closer to the next row.

"Talk to Mac. Maybe I'll go with you. I know some people there. Mother doesn't want me here."

"But Mac does."

Deidre nodded. "I know. That's why I stay." Her hands went still for a moment, and then she methodically began to pull the weeds, her face down, until the soil around the cabbages was cleared.

CHAPTER 39: THE MCDONNELL COTTAGE

Moira picked her way between the limestone rocks, down the steep path to the cove just below the McDonnell cottage. She was glad for an excuse to get out of the cottage.

She found Catriona adding driftwood to a fire in front of their temporary hut.

"'Tis glad I am you came to keep me company," said Catriona. "Did you see my Da and the boys at your place?"

"I saw them. They already started the meeting. The place is full enough without another meeting, mucking up my cooking."

The two young women laughed. "And what would you be cooking?" asked Catriona.

"Same as you, a bit of seaweed stew. Mac won't hardly eat it any more, he's so sick of it."

"Dougal neither. We're all bones, all of us."

The two young women worked companionably a while. "Shall I gather more driftwood or watch the fire?" asked Moira.

"You're not tired?"

"I feel fine," said Moira. "This baby's going to be a strong lad, just like his da." She smiled, but the small of her back ached. Moira looked at Catriona's smooth face. *No worries for her*, she thought.

"You watch the fire, then," said Catriona. "I'll bring what driftwood I can, and I'll check the traps."

Moira could feel the wind at her back as she warmed her feet on the stones set close by the fire. She stirred the driftwood fire and watched the pieces of wood break down into smaller red coals. She nudged the fire with her foot and closed her eyes a moment.

Bruce waved a broadsheet at the men gathered in McDonnell's cottage. "Mac, we dinna know what to do about this." Freya lay on a pallet close to the wall, watching the discussion. Jacob sat beside her on the floor, his arm just out of the makeshift sling she had fashioned from one of her kerchiefs.

"These sheets are posted everywhere," said Sean. "It's like he wants us all to leave for America."

"But how do we pay passage?" asked Jacob. "None of us has any money."

Bruce read from the broadsheet in the dim cottage light. "It says here, 'Farmers, laborers, carpenters, blacksmiths, fishermen, skilled family men encouraged to apply.' That could be any of us. And then it says, 'If applicants do not have passage fees, funds advanced will be reimbursed at indenture.' What does that mean?"

"It means you hire out as a servant once you're there," said Mac. "And he gets his money back right away. It's done through an agent. Your employer pays your passage, but you have to work for five or seven years. And no telling for who."

"Yes, but you're there, in America" said Jacob.

Freya grabbed Jacob's good arm. "You can't be thinking of going."

"Hush, hush. Not without you and not without the children."

Bruce frowned. "Maybe we have no choice about going or staying."

"And maybe they won't take us," Jacob whispered to Freya.

Mac turned to Dougal. "You've been talking with the Hudson's Bay Company. What do they say?"

"Aye, they've an agent over at Stromness. I've stopped by a few times," said Dougal. "The Hudson's Bay want men to clear wilderness, to trap and hunt, to trade with Indians, and to build forts. The work is hard, but they like us Orkneymen." He turned to the men gathered around him. "It's good pay and steady work. But they don't allow wives, so I'm just thinking on it."

"Thinking about getting wed, are you?" Jacob cracked a smile.

"Aye, sir, you know I am."

"I'd like to go," said Colin, his eyes alight. "I could hunt in the wilderness."

Dougal and Mac exchanged a glance. "Not now, Colin."

"This plan of Lord Gordon's is different. It says indentured servants wanted for farming in Virginia,' said Bruce. "That could be any of us crofters. We're not fishermen, and we have no land here."

"Virginia? I'm not ready to leave," said Sean.

"That's because they didn't come after you. Fishermen is one thing; farmers is another," said Bruce. "We've got all those people up at Quernshead to worry over."

The door to the cottage crashed open. Some fifteen guards burst into the room, guns lifted over their heads as they pushed into the cottage.

Freya screamed.

"Hey, you can't come in here," Mac shouted. "Get out. Get out!" Mac shoved at one of the guards, but a wave of men he didn't know bludgeoned their guns right and left, knocking crofters and fishermen to the floor. One of the guards grabbed Dougal's fiddle from the wall and smashed it over Mac's head.

Mac roared and grabbed a stool; it shattered as he bashed it against a guard.

Everyone howled and shouted. Freya screamed again and again.

Colin went down, his head bloodied. Mac stood over him, his legs on either side of Colin's body. "Ye bastards. Hitting a boy. Hit me. Hit me."

Two guards swarmed Mac, their guns raised. "He's the one. Get him."

Mac scrambled back against the wall and settled to fight stance. *Lord Gordon sent these men. We're going to lose.* He had no weapon, save his fists. "Come on, then." Mac punched the face of the guard closest to him and swung on the second. He choked the guard's neck, heedless of the blows that fell on his back.

A guard knocked Jacob into the hearth. He howled as he rolled over the smoldering peat and groaned as his arm hit the floor. They moved to Freya. She threw a basin at them, but they wrestled her to the ground.

"Help," screamed Jacob. "Help! They've got Freya."

Mac could hardly breathe. With a lunge, Mac shook free of the two men who had him pinned down and scrambled to his feet. *God help us. They're after the women.*

"Over here. We got him!" shouted the guard, grabbing at Mac's ankle.

The guards dropped Freya and rushed Mac.

"Dougal," yelled Mac. "Get her out." Mac punched at the guards, but they surrounded him once again. They battered him until he fell, and they kicked him unconscious.

Dougal picked Freya up, and shoved his way to the door. "Out! Let me out." He held Freya tight, for she was screaming in his ears, her screams a keening part of the melee.

"For God's sake, let me out." With a mighty push, Dougal broke through the crowded cottage and outside.

He set Freya down by the stacked peat in the side yard. "Stay here."

Dougal raced to the front door, now hanging by a hinge. He couldn't get in. He tripped on the bits of furniture that had been thrown out in the yard. Crofters and fishermen spilled into the yard, pushed out by the guards, but Mac and Colin were not among them. The roof of the cottage blazed afire. The noise mounted as guards smashed furniture and tore at the stone walls with pikes.

"Have you no shame," shouted Dougal. He ran back and forth in front of the cottage. "Let me back in. I just want to get our things out."

"Ye can't go in there," cried one of the guards, shoving him back from the door.

Dougal ducked as sparks flew from the roof.

Sean and Bruce pulled Colin from the house and laid him on the ground, unconscious, blood seeping from the side of his head. Jacob limped behind them.

Perkins rode up on a small black mare, surveying the damage, a smirk on his still bruised face.

"What in God's name have you done?" cried Dougal.

"You McDonnells. Always trying to better your betters. We have you now. No more meetings. No more protests." Smoke swirled up from the roof as Perkins called to his men, "Pull that roof down. I don't want anything left." Perkins looked around the yard, a tangled mess of men. "Where's Mac McDonnell?"

Two guards kicked and pushed Mac out of the cottage, half conscious, his face bloodied, his right shoulder at an awkward angle.

Dougal ran at the guards.

Perkins nudged his protesting horse between the two brothers.

"Stand back, Dougal, or you'll have the same. He's to be arrested," said Perkins. "You canna live here. This is Lord Gordon's property now."

Perkins waved his arm at the other men. "Disperse and go back to whatever hovel you drug yoursel' out of. There's to be no more meetings like this, or ye risk arrest."

"No," roared Dougal. "This is our own place, granted from me father to us, and from Grandda to him. You canna' just take it."

"That's where you're wrong, Mister McDonnell," sneered Perkins, leaning down from his perch on the black mare. "Yer cottage's being confiscated along with yer boat. And yer brother's being arrested for sedition. That's a hanging offense." He fingered his bruised cheek. "For all yer meetings and protests and fighting."

Dougal stood silent.

"What about the rest of us? We dinna have homes any more. We dinna have work," cried Bruce.

"Spread the word up at Quernshead," said Mr. Perkins, moving his horse closer to the men in the yard and raising his voice. "Lord Gordon wants you and your families gone to Virginia, where work is plenty."

"The bastard didn't have to do this," said Jacob.

"That bastard's willing to pay your passage, provided you sign indenture papers." Perkins grimaced. "You'd be wise to take his offer. I've set up an office by Scott's Mercantile. Tell those who are interested to sign by the end of the week, else you can expect more of this."

Perkins wheeled his black mare around as Mac stumbled along the path to Selkirk, a guard at either side.

The men milled around the small yard. They looked at each other and at the damaged cottage. The roof had fallen in. Peat still smoldered in places. Glass had been shattered out of the two small front windows. The out buildings had been pulled down. Several guards stood in front of the broken door.

Dougal wiped the blood from Colin's forehead and felt his chest, a slow heart beat. Colin shook his head and sat up, his eyes unfocused.

"Is he all right?" Sean asked.

Dougal stood. "I think so."

"Come to our place for as long as you need," said Sean.

"I don't know." Dougal rested his hand on Colin's head. "I dinna know what to do about the Brodies. There's some nine of us now."

"We'll find room."

"Aye," said Bruce. "The McDonnells will always have a place wherever we are." He brushed his singed arm and shook the ash from his pants.

"I can't quite take it all in," said Dougal. He sat suddenly on the ground next to Colin. "My fiddle's gone. Smashed. He said they took the boat too?"

"Aye. I guess Lord Gordon's after the fishermen as well," said Sean. "Mayhap we'll all be going to America. But for now, bring your family to my house."

"Later. We'll be there later." Dougal sat next to Colin, waiting for Moira and Catriona to come up from the cove. The yard was quiet. Two sea birds wheeled around the two brothers and then headed out to sea.

CHAPTER 40: STANDING STONES

The sun had dropped down into the sea, and the sky filled with pink and gray clouds. Dougal stood in front of Moira, Colin and Jamie. "I asked you up here because we have to talk, just us." He looked across the cove at their ruined cottage. "I figured here was as good as any a place to meet."

Moira sat on the ground, her back to one of the standing stones. "Where else is home?"

Jamie sat down close to her, his slight body shivering. They were silent, listening to the waves on the rocks below.

Colin kicked the base of one of the standing stones. "What's the point of doing anything if they just come and smash everything again." Colin's bruised face twisted in a scowl. "I hate them when they come into the store. I don't know what to do. I don't know how long Mr. Scott will let me keep working for him."

"I'm thinking we cannot stay, not any of us," said Moira.

"That's what I'm thinking too," said Dougal, hunching down beside her. "Mac's trial will be sometime in the next week or month, I don't know. We have to stay close, maybe here or over at the Mainland until that's over." He was quiet. "But there's nothing here for us. We could emigrate. Lord Gordon is calling for people to go to Virginia. It means they have us for seven years, but we'd be together."

"I want nothing to do with that pig," said Moira. Her thoughts were as dark as she could remember. She felt as if she couldn't move her arms, not even to shelter Jamie. "Never. And we'd go to America, all of us? What about

Dylan? How would he ever find us? And me with a baby coming?"

"If you sign the articles of indenture, they take you," said Dougal. "Pregnant or not. But if we go, you'd leave Dylan behind."

"That I canna do," said Moira.

"Then I'm thinking of the Hudson's Bay Company," said Dougal. "They're recruiting now. Their ships stop on the Mainland a little later in April. Colin and I could enlist and maybe send for you after we're established."

"And what's for us in the meanwhile?" asked Moira. "Stay here and starve?"

"Can't I come with you and Colin?" asked Jamie.

Dougal looked at Moira and Jamie, huddled on the ground together, sheltered by the largest of the standing stones. "Ah, Jamie, you're too young. But I'm not happy about you staying behind."

"We'll go to Inverness. There's work there," said Moira. "Jamie and I can stay together."

Colin stood as well. "Hudson's Bay? You really think they'll take us?"

"Aye, they'll take the two of us," said Dougal.

The clouds had turned to gray. Dougal's head lifted as the wind turned from the east. "Best we enlist before we're arrested ourselves for this or that."

Colin nodded.

Moira turned her back to the wind. She looked around at the standing stones so near the headlands and the sea below. "You'll see about Mac, when you go to Stromness?"

"Aye. Colin and I will go over with Sean," Dougal said. "The dory's not big enough for all of us. I'm sorry."

"Dinna be sorry for me," she said. "Send word as soon as you can."

"I'm truly to go with you tomorrow?" asked Colin.

"We'll go to the Mainland in the morning."

The four stood quietly together, looking out at the islands that seemed to float on the sea, the standing stones sheltering them from the wind.

"We'll be leaving all this," said Dougal.

"Aye," said Moira, holding Jamie's hand. "We'll be leaving."

CHAPTER 41: STROMNESS

Mac smelled vomit. Instantly he was awake. Every muscle in his body hurt. He remembered being marched down the hill to Selkirk, their house burning, Colin on the ground, and Perkins. Those bastards. And now here, in this stinkhole, a prison cell.

Mac stood up. His head hurt as he tried to see around him in the gray light that came from one small barred window near the ceiling. Men lay everywhere on crude shelves and on the floor, huddled together for warmth. Mac could trace the smell of vomit to the man next to him.

The man stirred, and Mac recoiled as the pungent smell of alcohol wafted towards him.

"Here, mate. Give an old man a hand. Don't let me lie in me own piss."

"They that smell least, smell best," said Mac as he pulled the old man up.

"Don't be babbling. Where's the bucket. I don't have me morning eyes yet."

A wooden slops bucket had been left near the barred door. "There," Mac pointed.

The old man shambled over to the bucket.

Mac averted his eyes and studied the stones on the wall, pockmarked with scratches. A cold draft came through bars that ran from floor to ceiling along one wall. "Where are we?" he asked as the old man returned.

"Ah, first time then?" The old man pulled his gray hair into a pony tail. "We're in Stromness, and you're in jail." He laughed a hearty laugh from his belly. "I'm Pete. They brought me in late last night. All I did was hit the bastard for taking me shore money. Then we all started fighting." Pete cleaned his teeth with his tongue and looked around the cell as if with new eyes. "Not so crowded as it was me first time."

"You been here before?"

"Aye. Last week when we landed. I'm cook's helper on the *Brilliant*. We're due to go to New South Wales in three months. Stopped here for crew. And who are you? I didn't hit you last night, did I?"

Mac laughed. The man barely came to his shoulders and had a banty swagger to his walk. Mac figured that came with hugging the deck of a ship. "I'm just a fisherman who got in trouble. The landlord's men evicted us, and I fought them. I'm in the devil's place now." He touched the bruises on his face. "How bad am I beat up?"

"They worked you over pretty good. Anything broken?"

"I don't think so. My arm went funny, but then it popped back." He winced as he touched another bruise. "You've been here before. What's next?"

"They'll fine us or put us in stocks. Maybe both. We'll be out of here by mid-morning if the first mate comes down." He peeled a scab off his hand. "But you, I don't know."

"God rot their souls."

"Hush. Talk like that gets you in trouble." Pete glanced at the men sleeping on the floor. "Maybe I can get you out with us. I hear good things about Orkneymen."

Mac felt hope for a moment. He didn't want to stay in this pigpen of a jail. How good it would be to simply sail away to anywhere, a new start with no landlord pushing and pushing at him. His stomach twisted as he thought of his family and Deidre. *Ah, Deidre. What was the point?* "Thanks. But it's not going to happen. They're holding me over for a trial. I won't forget you offered."

"We got many a man on board that way."

"I don't think it'll work." Mac settled back against the wall. Pete joined him. Together they watched the other men wake up as the cell lightened. Mac wondered how long it would be before he saw someone he knew.

CHAPTER 42: SCOTT'S MERCANTILE

Moira caught her shawl over her head. A light rain glistened on the stone cobbled streets of Selkirk as she walked to Scott's Mercantile. She found Deidre packing wool for shipment off island.

"This is lovely. Who made it?" asked Moira.

"Good morning." Deidre stopped working to give Moira a hug. She fanned her hand over a tightly woven length of gray wool. "This cloth came from the new sheep. You know Ronald McFadden, his wife and sisters? My father brought two looms all the way from Glasgow to get them started. They'll more than pay him back with these." She folded the woolens into a large wooden barrel, pushing them down tightly. "I saw Colin here earlier."

"Colin's been sleeping here, in the storeroom until he leaves." Moira began folding the woolens with Deidre. "Your father has been good to us."

"It's because of Mac. He likes Mac. Any news?"

"That's why I came. I feel funny. Here we are talking away, and this morning, they decide. Dougal said he's coming here after, if he can."

"Mac's trial is today?" asked Deidre.

Moira gave her a small smile. "It's easier waiting if I'm here with you."

The next few hours passed slowly. They folded the woolens. Colin moved a few heavy crates inside the store. Moira winced as Colin split the crates open, and the wood screeched. Deidre and Moira unpacked each crate and restocked the shelves with tea, tin pails, and needles wrapped in felt. No one came into the store.

Finally, Mr. Scott called from the front porch, "Someone here to see you, Deidre."

"Come on, Moira. It must be Dougal." Deidre rushed out of the store, Colin and Moira scrambling behind her.

Mr. Scott clapped Dougal on the back. "Go on around to the back. You'll have a bit of privacy there."

"What news?" said Deidre. "Tell us."

"You might as well know, Mr. Scott. The trial went better than we hoped," said Dougal. "It's over. He's to be transported to New South Wales."

"He's not coming home?" cried Moira.

"Did you see him?" Colin's voice ended on an awkward squawk.

Deidre swayed. "Is he all right?"

"Steady, daughter," said Mr. Scott. "'Tis still good news." Down the street, a group of guards walked toward the store. "Go around the back now. I'll cover the store." He stopped at the top of the front porch and waited for the guards.

"Were you able to talk to him?" asked Deidre.

Dougal followed the two women along the path at the side of Scott's Mercantile, around to the back garden. "Give me a minute." Dougal sat on a rough bench by the garden shed. "The court was crowded, every table full, every seat taken. I couldn't get close to the front, but I saw him."

"Tell us everything," said Moira, grabbing Dougal's hand.

"The judges were harsh to all, but they didn't sentence him to death." Dougal looked out over the garden. "Their verdict is final."

"There's nothing we can do?" asked Moira. "You're sure, Dougal?"

"The court was crammed with over a hundred cases. People crying out. Most were transported. A few were condemned to death. We're lucky they didn't hang him."

Dougal's words hung in the air for a moment.

"Aye, we're lucky then," said Moira.

"He'll be held at the Stromness jail a few more days. Then he'll be sent down to London and held there again to wait transport to Van Diemen's Land." Dougal looked at Colin and the two women. "If we're truly lucky, they won't come after any of the rest of us."

Deidre sank onto the bench beside Dougal. She fiddled with the watch pinned at her waist. "None of this can be changed?"

"I'm sorry, Deidre. I wish I had better news."

"Can we see him before he goes?" asked Deidre.

"I'd like to get something to him, maybe some food or clothes," said Dougal. "I'm not sure how."

"Deidre," called Anne, coming to the back door. "I need you inside."

"We should be going." Dougal stood. "Deidre, can you come by later?"

"I don't think that will be necessary," said Anne, her voice grating.

"Just a few more minutes, Mother."

"Dinna put us all at risk, then. Remember your sisters. Remember your father."

"I know, Mother. Leave us."

Anne turned away from the door, her straight back an accusation.

"I'm sorry," said Deidre. "All this has unsettled her. I had hoped for better news about Mac. Can we go over to Stromness? Tomorrow?"

"Maybe," said Dougal. "I wasn't able to see him before. Just at the hearing. I could bribe someone. We can try."

"I have a little money," said Deidre. "My own money."

Dougal was silent a moment, thinking. "Aye, I'll take you over tomorrow morning. We'll try to see him and come back the same day. Can you get away early?"

Deidre nodded. A little sun flickered on her face as she turned back to the house. "I'll come down to Sean's after supper."

Moira held Dougal's arm. Overhead, a single gull followed them as they made their way down on the beach.

"Have you heard anything at all from Dylan?" asked Dougal.

"The last I heard, he was looking for work in Inverness." Moira looked at Dougal. "I'm still not sure whether to go or to stay. There's not enough food at Sean and Lenore's. I'm not finding work, just dribs and drabs. A morning or two at Mrs. MacLean's."

"It's not going to get better," said Dougal. "The thing is we don't know what Lord Gordon will do next. It's a hard thing to say, but perhaps Mac being gone will help. There'll be no more protests up at Westness."

"What does that matter? I'm not working up there." Moira stared at the fishing boats coming in on the evening tide.

"We've signed on with the Hudson's Bay Company, me and Colin."

"You're leaving then? Off the island?"

Dougal nodded.

"Did you ask about Jamie?"

Dougal shrugged. "The Hudson's Bay Company canna take him."

Moira sat down on a large rock and rested her hand on her stomach. "What about Catriona? I thought that you and she would marry. Ah, that sounds silly to say now."

"I'll send for Catriona when I can. Tis the only way. The company sets aside two cabins for families, but they're already taken up by the officers." Dougal turned away. His face was set. "She won't be happy about this. Can you go up to Quernshead and ask her to come to Sean's tonight? I'm over to Pastor McPherson's to make arrangements."

"Aye," said Moira. "When does your ship leave?"

"By week's end. They only put in here twice a year. I know what you're thinking, Moira," said Dougal. "But there doesn't seem to be any other way. I don't like leaving you and Jamie, and I don't like leaving Cat. I'll send money as soon as I can."

"How will you know where we'll be?"

"God willing, if you'll both be in Inverness, Pastor McPherson's brother is there. I can write you in care of him. If you're here on Foulksay, I'll send it care of Mr. Scott. You have to decide before we leave."

Moira looked at her hands. "By Saturday you said?"

"I dinna like leaving any more than you," said Dougal. "Are you all right?"

"We'll manage, Jamie and I, and the little one to come. For certain it is we can't stay here. Colin's truly going with you?"

"Aye, and he's glad to go. For him, it's a grand adventure."

"I never thought to see my own brothers scattered so far." For a moment, Moira couldn't speak. "You'll be in Canada, and Mac, I can only thank God he's to go to Van Diemen's Land, for 'tis better than hanging."

They were both quiet. Dougal held his sister's hand. They watched the clouds fill the sky in the west and the gulls fly low behind the fishing boats coming in.

Moira thought of all her days on the island, the cool mornings with the fog lifting from the sea, her brothers coming in after a day of fishing, the smell of the sea in their hair and on their clothes, even the long walk to Westness over the hills and along the moor, and then coming home at night, with her brothers to meet her. She thought of the island, always the island, its rugged dark sandstone cliffs that she loved, and the standing stones, a mark of other people who had come and gone. Now their cottage, once home, was reduced to stones.

"I wish things could be other than they are." Moira brushed the sand from her skirts.

"I know," said Dougal. "It's like the music. Sometimes you play for others, sometimes you play for yourself. But you always have the music here." He held his hand over his heart. "Some things you don't forget." Dougal looked at his sister. "You should have told Dylan about the baby."

"I know," Moira replied. "All right. Jamie and I, we'll go to Inverness."

CHAPTER 43: CATRIONA

Moira paced outside one of the shelters at Quernshead. She shivered as the afternoon wind bit into her shawl. Several children played close to the fire where the women had gathered to cook seaweed soup in a large communal pot. Far below, the sea looked gray, and white capped waves followed one after another.

"You said they took both of them? Dougal and Colin?" asked Catriona, emerging from inside the shelter, a small knife and the onions Moira had brought in her hand.

"Yes," said Moira. "The Hudson's Bay signed them up yesterday. He sent me to ask you to come to Sean's tonight. Can you come?"

"He's really going?"

"Aye," replied Moira.

"It's been hard here." Catriona grimaced. "Perkins still comes around, threatening us all with arrests. Mother's some better. They've decided to emigrate to Virginia, and they want me to go with them. I dinna know what to do."

"It's Dougal, isn't it," said Moira.

"I would leave my family for him."

Moira was silent.

"What? He can't take me with him? Is that it?"

"He wants to tell you himself." Moira sighed. "The agent said only officers can bring their wives. Even that's rare, according to Dougal."

Catriona looked at her hands. "I can work as hard as any man. Why can't they take me?"

"Dougal said they're recruiting boys a little older than Jamie. That's why Jamie's staying with me. They've had the posters up for months. With the ship coming, they're really pushing right now." Moira smoothed the skirt on her belly. "I wish I had gone with Dylan."

The two women looked at each other. "What if I looked like a man?" said Catriona.

"You?" Moira looked at Cat's red hair and her heart-shaped face. "You can't."

"I think I can." Catriona thought for a moment. "Let's meet by the standing stones, just after the sun goes down. Bring me a cap. I think I'll have a surprise for Dougal tonight." She grinned. "Now, come with me and visit for a bit." She nodded at the group of women at the fire. "They'll be glad of these," she said, shaking the onions. "They'll go right in the pot."

"I wish I had more to bring," said Moira.

The women at the fire pit on the bluff took the onions with many expressions of gratitude, and then a silence fell.

"Dougal wanted me to ask how many of you are planning to emigrate," said Moira, as she looked around the group of women gathered at the fire.

"Not me and not ours," said Agnes MacGill, a black mass of hair piled on her head. She stirred the large pot of soup that rested directly on a smoking peat fire. "We're going to Glasgow as soon as we have the travel money from me sister."

"We're going, and we know of seven other families who've signed up," said Granny Lyttle, pushing white hair off her brow. "Us and all the children. It's not like we can stay."

"No sense looking back," said Catherine. "There's them that can go, and some will stay."

"It's been hard times without Mac," said Granny. "Some of the men went off to the mainland, and we've heard nothing of them, not a word."

"I know." Moira remembered the bodies she had found. *Hard times for all*, she thought.

"There's not enough food," said Granny. "You see how it is up here. People can't be living like this. And the guards coming around."

"They didn't come after you," said Agnes. "They came after my Maggie."

Moira leaned over to Catriona. "What are they talking about?"

"I'll tell you later," Catriona whispered back.

"So, how many are going to emigrate, do you think?" Moira asked again.

The two women ignored her.

"You didn't have to take her in, all bloody and muddied up. You didn't have to wash your daughter's tears from her face." Agnes used the large wooden spoon to push Granny away from the fire. "And you didn't have to bury your own daughter who was too young to be a woman. Aye, we're leaving." She spat. "We're leaving this bloody island. And we'll not be grateful for onions." She dropped her spoon into the soup and left the women standing by the fire.

Granny Lyle wiped a tear away as she retrieved the spoon. "You girls are too young to know what mothers suffer."

"I heard the guards found her alone and just took her there and left her for dead, covered over with a coat," said Catriona.

"Who? Maggie?" asked Moira. But Maggie was a pretty child, twelve or so, always good with the younger ones.

"Aye, Maggie," said Granny Lyle. "No need to say more."

Catriona pulled Moira away from the fire. "Everyone's upset. Some of the women have gone with the guards to get food, you know. Enough of them so the guards come up here all the time now, sniffing around. Maggie was found last week."

"Should Dougal talk with them?"

"It's too late. Nobody can do anything. It was the last push. Most of them have signed up to emigrate," said Catriona. "I'll tell Dougal how it is."

The two girls hugged.

"Be careful going down the path," said Catriona. "I'll meet you later by the standing stones. Just after night fall."

Moira walked slowly up the path to the standing stones, the smell of sweet sea pinks and flowering heather around her. Birds cried out in the early night as they settled on their nests along the cliffs near the sea. She leaned against her favorite stone as Venus rose in the west, low on the horizon, just above the clouds.

Moira watched a young boy make his way up the hill, scampering over rocks in the fading light. She smiled to herself to think of Catriona's plan to dress as a boy. She wondered if life were any easier as a man. *Certainly not for any of the McDonnells.*

The grubby boy came closer. With a shock, Moira recognized Catriona. "My God, you do look like a boy. How did you do this?"

Catriona smiled and circled in front of Moira, showing off her pantaloons. "Do you think Dougal will know me?"

"Well," said Moira. "I didn't know you, at first." She stared at Catriona in the fading light. "Let's see how you walk."

The two started down the hill. Moira laughed and poked Catriona's arm. "How can you wear those pantaloons? Don't they feel funny? Did your mother and father see you? What did they say? Oh, wait until Dougal sees you."

"No more questions. I can't answer you so fast," said Catriona. "When we get to Sean and Lenore's, you go ahead, and I'll follow. Tell him I couldn't make it tonight. Then I'll knock at the door." Catriona's face shone pale in the twilight.

"OK," said Moira. "Maybe put a little dirt on your face and hands."

They stopped by the path, and Catriona rubbed dirt onto her cheeks. "Better?"

Moira hugged Catriona. "I can't wait to see his face."

Catriona hesitated on the doorstep. It was fully dark now. She heard two guards coming down the street behind her. She knocked at the wooden door as she felt a rising frisson in her chest.

"Who's there," called Sean.

"Robbie." She said the first name that popped into her head.

Sean opened the door a crack. "What do you want this time of night?"

"They told me I should come down here from Quernshead. That you might have a place for me to stay," said Catriona. "My family's worried the guards will take me."

"Come on in, then," said Sean. He grimaced as he glanced up the dark, cobbled street. "We'll make room for one more. And why would they be after you?"

Catriona followed Sean in. She spoke to his back as he walked down the hall. "I dinna know. Maybe because we were evicted."

"You can sleep in the kitchen. We have some people who'll be leaving in a few days, but 'twill be crowded for now. You don't have anything with you? No blanket or food?"

"No, sir."

"Well, we'll manage. Here we are," said Sean.

The kitchen was full; everyone sat as near the fire as they could. Dougal was next to Moira, and Lenore held her sleeping baby. Dougal looked up quickly as they entered, then down in disappointment.

"Who's this," asked Moira.

"Robbie, from Quernshead. Another person who needs a place to stay, and a young one at that," said Sean. "Here, sit." He pointed to a chair next to Dougal.

Dougal stirred restively. "Didn't she tell you she was coming?" he asked Moira.

Moira nodded. "She said if she could get away, she would."

"Please, sir," said Catriona. "I heard you was going to Hudson's Bay."

"Aye. I'm going with me brother, Colin. He's about your age." Dougal's knee moved restively. "Do you know him?"

Catriona shook her head.

"We leave the end of the week." He looked around the room again. "Moira, did she say anything else?"

"I hear it's a hard life," Catriona kept her voice low. "Would they take someone as young as me, do you think?"

Dougal's eyes narrowed. "They might. They're recruiting pretty heavily." He stood up suddenly. "Cat, is that you? What have you done?"

"Ha! I did fool you. Dougal, I want to come with you."

"Don't be silly. 'Tis no place for a woman."

Catriona stood as tall as she could. "Dinna be so fast to say no. Can I not work as hard as any man?"

"Aye, but there's only men around. That's the problem."

Sean and Lenore stared at Catriona, but Moira was laughing, her hands cupped over her mouth. "You knew about this," said Dougal, pointing at his sister.

"I think Catriona's done it," said Sean. "You said they were taking boys near as young as Jamie. That's one way to solve the problem."

"Ah, come outside then, Cat. We need to talk," said Dougal.

As soon as they were outside, Dougal drew Catriona around the side of the house. "I was going crazy waiting for you." He pulled her into his arms. "I see you know already. They said no wives are allowed. Dear heart, I can't take you with me."

"Dougal, did you know me when I came in?"

"No, but . . ."

"Think on it. This way we can be together. No one need know other than our families. You can be my older brother."

"You'll never pass. You're too short. You're too pretty, and I'm not your brother."

"But we would be together. When our service is up, we can find our own place. We could maybe have some of that wilderness for ourselves."

"Don't be daydreaming. It won't work. You'd be surrounded by men all the time, people we don't know. People who don't know you. It's a rough life and dangerous, more dangerous than I've said. I wouldn't be able to protect you." Dougal tucked Catriona close in his arms. "Cat, I'll send for you as soon as I can."

Catriona pulled away. "That could take years and years, and it's not exactly safe here or there. You heard about Maggie?"

Dougal sighed. "Moira told me."

"It's not going to get better. What else can I do? Emigrate with my parents to Virginia? How would you find me then? Don't you want me to come with you?"

Dougal pulled her cap off and Catriona's hair fell down around her shoulders. He sniffed her hair and thought of how long it would be before he would see her again. "We'll never be able to pull it off."

"Take me over to Stromness. I'll go the whole way dressed like this. If no one discovers it's me, let me sign up. Give it a chance, Dougal. Can we try?"

"Are you sure about this?"

Catriona looked at Dougal. "I'm sure."

He lifted a lock of her hair. "Then, come with me tomorrow. God help me, I'm a crazy man to even think of it."

Catriona stood still, the enormity of what she'd decided just hitting her. "I need to tell my mother and father. They know nothing of this. I'll need to say goodbye."

"Tell them we'll be married first. That's the only way I'll go ahead with this."

"Are you asking me to marry you?"

"Yes, I am. Are you saying yes?"

"Ah, Dougal, I'm saying yes. My parents know you are an honorable man."

"Aye, an honorable man, one who entices you to the wilds of Canada. How honorable is that?"

"They're leaving as well."

"Your mother is strong enough for the trip?"

"She says she is. They want me to go with them, but . . ." Catriona paused to stare at Dougal. "I would rather be with you."

"Let's see if you still say that when we're slogging along the great Columbia River, fighting off Indians and mosquitoes bigger than your head. They said we're to go to Fort Vancouver, far on the west coast, maybe near to China for all I know."

"But I'll be with you."

"Aye, you'll be with me." Dougal tugged at Catriona's hair one last time. "You'll cut this tonight?"

"Aye."

CHAPTER 44: DEIDRE

"Good of you to come home last night," said Anne, pushing her needle through the thick wool of a new skirt. "'Twas very late for a decent person to be about."

"Mother, I'm so tired," Deidre leaned on the kitchen table. It was early morning, and she hadn't been able to sleep. "They wouldn't let me see Mac. Only Dougal could get in."

"And what were you thinking to go over to the Kirkwall gaol? You should leave well enough alone," said her mother. "Only bad comes from that direction, as you already know. I'm sure I don't know what your father will say."

"Mac's being transported to Van Diemen's Land, Mother. It was the only chance I could see him for years, maybe forever. I just wanted to see him." Deidre closed her eyes. She felt as if her bones would sink into the chair. She looked around the kitchen and laughed a little to herself. "We have enough to eat. We don't have to worry about the future. But, Mac and his family, they're torn apart. Everything's gone."

"Enough of this foolishness," replied Anne. "Put thoughts of that man behind you. You have a job and your family to concern yourself with, and the merits of that man are well known. Even Lord Gordon only has so much patience . . ."

"Don't say that name, mother," said Deidre. "He's ruined my life."

"What are you talking about, Deidre? Were you planning to marry that fisherman?" Anne's nostrils flared. "And live in a crofter's cottage to clean fish the rest of your life? When are you coming to your senses?

How do you think your father got you the job at the Grammar School? Through Lord Gordon. You were able to come home for the first time in many years, though I wonder why. Why do you have to associate yourself with that riff raff?" Anne pushed the needle faster through the thick wool.

"Mother, you haven't given him a chance. Everyone looks up to Mac. He is the kindest, most gentle man. Yes, he's a fisherman, but the people went to him when they were evicted from their homes. These are the people he's known always. How could he not speak on their behalf?"

Anne jabbed her needle into the wool. "You threaten everything for us because of your association with that man."

"Mother, I would marry him if I could."

"Bosh. That man is in jail and good riddance. Why can't you marry someone of our own kind? A nice merchantman like that Mr. Stanley. Why a fisherman?"

"There's no talking to you. You just don't understand."

"You're right. I don't understand. With your father and two other daughters to worry about, I don't understand. I have to worry about you as well, and you're old enough to know better."

Deidre wondered if her mother would ever forgive her, but it really didn't matter anymore. A cabbage soup simmered on the stove as her mother hemmed the woolen skirt. Things would never change here.

"It's a miracle we aren't all in jail ourselves," said Anne. "Go help your father downstairs before the girls are up with questions you can't answer."

"Mother, I want to go to Van Diemen's Land."

"What? Ouch." Anne pricked her finger with her needle. "What did you say? And how will you get there? You might as well wish for the moon in your pocket."

"I would take passage on a ship, Mother. It's not unheard of." Deidre could see herself leaning on the bulwarks of an ocean-going vessel, flags flying, the sun sparkling on the ocean, and Mac beside her. "Mac and I could be married. We could make a new life for ourselves."

"You don't know what you're talking about."

"I want to go."

"I don't understand you. I never will. Go to your father. Maybe he can talk you out of this craziness. I certainly can make no sense of this." Anne put her sewing away and stirred the soup on the stove. "Go, go to your father."

Deidre went down the stairs to the store, feeling lightheaded, as if she were on the brink of something entirely new. "Father," she called. "Where are you?"

"Here in the storeroom," called William. "Deidre?"

"Aye, father."

"You were late last night," he said. "We stayed up, Mother and me, hoping to see you home safe. Where were you?"

"I should have told you. I went over to Kirkwall with Dougal. We took some things for Mac, but I wasn't able to see him, Father. Only Dougal could get in. I left him a letter, that's all."

"I dinna like you going to the Kirkwall gaol. 'Tis good you're home."

"You know Mac's being transported."

"So I heard."

"He'll be sent south to London. Dougal said they'll keep him at a ship on the Thames until a transport ship takes him to Van Diemen's Land, most likely the end of the summer. Then he'll truly be gone."

"'Tis a hard sentence, daughter, but it could have been worse."

Deidre felt as if all she could see was her father's face, pale in the dim light of the storeroom. "Father, I want to go with him."

"You can't be going on a prison ship," said William.

"Maybe, maybe not. They said several ships will sail together, some carrying prisoners, like Mac, and some with emigrants. I could go on an emigrant ship, Father."

"Ah, you want to leave home then, for good this time?" William was silent for a moment, his hands atop a knotted rope. He cleared his throat. "You've just got home it seems."

"I tried to talk to Mother. She doesn't understand. She's angry," said Deidre.

"Never mind about your mother. So you'll be leaving whether I say yes or no?"

Deidre nodded.

"Well, then, how much is the passage? Did you find out?"

"Twelve pounds for a cabin and eight for a berth. That's what they told me in Stromness. I could go on a berth."

"That's steerage. I know something of this. You'll go in a cabin or not at all." William calculated quickly. "I have enough to give you sixty pounds. Is this what you truly want?"

"Yes, more than anything." Deidre's hand went to her chest; her heartbeat thrummed in her ears. "Mac doesn't know any of this. He doesn't want to even see me, Dad. But I have to go. I have to try."

"I only ask one thing. Wait until his sentence is served before you marry."

Deidre sat down suddenly as if her legs could no longer hold her up. She was leaving Foulksay Island.

Her father took her hand. "No more talk now. We'll work on this together."

Dougal and Catriona, her hair shorn, her face smudged with dirt, her jacket and pantaloons those of a young boy, stood together on the new pier, waiting for Sean's boat and the trip over to Kirkwall. From there, a cart would take them, or they'd walk the sixteen miles to Stromness.

Moira leaned close to hug Dougal and Catriona. She couldn't speak.

Dougal dipped his head to Deidre. "Thank you for coming to see us off."

"I wouldn't have missed saying goodbye," said Deidre.

"What about you, Deidre," asked Dougal. "Will you stay on with your parents, then, here on Foulksay?"

"I'm leaving as well, within the month." Deidre's face was paler than Moira had ever seen. "I'm going to Van Diemen's Land with Mac, one way or another. I won't have him going alone."

"What about your mother?" asked Moira.

"She'll never accept Mac." Deidre looked out to the sea, wondering if her mother would ever forgive her and knowing it wouldn't matter. "She hated him when he was a fisherman, and now she'll simply hate him."

Moira pulled Deidre and Catriona into a hug. "I've two sisters now, you and Catriona. Remember that when you're far away."

Moira took Catriona's hands in her own. "It's all going too fast. I can't believe you and Dougal are married. Are your parents all right?"

"They're hoping to leave when the ship for America arrives. It's been hard on them. They didn't want to come down to the pier to say goodbye, but they know my place is with Dougal." Catriona flushed. "They dinna like me dressing like a boy."

"I have to believe everything will work out, Cat." Moira turned to Dougal. "You'll write?"

"Aye, care of Mr. Scott," said Dougal. "Keep letting him know where you are. And you write us care of the Company." Dougal moved restively, pulling Catriona close. "I don't know if we're going to be able to pull this off."

Colin ran back from the edge of the pier. "Sean says it's time."

"No need to speak of it. You're breaking my heart," said Moira, clinging to Dougal and Colin.

"Safe passage," cried Deidre.

Moira and Deidre watched Sean's boat turn south toward Kirkwall, bumping along the white-topped waves, a few gulls screeching overhead.

Moira thought of the journey ahead for her two brothers and Catriona. First they'd go to Stromness, to the agent's station. They'd join the ship from Gravesend there, then sail direct across the Atlantic to Hudson Strait. She said a quick prayer and grabbed Deidre's hand. "It's hard to say goodbye."

The two women looked at each other and made their way off the pier, shivering a bit in the cool morning wind.

CHAPTER 45: MAC

Mac twisted the manacles on his wrists. He supposed he was luckier than those who had been sent down to Edinburgh for trial and most likely hanging. His stomach growled. He studied the locks on the large wooden door as he waited on the cold sandstone bench.

At least he would be out of this pit of a jail, worse than the dank, barred rooms set aside for prisoners in Stromness. He wished he could see Deidre, though as he looked down at his chained hands and his dirty clothing, he was glad she wasn't there.

The two guards dragged another prisoner down the dimly lit hall; they weren't gentle about it. They pushed their prisoner onto the grimy bench next to Mac.

"Move down there, McDonnell. We've got two more to bring," said Ranald, kicking at Mac. "This ain't the palace."

Mac flushed with rage, but he ducked his head and moved down. They wouldn't have treated him this way when he was free. He would have liked to return the many favors Ranald had given him since he'd arrived.

Mac felt along the side of his pants where three pieces of gold had been sewn.

"It's all we can do," Dougal had said two weeks ago. Dougal had bribed a guard to let him in and brought clothing and food from home, fresh oat cakes and a rare piece of meat.

Mac had shared some of the food through the bars with William, a twelve-year old who faced a flogging for stealing. Mac had made the oat cakes last as long as he could for the two of them, a precious bit at a time, for it was the right thing to do. He had savored every morsel, thinking of Moira and Deidre and his brothers back home.

"Thank you, Dougal," he had said. "'Tis glad I am that Deidre didn't come with you."

"But she did." His brother's face had creased with concern. "The bastards wouldn't let her in. I'm to give you this," Dougal had said, holding out a letter.

Mac had tears in his eyes that he didn't want his brother to see. "Thank you," Mac folded the letter into his pocket. "Tell her she should forget about me."

"She means to wait for you."

"A sentence of seven years, and she's going to wait for me? Look at me."

"You're alive, Mac. We heard some get pardons for good service."

"And I've heard not so many make it. I don't want her to waste her life waiting for something that may never happen." Mac felt like he was going to throw up. "Tell her I don't want to see her." But he had touched the letter again in his pocket, a thin sheet he already knew he would memorize.

Mac hadn't seen Deidre, not then and not now. He closed his eyes, the pungent smell of the man next to him crowding his nose. Today, he would leave Inverness for London, assigned to one of the prison ships on the Thames. *Work makes me valuable to the Crown,* he thought. *Thank God I'm strong. If I'm patient and steady, I'll get out of this, and Lord Gordon be damned.*

"These be the last two of the men," said Ranald. "Up with ye now. A nice carriage ride awaits you, all the way down to the docks." He pushed and shoved the men out of the stinking jail and onto a horse-drawn cart with a wooden cage affixed on the back. Two draft horses stamped their hooves on the cobbled street in front of the Sheriff's Jail as they waited for the cart to fill.

Just when Mac thought there was no more room in the cage, Ranald and two guards came back out the prison doors with a group of women and children, prisoners all, William among them.

"There ye be," Ranald said, when the cart could finally hold no more. "Accommodations fit for such as you, all nice and cozy." He shoved the door to the cage shut and locked it, amid groans and grunts.

"May God rot your soul," spat one of the prisoners through the bars.

Mac's gloom lifted even as bodies pressed around him so tightly he could barely breathe. The sky was bright above, and he could see Inverness about him, a city of churches, their spires lifting to the sky. The cart clattered along the Inverness River, past Old High Church, on narrow cobbled streets that bustled with carriages and people headed to market, strangers all.

Ah, sweet, sweet air. Mac, wedged in one corner of the cage, forgot the manacles that remained on his hands and ankles. He squeezed his head around to look back up the hill at Ranald standing in front of the squat pink stones of Inverness Castle. He'd never see that piggish face again.

The cart maneuvered by wagons and passersby along Bridge Street, down to the docks. It passed crammed rows of three-story buildings, their chimneys smoking, windows partly open. The smell of fresh bread from a bakery made Mac's stomach growl again. Four crows drafted on the afternoon wind. They circled and landed on the stepped gables above him. Mac turned his head away. *One crow for sorrow, two for mirth, three for a wedding, four for death.*

The cart wobbled past Mercat Cross at the center of the Inverness market, crowded with farmers, merchants, traders, sailors, and servants out for the day's shopping, clutching their market bags full of produce. Mac watched a few washerwomen leaning their laundry tubs on the Stone of Tubs, called the *clach-na-cudainn*, as they walked from the River Ness. Many believed if the stone remained, Inverness would continue to prosper. *Would that I had a piece of that stone to take with me,* Mac thought as someone elbowed him.

Closer to the docks, the crowds on the streets grew rowdier. Mac flinched as a few boys pelted rocks and shouted at the cart as it passed. The first floor shops changed to inns and taverns. Mac glimpsed a drunken sailor arguing with a woman in an alley.

The cart lurched to a stop. The pressure in the cage finally eased as guards hauled the prisoners onto the dock. They lined up by the *HMS Caledonian Rose*, an old war ship that had survived the Napoleonic Wars. Its guns had been removed, its ports boarded over, and its hold converted to carry prisoners down along the jagged east coast of Scotland and England, 500 miles to London.

Mac stood in line and took great breaths of fresh air, knowing it would be his last until London. He looked south. *If I were higher up, I could see Culloden Moor. The English. Bastards every one of them.*

He grimaced at the smart red uniformed guards as they methodically marched the prisoners on board and into the hold. Three sailors pulled the cover of the hold over the top, slamming it shut. As long as the *Caledonian Rose* remained in port, the prisoners remained below, without light or air. Mac settled himself against the wall of the hold, ignoring the groans and arguments around him. It was dark and dank. He felt something flit over his feet as an outcry went up.

"Rats," someone cried out. "God, they've rats in here."

Mac felt the ship move with the current and tried to imagine the route the *Caledonian Rose* would take from the mouth of the River Ness, past Fort George and into Moray Firth to the North Sea. Behind the ship, the church spires and the red sandstone towers of Inverness Castle gradually grew smaller, until only the green rolling hills of the Ben Nevis range remained. Below decks, Mac sat in the darkness and wondered if he would ever see home again.

BOOK 5: THE JOURNEY

SUMMER - FALL 1842

CHAPTER 46: INVERNESS

"It's bigger than Kirkwall." Despite the rain, Jamie hung over the side of the fishing boat and pointed at Fort George, his thin face bright with excitement.

Moira leaned next to Jamie, away from the netted pile of fresh caught cod, sea-weed lined crates of crab, and barrels of lamb meat stacked on the deck. They had spent last night wrapped in blankets in a cove close to Wick after passing Duncansby Stacks, sheer rock pillars several hundred feet high that rose from the sea near the headlands.

At dawn, the four-man crew had cast off, stepping around Moira and Jamie as if they were not there. The fishing boat then sailed down the coast, holding off at the mouth of the Moray Firth until the tide changed and swept them in to the port of Inverness.

Fort George took up the entire spit of land that jutted into Moray Firth. Pairs of red-coated and kilted soldiers patrolled the ramparts as hundreds of workers crawled along the muddy base of its stone fortifications. Men carted stones to masons who chipped them into place on fortifications three stories high.

"Can we go there?" asked Jamie.

"Perhaps." Moira touched the letter to Mrs. MacKinnon safely pinned inside her bodice. "God knows where we'll sleep tonight. I don't." She wondered again if they had made the right decision in leaving Foulksay.

Large fields scattered with sheep marked the rolling green hills that rose above either side of the mile-wide Moray Firth. The wind picked up, the waves swelled to bumpy white caps, and the boat edged to the side of the Firth. They passed the Black Isle and turned into protected bay fed by the River Ness. The banks narrowed as they approached Inverness.

Whitewashed buildings with crow-stepped gables gleamed in the afternoon sun, Their boat tacked into the dock area and joined a forest of masts. The crews shouted at each other as they angled for a spot to unload their cargo. Finally, they docked.

As she clambered ashore, Moira glimpsed the pink sandstone of Inverness Castle on the hill above the city. "Jamie. Keep close, now." Moira called her thanks to the crew, and they were on land again, for the first time in three days. She grabbed her bundle in one hand and Jamie's hand in the other.

The wharf was crowded with fishermen, sailors, and vendors. Men stood around, hoping to be hired for the day, and old men mended nets. Bare-footed children ran underfoot, begging for half-pennies or bread. Boys armed with brooms cleared the streets of horse dung.

"No, we don't need anything," Moira said again, pushing her way past a woman selling pasties, the smoke from her open grill spiraling upward. Finally free of the docks, they walked up the wooden docks to Inverness, past Fever Hospital, shaded by a giant sycamore, to Bridge Street, lined with inns and open shops.

Moira stood in front of a tailor's shop for a moment, looking up and down the cobbled street, busy with horse-drawn carts and carriages. People sidestepped around them, intent on their own errands.

"Excuse me, mum." Moira stepped in front of an older woman with a white cloth twisted over her hair who carried a worn straw basket filled with carrots. "Can you tell me the way to Academy Street?"

"You're nearly there," said the woman. She tucked her straw basket close. "Go over to Friars Lane, then go up to Academy Street." She waved her arm up the street and continued on her way.

Moira turned onto Friars Lane with Jamie pulling on her arm.

"Look at that." Jamie pointed to a tall brick tower ornamented with a clock.

"Later." Moira stepped around a drunken man asleep on the street. "Mrs. MacKinnon's school is somewhere along here. "

Finally, they stood across from the Claron School, a large two-story brick building facing Academy Street. Peaked turrets perched over the windows, while smoking brick chimneys implied warm fireplaces within. Two large bay windows jutted out from the front of the building. Greek revival columns embellished each side of the front door. A low rock wall and a small yard with two tall pine trees separated the school from the street.

"Are we going in?" asked Jamie.

"Just me. Wait here." Moira set her bag down next to Jamie's bundle.

Jamie pulled the bags to the side of a tree and settled down on top of them.

The house seemed bigger as Moira walked along the stone wall, past a large wrap-around porch, and through an arched stone gate until she came to a door at the back of the house. She rang the bell. A young woman entirely in black answered.

"I'm to see Mrs. MacKinnon, please, if she's in," said Moira.

"And you are?"

"Mrs. McInerney."

"Please come in. I'll fetch her."

Moira sat on a side chair in the back hallway and watched two young girls working in the kitchen. They added wood to the fire and brought pots and bowls out, directed by a cook that Moira couldn't see. A long trestle table was loaded with empty bowls, cheese and various greens. Moira smelled fresh bread and some kind of a stew cooking. She loosened her cloak and reveled in the warmth. Her eyelids felt heavy. *I should have brought Jamie in with me,* she thought.

An older woman tapped Moira gently. "I'm Mrs. MacKinnon."

Moira shook herself awake. "Yes, mum. I have a letter for you from Miss Scott of Foulksay Island."

"Hmmm." Mrs. MacKinnon sat next to Moira and read through the letter. She pursed her lips, looked at Moira, and read the letter again. She was a small, stout woman, with graying black hair piled in a crown on her head. Her black silk dress was relieved by a small white lace collar.

"When does the little one come?" asked Mrs. MacKinnon.

"I think winter, mum. Martinmas at the latest."

"I have nothing for you here at the school. Not as you are," mused Mrs. MacKinnon. "But Lady Thomas on Culduthel Road may take you in. Her husband is responsible for the Caledonian Canal. They always seem to be needing help. Let me write a note for you."

"Thank you, mum." Moira wondered if she could ask for some bread.

Mrs. MacKinnon hurried down the hall to her office and came back to the entry with an envelope. "First bells for class are to ring soon," she said. "Take this to Lady Thomas. Oh, I suppose you'd like something to eat?"

Moira nodded.

"Mrs. Bean," called Mrs. MacKinnon. "Make up a lunch for Mrs. McInerney."

"Thank you, mum."

"Lady Thomas is quite kind. Come and see us again when you can." With a quick, light step, Mrs. MacKinnon hurried out of the kitchen and returned, bringing a brown paper bag for Moira. "It's time for classes," she apologized.

Moira crossed Academy Street, the bag of food warm in her hand. Jamie had taken shelter under a large mulberry tree. Its leaves glistened with wet, but the rain had stopped. They sat on their bundles and ate thick bread crusted with butter.

"Are we staying?"

"No," said Moira. "I'm guessing it's another hour of walking."

A tall man stopped to cross the street, his face narrow under a black top hat.

Moira scrubbed her face with her sleeve. "Please, sir. Can you tell us the way to Culduthel Road?"

"The best way to go, miss, is this way," he said, pointing down the street. "Go down here until you get right by the River Ness. Stay on that road past the bridge. Then you'll be on Castle Road. You'll have to walk a good bit then and uphill. You'll see where the road turns to Edinburgh. Don't take that road. Keep going straight, and you'll be on Culduthel Road." The man tipped his tall silk hat as he continued his way.

"Did you see that?" Jamie hissed. "He tipped his hat at us."

"It don't mean anything. You can't eat manners."

The pair made their way along the River Ness, past the bridge that led to Inverness Castle, and marveled at how shallow and calm the river was. On the opposite side, fishermen pulled their nets, baskets nearby to carry their catch to town.

"Can we go there?" Jamie pointed at Inverness Castle.

"Maybe," replied Moira. "That's where Mac was held, there in the Sheriff's Jail."

"Right there?" Jamie looked again at the two-story pink castle with its high turrets and towers atop the hill behind the town.

"Yes."

"Will we hear from Dougal soon?"

"I don't know. Most likely not for a long while."

"They should have taken me with them," said Jamie.

They walked along Castle Road without talking and stepped off to the side when a wagon or carriage passed by, the horses sweaty and heaving as they trudged up the steep slope of Hangman's Hill.

At first, Moira asked everyone who passed for a ride, but no one stopped. Around them rolling hills, almost mountains, rose, now bright, now gray, as the clouds passed overhead. They passed small whitewashed farmhouses, their yards swept clean. They heard pigs grunting in the mud. Green shrubs grew everywhere as they picked their way along the rutted road, muddy in spots from the recent rain.

After several hours of walking, they came to Southcot House, a pink sandstone building dotted by large windows all along the front and a rounded tower on one side. Smoke rose from six chimneys; the house sprawled in an open area surrounded by formal plantings of juniper and pine trees. Moira and Jamie walked through the park and up the rounded graveled lane that served as an entry way.

"It's a grand house, grander than Westness." Moira brushed the dust from her skirts and resettling her hat over her hair as they stood under a pine tree. "How do I look?"

"Look? You look hungry," said Jamie. "Do you think we'll get something to eat here?"

"Just wait here. I'll do the best I can." Moira gave a final brush to her skirt and walked around the colorful two-story corner tower, careful not to glance in any of the windows. At the back of the house, she found a gated kitchen garden. Two gardeners with worn jackets and caps were digging up the back garden. Their spades piled up mounds of cabbages.

"Go on and ring the bell, miss," one of the gardeners called.

Moira rang the bell. A young woman wearing a lace cap and a lace apron opened the door as if she had been watching. Moira looked at her face. *She has such pretty white skin.* Her heart sank. *I'll never be so clean again.* "I've a note for Lady Thomas."

A look of displeasure crossed the woman's face. "Stay here. I'll take it to her." She closed the door.

Moira stood on the porch, shifting a little on her tired feet, and watched the gardeners work up one row and then the next.

Inside, the maidservant skimmed the note as she went down the hall. "Lady Thomas," she said as she entered the bedroom. "I have a note for you."

"Read it to me, Mary. You know I have one of my headaches." Lady Thomas reclined on a side chair, a silk handkerchief dappled with perfume spread over her forehead, her eyes closed.

"Yes, mum. It's from Mrs. MacKinnon at the Academy." Mary cleared her throat. "Dear Lady Thomas, I know of your kind generosity in the parish and hope you will find a place in service for Moira McInerney and her brother, newly come to Inverness. She is of good character, has a letter of reference, and can work in the kitchen or anywhere you wish. Her child is to be born . . . ." Mary stopped reading. "Mum, she has a child coming."

"You saw her, Mary. What do you think?"

"She was quite dirty, mum." Mary made a face. "McInerney is an Irish name, isn't it? And she smelled of fish."

"Never mind that." Lady Thomas stirred restlessly. "We can't take on any more staff. Take a shilling from my purse there. Give her that and tell her we don't have any work for her. I just can't do any more."

"Do you want to send an answer to Mrs. MacKinnon?"

"Put the letter on the desk, Mary. I'll try to write something later." Lady Thomas put her handkerchief back over her eyes.

Mary stopped in the hallway. She slid the shilling into her pocket, smoothed her lace apron, and opened the back door. "Lady Thomas says we don't have anything for you."

"But Mrs. MacKinnon sent us."

"There's nothing here." Mary studied Moira's dress. "Try the Ardkeen House."

Moira fought to keep her disappointment from showing. "The Ardkeen House?"

"The house with the tower. It's on the turn to Culduthel Road. You passed it on the way here. You know where that is?"

"Yes. I know the way," said Moira.

The door closed in her face with a final snap.

CHAPTER 47: THE THAMES

Mac braced himself against the side of the longboat packed with prisoners and prayed it would not sink. He was outside at last, not crammed in a cell, chained in a wagon, or stuffed in the hold of a ship.

A low haze hung over the Thames; its vivid tints glinted in the afternoon sun. The river swarmed with steamships, barges and small boats. The stench of offal stung Mac's eyes. He stared at three prison ships moored bow to stern on the north shore, across from Woolwich. A fourth lay aground on a bank of muddy marsh.

"You don't want to go there, mate," said the waterman, noting his glance. "That's the *Justistia*."

"Thanks." Mac looked south at a cluster of buildings. "What's that?"

"People call that the Warren," the man replied. Gray water beaded along his oars and ran into the boat. "If you're lucky, you'll be assigned to work in one of their warehouses or at the Arsenal." He steered the small boat away from a steamer moving west from Woolwich to London Bridge.

"What about over there?"

"That's a foundry and those are barracks, wood yards and workshops. All support the Arsenal." The waterman spit in the Thames. "Downriver is where they dredge. Most likely you'll wind up there. 'tis ten hours a day now. In the winter, you won't have to work so long."

"I'll not be here come winter."

"God willing, you might say." The waterman laughed, a short bark. "Some have been here longer than that. God forgot them."

The small boat came alongside the *Warrior*, once a 74-gun ship of the line, purchased by the hulk authorities in 1840. Its massive frame listed slightly to one side. The *Warrior* was no longer seaworthy.

Long practice led the watermen to tie up their boats to the side of the *Warrior* efficiently. Their longboats dipped and crowded together. The watermen shouted at the prisoners to climb up the rope ladders hanging down, over the side of the *Warrior*, on pain of taking a swim in the Thames.

Amid shouts and taunts, the prisoners made their way onto the decks to be greeted by guards who shoved them along the deck. "Clothes off. Get moving." Cuffing those who weren't fast enough, the guards herded the men into large tubs, where they were washed down with harsh yellow soap. Mac held back at the end of the line.

"You there, off with your pants."

Mac tore at the side seam where he had hidden his coins. He couldn't get the seam open.

"What have we here?" cried one of the guards, coming over to Mac. "Are ye holding something back?"

"Nothing, sir." Mac ripped two sovereigns from his pants just in time and feigned a fit of coughing. "Nothing at all." He held his hand over his mouth, and quickly palmed the two coins inside his cheek, continuing to cough as he held his pants out, smelly and dirty from two months in prison. "Just trying to get them off, sir."

"Don't give me that worthless crap. Get to the tubs and wash yourself well. We don't want no stinking pigs on our lovely ship." He poked Mac in the ribs. "And a skinny pig at that."

Mac bristled. He followed the guard down the deck to the tubs. The soap stung his eyes and the sores on his body, but he was grateful to be clean.

The wet and shivering men slowly moved along the deck where two guards handed out canvas shirts, pantaloons and shoes. "Not enough for everyone to have everything," said one of the guards, his fat cheeks jiggling. "But you can get more if you work hard."

"We're out of shirts." The second guard shoved pantaloons and rough shoes at the prisoner in front of Mac. "We're nearly out of shoes." He pushed a ragged but clean pair of pants at Mac. "You look like a strong one. You get a pair of pants. Maybe you'll get shoes after you prove yoursel'."

Mac guessed he was lucky to have the pants. Made of rough homespun, they were clean but threadbare.

"Go on, now. Get your clothes on." Another guard moved in, waving a thick stick. "No need of persuading, is there?" He shoved the man behind Mac to the deck and clubbed him. "Don't look at me cross-eyed, get it?"

The prisoners shuffled quickly down the line.

Mac shivered as he pulled his pants on. He could hear the clank of irons ahead of him. He knew what was next.

"We got three types of irons here," explained a wizened little man, his hairy eyebrows well salted with gray. "We got leg irons. Everyone gets those. We don't want no one to go swimming tonight. We got hand manacles for the rowdy ones. Only a few get the waist shackle." He looked at Mac and squinted. "Looks like you'll get two out of three. Put your hands up on the barrel."

Mac stood still as the little man's hammer knocked the shackles into place.

The prisoners were herded into a large room with wooden benches facing a podium, rather like a rough church. "Sit. This here's our chapel." The guards laughed.

"Quiet," called out one of the guards. "Lieutenant Evans's comin'."

The men sat on the narrow, rough-hewn benches, Mac among them. Mac rubbed his wrists, already tired of the weight of the shackles. He guessed the large room was once a mess hall. The men eyed each other, but nobody talked.

A tall, heavyset man in full uniform, gold braid at his shoulders, ascended the podium. "Men, you've been assigned to the *Warrior.*" He scratched his neck casually, the lace falling away from his wrist. "Know this: Any attempt to escape will be punished by flogging and solitary confinement. A second attempt? Hanging. No trial. No remedy."

"You are here to work." Lieutenant Evans' voice boomed out into the chapel. "Most of you will load or unload cargo at the docks. Some of you will muck out the canals. Some of you will bring ballast from upriver. If you have carpentry skills or such, speak to one of the guards. But you will all work. There will be no slackers from the *Warrior.*"

Evans stared at the line of men looking up at him. "Aye, I see you're in shackles now. And so you will stay. Work hard. Follow what the guards say, and you'll not taste the cat. No fighting. No gambling. No stealing. No taking of someone else's food." Evans flicked his wrist at the guards. "Get them below."

"Stand up," called one of the guards. Mac heard shackles clank all around him as the prisoners rose to their feet.

"Fall in," called another guard. The men followed him out of the chapel. One by one, they climbed down into the hold. The smell that met Mac made him gag. He could almost see a green haze. A prisoner behind him began to retch.

The guard herded them down a narrow hall, past a barred door, and into a large open space with a low ceiling. No windows. No bunks. A few men lay rolled in blankets, while others sat, their backs against the sloping wall of the ship. One man lay sprawled in the middle of the room, naked.

"Down here, you answer to them. And then you answer to us." The guard dipped his head as he stepped outside the barred door and locked it. "Sleep well. We'll be back at dawn."

Mac could barely stand erect. He stood with his back against the barred door and watched as a few prisoners approached them.

"You got any food, anything tucked away?" asked a tall man with dirty blonde hair.

"Anyone from Bristol?" asked another.

The new prisoners huddled together.

"Well, I'm Jack Doherty," said the tall man. "And one thing you got is new clothes, so hand them over. We'll have a little trade."

The new prisoners began to back up tight against the barred door. They pushed Mac to the front of the group.

Jack stepped close, the stench of his body adding to the hot stench of the dark room. His eyes gleamed. His thin arms were covered with bruises and scars.

"You're not taking me pants," said Mac. He braced his feet as well as he could and lifted his shackled hands in defense, the chain swinging.

"Thinking to keep those fine pants, are you?"

Jack kicked Mac and knocked his feet out from under him. Mac's breath whooshed out as he hit the deck. He was naked within seconds. Jack held the clean pantaloons aloft and crowed.

Mac clenched his mouth closed to keep his coins from spilling out. He grabbed Jack's ankle and pulled savagely. Jack banged to the floor with a thump and rose on his hands and knees, glaring at Mac and ready to throw another punch.

"Fight. Fight," someone cried out.

"No fighting," shouted a man from the corner. "Leave the new ones alone, and give that man some pants."

Grudgingly, Jack threw a pair of dirty pants to Mac. He rubbed his hip. "Dinna worry, a new batch comes in next week. You'll have a chance to get some clean ones then."

Mac grimaced and put the pants on. His forehead stung where it had hit the floor. Mac pushed his tongue against the coins in his cheek and wandered over to the man who'd stopped the fight. "Thank you."

"Call me O'Toole," the man answered. "Been here long enough so they listen to me. Sometimes. It's just that all dogs go down on a strange dog."

O'Toole gestured for Mac to settle next to him, his back against the wall. "Sleep here tonight. You'll be safer if you stay close by."

Mac eyed O'Toole's double chains. "Thanks. I'm from the Orkneys."

"Ah, an Orkneyman. What led you here?"

"Our landlord brought in sheep. I got up a protest. You know the rest. I'm to be transported to Van Diemen's Land. Sometime soon, I hope."

"The ships go out the end of summer, so you'll be here awhile. That is, if you can stay out of trouble. You have a temper?"

"'Tis likely how I came here."

O'Toole looked him over. "You're strong enough, but you need clothes. Mel," he called. "Bring me some shoes. And a shirt, if you can manage."

"Aye, sir." A short man with gnarled hands and a twisted leg, hopped up. "Will these do?" He held a pair of shoes up, their soles rat-chewed and worn.

"Better than none. Thank you," said Mac.

"Don't ask where they came from," said O'Toole. "You got a shirt?"

The scrawny man stripped the shirt off his back and handed it over. "Take this, mate."

"I couldn't."

"Don't worry. I'll get another one tonight." Mel snickered. "Just say I'm good at cards."

Mac put the shirt by his side.

"Better put that on or you'll lose it," said O'Toole.

Mac put the shirt on, still wet from Mel's body, and left it open in the front. He leaned back against the wall. "Does it get cooler?"

"Not much. Tomorrow, stay close to Jack. He's the one who took your pants. He digs ballast over by the Arsenal. That'll be easier than working the docks."

"And you?" Mac asked.

"They don't let me out much just now," said O'Toole. His arms clanked as he held up the blanket that covered his legs. Shriveled flesh and burns marked both legs. O'Toole picked a maggot off his leg and crushed it. "My job is to keep the rats away." O'Toole's mouth turned down. "I'll be okay in another week or so." He dribbled a little salt water from a bottle onto his legs. "Watch the guards. Better to be a coward than a corpse."

Mac nodded.

"Don't say much, do you."

Mac shook his head, wondering where he could put the coins he still held in his mouth.

"Well, you'll get some food in the morning. Try to eat apart from the others, or you'll lose what little you get. They don't give us much, and what they give us has got worms that wiggle in your belly. Scrape 'em off, and you'll be fine."

Mac looked at O'Toole.

"You want to tell me?" O'Toole said. "I know you've got something in your mouth. Spit it out."

Mac shook his head.

"You don't have a choice, man. Spill it, or I call someone over."

Mac spit two sovereigns into his hand. "You're not taking these without a fight."

"I'm not taking nothing. I'm offering you protection. You're a dead man if the others find out you're hiding those." O'Toole adjusted the blanket on his legs with another clank. "Give them to me. I'll charge you one coin and give the other back to you afore you leave."

"What's to prevent you from keeping them outright?"

"Do I look like I'm going somewhere?" O'Toole opened his hand. "You want to keep them, hand 'em over."

Mac looked around the room at the men sleeping on the floor. Their fetters clanked as they rolled over. The smell of vomit clung to his nose. "How do you stand this," he asked as he handed the coins over.

"One day at a time," replied O'Toole. He lifted his lips in a toothy grin. "Better bend than break."

Mac eased against the wall near O'Toole. He could barely imagine the Orkneys, the *Star,* his brothers, or Moira. And Deidre. Her letter was long gone, but he yet knew every word. *I will bend*, he thought.

At the end of the room farthest away from the barred door, a few men gathered around a candle. Mac could hear their whispers, Mel at the center, and the occasional curse mixed with the rattle of dice. He closed his eyes and slept.

It was still dark when the guards entered the prisoners' lockup. "Get up, you scum."

The men lined up quickly, a few moaned on the floor. One lay on the floor, silent and still. Mac saw Mel cut into the front of the line. No one protested.

When Mac's turn came, the guard shoved two green pilot biscuits at him, one covered with thin oatmeal gruel, the other squirming with worms. Mac brushed them off.

"Move on," said the guard, not looking at him.

"You there. Get this aboveboard." Another guard pointed at the dead body. Two prisoners behind Mac seized the dead man by his feet and hands and carried him away; his fetters dragging on the pitted floor.

Jack came over. "O'Toole told me to look after you. Just follow me. Don't talk to me, and don't mess with me. And get that crap down quickly afore someone takes it away from you."

"How did that man die?" Mac asked.

"Gaol fever. Don't worry. It's too soon for you to get it. Just stay away from the guards as much as you can. They're always looking for bodies to sell to the dissectors."

Mac nodded.

The guards herded the men up on the deck of the *Warrior*. Mac took deep breaths of the cold morning air, and he was grateful for Mel's shirt. Once separated into work gangs of about fifteen men each, the men climbed down rope ladders into the waiting longboats. If they lagged, the guards shouted at them and tapped their clubs on the deck.

The boats spun away from the *Warrior* and headed in different directions on the Thames. As Mac's boat passed the Arsenal, several gangs of men hauled rocks to repair the walls, while others drove posts into the ground to protect the riverbanks from erosion. About a mile below

Woolwich, the waterman tied his boat up to a small landing. At low tide, the muddy banks swarmed with crawling, squirming red worms.

"Blood worms," someone muttered.

"OK, everyone out," called the guard.

Mac grabbed his chains and heaved himself out of the boat, steadying himself as best he could once he was on land, his feet sinking into the mud. Ahead of him, a guard tapped his club against the legs of two men chained together to move them along a little faster.

Mac followed the man in front of him, keeping an eye on Jack, as the guard handed out shovels. The rest of the morning, Mac dug dirt from the banks, filled wheelbarrows, and dragged them to a barge moored at the landing. A steady rhythm of work ensued, marked only by the curses of the guards as they walked along the line of workers.

"What happens to all the dirt?" Mac asked the man next to him.

"Gets taken to Woolwich, by Target Walk," the man muttered.

"And what then?"

"No talking over there," called a guard.

The man shrugged and continued to shovel the dirt into his wheelbarrow, his head down. "Some is sifted out. Some is spread on the bank," he hissed in a low voice. "Keep your head down so they don't know you're talking."

Mac dug in his shovel. "Anyone escape from here?"

"Don't even think on it. You'll wind up on the *Justistia*." The man continued to work at a steady pace. Mac did the same.

One of the men fainted. His wheelbarrow tipped and fell into the Thames.

"You stupid piece of carrion," cried one of the guards.

The dirt spilled out in a large circle of muddy water while the man lay unconscious. The guard beat him methodically. All Mac could hear was the rhythmic thud of the club hitting the man's flesh over and over, as the guard grunted.

"You there, get back to work, or get the same."

Mac pushed his wheelbarrow past the prisoner who now lay in a pool of blood. The man looked dead.

"Another body for Rat's Castle," the man next to Mac muttered.

Mac wanted to smash the guard's face and twist his neck until it popped. But he kept his head down and worked until a lunch break was called. Each man received a cup of brackish water drawn from the Thames and two ship's biscuits, green with mold.

"Same as breakfast," said Mac, pushing the worms off his biscuit.

"Dip it in your water," advised Jack, sitting on his haunches next to Mac. "It don't taste so bad. Tonight, 'tis Saturday. We get beer and a bit of boiled ox-cheek. Most likely tis salt horse." Jack tapped his biscuit against his tin cup. A few worms fell onto his leg and he brushed them away.

"I can hardly wait," replied Mac.

Jack chortled. "Eat up. They don't give us all day here."

The guards clustered around a small fire. Mac smelled meat cooking and saw them passing a flask. "When do we get what they're eating?"

"In your dreams, sweetheart." Jack spat out a piece of biscuit and stood, rags twisted in his chains, his tall body emaciated. "In your dreams."

CHAPTER 48: ARDKEEN HOUSE

Moira could hardly see the road in front of her as she and Jamie walked back to Inverness.

"Why can't we go back to that school?" asked Jamie. His bag slipped down on his back. They gave us food."

"Remember last summer, when I went harvesting? We slept in the fields in boothies. We'll make a shelter for tonight. Tomorrow, I'll ask for work at that farmhouse we passed. And if that doesn't work, we'll try that place the maid told me about."

"I wish we were home."

"If one door sticks, another opens," said Moira. "We'll find a place."

Together they trudged off the road and up a ravine until they found a copse of birch trees. They gathered a few fallen limbs and made a three-legged shelter, pulling branches around to fill the gaps.

"It won't be that cold," said Moira. "But it may get a little wet."

They sat on their bundles, and Moira spread her shawl over them. Above and between the scudding clouds, they could see stars. Long after Jamie fell asleep, Moira sat awake, wondering what the future would bring. She stroked her stomach, amazed again at its size, and felt fluttery kicks. *Settle down, little one. I will take care of you.*

The next morning, Moira and Jamie were back in Inverness and hungry. The farmer's wife had been kind, but offered no food or work. "There's too many of you," she apologized as she turned them away.

Once again, Moira and Jamie stood outside a sprawling three-story stone house set back from Edinburgh Road behind a high stone wall. Moira knocked on the freshly painted green door of the small gatehouse.

"Yes," called the watchman. "I'm coming." He opened the grated window on the door. "What do you want?"

"Is this Ardkeen House? They told me you have work here." Moira pushed her face close to the grate.

"Work for young women." The porter looked at Jamie through the grate. "Not him."

"But he's my brother."

"And sure I'm St. Peter," replied the porter. "No boys allowed."

Moira and Jamie looked at each other. They turned away and began walking back down the hill toward Inverness Castle, when the man called after them.

"Did the constables send you?"

"No. What would they have to do with us?"

"Never mind," said the man. "Come in. Maybe Mrs. Harcourt will make an exception." He swung the gate open. "Go up the path to the tower room." He pointed to Jamie. "But he stays here with me."

"All right. Jamie, wait for me."

Moira followed the path past a small flower garden with newly budding cornflowers and a planting of roses. She found a thin woman, her hair twisted on top of her head, sitting at a desk in the first floor of the tower room. The woman looked up from a sheaf of papers, a magnifying glass in her hand. "Hello."

"Mrs. Harcourt? We've come to see about work, my brother and me."

"The gateman didn't explain?" Mrs. Harcourt set her glasses on her desk. "We offer refuge for young women. No men or boys. If you live here, you work in our laundry and take all your meals here. Once you've been trained to enter service, we find you employment.

Through prayer, we help you to leave your life of sin behind."

"But I'm not living a life of sin," Moira protested.

The woman arched her eyebrows and stared at Moira's stomach.

"My husband was hoping to be taken on by the boatyards here. It's just that I haven't found him yet. He may have gone over to Glasgow."

"You're not from here?"

"We came from Foulksay Island, up in the Orkneys. I already know how to work in a great house. I was a servant at Westness in the kitchen, doing whatever we was told. I need some employment for me and my brother."

"Perhaps we can do something. You said McInerney's your name. Are you Catholic?"

"No, mum."

"How long have you been in Inverness?"

"Two days."

"Have you been down in the docks?"

"That's where we arrived, mum."

"Were you at the Fair?"

Moira shook her head. "I don't know of any fair."

"The Fair tempts far too many of our young people," said Mrs. Harcourt. "Especially our young women. The Magistrates won't shut it down. Tradition, they say, from the fourteenth century. Andrewmas now and Marymas coming. The fairs bring trade to the town, but at a great moral cost. A great moral cost."

"I wouldn't know about the Fair, mum."

"Do you know anyone here in Inverness?"

"I had a letter for Mrs. MacKennon at the Claron School. She sent me to Southcot House, but they wasn't hiring. They said to come here."

Mrs. Harcourt stood up. "I'll see what I can do. Wait here."

Sunlight came through the windows as Moira leaned her back against the wooden chair. The old oak desk was littered with papers. White lace curtains hung at the windows. No fire had been set in the grate, but vapor still rose from Mrs. Harcourt's forgotten teacup.

Moira's stomach turned at the smell of the tea. If there's no place here for us, we'll go back to Mrs. MacKinnon.

Mrs. Harcourt returned with Jamie and a young woman, also pregnant, who carried a tray heavy with two bowls of hot soup and brown bread.

"Here you are," said Mrs. Harcourt. "Sit next to your sister."

"Thank you, mum." Jamie took a bowl of soup and sopped his bread in the rich brown gravy without another word.

"There's someone who's hungry." Mrs. Harcourt held out the other bowl to Moira. "I've sent a note over to Mr. Dunleigh at the woolen mills. He may need an apprentice, just like you, young man."

Jamie and Moira looked at each other. "You have work for us?" asked Moira.

"In a manner of speaking. If Mr. Dunleigh approves, your brother will work at the mill, with room and board, and half-day Saturdays. He'll have Sundays off." She smiled at Moira. "You will stay here until your baby comes." She drew the young woman forward. "This is Mary. You can see you'll have company."

Mary ducked her head.

Mrs. Harcourt continued. "All we ask is that you attend classes and work in our laundry."

Moira felt a wave of relief so strong she nearly dropped her soup. She had found a place for her and

Jamie. "Mrs. Harcourt, I am so thankful. I will work very hard for you."

"I'm sure Mr. Dunleigh will approve the arrangements. For now, eat your lunch." Mrs. Harcourt swept from the office, her black silk skirt swishing behind her. Mary bobbed her head again and followed Mrs. Harcourt down the hall.

Night had fallen. Moira sat on a small iron bed on the third floor. She hoped Jamie's quarters were as good. A lantern hung by the door flickered in the large room, lighting two neat rows of beds made up with blankets, each bed with a trunk underneath. She counted thirty beds as the women chattered around her. They talked so fast, they interrupted each other, for once the light was put out, no one was allowed to talk.

She wasn't sure whether to be afraid or excited about tomorrow, her first day.

"Ah, they'll work you here, but you can leave. That is if you have a place to go," said one woman with a bruised cheek.

"Don't be giving her a hard time. They feed us. They give us clean clothes. They lead us in prayer. Lots of prayer, but we can leave when we want to." Another woman, heavy set and with one crossed eye, leaned close. "See, I'm having a bit of a rest here. It's rather nice to be sleeping alone for a change." A few of the women laughed.

"I'm leaving as soon as I get word from my family," said the young woman Moira had met earlier.

"Right you are, Mary. And is that after you have the baby?"

Mary was silent.

A matron Moira didn't know came in and closed the lantern. "Rest with God's peace," she called, as she closed and locked the door behind her. Each woman returned to her own bed. All was quiet. Moira lay in her bed, too excited to sleep. She listened to the women around her settle down. Someone was crying softly in a bed near hers, but she couldn't remember who slept there.

"Shush," said a woman two beds over. "They'll come and take you away."

The crying stopped.

"Religion is the answer to immorality, don't you agree?" Mrs. Harcourt presided at the head of the breakfast table. Baskets of bread lined the middle of the table, and each woman's place had been set with a bowl of thin oatmeal and a mug of tea. The women and girls sat crammed on stools along both sides of the long table.

"The path sinners must follow to redemption is through work and prayer," she continued. "God sent you to Ardkeen House for redemption through Christian kindness, so work with a willing heart. Today we'll spend in silent reflection. Let us pray."

Long moments of quiet followed. Spoons clicked on bowls as the women ate in silence. The warm porridge tasted salty, reminding Moira of home.

"Moira, come with me," said a thin woman. Her dark eyes protruded slightly. She wore the same white pinafore over her black dress to protect it, but her hands were soft, and her dress was of silk, like that of Mrs. Harcourt. "Today is your first day?" the woman asked quietly, turning down a side hall.

"Yes, mum."

"In here, please." The two women sat in a corner of the office Moira had visited the day before.

"I'm Mrs. Hodkins. Welcome to our home. You know we are modeled after a Catholic charity, the Magdalene House."

Moira shook her head.

"Didn't Mrs. Harcourt explain this to you?" Mrs. Hodkins looked more sharply at Moira. "We are quite pleased to be in our new building. Here, under one roof, we run several charitable services, the Juvenile Female School, the Inverness Infant School, and the program Mrs. Harcourt has recommended for you, the Work Society." Mrs. Hodkins blinked and pulled a lace handkerchief from her sleeve to wipe her nose.

"You're very lucky, you know. We never have more than forty women at a time. We have women from the farms, the docks, insubordinate girls from the mills, and some orphans. Some have been rescued from imminent danger." Mrs. Hodkins frowned and blinked again, her eyelids almost a nun's coif. "Some are brought here by their families. Some, like you, are pregnant. We find homes for the babies. Some girls stay for a short time, and some have been here already several years. Most find Ardkeen House a haven."

Moira nodded.

"When a woman comes here, like you, without a home or family," Mrs. Hodkins continued, "we ask that you commit to remain at Ardkeen House for three months. Can you do that?"

"I believe I can," said Moira. "Unless my husband comes for me. The women last night said we could leave at any time."

"But he is not here now, is he? And if you leave, where will you go? Here, you have a safe place to stay. You'll have an opportunity to leave if your husband comes for you." Mrs. Hodkins smiled. "We can help you find gainful work in domestic service or the mills after the baby comes."

Moira rubbed her fingers over her work-roughened palms. "I will stay."

"Good. Do you have any questions?"

"My brother. I was wondering when I could see my brother."

"He can come to Ardkeen House to visit on his off days. That would be on Saturday afternoon or Sunday."

"I won't see him until then?"

"No, I can't imagine you would," Mrs. Hodkins replied. "Shall we go to the laundry?"

CHAPTER 49: EDINBURGH

Alice hurried from the parlour to open the door at Mewston Place. "Gordon, I didn't expect to see you here in Edinburgh."

"I've been here this last week. Staying at the club." He leaned forward. "I've missed you, Alice."

"Mother is not well. I wrote you." She glanced back into the house.

"I've received your letters, but it's summer. You've been gone since February."

"We can't really talk here, Gordon." Alice looked out past the front walk to Ladysmith Road. A few students wearing university robes passed by, their heads hunched together. They ducked between carts and carriages, on their way to the University. A tall student slipped on the wet flagstones.

"Come in. How have you been?"

"Well enough." Gordon stood in the vestibule. Rain dripped from his cloak onto the black and white tile floor.

Alice took his wet cloak and hung it up. She should have known he would come to Edinburgh. How different he looked. So much more vibrant. She sighed. "Mother and Father will be pleased to see you."

"Will they?"

"Yes."

"And you? Are you happy to see me?"

"Perhaps."

"Dammit, Alice. You're not being fair."

"I tried to talk to you at Westness. You never listened, yet here you are. What do you want?"

"I want you to come back to me." Gordon leaned on his walking stick and gazed at Alice without blinking.

"I don't think that's possible. Mother is better, but she still needs me." Alice folded her arms. "I wrote you."

"Your place is with me. I need you." Gordon was silent, as if by his very presence he could persuade her to return.

"I don't think anything has changed."

Gordon reached out his hand. "I'd like to think so. Give me a chance to explain."

Alice turned away. "Come to the library then. It's quiet there. I suppose we have to talk."

She could feel his presence behind her as she led the way to the back of the house. She gestured to the settee and leaned against one of the bookshelves that lined the wall. Behind him, the windows were open, letting in the cool morning air and the smell of rain and her mother's garden. "I don't want to return to Westness."

"You don't have to. That's what I mean to tell you." Gordon sat on the coffee-colored settee as if he owned it. He stretched his bad leg out and rested it on a small stool. "The last ship arrived safely. The estate is finally doing well. Our sheep are thriving. We can stay anywhere you like, here in Edinburgh. In London. Wherever."

Alice stared at Gordon. "I'm remembering when we first met. You said so many things then about making improvements. I wasn't prepared for Westness. All those people evicted from their homes. They were starving."

"But that was the problem. There were too many people on the land. There wasn't enough work to go around. I couldn't support them all, not as dependents. They're no longer on Foulksay Island, Alice. They'll have a chance at a new life, a more productive life. Perkins writes that the sheep have done well since the spring. That will bring new industry to the island." He shrugged and looked up at her. "You know my plans. Even Hume says we cannot have social progress without economic prosperity."

Alice's black silk skirt swished as she began to pace. "I've heard his arguments, Gordon. It's not just about prosperity for us or even for those you transported. I can't forget their suffering. We did nothing."

"Nothing? How can you say that? I'm not the only one who's trying to improve the land. You met Ross from Shapinsay. And there's Sutherland, Campbell, MacDonald. All have gone before me, showing me what's possible."

"I've been reading the papers, Gordon. People are streaming into the cities, looking for work. They're from the country; they're coming over from Ireland by the thousands into Glasgow and Edinburgh. They're crammed into the tenements over in Bogtown. Father says the whole area is ripe for cholera. Now that it's summer, we're hearing of scarlet fever. When I go with Diana or Father, I see such poverty. There's no helping them. Too many of them die."

"You should not be going into the tenements, Alice. There are other ways to help the poor. They need industry. They need jobs. Ah, you're too thin. I would take better care of you, Alice. Come back to me."

Alice began to shake her head.

Gordon reached out his hand to stop her. "Don't say no. Remember what we have done together, what we talked about when we first met. You helped me, Alice. If we settle here in Edinburgh, you would be close to your family. I can make certain investments now, Alice, investments you would approve of. But I don't want to do it without you. Without you, I lose my will."

Alice moved restively. "My parents don't understand why I'm here at home instead of with you. Even Diana doesn't understand. Sometimes I don't understand. You are still my husband."

"Don't say anything more. You are still my wife." His face crumpled. "What do you want, Alice? Tell me."

Alice felt lighter than air. She wasn't sure what she wanted any more. "When we first met, it seemed we could have what my parents have. But you never included me. Gordon, I don't think you've changed. You've been so angry."

"I was never angry at you."

"I suppose I knew that." Alice shook her head. "There were people about always. But you were so withdrawn. I used to wait for you to come to me. Then when you did." She stopped speaking.

"I'm sorry, Alice."

"That's not everything. You know I wanted a child. Your child. When I lost the baby, it was a very difficult time." She remembered her rooms at Westness, the stilted conversations with Mrs. MacNaught and Pastor McPherson, her walks on the hills near Westness. "You wouldn't let Diana come to visit. I needed my sister in a way I don't think you could ever understand."

"Foulksay Island isn't Edinburgh. Your sister never would have been comfortable there."

"That's not the point, Gordon. I needed her, and I needed you. Please don't leave me on the outside."

"You are never on the outside." Gordon reached his hand up to Alice. "I'm so very tired. Please come back to me."

"I wanted to be a good wife, Gordon."

"Then, come back to me. Let us try again."

"It can't be the same."

"I know. Stay with me, Alice. I need you."

Alice remembered every line of his body, every hope he had held for their future. Now he was alone as she had once been. How could she not return to him?

She sat next to him on the settee and leaned on his shoulder. Outside, the sun glinted on her mother's garden. Together they watched the soft rain fall.

CHAPTER 50: THE THAMES

Mac awoke in a sweat in the darkness. His stomach roiled, and he leaned over to vomit in the slops bucket someone had put by his head.

"What are you doing, Mac?" hissed O'Toole. "Ye can't come like this. You'll not be able to keep up."

"Don't think it. I'll keep up." Mac sat up, propping his back against the wall of the common room. He could see just the outlines of O'Toole's face as he bent down, cradling his manacles so they wouldn't make a sound, his head barely clearing the low timbers.

O'Toole put his hand on Mac's forehead. "Ye've got it pretty bad." He looked around. "The guards will be coming round in another few minutes, and then we're going. But ye can't come with us."

"If I get on deck, my head will clear." The hairs on Mac's arms stood up as another wave of cramps hit his stomach.

"I've seen this before. You're sick, man. Ye'll be puking up your guts for three days and barely able to walk, let alone run. Ye'll be lucky if they leave you alone."

Mac finally nodded. "Go with Godspeed then."

"Take this." O'Toole handed over a small leather pouch. "There's no safe place really, but you can tie this under your clothes."

Mac felt the pouch. "There's two coins here. You were supposed to keep one. Take it back. You'll need it."

"I'm sorry, Mac. Truly." O'Toole palmed one of the coins and grinned. He cradled his chains in his arms and crept back to his corner to wait for the guards to pass.

Mac could barely see O'Toole through the shadows. Mac shut his eyes. He knew he stank of vomit. He wished he were topside and then swimming in the Thames. He would sink, and no one would care. Another wave of cramps hit his stomach. He retched, but there was nothing left. He glanced over at O'Toole's corner. O'Toole was gone.

"Up, you sons of whores," cried Hyde, as the guards walked through the commons. He walked over to where Mac lay. "Sommat wrong this morning? Yer not getting up?" He nudged Mac with his boot and then kicked him in the ribs. "Get up, you misbegotten son of a bitch." He grimaced. "Here's another one."

"Lieutenant said we should leave them be if they're truly sick," said Simmons.

"I'll leave him be." Hyde angled around Mac's body, getting ready for another kick. "He's always trying to get sommat for nothing."

"I know this one," said Simmons, leaning over Mac. "He's a good worker. Been here a month. Hasn't been sick before."

"What do I care?" Hyde shrugged and walked away.

"Can ye get up, Mac? Up on deck for the count?" Simmons looked around. "Here, you two, help this man on deck."

Lieutenant Evans looked at the ragged men lined up on deck, bent over, shivering, their arms pressed over their stomachs. He was not pleased. "Simmons," called Evans.

"Aye, sir."

"If any men are too sick to send out today, have them pull the bedding and dredge out the sleeping quarters." Evans paced along the poop deck. "These men are not here to lay about. A bit of work will warm them up."

"The count's off by four, sir," said Simmons.

"Count them again."

"We did, sir. There's four missing."

Lieutenant Evans grimaced, deep lines appearing on each side of his mouth. "Since this morning? Was the count done last night?"

"Aye, sir. All present at midnight, sir."

"Someone has to know something. Simmons, find out who's missing. Promise light duty for any information." Lieutenant Evans called to Villard. "Take four men and search the ship. And count them again."

Three longboats bobbed up and down in the choppy Thames, close to the *Warrior*. One of the watermen called, "Are they coming down? It's bloody cold down here."

Mac clung to the bulwarks as the guards pulled the prisoners out of the line and questioned them roughly. Some of the prisoners hung over the side, vomiting into the Thames. The count remained four men short.

A shout went up, and Simmons hurried over to the Lieutenant. "One of the prisoners saw them leave, four together. O'Toole, Doherty, Cassidy, and Menzies. He thought they had a boat waiting."

"Bloody Irish. I want you to take a detail to Woolwich immediately and inform the watch," Lieutenant Evans commanded. "Even with a boat, someone would have seen them." Evans paced a moment more on the foredeck and waved his hand. "Release the men for work."

"What about those who are sick?"

Evans wheeled on Simmons. "I said release the men for work." His face flushed red, and spittle specked his lips. "All of them. I'll have a report ready for Lord Penrose within the half-hour requesting a detachment. He will not be pleased, and neither am I."

The order went down the line. One by one, the prisoners were forced into the waiting longboats, Mac among them, half falling down the rope ladder. He lay on the bottom of the small boat, dizzy but breathing fresh air, knowing somehow he must work today, else he would wind up beaten or dead.

The longboats passed the prison hulks, their rigging hung with bedding and ragged laundry instead of sails, the hulks lining the river like a stinking, floating shantytown. They passed the *Justistia*, moored on the north side of the Thames near a swamp, farthest from Woolwich, a floating hell for the most incorrigible prisoners, most held in solitary confinement.

Hyde nudged Mac with a boot. "Pitiful scum, aren't you. You know something, and you're going to tell me afore the day's done."

Just as the sun faded to dusk and fog began to rise over the Thames, a squad of red-coated soldiers brought back Jack Doherty, Mel Cassidy and John Menzies, heavily chained, their faces blank with despair. Mel cradled his left hand as if it were broken.

"Tie them to the yardarm. Call the men on deck," called Lieutenant Evans.

Mac stumbled onto the deck, hoping they hadn't caught O'Toole. He saw Jack, John, and Mel trussed up for flogging. Their bodies slumped next to a pitiful row of laundry hung on the rigging. Hyde shook out the cat o'nine tails. Each whip end tipped with lead clicked on the deck.

Mac made his way to where the prisoners had gathered. "Hang on. I'll help you later," he hissed as he passed his friends.

The punishment began – eighty lashes for each and a sentence to the Black Hole. Hyde took his time. He set his feet on the deck before each blow. Mac winced as the screams began. Finally the three men were cut down. They lay on the deck, bloodied and unconscious.

"Give them a salt bath and then take them below to solitary," commanded Lieutenant Evans. "Five days. Then transfer them to the *Justistia*." He swung back to the assembled prisoners. "Your government seeks to rehabilitate you, to prepare you for that awful day you face your Maker. But not to coddle you. Any escape will be punished, in the name of God, Queen, and country." He turned and left the foredeck.

Mac knew he wouldn't see Mel or Jack for five days, if then. He didn't really know Menzies, but he felt sorry for him. Mac took the last sovereign from his leather pouch and sidled over to Simmons.

"Can you do something for those men, sir?" Mac asked.

"What's it to you?" Simmons said, not meeting Mac's eyes.

"Maybe a bit of food, something to drink and something for their backs?" asked Mac, putting his hand out as if to grasp onto Simmon's sleeve.

Simmon's eyes widened. He quickly took the coin and nodded. "Get along with you there. Back to your cell." He turned away.

Mac stopped to stare at the Thames, crowded with prison hulks on the south and north sides. At the Royal Arsenal to the east, a mess of boats and barges unloaded crates of food and supplies. A slight wind kept the smell of swill from rising up from the river.

Bend, don't break, he thought.

CHAPTER 51: ARDKEEN HOUSE

Moira didn't like the look Jamie gave her or the way he slumped against the wall. Outside the gatehouse fronting Ardkeen House, rain pelted the cobblestones of Edinburgh Road where few traveled this gray morning.

"It's not so bad, is it? At the mills?" Moira's back hurt, and her feet were swollen. The baby was due nearly any day now, and she was tired of the laundry rooms and tired of stirring tubs of hot wash until she was nauseous.

"It's all right." Jamie picked at his sleeve. "Some of the kids don't have shoes. They get them as soon as they can." He straightened up a little. "I'm already a piecer. I'm not tall enough to be a spinner. They earn more money."

"I got a letter from Dylan through Mrs. MacKinnon at the Claron School. Deidre sent it from home. He's in Edinburgh."

Jamie twisted away from Moira. "I'm hungry."

"He doesn't know we're in Inverness."

"But I'm not with you. I'm over at the mill. Mr. Dunleigh gets paid for taking children from the poorhouse, the younger the better. Some of them are sick. He don't care. He works us all. Every day except a little bit of today and Sunday."

"We have to work, Jamie. Both of us."

"I know. But it's not like home where I could go all over the island, down to Selkirk and the new pier and over to the farms or out on the boat with Mac and Dougal. I was working then too. Mr. Dunleigh, he locks us in before it's light. I don't like the steward. Mr. Bean has a stick he calls his walking stick, but I've seen him hit the workers when Mr. Dunleigh isn't there. It's not a good place."

"Has he hit you?"

"I don't want to say."

"It's all we've got right now." Moira pressed her stomach again. She knew that tomorrow she'd be back at work, singing hymns and bending over dirty laundry. She looked at her hands reddened by soapy water, her fingernails soft to the touch. Not so different from cleaning fish. "They feed you, don't they?"

Jamie snorted. "It's oatcakes and gruel, oatcakes and gruel. Some of the bigger ones take food from the little ones. I'm going to run away."

"You can't."

"I can. I could go today. Right now. Mr. Bean smiles when he hits us. I would be better off back on Foulksay."

"We tried that, Jamie. There's no work."

"Maybe I'll do better if I go off on my own."

Moira felt as if the cold stone walls of the gatehouse were closing in on her. Her back ached. "I'm going to write Dylan. I want him to know about the baby. If we don't hear again, we could try Edinburgh. It can't be worse there."

Jamie looked at her with the eyes of an old man. "Did he send any money?"

"Come next Sunday, will you?" replied Moira.

The next Sunday, Moira sat in the gatehouse. In her arms she held her daughter, bundled in the white blanket that Mrs. Harcourt had given her. She was tired, but she couldn't get over the miracle of this little life.

"She's awful small," said Jamie.

"Of course she's small. She's four days old." Moira held her baby close. "They told me they have a family that will take her."

"You're going to let her go?"

"I can keep Rose with me if I leave. They said I could go to the poorhouse down the hill."

"For how long?"

"Until we hear from Dylan again? Until I can find some work and some way to care for Rose? I don't know, Jamie."

"I'm going to the docks," said Jamie. "I'll find something there. I can't stay at the mill."

"Could I get on at the mill?"

"And what would you do with Rose? Anyway, you don't want to. It's hard work, Moira."

"Harder than stirring laundry all day?"

"Maybe Mr. Bean won't hit you. But he goes after the older girls."

"We should have stayed on Foulksay."

"I'm not waiting anymore," replied Jamie. "I can find a ship that will take me on as a cabin boy. Micah told me." He reached out to hold the baby.

"Can you wait, Jamie?" Moira watched Jamie rock the baby back and forth. "Dylan will write again as soon as he gets my letter. I know he will. He'll send money, or he'll come for us. You don't have to go now, do you?"

Jamie stood up. His thin legs jutted out from below his pants. He held the baby close. "You wouldn't want me to stay if you knew how it was at the mill."

Moira was silent. "Give me another week, Jamie. Come next Sunday."

Jamie nestled his head close to Rose. "All right. Another week. But no more."

Moira sat alone in the gatehouse after Jamie left. The baby lay heavy on her lap. She hummed the lines of an old ballad.

Dae ye see yon high hills a-covered with the snow?
They've parted many a true love, an' soon I'll have to go.
Bide, bide, me bonnie, an' I'll come again one day,
An' I'll take ye to our island, dear, home to Foulksay.

She felt so tired. She touched Rose's cheek. The cold from the stones of the gatehouse seeped through her shawl into her bones. Moira wrapped the baby tight in her shawl and turned back to Ardkeen House.

CHAPTER 52: EDINBURGH

Lord Gordon finished the last of his correspondence and rose from his desk, another letter from Perkins in his hand. He glanced around his office, glad he had brought the sculpture of Wellington with him to Edinburgh, for they would not be returning to Foulksay Island, at least not until the spring. *Only if Alice is willing*, he thought. He reread the letter from Perkins, pacing in front of the coal fire in the fireplace.

Honorable Lord Gordon, sir.

The sheep shearing in April went well. We continue enclosing fields with stone walls which bodes a good harvest. Demand is high for woven goods. Pastor McPherson reports no additional men or women admitted to the workhouse. Pier fees have been paid. Rents are enumerated on the enclosed report. Income has been deposited through the Edinburgh bank you noted. Should you wish Westness reopened, please advise. Note that the island population is now at 237 souls, including Selkirk.

Your humble and obedient servant, Geo. Perkins.

Gordon looked over the profit report from the sale of the wool. His breeding program had been successful. The flock had doubled in under a year.

Gordon shook his head. *I'll visit Foulksay, perhaps once a year, but I do not have to live on that island again.* For a moment he remembered the summers of his youth, scrambling on the cliffs near Westness. He nearly crushed the letter in his hand. *I'll talk with Alice tonight.*

Lord Gordon strolled downstairs, amused at the noise as servants prepared the house for tonight's dinner party. Calling for the cabriolet, he admired the orderly planting of shrubbery at the front of the house. Alice had made a difference. They had a home. "To the club, Charles," he called as he entered the cabriolet.

Charles, resplendent in green and blue livery, closed the door to the one person carriage and flicked his whip at the horse as they made their way out of New Town and negotiated the crowded streets along Princes Street. Gordon peered out as they passed the partially built Scott Monument. Day laborers gathered at its base, setting up tiers of scaffolding. As the cabriolet turned onto the crowded North Bridge to High Street, Gordon glanced at the works begun for Waverly Station.

"I'll walk from here," called Gordon.

He passed a long line of women waiting to fill their pails and wooden buckets from the Netherbow wellhead and continued up the hill past St. Giles Cathedral. Finally he was at the door of the East India Club tucked in the Wardrop's Close, just down the hill from the towers of Edinburgh Castle. He sniffed at the open sewage. *Auld Reekie. Edinburgh's well deserved nickname.*

Gordon spent the afternoon at the East India Club with newspapers from New Delhi and cigars from Spain made with Cuban tobacco. He relaxed in the large downstairs reading room, nodding to acquaintances. He was content to sit quietly, not taking part in the latest arguments that flared over Peel's proposed income tax. He relished the smooth taste of Scottish malt whisky that burned his throat slightly.

Sunlight from a nearby window played on the dark amber spirits in his crystal glass. He closed his eyes as the familiar pain snaked down his arm. He waited, concentrating on his breathing, but this time, the heaviness grew in the center of his chest, pressing down tighter and tighter. Gordon felt he could not breathe. The pain eased, but he knew it would come again. He would have to tell Alice.

That night, as the formal party at home began, Gordon was pleased to see several families of the men he knew from the club. The bright silk gowns of their wives and daughters gave a festive air.

"A small party," he had told Alice. "Limit it to forty guests. You will know whom to invite. The head of the university. The mayor. Someone from the church."

Gordon nodded to the guests as he moved through the crowd. Their chatter rose around him. Her father and mother were here, of course, as were her sisters. He frowned. Both young women unmarried still. A quartet of musicians played traditional Scottish airs in the corner of the ball room where the young people had gathered. He looked for Alice everywhere.

Gordon strolled into the entry hall. The Greek fresco of black and white tiles distracted him. *Where was she?* His right hand began to twitch. He glanced up to see Alice walking down the circular stairs, a white silken shawl draped over her shoulders, the lines of her evening dress revealing her slightly rounded belly.

My God. She's pregnant. A rush of feeling came over him. For a moment, he couldn't breathe. *An heir. Finally, an heir.* He reached out for her hand.

"You look lovely, my dear."

CHAPTER 53: DEIDRE

Deidre followed the steward and the other passengers along the narrow wooden passage, stumbling slightly.

Once a military transport ship, the *Brilliant* had been refitted for emigrants to Australia. The ticket master had told her she had been assigned to a commodious and private cabin. She sniffed. The narrow hallway wasn't looking commodious. She knew only that she would have her own berth, as Father had required.

William Scott had paid twelve pounds for passage on the *Brilliant*, one of three ships in the flotilla commanded by Captain David Sinclair. The *Mermaid* and the *Alexander* would join them at Gravesend. He had arranged the ticket for Deidre through an agent in Stromness, after learning that Mac would be transported to Van Dieman's Land on the *Mermaid*.

The steward, a slight man with pale hair, turned around. "In here, ladies." He gestured to the right and read from a roster: "Mrs. Fraser, Mrs. Miller, and Miss Scott. We leave on the morning ebb, so best to settle in quickly. The rest of you, follow me." He hurried down the narrow hallway, a silent group of women and children draggling behind him.

The three women hesitated outside their new quarters. The small cabin had no windows. An oil lantern hung from the middle of the ceiling. Three bunk beds crowded the room, each with white canvas curtains to pull for privacy and a chamber pot underneath. Boards had been added to the sides of the bunk beds, making it difficult to climb in or fall out. Three stools hung on the fourth wall, over a small collapsing table. The floorboards smelled of vinegar.

Deidre followed a large woman wearing a heavy navy coat with silver buttons into the cabin. The woman huffed and set her portmanteau and a wooden case down in the center of the cabin as did Deidre. The third woman crowded behind them.

"I don't think we can fit in here if we're all standing," said Deidre. She sat on the lower bed of the nearest bunk bed; the board cut into her legs as she shoved her case underneath.

"Ah, but this is bigger than I expected," said Mrs. Fraser.

"Bigger?" Mrs. Miller snorted and set her bags underneath the bunk bed next to Deidre's. "This isn't any bigger than a flea's house. Six of us in here? Where shall we sleep?"

"I, for one, can only sleep on the lower berth," said Mrs. Fraser.

"That's good, for I prefer the top," replied Mrs. Miller.

"At least we'll be warm," said Mrs. Fraser, unbuttoning her navy coat and laying it on the bottom bunk opposite Deidre. "And we shall come to know each other. I am Mrs. Isabella Fraser and you are Mrs. Miller?"

Mrs. Miller nodded. The two older women turned to Deidre, their eyes curious and a little hostile.

"I am pleased to meet you," said Deidre.

The three women looked at each other.

"Come along. We're late enough." A stout woman with over-red cheeks half pulled a young girl into the cabin. "This is Miss Amalie Chalmers. I am her guardian, Mrs. Arbuckle." She peered at the cabin. "We will require one of the bunk beds, for I promised her father I would look after her."

"The top is all right for me, auntie," said Amalie. Her wide blue eyes reminded Deidre of Mac.

Deidre sat on her bunk bed and watched as the women organized their boxes and bags. *If it weren't so crowded, I would think this funny,* she thought, as the women muttered, and bumped into each other. The bed above her remained empty.

"Did anyone bring food? I think we should set a common store," said Mrs. Arbuckle, smoothing her ample front.

"Can we go topside to watch them cast off?" asked Amalie.

"I do not wish to share my food." Mrs. Miller pursed her full lips.

Deidre heard a knock at the door over the commotion. She opened the door to find the steward propping up another woman.

"This is Miss Dallow," he said. "Can ye get her to a bunk?"

Deidre half-carried the young woman to the bunk she had been sitting on. *So much for a lower bunk for me.* She pulled a blanket over the woman who remained asleep, her head lolling to the side. Deidre noted bruises on her face.

"Who's that?" asked Mrs. Miller. "Not someone else?"

"She smells of drink," Mrs. Arbuckle's eyes narrowed. "Not a proper companion. I will speak to the captain."

"The steward said she had a berth here," said Deidre. "Where else could she go?"

"Down in steerage for all I care." Mrs. Arbuckle sniffed and covered Amalie's ears. "She could be a woman of the streets."

"Let's not jump to any conclusions," said Deidre.

"We can talk to her when she wakes up," said Mrs. Miller.

Deidre stood protectively in front of her bunk. "We don't know the details yet. For now, let's go aboveboard and watch them cast off. I would like one last look at Portsmouth."

"But she doesn't have any luggage, not even a box."

"We don't know that. Maybe they'll bring it later," said Deidre. "May I take Amalie up to the deck?"

"You might as well," said Mrs. Arbuckle. "But I'm not leaving our things unattended with that woman here."

Deidre glanced at the woman who lay on the bunk unmoving. "Anyone wish to join me?"

"I certainly would like one last look at the motherland before we leave its shores," said Mrs. Fraser. "Please call me Bella."

The two women made their way along the narrow hall, Amalie trailing slightly behind them. As they came out on the foredeck, a burst of noise met them. They pushed their way to the bulwarks, as passengers called down to family and friends.

Officers on the above deck shouted commands, and sailors worked frantically to finish loading the ship. Some of the crew, bent over with boxes, pushed wheelbarrows up narrow planks laid all along the side of the *Brilliant*.

A sailor roped a crate of chickens on his back while another pulled and shoved five Merino rams up a plank. A third sailor led a short-horned cow on board. *Milk for tea*, Deidre thought.

Two planks had been reserved for the emigrants in steerage. A steady line of people edged along the planks and disappeared into the hold of the ship. One man carried an accordion with a pack on his back. A woman followed closely behind, carrying two small children wrapped in a shawl to cover their eyes.

Finally, the ship was loaded. The noise peaked as sailors pulled in the planks all along the sides of the *Brilliant* and awaited orders. Two sailors stood by the anchor. When the command came, a thrill ran through Deidre.

"Cast off. Cast off," cried the first mate. "Weigh anchor."

"Hurrah! Hurrah!" shouted the passengers.

At first the ship seemed not to move, and then the *Brilliant* slowly lifted up and dipped into the bay, past Margate, into the Channel, down along the Straits of Dover, headed to the Isle of Wight, its foresails billowing in a slight wind from the west.

Deidre held Amalie's hand tightly. "We've a long journey."

"You don't want to go below, do you?" asked Amalie.

"We'll stay up here, as long as we can." Deidre pointed to the coast. "We'll follow this coast past Plymouth to Gravesend, where we meet the other ships coming with us. Then we sail all the way to Van Diemen's Land. You've done this before?"

"Yes, but I only remember being sick. Last time was two years ago. 'Tis better this time," said Amalie. "I'm going home."

The wind scattered drops of foam that shone in the sun as the ship dipped and slid along the waves in the Channel. The westerly wind filled the sails, pulling them along the coast and out toward the sea. Deidre held Amalie's hand. Together they stared at the land until only a smudge of dark green and white could be seen.

CHAPTER 54: MAC

Mac spat into the Thames. The *Warrior* looked nearly empty, though the guards paced along her foredeck, and laundry still flapped on her yardarms. Nearly two hundred men had been offloaded from the *Warrior* and the *Justistia* onto longboats, and then ferried to the *Mermaid*, its red and white pennant flicking in a brisk wind. They were headed Bay side, first to Gravesend where the wives and families of the guards would embark, and then to Hobart Town in Van Diemen's Land.

Mac had marched with the other prisoners below decks to his new quarters, naked and shivering from the bath of sea-water they'd been given immediately on boarding the *Mermaid*.

Each prisoner had been issued a regulation parcel of clothing as well. Now, like the men around him, he opened his parcel to find a cap, two shirts, a smock, trousers, drawers, stockings, and, he hoped, shoes that would fit him. Murmurs of surprise arose around him. Though the fabric was coarse, it was clean and sturdy and would keep him warm. Mac fingered a towel, a brush, and a comb. For the first time, he felt hopeful about the voyage to Van Diemen's Land, a place that seemed beyond the end of the world.

The men would sleep on wooden shelves built all along the walls in a large room that had once held cargo. A board some ten inches high separated each man's bed, and a clean mattress, pillow and two blankets were neatly rolled at the end of each berth. Several lanterns affixed to a top beam that ran along the length of the room alleviated the gloom somewhat. A group of ship's men in uniform stood at the far end of the room. One stepped forward and looked over the men as they quickly pulled baggy trousers on. Mac was glad to see Menzies and pushed his way to stand near him.

'Line up," shouted one of the ship's men. The transportees stood in front of their wooden bunks, half-dressed.

'Once the ship gets underway, you'll be allowed on deck," First Mate Dickerson began. "But that is a privilege. When the seas run high, you'll go below, and the hatches will be closed and locked. Ship's bells begin the day at 6. On fair days, you are to roll up your bedding and take it on deck. You'll have bread sometime between 6 and 7 above deck, if the weather allows it. Dinner's at twelve and supper at 4. You'll have a ration of boiled beef once a week, again, conditions permitting. You'll be locked in for the night at 5:30. Lights out by 8 o'clock. When it's warm enough, salt-water baths will be provided before first bell. Soap and razors will be allotted for shaving twice a week. Captain?"

Captain Meredith brushed an imaginary speck of lint from his sleeve. He walked to the center of the room. "Regardless of what you may have heard, the *Mermaid* is a transport ship. You are prisoners, and you will remain prisoners until we dock in Port Arthur, and you are released to the authorities there.

"Our voyage will take about three months. I believe discipline will help us all make this voyage safely and efficiently. All of you will report for work by 9 o'clock. Most of you will be assigned to sewing or mending sails. A few of you may be recruited to work on repairs." He paced along the line of men. "There's to be no fighting, no drinking, and no gambling. You will be encouraged to attend Sunday services on deck. If any of you are sick, inform First Mate Dickerson at once." He motioned to the first mate and a man in a black frock coat standing beside him. "Go ahead, Dr. Mayhew."

Mac rubbed his wrist and whispered to the man next to him. "'Tis already better than the *Warrior*."

"Wait until we're out on the open sea. Tell me that when you've got men vomiting up their toenails. How long were you on the *Warrior*?"

"Four months, I think," said Mac. "You've done this before?"

"My third trip," the man replied. "Captain Meredith's not so bad, but you have to follow his rules. Try to get assigned to a work detail as fast as you can. It will get you out of here when the storms come."

"Thanks. I'm Mac. This is Menzies."

"Call me Davis. And don't believe what they said about gambling."

CHAPTER 55: DEIDRE

Deidre stood alone on the foredeck of the *Brilliant*, grateful for the fresh air. She had awakened at dawn to find the ship wallowing as the English Channel widened. Everyone had been sick below, especially the mysterious Kate Dallow. No one gave thought to breakfast. Bella and Mrs. Arbuckle had fought over the slops bucket, each one protesting she needed it more. Finally, Deidre escaped to the deck.

Deidre searched the horizon, but she couldn't see the other two ships that travelled with the *Brilliant* as it bucked and lifted over the swells. The seas rose and fell in a steady rhythm.

"There you are," cried Amalie, properness forgotten. The ten-year-old bounced up the stairs to the foredeck, her skirts flouncing.

"How are they all below?" asked Deidre.

Amalie shrugged. "It smells horrible down there."

"You're better off up here with me, then."

Deidre and Amalie leaned over the railing on the foredeck and tried to decode the routine of life aboard the *Brilliant*. Women on the steerage deck gathered pots for breakfast and stumbled as the ship lifted with the waves. Above them, sailors climbed up the rigging to let out more sails that billowed out and caught in the wind.

Occasionally Deidre felt nauseous. She fixed her gaze on the horizon of the sea, and the nausea passed. "I heard there's to be a school. Shall you go?"

"With the children from steerage?" said Amalie. "I'd rather be a sailor. I could curse then, by God's breath."

"Amalie." Deidre laughed. "I don't think your aunt would approve."

"She's not my real aunt. She's truly just my traveling companion." Amalie leaned forward on the railing. The boat was surrounded by gray waves topped by white caps. No land was to be seen. "I miss home."

"What is home like?"

"We live across the bay from Hobart Town. It's so pretty they named it Bellerive. That means beautiful river."

"I know," Deidre replied.

"My father used to take me down to the bay early in the morning. If we were lucky, we'd see kangaroos gathering by the water." Amalie leaned further over the balustrade. "There's not much to do here, is there."

"I imagine the days will pass pretty quickly. Did you like the music down in steerage last night?" asked Deidre. "It was fun to see the men twirling while the ladies stood by and watched. Their feet were tapping, and so were mine. The fiddling reminds me of home."

"Good morning, ladies." Reverend Baxter joined them at the railing. "And a fine morning it is, beauteous and full of God's grace."

Murmuring assent, Deidre thought the confusion and smell in their cabin below was not full of God's grace, though she could agree the sunlight dappling the ship as it cut through the waves was beauteous. "I can't see the other ships travelling with us, Reverend."

"They're out there, never fear." His eyes shut, the Reverend fell into prayer. "May God's hand protect all innocent souls on this journey." Deidre and Amalie shut their eyes obediently, but Deidre wondered if the Reverend had already heard of Kate Dallow.

"It's an amazing sight, all those people crammed together, while we are stand here in comfort," the Reverend said, with a sweep of his hand from steerage to the foredeck where they stood. "God's will is inscrutable."

The women in steerage had fed their families on the main deck and were now wrestling their children in and out of great barrel tubs filled with sea-water. A few men sat on the deck in small circles, playing cards. Others, amid much teasing, climbed clumsily into the rigging to help the sailors.

The boatswain started a chant and the men pulled at the sails rhythmically, resting between the beats.

Way haul away, way haul away,
we'll haul away the bowlin'.
Way haul away, way haul away,
the ship she is a rollin'.
Way haul away, way haul away,
we'll hang and haul together.

Deidre and Amalie looked at each other and giggled.

"Shark, ho!" Several men raced along the deck, lashing a rope to a harpoon as they ran, their bare feet slapping on the deck.

"Lower the boat," cried the first mate. A small longboat was lowered over the side. Three men and the first mate stood in her, tense with excitement. The boat hit the water and tipped in the heavy seas, then righted.

"Kill the blighter," called a sailor hanging from the side of the ship. "Don't let that death head follow us."

Everyone rushed to the bulwarks to watch the longboat chase the shark. Deidre could barely see the men in the small boat. The boat rocked on the top of the waves and then disappeared. It reappeared on the crest of a wave, and the men shouted incomprehensible words back to the ship. Deidre twisted her hands. The men would die before her eyes.

"Not to worry," said Reverend Baxter. "They'll return safe. These sailors are a superstitious lot. They believe the shark is waiting, you see, for a body, dead or alive. The sailors say the shark will follow the ship until it's fed." He cleared his throat. "I mean to say, they believe the shark is an evil omen."

The first death occurred two days later, as the *Brilliant* held off the islands of the Canaries. A little girl from steerage died of dysentery. The ship's surgeon wrapped her small body in a white canvas shroud and attached a bag of stones at one end to weigh it down. He held the body balanced on a piece of board over the bulwarks. Her parents stood by while Reverend Baxter read the Burial Service, his voice booming through the ship to all hands assembled. At the words, "Ashes to ashes, and dust to dust," her body slid into the waters below. The mother slumped.

Deidre looked down from the foredeck and wondered if the little girl had been one she'd watched playing. Now the little girl was dead. Deidre no longer wished she were traveling in steerage.

When conditions permitted, Deidre found a corner near their cabin to begin a letter home.

17 August. Dear Father. We have left Portsmouth and have now been at sea for seven days, well on our journey to Van Diemen's Land. We travel with two other ships, the *Mermaid* and the *Alexander*, though they are rarely with us. I write with hope that you and Mother and the girls are well.

Our cabin is quite cozy with four other women and a young girl, Amalie, but I have my own bunk, and the company is agreeable. We've shared our stores and eat salty meat with pickles nearly every day. During the day, I read or walk on the little deck near our cabin. At night, we hear fiddles from the emigrants, reminding me of home. The ocean changes every day. So far we've not encountered bad storms, yet Reverend Baxter says they're coming. I will continue this letter until we meet a passing ship.

25 August. We passed the Canary Islands and Mount Pala, the largest mountain I have ever seen. This morning I was up at 6 and had a good walk alone on the forecastle deck, though we still see nothing of the ships that accompany us. It's now thirty-four days since I left home, and fifteen days since Portsmouth. This afternoon, rain fell, and everyone ran out with buckets, pots, pails, and blankets to soak up this precious gift of fresh water, as it is much sweeter than ship's water.

30 August. This morning we stopped at the Cape Verde Islands to take on stores and replenish our water. We were allowed off ship briefly, and we gorged on oranges and fresh meat. After we passed the islands, a brisk wind threw our vessel nearly on her side. Many of us were sick, but Doctor Meriwether handed out salt pills. I continue in good health and spirits. The Captain says we are making good progress.

6 September. Today we saw a large albatross following our ship. Some of the men tried unsuccessfully to shoot it. The sailors put lines over to catch fresh fish, which were then boiled into a stew for supper, a welcome change to boiled meat. As the heat continues, the captain ordered wind sails directed into the hatchways to push fresh air below decks to everyone's gratitude. Last night, lightning marked the skies, and we had scant rain. Often our ship is alone on the sea, and I can only hope the *Mermaid* and the *Alexander* continue safely. I do not know if Mac is alive or well, and despite the company I'm traveling with, I feel very far from home. I wonder if I will see Foulksay again but cast off my melancholy thoughts, for the journey is taking me far south, and I have to believe that Mac and I will be reunited somehow.

17 September. Last night Doctor Meriwether told stories about the new stars which have filled the sky. We had our first glimpse of the Southern Cross. Father, I close now with love, for we are approaching a ship sailing north, and Captain Sinclair has promised a packet of letters will be sent over. I send loving thoughts to all of you and pray you continue in good health. Your devoted daughter, Deidre.

CHAPTER 56: THE *MERMAID*

Mac hurried along the deck of the *Mermaid*, grateful to be out of the hold. The cries of the men below, some still sick after two months aboard, rang in his ears, and the foul damp air pressed on his face, the stink of too many people in one place. They lost another man yesterday, his body slipped into the sea, anonymous.

This morning, Mac had marked another notch on the wall beside his shelf. He refused to call it a bed. Of 224 original passengers, including the families of the guards in the two cabins above, and adding the eighteen crew members quartered in the forecastle, some ten had been lost to sickness or accident, including four children and one woman.

He was one of the lucky ones, strong enough to help the crew and quick to volunteer. This earned him a little extra food, though the steady diet of sea biscuits and a bowl of potatoes and boiled beef twice a week had kept his body at bare sinew. Even after these weeks at sea, he was grateful to be free of shackles and out of the hold during the day.

The *Mermaid* lumbered against the wind with shortened sails and a double-reefed foresail, unable to make headway. The ship was sloppy with water. Mac clambered below to work bilge pumps in the front hold. Mac pumped next to Jack, whose sly grin said he had got his precious flint back gambling. Sweating, they worked the bilge pump nearly eye to eye.

"I hate this stinking ship," said Jack. "Not a drop of grog or a smoke."

Mac kept his head down. "Nobody should be smoking, Jack. Not even you."

"Ah, I'll get mine. That stinking mate. I got ways." Jack stopped pushing his side of the pump and leaned against the sloping side of the ship. He watched Mac. "Go on, work your heart out, you stupid cluck." Jack slipped a cheroot out of his pocket and turned it over in his hands. He ducked back to pump as the first mate climbed down the ladder.

The next day, ship's carpenter patched the leak, but Mac continued to climb down into the lowest parts of the ship to work the bilge pumps. Instead of Jack, Menzies worked steadily beside him, bare-shirted and silent. His back was slippery with sweat and scarred over from his flogging on the Thames.

When the wind shifted, the first mate called for the crew to set the topsails. The *Mermaid* was truly on her way, past Gibraltar, and along the coast of Africa to the Canaries. A dry hot wind blew out of Africa, and the men hung the bedding and their laundry along the lower rigging. Mac couldn't wait to have dry clothing again.

The rain held off for the next week as the ship slowly dried out. Jack grumbled about the first mate as he pondered his cards at the end of the day and twirled his slender cigar. "Wait until we get to Cape Town," he said. "Then we'll find out who's the better man."

Menzies looked at Jack. "Why do you want to pick a fight?"

"Do you have to ask? He's always after me." Jack, his face bruised, put his cards face down on the deck and leaned close to Menzies. "When you look at me, do you see a broken down sailor, somebody without a place to go? That's what the first mate called me, a wastrel and a layabout. As long as I got these," he shook his cards in Menzies' face. "I'm a gentleman. And don't you forget it. They brought me here by force, dragged me right out of Chauncey's Inn. They should'a sent me to Plymouth.

That's where I belong. Not on this god-forsaken floating prison going to god-forsaken Van Diemen's Land, for God's sake."

"I'm with you, Jack." Davis fanned his cards. "These pigs don't know nothing. We'll get him. By Cape Town."

"For God's sake, I hate the man."

"Settle down, Jack. Play your cards. We got the night." Davis smiled. The men hunched close on the open deck.

Late the next afternoon, Mac stood in line at supper, his dinner pail empty. Tired after working in the bowels of the ship, he savored the smell of the sea. Curious yellow clouds lay along the horizon, directly in front of the *Mermaid*, but there was no wind. The ship was becalmed. Now and again he caught a whiff of smoke. They broiling the beef, he thought, and his stomach growled.

"All hands, all hands!" The first mate shrieked. "Fire! Fire below."

Black dense smoke poured from the forward hold next to the gunroom.

Everyone dropped what they were doing and came running.

"We're afire," someone shouted.

"I'll kill Jack, that son of a bitch," cried the first mate. "Bucket brigade now!"

Every man grabbed a bucket. Two lines formed immediately. In one line, the men passed buckets filled with sea water down into the hold. In the second line, the men passed the empty pails just as quickly to the bulwarks.

"Faster, men. Faster," yelled the mate again and again, running along the line.

Mac was in the middle of the line. Salt water splashed around his feet and on the deck, while his heart hammered. He passed the water-filled buckets as fast as he could. His knuckles scraped on the handles, and cold water sloshed on his pants.

Rats streamed out of the hold as the men sent the buckets down, one after the other. Flames shot up from the hold. The men groaned and cried out.

"Fall back," shouted the first mate.

The first mate climbed up into the rigging with his glass and scanned the sea for either the *Alexander* or the *Brilliant*. "Ship on the horizon," he called down as he quickly slid back to the deck. "Can't tell which one."

Where a moment before the sea had been calm, the waves now built to long rows of swells. The sky darkened, and black smoke from the ship billowed up into the clouds.

"Ready the longboats," Captain Meredith shouted. "Passengers first."

The sailors swore and lowered the two longboats, bumping and scraping them on the side of the ship. They tied the wives and children of the guards together and lifted them down, their cries and screams lost in the commotion. The crew began throwing barrels and casks overboard, anything that would float.

Transportees gathered on the deck, Mac among them, the stink of fear mingling with sweat as they pushed to see what was happening. The guards and a few sailors climbed monkey-wise down the rope ladders in the fading afternoon light.

"Over you go, men," cried the mate. "Swim, and if you can't swim, hang on as best you can."

"Abandon ship," shouted Captain Meredith, eyeglass clenched in his fist. "The *Brilliant*'s coming. God willing, she'll pick us up."

Dark plumes of smoke rose up from the ship, carried off by the increasing wind. The overloaded boats nearly swamped in the heavy waves. Men bobbed and swam in the water next to the boats, Mac and Menzies with them. A few clung to the floating casks.

The salt stung Mac's eyes and nose. He swam behind one of the boats and hoped he wouldn't drown. The men rowed the boats away from the *Mermaid*. Behind them, the fire spread quickly fore and aft, and the *Mermaid's* sails burst into great sheets of flame.

"Mac, I can't make it," called Menzies. His face submerged and disappeared beneath the waves.

Mac swam toward Menzies and grabbed his shirt. "Hang on. I've got you."

A series of explosions rang out behind them as the *Mermaid's* store of ammunition caught fire.

The *Brilliant* came in fast, like a giant seabird. Their crew pulled in some of their smaller sails, just as they passed the *Mermaid*, ablaze with fire, a few hundred yards away. The *Brilliant* stood by, a fine sight, her white sails catching the last light of the setting sun as clouds moved in. Her crew lowered boats to pick up the men still floating in the ocean, and the boats from the *Mermaid* rowed to the *Brilliant*.

The men from the sea were brought aboard, shivering and wet. They lay on the deck under temporary shelters of canvas, covered with rough blankets.

Captain Sinclair ordered the wives and children of the guards to be parceled out among the first class cabins. The crews of the two ships mixed together in the forecastle quarters, and the transportees slept on the deck, apart from steerage for now. Jack and the first mate were missing.

As night fell, Mac watched Captain Meredith pace alone along the deck by the temporary canvas shelters. No one spoke. Only the hiss of the wind in the sails marked the progress of the *Brilliant*.

CHAPTER 57: THE *BRILLIANT*

A sailor, his red hair cropped close to avoid lice, stepped over the sleeping bodies on the deck of the *Brilliant* to nail a notice on the masthead.

"Any chance of work?" asked Mac, sitting up from his blanket on the deck.

The man scratched above his ear and looked at Mac. "Transportee?"

Mac nodded.

"Maybe." He pointed to the notice. "You read?"

Mac nodded again.

"Read it."

Mac stood by the masthead. "Any one caught smoking below decks shall be liable for each offence one month's confinement and a fine of 2 pounds sterling."

"Come talk to me, then, after we've got this mess straightened away. Ask for First Mate Banks." His eyes crinkled. "And pass the word. Captain Sinclair don't want no smoking aboard ship. None."

The next days passed slowly as Captain Sinclair limited water and cut the daily ration to accommodate the increased load on the *Brilliant*. The transportees were moved from the deck and locked in the hold. They were kept under heavy guard, allowed out twice daily for exercise, once at dawn and once in the evening.

When the *Alexander* caught up, Captain Meredith and half of the transportees were transferred to the other ship. Stores were shared between the two ships. Despite protests from the emigrants, the crew built a temporary wall dividing steerage into two sections to accommodate the number of transportees. Those in steerage complained loudly about their newly crowded berths, for they had paid for their passage.

Menzies, Davis, and Mac remained on the *Brilliant*. Mac was relieved when the manacles were removed and the hold left open during the day, weather permitting. Mac and Menzies made themselves useful whenever and however they could. Banks called them to work nearly every morning.

Mac had just come above decks when he saw her on the foredeck. His heart nearly stopped. He couldn't believe what he was seeing. "Deidre," he shouted before he thought. "Over here."

Deidre turned and peered over the railing.

"Watch it, man. Banks is coming this way," said Menzies, pulling Mac away from the stairs to the upper deck.

"But it's Deidre." Mac struggled against Menzies.

"It's not worth it, Mac."

"What's going on here?" said Banks, his face as red as the hair on his head. "You were supposed to work forward."

"Sir, nothing, sir," said Menzies. "We was just . . ."

"'Tis Miss Scott." Mac interrupted, his heart pounding. He could hardly breathe. "She's there, on the deck."

The three men peered up at Deidre, leaning over the railing.

"Mac?" Deidre waved her arms excitedly. "Is that you?"

"What foolishness is this?" Banks scowled and grabbed Mac's arm. "Do you want to be put in irons?" Banks shoved Mac against the bulwarks. "Are you listening?"

Mac broke free and raced up the ladder.

The first mate shrugged and rubbed his head. "His funeral. I'm going for the captain."

Menzies leaped halfway up the ladder. "Mac, come back."

Mac ran along the upper deck and took Deidre into his arms. She was here, next to him, and she smelled glorious. "I can't believe you're here. Dougal never said a word."

"I knew you were on the *Mermaid*." Deidre burrowed into Mac's body and pulled back to look at him. "I was so worried when the fire . . . ."

"Hush. You shouldn't be here." Mac touched Deidre's face gently.

"Mac, I'm coming to Van Diemen's Land."

Mac's eyes filled with tears. He couldn't resist any more. He took her in his arms and held her. He could feel her trembling.

"Get off that woman. What are you doing up here?" Reverend Baxter's voice rang out. "Help! I say, help!" He beat Mac's back with his walking stick, the spittle flying from his mouth.

"Stop it. Reverend, stop!" cried Deidre. "This is Mr. McDonnell. I told you about him. He was on the *Mermaid* and escaped that fire somehow."

"You're one of the convicts and up on our deck?" The Reverend lifted his walking stick again. "Off! I say off."

"Stop it, Reverend." Deidre stepped between Mac and Reverend Baxter. "God has protected him and brought us together."

Mac edged in front of Deidre.

"Don't be blasphemous, girl."

Deidre clung to Mac's hand. "If we can't be here, I'll go to steerage."

"She doesn't know what she's saying," said Mac. For the hundredth time, Mac was ashamed of what he had become. He looked down at her hand, but he couldn't let go.

"You're alive," said Deidre. "We're going to Van Diemen's Land. That's all."

Captain Sinclair and First Mate Banks came running up the promenade deck.

"What did I tell you?" said Banks. "You can't be up here."

"That's what I said," sputtered Reverend Baxter. His neck jiggled with outrage. "He won't listen."

"Captain Sinclair, I'm so glad you came," said Deidre. She spoke as if she were in the assembly room. "This is my fiancé from home, a fisherman from the Orkneys. Mr. Malcolm McDonnell. He was on the *Mermaid*."

"Yes, Miss Scott, but what is he doing on my promenade deck?"

"I didn't know he was alive, and then I saw him. I called him up," said Deidre. "Was that wrong?"

The two stood before the captain, still holding hands.

Mac braced himself. He could feel Deidre's hand warm in his. "I'm sorry, sir," said Mac. "I know I'm supposed to be below."

"Damn right you're supposed to be below," said Banks and darted a look at Deidre. "Excuse me, miss."

"A fisherman, you say?" asked Captain Sinclair.

"The best," said Deidre.

"I've seen you about. Is he a good man, Banks?" asked Captain Sinclair.

Banks nodded reluctantly. "Aye, sir. We've used him."

"Then, put him to work." Captain Sinclair stared at Mac. "You can run lines aft for the cook. But as for coming up here, you cannot." He lifted his hands to shush Deidre. "He cannot come up here again, Miss Scott."

"Then, I shall go down. There's nothing to stop me, is there?"

"No, miss. But I can't have you down among steerage or around the crew." Captain Sinclair stared at the couple. "Very well. You may walk on the foredeck, but only within strict boundaries, or I shall have you, Miss Scott, locked in your cabin, and, you, McDonnell, back in irons. Trust me. That will not be pleasant for either of you."

"Deidre, we can wait until we're in Van Diemen's Land. It all changes then anyway."

"Listen to your fiancé," said Captain Sinclair. "He'll go into quarantine once we land at Hobart Town. No one knows yet where he'll be assigned."

"I'll find him."

"And I hope you do," said Captain Sinclair. "For now, McDonnell, keep to your work. You may walk together in the evening only. Once it's dark, and I mean past seven bells, you are not to meet. McDonnell, are you listening? Is that clear?"

"Yes, sir," said Mac.

Sinclair waved his hand at the couple. "Take a few moments, then. I was young once."

"Thank you, Captain." Deidre led Mac to the far corner of the promenade deck.

Banks grimaced. "'Tis not a good example, sir."

Captain Sinclair turned. "Did I hear you say anything, Banks?"

The *Brilliant* and the *Alexander* followed the trade winds southwest across the Atlantic to Rio for provisions. Once they made port, the transportees were locked below. Given the heat and the close quarters, everyone was relieved when the ship stayed in port for a mercifully short week. Once they were underway, the ship's routine resumed. Captain Sinclair charted their journey southwest to Cape Town, hoping to stay above the violent storms of the "roaring forties".

As they sailed back to southern Africa, the wind scorched the ship. Complaints grew, and fights broke out. Mac came on deck one evening to find a sailor manacled and chained to the mainmast, his eyes blackened. The sailor had been found asleep in the women's quarters. He was to be locked in the forward brig until Cape Town.

Their ship passed a slaver, far on the horizon, headed to Brazil. Occasionally, the *Brilliant* sent a longboat over to the *Alexander*. Whenever they passed a ship sailing north to London, they exchanged letters, including letters from Deidre back home. The hot winds continued.

The women in steerage put up small scraps of canvas on deck for shade, but the children sickened. It became nearly unbearable to stay on deck, but conditions were worse below. Another child died, some said of starvation.

Captain Sinclair limited the fresh milk to the youngest children only. Weevils appeared in the bread. The salty meat was a dark mahogany color, impossible to eat, yet eat it they did. In the following week, two children died, and then another infant, with the mother dangerously ill.

Mac held to his promise to the captain, knowing that he could see Deidre every day. He set lines at dawn, each day pulling in fresh fish, which Musa, a bow-legged Malay, boiled into a kind of stew.

"You, Mac, get me flour." Musa tossed Mac a set of keys for the ship's stores. "Two kegs."

Mac grunted assent and ducked down the ladder from the galley into the dank, hot bowels of the ship. He made his way by feel and unlocked the door to the ship's stores, a small room crammed with barrels of food and water.

"Get the hell out," cried Davis, lifting a candle that dazzled Mac's eyes.

"Who's that?" cried another transportee, one Mac barely recognized.

"You're not supposed to be down here," said Mac.

"Ah, shut up," said Davis. "I know him. Always sniffing around. Well, Mac, you can join us and have a bit of rum, or you can die, right now." Davis tossed the candle to his friend, drew a knife from his waistband, and hunched down, slicing the air in front of him.

Mac felt behind him for the door, the latch cold on his fingers.

Davis advanced, bracing himself as the ship swayed.

Mac slipped through the door, slammed it shut and leaned against it. "Help!" he called. "Help!"

He tried to lock the door, but the two men inside pushed and battered the door. "Let us out, you bastard!"

First Mate Banks ran up with a sailor behind him. "You again. What's all this?"

Mac barely held the door closed. "There's two men inside, sir. I don't know how. Musa just sent me down with the keys."

"Ah, God's teeth. This is a hell boat," grumbled Banks. He yanked the door open to find Davis, knife ready, poised to leap.

"Drop the knife. You want more troubles, do you? What the hell are ye doing down here." He sniffed. "Guess I already know. Drop the knife."

Davis smirked and let the knife fall. "Leave her, Johnny, leave her," he sang in a high falsetto.

"None of that now. Take them up and shackle them" He pointed at Davis. "Yer a troublemaker. Meat for the captain's pleasure."

The two men were dragged above board, kicking and shouting all the way, "Leave her, Johnny, leave her."

Banks turned to Mac. "I'll remember this."

"Last thing we need is another fire."

No one found out how the two men got into the store room. They were whipped for stealing grog and whipped again for having a lighted candle below. Mac stood amid the sailors, wincing as the blows fell and Davis screamed.

Captain Sinclair ordered the two men chained to the masthead for twenty-four hours. He approved a ration of grog for the gathered crew, who stood muttering in groups of three and four. The men drank their cups quickly, but they were not so quick to jump when the First Mate called them back to work.

Mac heard the chantey start up as the men pulled the sails up into the rigging. He knew the song. He had heard it on the *Mermaid* when the sailors had been angry at the captain. The song echoed throughout the ship as they continued south to Cape Town.

I thought I heard the Old Man say,
leave her, Johnny, leave her.
Tomorrow you will get your pay,
an' it's time for us to leave her.

The work was hard, and the voyage long,
leave her, Johnny, leave her.
The seas was high and the gales was strong,
an' it's time for us to leave her.

The grub was bad and the wages low,

leave her, Johnny, leave her.
The wind was foul and the sea ran high,
leave her, Johnny, leave her.

We'd be better off in a nice clean gaol,
leave her, Johnny, leave her.
With all night in and plenty of ale,
an' it's time for us to leave her.

Leave her, Johnny,
ye can leave her like a man.
Oh, leave her, Johnny,
oh, leave her while ye can.
An' it's time for us to leave her!

CHAPTER 58: EDINBURGH

Alice sat beside Gordon's bed, the curtains pulled back, one candle lit. She didn't want to leave him alone to face what would come. Doctor McKenzie had left long ago, with promises to return in the morning when he made his rounds in New Town.

Outside a carriage passed, the horses clattering on the cobble-stoned street. Edinburgh was never really quiet, not even in the middle of the night. Gordon slept now, his hand in hers, his breathing labored. Gordon startled awake and pulled at her hand. "Alice, is that you?"

"I'm here, Gordon."

He shifted his head fretfully. "I need my papers. Bring them, will you?"

"Darling, rest. Let's worry about the papers in the morning."

He stared at her, his pupils contracting, and then his eyes closed.

Alice hesitated. "Do you want me to send for Alexander?"

Gordon began to laugh, but it ended with him choking. "All the way from London? He would never arrive in time. Don't coddle me, Alice. I'm dying."

Alice was silent. All she could do was hold his hand.

"I'm not afraid. I've done what I could. It's all written down. Be sure to meet with Gray, but don't trust him." Gordon's eyes closed for a few moments, and the room was filled with the sound of his harsh breathing. "You'll have to go to Foulksay. See about Perkins."

"Don't worry about that now."

Gordon sighed. "Just go after I'm gone. Close the house. Tell them what you like. My only regret is that I won't be here when our son is born."

"It's not so long to spring. Our child will be born then."

"I won't be here."

"You can't know that."

"I know."

They were silent for a moment.

"You have given me heart's ease, my dear," said Gordon. "I am grateful."

Alice couldn't speak. She grasped his hand tightly.

"Be sure he goes to a good school. Alexander can advise you. Take him to Foulksay in the summers. Let him know our heritage." He coughed again.

"I promise." Alice stared at their hands entwined. As difficult as their marriage had been, here in Edinburgh, Gordon had become the husband she had dreamed of so long ago. *What would my life have been without him?*

Gordon closed his eyes. "I would not take any of it back."

"Neither would I." Alice lay her face on his hand.

CHAPTER 59: CAPE TOWN

The passengers spilled onto the deck and lined the bulkheads as the *Brilliant* sailed slowly into Table Bay. Deidre and Amalie squeezed in between Bella Fraser and Mrs. Arbuckle. Just as the anchor splashed down, Reverend Baxter joined them.

"I never thought to see such a mountain. It's so very beautiful. Beyond my imagination," said Deidre.

Table Mountain stretched hundreds of feet above them. Lion's Head marked one end of the mountain, and Lion's Rump the other. On the far right, permanently encased in clouds as wispy as smoke, Devil's Peak rose over the fast growing port city of Cape Town.

"Oh, it's pretty all right." Mrs. Arbuckle moved restively. "I can't wait to get ashore."

"When can we go?" cried Amalie.

"Not to worry," said Reverend Baxter. "They'll take us ashore as soon as the paperwork is filed with the dockmaster. We'll be sleeping on land tonight, at the latest, tomorrow, with fresh meat and drink." Reverend Baxter smoothed the front of his waistcoat and rocked back on his toes. He was considerably slimmer now than at the start of the journey some eight weeks ago.

"What about them?" Mrs. Arbuckle pointed to the men and women on the decks below. She glanced at Deidre. "What about the transportees?"

Reverend Baxter turned red. "They'll let as many ashore from steerage as can afford to go. I heard the transportees will be locked up again."

"Not Mac." Deidre stiffened. "Surely they won't lock him up."

"Hush, now." Bella glared at Reverend Baxter. "We can't be worrying about what we don't know."

The small boat of the dockmaster made its way out to the *Brilliant*. Captain Sinclair stood at attention on the main deck, in full uniform, the feathers on his hat blowing in the wind. First Mate Banks whispered in his ear.

"At least we'll be able to go ashore for today." Bella patted Deidre's arm. "Come, dear. Let's get our things ready." The two women walked below, not looking back.

Mac and Menzies, locked in the empty forecastle cabin, peered out of porthole windows, as sailors tied the *Brilliant* up to the long quayside dock crowded with ships. People swarmed the docks. Vendors, men from other ships, and a few merchantmen and soldiers squawked at each other in a mélange of languages: French, English, Spanish, German, Indian, and African. A few fat seals lay about the dock, hoping for a handout.

Menzies ran his hand over his freshly cropped head, as if he were not used to its stubble. "They're going to keep us locked up."

"It's enough we're here and not down in the hold with the rest."

"It's not enough."

"What are you thinking, man?" asked Mac.

Menzies looked around. "I want to run. Will you come with me?"

"Run? Run where? There?"

They looked at Table Mountain. Menzies shrugged.

"When?" asked Mac.

"When we can."

Mac peered out the window again. He saw Deidre link arms with Mrs. Fraser, who carried an umbrella against the heat. They skirted around the seals laying on the pier and ignored the vendors. Deidre stumbled as she walked on land for the first time.

"I'll think on it."

Banks came to the forecastle late. He eyed the hammocks that swung empty around them and shook his head at the close air. "We're short-handed. A few will straggle back tonight. The patrol will find the rest." He spat. "You two can work for me, sleep up here, and be locked up each night, or you can go below with the other transportees for the next three weeks. You can stay here if you give me your word that you won't try to escape."

Mac and Menzies looked at each other.

"I'd rather work than go below," said Mac. "I give you my word."

"My word's as good as any man's," said Menzies.

Banks nodded. "Get some sleep then. We start early."

Captain Sinclair ordered the ship's stores of food and water replenished, its sails hauled down and repaired, and the ship itself cleaned rigorously. At dusk, the crew took turns going to town, a portion of their pay in their pockets. Some of them returned to the ship late at night, singing. The wine was cheap. The women were beautiful. Some never returned.

Every night, Banks locked Mac and Menzies into the hot, airless forecastle cabin. The few sailors assigned to stay on board tied their hammocks on the deck and slept under the stars. Every night, Mac lay in his hammock and worried about Deidre. Seven years of indenture faced him. What future did they have? Yet when Menzies tried to talk, Mac rolled over in his hammock.

By the end of the first week in port, Menzies was gone. So were six men from the crew.

Martha Arbuckle also left. Heartily sick of the crowding in the first class cabin, she had found work as a governess on their first day in port. She took her bustle and her baggage to one of the large Dutch colonial mansions that lined Buitenkant Street, near the Castle of Good Hope.

The women gathered again at the forecastle deck to watch Mrs. Arbuckle leave.

"I never want to see her again," said Amalie.

Deidre and Bella shared a look over Amalie's head.

Bella tucked the letters from Mrs. Arbuckle to Amalie's father into her reticule and sniffed. "Never you worry, child. We'll make sure you're safe home to your father."

Deidre came to the forecastle cabin that night. Mac could barely see her face in the deepening night as they talked through the bars covering one of the porthole windows. She told Mac the cabin seemed much larger with Mrs. Arbuckle gone, though she worried about Kate Dallow, who spent much of the day sleeping. "I don't know where she goes at night," Deidre confided. "Her bunk is empty, but no one says anything."

Mac didn't want to tell her that he knew where Miss Dallow slept, up on the deck with the sailors. He didn't tell her he dreamed of the two of them running away to Table Mountain. "Banks says we can't meet anymore," he said. "Not 'til we're back at sea."

"I know. That's why I came. We're moving off ship tomorrow, Mac. I will miss you."

"But you'll come back?" Mac knew he couldn't bear to lose her again.

"I'll be back."

Mac was put to work loading the ship with provisions, crates of oranges and lemons, and fresh supplies of beef, lamb, and flour. He rolled endless barrels of water up wooden planks from the noisy dock and then down into the hold. He layered salt and fresh yellowtail and Cape salmon into wooden casks. He scattered the salt over the pink and green specked salmon and pressed another layer of fish down into the cask, then added a final thick layer of salt at the top, and tapped the wooden lid tightly into place. The heat was constant, and the salt had worked its way into his hands, stinging tiny cuts there.

Mac half listened to the stream of words around him. Most he could understand, English mixed with German, Dutch, and Malay. Each day, he hoped for a glimpse of Deidre, but she stayed on shore. Each night, Mac fell into his hammock exhausted, now alone in the forecastle cabin.

Captain Sinclair requested patrols be sent out from the garrison at Barrack Street. They brought back a few of the crew, who told stories of others who escaped to Table Mountain to live in a honeycomb of caves. They had feasted on dussies, a kind of rock rabbit, and ate walkie-talkies, a fried cake made of birds' beaks and feet. The sailors spoke of baboons that shrieked and chased the sailors as they climbed up out of Cape Town, and how, a year before, a terrible fire had swept Table Mountain, started by a cave dweller. This was a dangerous time to go up Table Mountain, they said, until the rains began in the spring. Mac worried about Menzies.

The deserters, their eyes blackened, their limbs slack from drunkenness, were chained to the masthead and lashed. Yet as soon as they had permission, they were ready to go ashore again to sit in the grog shops that dotted wharfside, doxies on their laps. Captain Sinclair let them go. When their money ran out, they came back to the ship and worked next to Mac silently, the grog smell sweating out of their bodies like a broken promise. Menzies never returned.

Mac wondered over and over if he had made the right decision. Each day, he worked. Each night, Banks locked him in the forecastle cabin. Finally, a surge of activity told him departure was near. Soon they would face the Indian Ocean.

Captain Sinclair hoped for an easy sail nearly 7,000 miles due east to Australia, but strong winds and heavy seas, larger than any seen before, terrified the passengers and crew alike. Steerage was locked down for several days as the *Brilliant* teetered and skidded through mountainous waves. Waves battered the ship and would have washed the crew over board had the men not been roped to the ship.

Captain Sinclair hoped to avoid the worst of the gales. He resolved not to go further south than 40 degrees. Strong breezes with some rain ensued, interspersed with a few days of sun. At the first sign of good weather, Captain Sinclair ordered all bedding and clothes on deck. The crew cleaned cabins and berths, sprinkling vinegar and oil of tar where the air had not circulated freely. All were thankful to spot a humpback whale at sea, its spout glistening in the sun.

Cape Town might have been a million miles away. No land at all was in sight.

Deep in the Southern Ocean at the end of the second week, dark clouds lay again on the horizon, and a second severe storm hit.

Deidre could hardly stand as waves battered the ship, each more fierce than the one before. A hurricane force gale again terrorized the ship. Half the passengers huddled in bed, incapacitated as the ship trembled and shuddered. Those who were able did their best to empty slops buckets for the sick. Those who were locked below decks suffered greatly. In the cabins, chests, boxes, and dishes slid and scattered on the floor. Amalie crept into Deidre's bunk, and they huddled under the covers, braced against the ship's swaying.

The next day was calm. Grateful and weak-kneed, crew and passengers carried buckets of water out of cabins with bilge pumps working below decks and in steerage. Two from steerage had died in the night. Reverend Baxter led a small group in prayer as their bodies were tilted over the side into a now quiet sea.

Following services, First Mate Banks announced, "We're cutting the daily ration. Our food stores are soaked." A thin gruel was issued to all, despite angry protests. Deidre and Amalie couldn't eat the gruel after Mrs. Miller said the little bumps were weevils and not oatmeal. Kate Dallow disappeared once again. She said she knew where there was better food, and they'd come with her if they knew what was good for them.

The next morning, they spotted the *Alexander*. After exchanging signal flags, the *Alexander* sent a small boat over to the *Brilliant*. Captain Sinclair was able to replenish ship's stores. He immediately issued an extra allowance of biscuits, pickles, raisins, and suet to the passengers and crew. All were pleased, and the transportees were once again allowed on deck twice a day.

Mac kept an eye out for Deidre. He was still amazed they were on the same ship. If only the storms weren't so intense, the ship less crowded, and fewer passengers were sick. When he thought of the trial and all those back home, if he hadn't been filled with humiliation and sadness, this would be a grand adventure.

Mac met Deidre midmorning, by the stairs that linked the main deck to the foredeck. "How fare you this impossibly beautiful morning?"

Deidre laughed, but fatigue marked her face. "Mac, you are the one who's impossible. Don't you see those clouds?"

"Banks thinks another storm is coming, but the ocean is behind us. We're close to land." He held her hand, taking comfort from just these few moments together.

"Did he say how much longer," asked Deidre.

"Maybe another week before Hobart Town."

"I'll be grateful to feel land under my feet again. Are you getting enough to eat?

"I'm fine. Remember, Musa slips me an extra bit now and then. If the storm's bad, stow everything away and lash yourself to your bed and stay there." Mac shook his head. "I worry about what's next, Deidre."

"Hush. Don't worry about what's to come. The worst may be handled when it's known. Even after we land, 'tis only a matter of time before we'll be on our own and together again."

"Dinna count on us being together," said Mac. "'Tis best to be prepared."

For a few minutes they watched the swell of the waves lift to whitecaps as the *Brilliant* skirted along the southern coast of Van Diemen's Land, nearly at the mouth of D'Entrecasteaux Channel.

Banks was right. Another storm darkened the sky above them lashed the ship with rain and strong winds. They could no longer see the shore. The *Brilliant* ran before the wind, picking up speed, her sails taut.

"Secure the deck," cried Banks. "All below 'til this is past."

CHAPTER 60: THE STORM

"Batten the hatches."

Mac heard the voices overhead. He dreaded that moment when the sailors nailed the hatches shut once more, leaving those below in absolute dark. All lights had been doused. People fell out of their crowded bunks and mumbled curses. A child's high-pitched scream cut through the dark. Many were sick again and again through the long night, for the waves pitched the *Brilliant* around as if she were a moth in a high wind.

Mac could no longer tell what hour it was. Finally, he slept, braced against the wall, prayers for Deidre and a safe passage on his lips.

Mac woke when fresh, cool air filled the hold.

"Hey," called Banks. "I need a few men."

Mac lurched from his berth as several men rushed to the ladder.

"Easy now. Robert and Mac, you come up. Grab the ropes and tie yoursel' good," said Banks, as he threw two ropes down the open hatch. "Tis a bastard of a storm."

Thomas shoved past Mac and climbed the ladder, only to be washed down the sharply listing deck by waves the moment he lifted himself off the ladder.

"Grab that man!" Banks shouted. "You below, tie up tightly and come up now."

Cold sea water splashed down the ladder as Mac knotted the rope around his waist. The transportees shouted and screamed as the ship rolled, and a few more men tried to climb the ladder behind him.

Mac climbed up out of steerage, close after Robert. They were instantly knocked to the deck by a fierce wave, chilling Mac to his bones. He scrambled to his feet, struggling to keep his balance as the deck listed sharply to starboard.

"Close her up," cried Banks.

Mac helped to pound the wooden hatch shut as more waves sluiced over them.

"Hold on! Hold on to the side," shouted Banks. "Go forward now. Go fast and hold on." His shouts were lost in the wind as the men crawled toward the front of the ship as best they could. The waves heaved and pounded around them, breaking over the deck and over their backs.

"Thomas, go to the helmsman. Simpson, take Robert and Mac forward. Make sure all hatches are secured and report back," cried Banks over the rising wind. "God help us, we'll get through this."

Mac's stomach churned. He could barely see in front of him as the waves came one after the other, rising up like mountains around them. The *Brilliant* wallowed and tipped, most of her sails tied tight to lessen the wind. The waves crashed over her and drenched the decks. Water streamed from the scuppers as the *Brilliant* shuddered.

"Bring her around," screamed Banks. "God, bring her around."

With a slam, the *Brilliant* struck the rocks, aground at the mouth of the channel. She rocked once as if her very bones were undone, settled and dipped slightly at each wave. The wind whipped white spray over waves that crested as fast as they were formed, and jagged black waves crashed onto the decks.

Mac fell to the deck, his breath knocked out. He felt the ship shudder as the waves battered her. He crawled forward.

Banks clung to a guy rope on the poop deck, close to the captain. "We need to let out the sails. We've got to try to float her off, or the wind will batter us to death on these rocks. We'll lose her."

"Pull the rest of the sails in, and send the men up to cut away the foremast and mizzen," Captain Sinclair shouted over the wind. "If we cut away, she'll hold. She'll stand the wind."

Banks yelled. "We don't have a chance unless we float her off."

"Do you not hear that groaning, man," cried the Captain. "She's got a hole in her belly. I don't know how big. We've got to hold on. Our only hope is the wind will ease."

Captain Sinclair waved to the sailors waiting by the rigging, and they went up, locking their feet in the ropes as they climbed. The ship swayed and the wind howled as the sailors struggled to pull the remaining sails in and tie them to the masts.

Mac felt the beams of *Brilliant* shudder with each wave. She held still in one spot, while the waves and wind from the southeast buffeted her steadily. A mighty crack and the main mast broke, crashing down to the deck, bringing sailors and sails with it.

"Cut away as quickly as you can," Banks shouted. "Move it, lads."

The sailors and the men from below swarmed over the main mast. They dragged the men who'd fallen to safety and tore at the wooden mast with axes. As fast as they cleared the mast, they heaved chunks overboard. Mac and Robert hacked at the sails and ropes, all hopelessly twisted and useless. The deck shifted beneath their feet and the wind howled.

Mac shivered as he realized they might all drown, but he kept pulling the sails away from the mast. The Captain was in their midst as well, throwing parts of the mast overboard. He stopped finally and cried, "We've got to get ashore. Now. Bring the passengers on deck. All of them." He pointed to land just visible as the sky lightened around them. But along the southern horizon, the sky and the ocean remained entirely black.

"What's he saying," Mac asked a sailor near him. "He canna bring the women and children out on deck, can he?"

"Martin, take three men and ready the longboats," cried Banks. "We'll link ropes to the shore, and we'll offload that way. I need a few of you to go below and bring up every rope you can find."

The sailor nodded, for he had seen this before, but Mac cried out, "We can't bring the passengers up. We don't have enough rope. They'll be swept overboard."

"They'll die if we don't bring them up. They'll die if we don't get them off the ship," yelled Banks in Mac's face. "Go below and bring that rope up now."

Mac's stomach lurched. *Deidre*, he thought. *God help us*. He turned and went with the small group of sailors. The ship heaved beneath their feet at every step as they made their way down the small entryway into the forward hold.

Some of the cargo had come loose. With each wave, heavy boxes slid across the bottom of the ship with a crash. Water sloshed around their feet.

"Go on," cried the mate. "Get the ropes. We'll need them all."

Robert climbed on top of the cargo and began throwing coiled ropes over to the men who looped the ropes around their bodies and one by one, went above, back to the deck.

The ship wobbled and the cargo shifted. Robert slipped.

Before the crates and boxes had a chance to shift back and crush him, Mac climbed the crates and grabbed his arm.

"Out of here, man," he cried, giving a mighty pull.

The ship jerked and settled. The cargo shifted back, missing Thomas by inches.

"This is the last of it," cried Robert. He thrust a line at Mac, keeping one for himself. They crawled up out of the hold, the ship tipping the cargo behind them. They raced up the ladder to be greeted by still howling winds.

"Tie it like them." Banks pointed to the other sailors. Mac and Robert watched closely. They crisscrossed the rope around their shoulders and looped the ends around their waists. When they were done, they stood by the railing.

"Go two at a time," said Banks. "Make for that shore." He pointed to a bit of land marked by heavy surf, some two hundred feet from the *Brilliant*.

Two of the seamen plunged over the side of the ship into the roiling icy water. They swam toward shore, one end of their rope tethered to the ship. They got ten feet out and then disappeared beneath the waves.

"Pull them back. Next," cried Banks, as the sailors pulled the nearly drowned men back. "Robert, Mac, go ahead. Swim as if the very devil were after yer bones."

Mac heard ominous cracks behind him as he leaped into the sea, and then it was cold, colder than any water he'd ever felt. He swam, his arms and legs aching. He swam against the waves, and then with the waves. His arms ached with cold. The salt stung his eyes as he fought through the waves, the rope pulling him down.

For Deidre, he thought. *For Deidre*. He willed his arms and legs to keep moving and then he felt it, the hard rocky beach under his feet. He scrabbled toward shore, and a final wave pushed him onto the beach, face down.

Mac turned to see Robert beside him in the shallow water on the beach. They both had made it. They stumbled up the beach, looking to tie the other end of their ropes to anything.

Their ropes secured to a large rock, four more sailors quickly came to shore, clinging to the ropes as they came. They uncoiled the ropes wrapped around their bodies and tied them down.

At once, men began to make their way off the ship. Waves and the cold sea swept a few off the lines, but they continued to swim ashore, a few at a time, using the ropes as guidelines. The captain's launch and two longboats carried heavy loads of women and children to the beach, the surf near swamping them. As soon as the boats were emptied, the sailors turned back to the ship, their bodies shaking with chill.

Mac watched in horror as one of the lines snapped, and the heads of the passengers and sailors went under. At the edge of the breakwater, the ship careened to one side more sharply. He knew they only had a very brief space of time. Mac ran to the water's edge. *Deidre*, he thought. *For God's sake, come to me now.*

Several sailors came along the ropes, some with children tied around them; others with women holding tightly behind. As soon as they reached the beach, Mac helped to drag them from the surf to huddle with the wet and bedraggled survivors. He couldn't find Deidre.

Mac heard a shout behind him. Several men on horseback raced along the beach toward them.

"Thank God," one of the sailors said.

"Mac! Over here," cried Deidre.

Mac could hardly believe his eyes. She was alive.

Deidre waved her arm wildly at Mac. She held Amalie in her lap, unconscious and colder than the sea itself. Amalie's lips were blue. Her black hair streamed down, all plastered to her head. Her tiny body shivered uncontrollably in the cold.

"I can't get her to wake up," said Deidre. "Please do something."

"Thank God I found you." Mac held Deidre and Amalie close. "Are you all right?"

"Well enough. I'm a little dizzy. I think I hit my head." Deidre pressed her forehead where a large bruise had already formed. "It hurts here."

Mac shivered violently and pressed his lips to her cold cheek. He wished they were any place but here, even back on Foulksay Island. Tears leaked from his eyes. She was alive.

"Out of the way, man."

Someone tried to shove Mac away from Deidre. Mac held Deidre and Amalie tightly. He didn't move.

"For Christ's sake, Mac, you know me." Doc Harris said. "Let me examine her. I've no time to waste."

Mac placed Amalie on the sand. The doctor quickly probed the girl's head and limbs. He put his head to her chest and listened to her heart. "She'll be all right. She's just cold."

Mac nodded, although he wasn't sure what he could do.

"Carry her to that hollow in the dunes, over there with the others. You, Miss Scott, go along with him. Stay with her and try to keep her warm. Get her on the first cart when it comes. Mac, then you come back down here and help me."

"Yes, sir," said Mac.

Mac carried Amalie up the beach, holding her close to his body as if he could warm her by the strength of his will. She felt too light in his arms, lighter than air.

Mac sat on the ground, with Deidre on one side and Amalie on his lap. He murmured in Deidre's hair, "We made it, love. We're on land now."

"Mac, I can't believe we're here. What's ahead of us now?"

"Hush, dear one. 'Tis enough we are here and alive."

Amalie opened her eyes and began to cry. "I never want to go on another ship in my life. I don't care where we are, I'm not going on another ship."

Mac patted Amalie. "Dinna worry, lass. Your father will be grateful to see you, so grateful he'll build you a palace right here. Hush now. You'll get warm. We'll be all right."

Amalie snuggled closer. "Let me stay with you, please."

"Aye, you can stay."

Someone gave Mac a drink of whiskey, fiery hot down his throat. When it was her turn, Amalie choked, but her cheeks took on a little color.

"I've got to be helping the others," said Mac.

"Don't worry, Mac," called Deidre. "I'll stay with her."

"I'll come as soon as I can," yelled Mac. He ran down the sand dunes to the sea and began helping passengers up the beach and out of the wind. A great howl went up from the assembly as the ship broke in two and sank before their eyes. Mac knew full well he was one of the lucky ones. Deidre and he were alive.

Mac went from group to group, helping where he could. Less than half of those aboard and two-thirds of the sailors had made it to shore. The Captain and First Mate Banks were missing. So too were Mrs. MacKinnon and Mrs. Miller. His berth-mates, Davis and Thomas, were nowhere to be found. Mac stood on the beach and stared at the reef. People swarmed around him, crying out for their companions.

The storm clouds passed. The sun came out, and the sea sparkled blue. For the first time, Mac realized he was standing on land. He laughed and nearly fell down. No matter he was a prisoner. No matter he now faced Van Diemen's Land. He stared at the blue sky and the blue sea. No matter anything. Deidre was alive.

CHAPTER 61: ARDKEEN HOUSE

"We should have stayed on Foulksay." Moira fussed with Rose's blanket. "Someone would have taken us in."

Jamie turned away from his sister and stared out the door of the gatehouse at the empty street in front of the Ardkeen House. "I'm not going back."

"Jamie, we'll manage. Never doubt it."

"I've got a chance to go on a whaler." He lifted his thin shoulders defensively. "Don't look at me that way. Gibson went whaling and came back with a pile of money. So did Sturgess."

Moira's mouth went dry. "You're too young."

"Don't be saying that. I'm old enough to work, and I'm old enough to go hungry."

"Come home with me. We'll manage, the three of us."

"I talked to them already. I'm leaving Thursday."

"Ah, you don't have to go." Moira held Jamie close, Rose between them. Jamie rested his head on her shoulder. "All right, then, but I'm going home." For a moment, she faltered, remembering the woman she'd found on the path to Selkirk. "We'll wait for you there, me and Rosie."

Jamie touched Rose's cheek. "She'll be walking afore I see her again." They both looked at Rose, bundled against the cold morning in Moira's shawl. She slept, her mouth slightly open. A crystal of sleep hung on her eyelash. Moira brushed it away, and the baby lifted her hand up, still sleeping.

"Aye, but she'll know her uncle."

"Some day I'll get our house back. I promise." Jamie turned away, and then he was gone from the gatehouse, striding down the empty street, his hands jammed in his pockets, his head down.

Moira sat in the stone gatehouse, the baby warm against her breast. She felt as if she could never move again. Jamie was truly gone. Dylan, Mac, Dougal, all somewhere far away. Who here would help her? She was alone. The baby turned in her sleep, nestling close. *Ah, Rose*, thought Moira. *I will not take you to a workhouse.* She remembered Granny saying 'What cannot be helped must be put up with.' *So be it. I'm going home to Foulksay.* She wondered who she might stay with and how the island had changed.

The morning fog lifted. Two women with market baskets walked by the gatehouse, their heads together, their arms entwined. Moira patted Rose, tightened her shawl, and followed the women down the hill to the bay where the ships docked. *It was time to make arrangements*, she thought. *Well enough time to go home.*

"You can't be leaving us." Mrs. Harcourt nodded to Mrs. Hodkins. "Where are you going?"

"But you're not recovered from the baby," Mrs. Hodkins interjected. "And you're barely able to work."

Mrs. Harcourt frowned and picked at the finely embroidered shawl wrapped around her shoulders. "We made arrangements for your little one. She would have a good home."

Moira rocked Rose in her arms and knew if she stayed, they would take the baby from her. "Enough. It's enough that I was able to stay with you when I needed a place more than anything. I'm thankful, but my brother's gone. He's off whaling, and he's too young to do so."

"We can't be responsible for that. We found him work."

"Aye, work of a kind. Locked in that factory and him thinner every week. We just as well have stayed on Foulksay. Home. That's where I'm going."

"We have only the best of intentions for you. We want you to leave your sinful ways behind you. Here we can help you lead a virtuous life."

"You don't understand." Moira thought of Foulksay, her hill and the standing stones, the path she walked up to Granny's house, the stories in the twilight that Mac and Dougal told as they all sat around their peat fireplace, the fish smoking slowly on the dampened rocks, oatcakes cooking in a flat pan nearby. "I want to go home."

"But you told us your family was gone."

"Aye, they're gone now. But they'll come back. I have people there who know me and who'll take me in."

"Well, then, you should have stayed there."

"Yes, so I should. My daughter will grow up on Foulksay, not here. I thank you for all you've done, but me and Rose, we're leaving."

"Once you leave, you cannot return." Mrs. Harcourt wrote another line in her account book and closed it. "You may stay until the end of the week, then."

Moira looked down at Rose. Three days and then home. "Thank you, mum."

Upstairs, the women of Ardkeen House gathered around her.

"You're leaving us already? The baby's not even a month yet."

"Hush, Margaret. 'Tis time. They'll take her child if she stays."

"Do you have a place to go to?"

"It's all arranged. I'm leaving Sunday. Gibson, a fisherman from Foulksay, he'll take me home. I'll find a place there. Mac, me brother, he had friends. And that's where they'll all come back, and I'll be there on Foulksay with Rose."

"Good on you," said Maddie. "I wish I could be going home. I hate the city."

"You don't hate it on Saturday night." The women laughed and drifted away, leaving Margaret behind with Moira.

"Take this," Margaret said. "I've put a little by. Enough to give you this."

"You shouldn't." Moira looked down at the shilling and six pence in her hand, enough to buy a week of food.

"Aye, I shouldn't. But I did. Just take it, and think of me now and then." Margaret touched her head where the last of a yellow bruise colored her forehead. "I wish I could go home."

"Maybe someday," said Moira.

"Yeah. Someday." Margaret turned and went to bed, pulling the covers over her head.

Sunday morning came soon enough, but Jamie wasn't at the gatehouse. Moira said her goodbyes and was surprised to see some of the women had tears in their eyes.

"You remind me of my daughter, the one who ran away." Sarah pushed to the front and hugged her. "God go with you and keep you safe. Take care of the precious bairn, and here, take this for your journey." She put a small bundle under Moira's arm. "Just a little food," she whispered with a last hug. "On your way now. It won't do for you to be staying too long. They could change their minds. It's happened before." Sarah gave Moira a little push out the gatehouse door.

Their goodbyes echoed in Moira's ears as she walked down the hill, past the pink sandstone of Inverness Castle, the row of shops, and to the docks.

At first, she couldn't see Gibson's boat among the hundreds of boats tied up on Thornbush Quay. His boat was smaller than the *Star*, after all. She stepped around the old woman selling fried fish, past the fishmongers shouting their wares, fish eyes staring out of the large baskets, and past the old men who mended nets along the dock, their fingers flashing in and out of the coarse thread. She walked quickly along the quay, ignoring the catcalls of the boatsmen.

"Come along with us, sweetie. We'll use that bundle you've got for ballast."

"Aye, and we got a use for you too."

Finally, Moira spotted Gibson, ear deep in argument with another fisherman. "Take that shark fish and shove it right up your nose," cried Gibson. "That wasn't in our catch, and you can't be saying it was, you bag of scuttlebones."

"Throw it over the side then. Don't be saying I put it there."

"Mr. Gibson, you still going over to Foulksay?" Moira called out.

Both men turned to look at her.

"Aye, I'm going. Come on aboard. And you," Gibson shook the shark fish over the side. "You don't want my fish, I'll sell them to someone else."

"Yeah, and who would that be." The two men hopped off the boat and stood nose to nose, still arguing. Moira tucked Rose under her arm and climbed aboard. She stepped around the pile of rock cod in the center of the boat, until she found a seat near the prow.

Another hour passed. Gibson and a few scrawny boys from the wharf emptied the boat of cod and loaded several heavy crates. "Two more of salt and that'll do it." He tossed a coin to the leader of the boys and turned to Moira. "'Tis good you came now."

Gibson untied the rope holding his boat to the dock and shoved off, oaring past the other small boats nearby. "Fasten yoursel' down, girl. We're going home." He pulled the center sail up, and the tiny craft sailed out of Inverness Harbor, past Cromwell's Tower, pulled to the sea by a strong wind and the outgoing tide of Moray Firth.

Moira tucked the blanket more tightly around Rose and looked ahead. A steady row of waves met her gaze, the waves breaking, swelling and rolling, shimmering in the morning light, the fog lifting like a mermaid's siren song. *We're going home*, she thought. *Home.*

They sailed up the coast and stopped for the night at Wick. Early in the morning, Gibson piloted the boat past Duncansby Head, timing his trip for the ebb of the tide before crossing Pentland Firth. "I'll not fight the Merry Men," cried Gibson.

Moira nodded. She knew well the tides of the Firth from stories Dougal had told. Her favorite she would tell Rose one day, of a Norse king's magical quern, stolen and then lost in the sea, said to lie at the bottom of the Firth, still grinding away, salting the sea.

Gibson piloted the little boat west of the Pentland Skerries, then straight north across the Firth, up past Burray and then to Copinsay, where gray seals lined the island's rocky beach with their white pups. He turned the boat at Grimness, and then east to Foulksay.

Moira fed Rose, her back against the wind, and watched the familiar hump of Barr Auch grow larger as they approached Foulksay Island. She wanted to stand on the beach at Selkirk, to feel the ground with her own feet, to see the men laying nets while the women cleaned the day's catch. She wanted Dylan to come home to her. She looked down at her hands, swollen from the laundry and scarred from gutting fish. They would smell again, and she would be dirty. She hugged Rose tight. "We'll not go hungry, you and me. We'll manage."

CHAPTER 62: WESTNESS

"They've left. All that paper work is done, and your staff is settled. Come, Alice. It's time to go home to Edinburgh." Diana stood at the door to the front drawing room at Westness.

Alice looked around the great room, its furniture and paintings covered with sheets, the candelabras packed away with the Indian and Chinese sculptures she had loved.

"Your trunks are already at the landing. Everything's ready."

"I'm not sure I'll be able to leave Foulksay now the time has come," said Alice. "The house seems like it has its own life, even with everything covered up. You saw Moira's baby with Mrs. MacNaught? A pretty little girl. I think her name was Rose."

Alice held the curtains open. Outside a brisk wind blew along the garden paths so carefully laid out. Her roses, protected by Gordon's stone wall, had been mulched. She felt balanced between two worlds, one in the past, known, but not quite what she had wanted. The other world lay ahead as misty and gray as the sky above her.

"We've a long journey home," said her sister, glancing at her watch. "We need to be down to the ferry by three. I'm told the strait is choppy today."

Alice moved around the parlour, her long black skirts rustling, a widow's hat of black bombazine dangled from her hands. "You know we weren't all that unhappy," she said. "It just seems strange now that he's gone, his fondest wish will come true." She didn't want to remember his last weeks in bed, his hands restless and grasping, the doctor's whispered consultations, and finally, that last, awful night when Gordon ceased to breathe.

"Don't dwell on the past," said Diana. "You have the future to think of now."

"I'm not worried about the future. His investments were brilliant. Even here, he kept up with the latest innovations. He had a schedule for everything. You know he hoped to return to India one day. His moment of triumph. Listen to that wind."

Diana shrugged as the wind rattled at the window.

"You don't know how much time I spent in that garden and here in my rooms, worrying about that wind." Alice turned away from the window. "Even at night."

"Don't let the wind worry you, dear," Diana said.

"There's little enough wind in Edinburgh," replied Alice. "I've decided to keep the house in New Town. You can stay with me, if you like." She looked at the high ceilings painted in the baroque Indian style Gordon had so admired. The wind rattled at the windows again. "He would want me to bring his son here." She smiled. "Or his daughter."

Alice fastened her hat and tied the bow. "I can't believe this is the last day. That he won't come through that door again, barking orders, a sheaf of plans tucked under his arm."

She walked to the window again and looked through the curtains. "What I mean is this island is beautiful in a melancholy and fierce sort of way. The people here are indestructible. They have their land again. They will raise sheep, and the fishermen will fish." She shook her head. "I'm so very glad Perkins is gone. I think I came to hate him," she mused.

"It's time, Alice."

"Yes, they'll be all right here. We'll come back in the summers to visit this island and the standing stones." She turned to her sister. "I'm ready now."

The two women gathered their cloaks and purses. Alice took a last look around the drawing room and closed the door.

AFTERWORD

Foulksay Island, the home of Mac McDonnell, is entirely imaginary. Only one clearance took place in the Orkneys – at Trumland on the island of Rousay in 1845, though clearances occurred throughout the highlands in 19th Century Scotland.

The Industrial Revolution did transform estates from small holdings worked by small crofters to vast sheep runs. The crofters, evicted and without jobs, starved. Some managed to emigrate. The resulting *diasporas*, exacerbated by the potato famine in mid-19th Century, sent Scots to the railroads and factories in cities throughout England and around the world – to the cities in Great Britain, India, the United States, Canada, and Australia. But the abandoned stones of crofters' cottages still dot the Scottish landscape.

Standing Stones began as a short story on selkies, but as I began research on the Industrial Revolution in Northern Scotland, the story of the McDonnells began to emerge.

Many books and online sites contributed to my understanding of this period in Scottish history. Most useful: Erick Richards, *The Highland Clearances*; T. M. Devine, *The Great Highland Famine*; T. C. Smout, *A Century of the Scottish People*; John Prebble, *The Highland Clearances*; John McFee, *The Crofter and the Laird*; and Nancy C. Dorian, *The Tyranny of Tide*. The online site, *Orkneyjar: The Heritage of the Orkney Islands*, offered fascinating insights into 19th Century everyday life.

As an avid quilter, I couldn't resist adding a scrap of history about the Rajah Quilt, now held at the National

Gallery of Australia in Canberra and taken out once a year.

In 1841, at the invitation of famous prison reformer Elizabeth Fry, Kezia Hayter did serve as matron to a group of women prisoners being transported from England to Van Diemen's Land on the *Rajah*. The British Ladies Society for the Reformation of Female Prisoners, a Quaker group, donated sewing kits and scraps to the women, and the Rajah Quilt was sewn on that four-month voyage. Because of heavy storms, Captain Charles Ferguson did take the *Rajah* to temporary shelter in Stromness.

Although online and library resources were excellent, I was thrilled to travel in Scotland for two months to visit Kirkwall, Inverness and Edinburgh, exploring further the sites and history of *Standing Stones*. I now hold library cards from each of these cities and found their help unforgettable.

Ardkeen House (1834), Culduthel Road, Inverness (Camp 2009)

ACKNOWLEDGEMENTS

Along the way, encouragement and critiques kept me researching, drafting, and revising. Thank you, Jane White, Linda Smith, and Natalie Daley, intrepid critics and Scrabble ladies. Beta readers Ruth Nestvold, Carol Kean, and Judith Quaempts provided excellent feedback, as did Rick Bylina and Karen Rice, the intrepid members of ROW80 (A Round of Words in 80 Days) and the NOVELS-L group on the Internet Writing Workshop. Closest to my heart, comments from my husband, Allen, and daughter Rachel.

Grateful acknowledgement is also made to the readers and judges of the Pacific Northwest Writers Association for recognizing *Standing Stones* with an award for historical fiction in its annual writing contest, 2010.

ABOUT THE AUTHOR

I grew up on the West Coast of the United States, attending some 14 high schools from Seattle to Phoenix. That pattern continued as I worked my way through college -- as a hospital admitting clerk, an international banker, and a social policy analyst, among many other jobs. After earning my master's degree, I taught English, technical writing, and humanities at Linn-Benton Community College and served as Department Chair there.

Standing Stones began with "My Selkie," one of the stories in a collection of short stories, *The Mermaid Quilt & Other Tales*. Shaped by my interest in the Industrial

Revolution, somehow this short story morphed into a trilogy that follows the McDonnell clan from the Orkneys in Scotland (*Standing Stones*), to Van Diemen's Land (*Years of Stone*), and the Great Nor'west (*Rivers of Stone*) in the 1840s.

You may read an excerpt of the next book that continues the story of Mac and Deidre in *Years of Stone*, that follows in the next pages.

If you enjoyed reading *Standing Stones*, please consider leaving a review on Amazon. I do love hearing from readers, so please send me an e-mail, if you like.

Beth Camp
bluebethley@yahoo.com

Writingblog: **http://bethandwriting.blogspot.com**
Travel blog: **http://bethcamp.blogspot.com**
Amazon: **http://www.amazon.com**

PREVIEW *Years of Stone.*
Book 2: The McDonnell Clan
Anticipate publication: Spring 2014
Cover design by Natalie Daley

SUMMARY: YEARS OF STONE

In 1842, Deidre Scott leaves her island home in the Orkneys to undertake a perilous four-month journey to follow the man she loves. Mac McDonnell has been sentenced to seven years in prison for resisting the clearances. Not realizing Deidre intends to follow him, Mac has been sent to the hulks on the Thames in London to await shipment to the penal colony in Van Diemen's Land.

Once underway and reunited, Deidre and Mac survive a shipwreck, only to be separated as Mac begins work on a road gang, while Deidre cobbles together a job. Befriended by Lady Franklin, the wife of the Lieutenant-Governor and world-famous explorer, Sir John Franklin, Deidre begins teaching at the Cascades Women's Factory, and tries to improve conditions for the women there and for Mac.

Through Deidre's efforts, Mac is re-assigned to Doc Morrell in Hobart Town, but even Doc Morrell is unable to help him, once Mac is transferred to the dreaded prison at Port Arthur. Will Deidre and Mac find a way to build a new life for themselves in this strange and new land beyond the seas?

YEARS OF STONE
CHAPTER 1: SNUG HARBOUR
(NOVEMBER 1842)

The ship's foredeck tipped at a steep angle beneath Deidre's feet as the *Brilliant* leaned to one side. Almost to Van Diemen's Land, the ship, pushed by onshore winds, had run aground. Sailors stumbled over tangled sails and a fallen mast, trying to cut it free. Sea water sloshed over the deck from waves pounding the windward side.

Deidre swallowed the bile that rose in her throat and steadied Amalie, the little girl from her cabin. Rough hands jostled them back in place as another rush of water sluiced over the deck.

"Don't push me," Deidre snapped. "I know my place."

The sailor ducked an apology and moved back along the line of women and children who waited their turn to be carried ashore. Two overloaded cutters ferried passengers off the ship, but just an hour ago, the Captain had sent Mac and several volunteers over the side, wrapped with ropes to tie a line from ship to shore.

Ah, Mac, Deidre thought. *You told me not to follow you. Will we even live another day?* The wind buffeted her wet hair. *God protect us all.* She grabbed the bulwarks and peeked over the side as another wave battered the ship.

Far below, a sailor held fast to one of three ropes strung from the ship to the shore through choppy waves and surf some eighty yards away. As soon as a passenger was lowered, he pulled his way along the rope to shore, the passenger hanging onto his back. Once they started underway, another sailor crabwalked down a rope ladder on the side of the ship to wait for the next person.

The ship settled again.

The woman standing next to Deidre moaned and sank to the slanted deck.

"Not now," Deidre pulled the woman to her feet. "There's only one person ahead of you."

"Steady," called First Mate Banks.

Amalie grabbed Deidre's skirts and burrowed close. "I'm scared."

"Hush, child. Look there," said Deidre. "That's where we're going. Mr. McDonnell will be waiting for us." The cliffs that lined D'Entrecasteaux Channel rose dark above the surf and a small line of rocky beach.

Before she knew it, Deidre was at the head of the line, Amalie clinging to her skirts.

"Let go." First Mate Banks pried Amalie's fingers from Deidre's skirt. "Don't worry. Miss Amalie. You'll be next." He looped a Spanish bowline around Deidre's waist. "Miss Scott, you sit in this like you was sitting in a chair. Just slip out of the rope once you're in the water and hold onto the sailor. He'll take you to shore. You can do this."

"Wait. I'm not going without her." Deidre pushed Amalie forward. "Can you tie her on me like you do for the sailors?"

Banks grimaced. "You'll drown with her on your back."

"I'll take my chances."

Banks shrugged. "We got no time to argue. If you kin take her, do it."

Deidre turned to Amalie. "I'm taking you with me. Don't let go, no matter what."

The ten-year-old nodded.

Banks lifted Amalie onto Deidre's back and, with a short piece of rope, linked the two together. Deidre grunted with the weight, choking as Amalie threw her arms around Deidre's neck.

"Not my neck, Amalie. Grab my shoulders." She gasped as the pressure eased. "Promise me you won't let go." Deidre felt Amalie's nod against her back.

Banks and another sailor lifted the two up on the bulwarks. Deidre and Amalie bumped down the side of the ship, the wind a steady blast, waves splashing at their feet as Banks lowered them to the waiting sailor. Deidre gripped the bowline with one hand and steadied Amalie with the other.

Deidre reached out for the sailor and missed, her skirts billowing up as she fell into the sea. She and Amalie went under. Water coursed into her nose, and her heavy skirts pulled her down into the dark, churning waters. The rope around her waist jerked. Deidre kicked back up and grabbed the sailor's arm.

"We're going to die," shrieked Amalie.

"Hold on," Deidre shouted. Deidre, now free of the bow line, clung to the sailor's back, and Amalie clung to her.

Arm over arm, the sailor pulled his way to shore along the rope, the cold waves a steady roar around them. *I'm not going back under*, thought Deidre, *and neither is Amalie.*

The sailor called out, but Deidre couldn't hear what he said. She tried to call out, but her mouth filled with salt water. Amalie's hands tightened on her neck. Deidre coughed and shook her head. She slid her arm behind Amalie and pulled her close.

Deidre closed her eyes to slits. *We will make it ashore.* Deidre clutched the sailor, buffeted by the sea, her shoulders aching where Amalie clung to her. They rocked forward as the sailor hitched along the rope.

Salt stung her eyes, and she struggled to catch her breath. Deidre was so cold she could not close her hands. The undertow pulled at her skirts, then eased, and pulled again.

A giant breaker ripped them from the sailor. Deidre and Amalie tumbled into the surf, rolling over and over. Deidre's head hit a rock. Pain sliced through her, and her feet touched bottom. Another wave tipped Deidre over. She was on her feet again. She fought her way through the surf and collapsed on the sandy beach, the waves tugging at her feet.

Amalie, where was Amalie? Deidre pulled herself to her knees. She wanted to lay down on the sand, grateful to breathe, but Amalie lay at water's edge, unmoving. Deidre crawled over to her, grabbed her skirt, and dragged her up on the beach above the waterline.

Was she alive? They were safe on land, but the little girl didn't move. Deidre brushed the sand from her face and her eyes. Deidre leaned her head against Amalie's chest; she couldn't hear a heartbeat.

"You all right, lady?" A sailor ran by, carrying a young boy on his back. "I'll send the doc over."

Deidre pulled Amalie onto her lap. "Wake up," she whispered.

Amalie's black hair streamed down, plastered to her head. She looked as if she were sleeping.

"We'll manage, little one. We've made it this far." Deidre hunched over Amalie, trying to shelter her from the steady wind.

The storm lifted. Seagulls swooped and dove along the surf, and the waves sparkled blue. Exhausted passengers and transportees gathered in small groups along the beach; a few lay on the sand. Men ran to the water to help as more came in from the sea. Sailors pulled their way along the two ropes that yet linked the ship to the shore, carrying women and children on their backs. Others swam through the choppy waves; some slipped beneath the waves, their cries lost.

"Mac, over here," cried Deidre. At last. None of it mattered. The horror of the storms. The four month journey on a crowded ship, leaving her sisters and father behind, saying goodbye to all she knew. Mac was alive.

Amalie lay still, barely breathing, colder than the sea itself.

"Thank God." Mac knelt down on the sand and held Deidre tight. "I didn't know where you were. I thought

I'd lost you." He shivered and pressed his lips to her face.

"Oh, Mac, she's so cold," said Deidre. "She's got to wake up." For a moment, Deidre leaned her head into Mac's shoulder, Amalie tucked between them.

Someone tried to shove Mac away from Deidre and Amalie, but he wouldn't let go.

"For Christ's sake, Mac," said Doc Harris. "Let me examine her." He probed Amalie's head and limbs and listened to her heart, then rolled her on her side.

Amalie choked and vomited sea water.

"There you go. You'll be all right," Doc Harris patted Amalie and turned to Deidre. "You just need to get warm, the both of you."

Mac nodded, but he didn't let go of Deidre.

"Mac, take them up by the dunes with the others, then come back to me," said Doc Harris. "Miss Scott, you take shelter in the dunes. Tend to those you can." Doc Harris worked his way through the survivors. A small group of men moved with the ship's surgeon as he barked orders.

Mac carried Amalie up the steep beach. They reached a clear space where tough grass protected them from the wind. Cries and groans rose around them as he put Amalie down with the other survivors.

"Will she be all right?" asked Deidre.

"I think so. Try to stay warm," Mac said. "I don't want to leave, but I have to be helping the others."

"Don't worry, Mac." Deidre pulled Amalie close. "I'll be here."

One of the ship's two cutters came in low in the water; the people jammed aboard her screamed and shouted as the surf tipped the boat and spilled them into the heavy waves.

"Oh, God," cried Mac. "I'll be back." He ran down into the surf and carried people to shore.

A great howl went up from the assembly as the *Brilliant* broke in two and sank before their eyes.

Mac stared at the reef where the ship had been. People swarmed around him, crying out for their companions. The body of a young boy bumped against his legs.

"Mac, help." Robert staggered as he tried to carry a woman up from the beach. "This one's alive."

Mac pulled the boy's body out of the sea, laid it on the sand, and ran to Robert.

"You see Doc Harris?" asked Robert.

"Up there." Mac grunted as he took part of the woman's weight.

They linked arms and carried the unconscious woman up to the dunes, her wet skirts dragging in the sand.

"I know her," said Mac. "'Tis Kate Dallow. She was in the cabin with Deidre."

A bruise covered half of Kate's face, and one of her arms hung disjointed. She moaned and opened her eyes.

"You're safe, Miss Dallow," said Mac.

"God's bones, I hurt." She moaned again. "Watch my arm, you oafs."

Mac looked at Robert. If he started laughing, he would never stop. They settled her on the ground with the others who'd been pulled from the sea and close to where Deidre yet held Amalie. Mac could not resist touching Deidre's arm as if he could not believe she was alive.

Nearby, Doc Harris bent over a man stretched out on the ground. He closed the man's eyes and covered his face, then spotted Mac and Robert. "Hey, Mac. Get back down on the beach. If you see the Captain or First Mate Banks, send them to me."

Mac turned away from Deidre to survey the rocky cliffs rising from the beach. Other than the survivors, no one. No houses. Nothing indicated anyone lived near. Only the blasted sun burned the clouds away and warmed his back. He shook his head and made his way back to the beach.

Doc Harris felt Amalie's pulse. "She's doing fine."

"What about me, Doc?" croaked Kate. "You gonna do somethin' about me shoulder?"

BETH CAMP
bluebethley@yahoo.com
http://bethandwriting.blogspot.com

30069131R00222

Made in the USA
Charleston, SC
03 June 2014